Praise for
and The Wi

"Erica Ridley is a delight!"

—Julia Quinn, *New York Times* bestselling
author of *Bridgerton*

"Erica Ridley's love stories are warm, witty and irresistible. I want to
be a Wynchester!"

—Eloisa James, *New York Times* bestselling
author of *My Last Duchess*

"Ridley's motley crew of Wynchester siblings is as charming as it is
unforgettable."   —*BookPage*

The Duke Heist

"This entrancing Regency . . . is a knockout."

—*Publishers Weekly*, starred review

"Schemes, heists, and forgeries abound in this charming series starter.
This unconventional and quirky Regency will have readers falling
for the plucky family and rooting for Chloe and Lawrence to buck
tradition."   —*Library Journal*

The Perks of Loving a Wallflower

"A plot full of mystery, high jinks and tender personal revelations."

—*New York Times*

"The holy grail for Regency fans: like Georgette Heyer, but with sex . . . a feminist fairy tale readers will rejoice in."

—*Publishers Weekly,* starred review

"Completely enchanting." —*Kirkus*, starred review

"An exquisitely written, utterly transcendent romance that perfectly captures the joy of being loved for who you truly are . . . pure reading bliss." —*Booklist,* starred review

"This clever novel will delight readers."

—*Library Journal*, starred review

"A sapphic Regency romp that radiates all the good, fuzzy feelings readers want in a romance." —*BookPage*

Nobody's Princess

"Ridley hits the sweet spot of tickling readers' funny bones and pulling on their heartstrings in equal measure. This is a joy."

—*Publishers Weekly*, starred review

"Writing with plenty of panache, a flair for thoughtful characterization, and an exhilarating sense of humor, Ridley deftly delivers another marvelously imaginative addition to her Wild Wynchesters series that proves to be another perfect dose of reading joy."

—*Booklist*, starred review

"The story is fun and playful, but weighty topics are deftly mixed in . . . Another pleasing and joyful addition to the Wild Wynchesters series." —*Kirkus*

"Ridley, who has a deft hand with dialogue and detail and crafts bookmark-it scenes and byplay, is fast becoming an auto-buy author and makes a good read-alike suggestion for fans of Lisa Kleypas, Grace Burrowes, and Elizabeth Hoyt."   —*Library Journal*

"Swift pacing, sleek prose, lively characters, and much humor make for a fun, flirtatious romp that weaves fantasy and joy into a book with real heart."   —Historical Novel Society

My Rogue to Ruin

"This Regency romance will have readers speeding through the pages and smiling all the while."   —*BookPage*

Hot Earl

SUMMER

Books by Erica Ridley

The Wild Wynchesters

The Duke Heist
The Perks of Loving a Wallflower
Nobody's Princess
My Rogue to Ruin

The Dukes of War

The Viscount's Tempting Minx
The Earl's Defiant Wallflower
The Captain's Bluestocking Mistress
The Major's Faux Fiancée
The Brigadier's Runaway Bride
The Pirate's Tempting Stowaway
The Duke's Accidental Wife
A Match, Unmasked

Rogues to Riches

Lord of Chance
Lord of Pleasure
Lord of Night
Lord of Temptation
Lord of Secrets
Lord of Vice
Lord of the Masquerade

Magic & Mayhem

Kissed by Magic
Must Love Magic
Smitten by Magic

Heist Club

The Rake Mistake
The Modiste Mishap

Regency Fairy Tales

Bianca & the Huntsman
Her Princess at Midnight

The 12 Dukes of Christmas

Once Upon a Duke
Kiss of a Duke
Wish Upon a Duke
Never Say Duke
Dukes, Actually
The Duke's Bride
The Duke's Embrace
The Duke's Desire
Dawn with a Duke
One Night with a Duke
Ten Days with a Duke
Forever Your Duke
Making Merry

Gothic Love Stories

Too Wicked to Kiss
Too Sinful to Deny
Too Tempting to Resist
Too Wanton to Wed
Too Brazen to Bite

Heart & Soul

Defying the Earl
Taming the Rake
Chasing the Bride
Undressing the Duke

Wicked Dukes Club

One Night for Seduction
One Night of Surrender
One Night of Passion
One Night of Scandal
One Night to Remember
One Night of Temptation

Standalone

Mistletoe Christmas
The Protégée

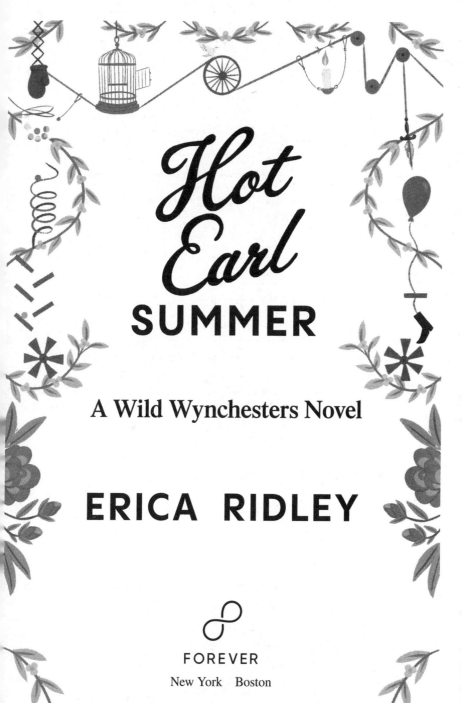

Hot Earl SUMMER

A Wild Wynchesters Novel

ERICA RIDLEY

FOREVER

New York   Boston

Forever
Hachette Book Group
1290 Avenue of the Americas, New York, NY 10104
read-forever.com
@readforeverpub

First Edition: August 2024

Forever is an imprint of Grand Central Publishing. The Forever name and logo are registered trademarks of Hachette Book Group, Inc.

The publisher is not responsible for websites (or their content) that are not owned by the publisher.

The Hachette Speakers Bureau provides a wide range of authors for speaking events. To find out more, go to hachettespeakersbureau.com or email HachetteSpeakers@hbgusa.com.

Forever books may be purchased in bulk for business, educational, or promotional use. For information, please contact your local bookseller or the Hachette Book Group Special Markets Department at special.markets@hbgusa.com.

Library of Congress Cataloging-in-Publication Data
Names: Ridley, Erica, author.
Title: Hot earl summer / Erica Ridley
Description: First edition. | New York ; Boston : Forever, 2024. | Series:
    A wild Wynchesters novel ; book 5
Identifiers: LCCN 2024001542 | ISBN 9781538726150 (trade paperback) | ISBN
    9781538726167 (ebook)
Subjects: LCSH: Aristocracy (Social class)—England—Fiction. |
    Castles—Fiction. | Swords—Fiction. | England—Social life and
    customs—19th century—Fiction. | LCGFT: Romance fiction. | Novels of
    manners. | Novels.
Classification: LCC PS3618.I392255 H68 2024 | DDC 813/.6—dc23/eng/20240118
LC record available at https://lccn.loc.gov/2024001542

ISBNs: 978-1-5387-2615-0 (trade paperback), 978-1-5387-2616-7 (ebook)

Printed in the United States of America

LSC-C

Printing 1, 2024

To anyone who has ever felt lesser for being different:
You're perfect just as you are.

And to Roy, for everything

1

Miss Elizabeth Wynchester lay in wait in the shadows of a purported hackney carriage. The handsome Black man at the reins was actually her brother Jacob. The brown-haired woman perched on the bench opposite Elizabeth was their sister Chloe.

A small frown creased Chloe's brow. "You remember the plan?"

"I always remember the plan."

"The *real* plan. Not your bloodthirsty agenda."

"It ought to be the real plan," Elizabeth muttered. At her sister's sharp glance, Elizabeth added, "I know, I know. Resorting to violence is a contingency."

"A distant one," Chloe said firmly. "And only if I tell you it's time for contingencies."

Today, Chloe was not dressed as the flamboyant Duchess of Faircliffe, but rather as the unassuming, practically invisible pickpocket she'd once been before falling in love and marrying a duke. Now she only used her past skills in the service of bringing justice to one of the Wynchesters' deserving clients.

Elizabeth preferred to mete out justice with the blade of a sword.

"I just want to poke him a little bit," she tried again. "When he bleeds, it'll be simple to snatch the key."

"It will already be simple to snatch the key. Having him slippery with blood makes things harder. Plus there's no room to swing a sword inside the carriage."

"Not a problem," Elizabeth assured her sister. "Kuni has been teaching me to throw knives."

Chloe covered her face with her hand. "God help us all."

"No murdering!" Jacob called through the sliding panel that separated the driver from passengers.

"Except as a last resort," Elizabeth reminded her pacifist brother. "Or if the perpetrator deserves to die."

"My carriage, my rules," Jacob shot back.

"Absolutely no bloodshed allowed," Chloe put in quickly, "because Tommy and Philippa need to use this carriage for *their* mission, as soon as we've finished with ours."

Elizabeth let out a long-suffering sigh. "I'm being oppressed."

"Places!" Jacob hissed through the sliding panel. "He's coming out of the bank now."

Elizabeth and Chloe both shot up ramrod straight, then arranged themselves in carefully casual positions.

"If he sits next to you . . ." Chloe whispered.

"I know, I know." Elizabeth gripped the handle of her sword stick. "Shove him in your direction."

"*Subtly*," Chloe admonished.

The door cracked open. A male voice gave directions to an address on the opposite side of nearby Hyde Park.

Elizabeth tensed with delicious anticipation. Mr. Bunyan was a liar and a thief . . . and shortly to receive his comeuppance. The young ward he'd been stealing from would not only have her inheritance returned, but also need no longer fear the volatile temper of a knave who—

"I'll have you there at once," came Jacob's clear voice.

Almost time. Elizabeth was certain there was more than enough room in the carriage to unsheathe her sword. However, she didn't want to be the one who ruined good carpet before her siblings' next mission, so she heroically stifled her bloodlust and prepared to give the thief a nice, friendly shove instead.

Mr. Bunyan leapt into the carriage. The horses took off at top speed, causing the loose door to swing shut behind Mr. Bunyan. Off-balance and floundering, he fell heavily into the first available seat—which happened to be the bench next to Elizabeth.

"Who are *you*?" asked Mr. Bunyan, visibly startled.

Elizabeth opened her mouth to say "Your worst nightmare" before catching her sister's eye and remembering to stay on plan. Elizabeth was meant to appear even more afraid of this scoundrel than he was about to be of her, thus providing a reasonable cover for panicking and pushing a strange man away from her.

"Aaahh!" she screamed in faux hysteria, then gave him a mighty shove.

At that moment, the carriage jerked to one side, as Jacob presumably was forced to avoid some obstruction on the street. Rather than tumble across Chloe's lap as planned, Mr. Bunyan stumbled across the carriage to thump against the inside window.

The coach hurtled down the road even faster.

"What is this?" Mr. Bunyan sputtered, eyes wide. "Who are you people?"

Behind him, Chloe's hand reached up toward his coat.

Elizabeth gave a winning smile to distract him. He recoiled as if a cobra had just flashed its fangs at him. Which, to be fair, was often how people described Elizabeth's smiles.

Mr. Bunyan gasped in terror. "You're not... You're not *Wynchesters*?"

Elizabeth blinked. "That was quick."

Usually it wasn't until well *after* any given maneuver that their villainous targets realized they'd been hoodwinked. But the Wynchester family had taken on so many new clients as of late, and developed such a following, that Elizabeth supposed it was only reasonable for a felonious blackguard to live in fear that he should one day find himself flat against a carriage window in the middle of—

With a scream, Mr. Bunyan leapt across the carriage, shouldered open the door, and threw himself onto the crowded pavement.

"Shite." Chloe shook her fist at the swinging door. "A runner."

Jacob stopped the horses at once. "Go."

Chloe clutched her chest. "I can't. Elizabeth?"

"I'll do my best."

Chloe was breastfeeding a baby every three hours like clockwork, which did not currently allow for sprints through the park to tackle miscreants.

Justice was up to Elizabeth.

Mindful of her sometimes rebellious joints, she scrambled out of the carriage and raked her gaze over the milling throngs. She stood in front of an entrance to Green Park. Now, where on earth was... *There*, trying his damnedest to disappear amongst the trees and picnickers, was Mr. Bunyan. She lifted the handle of her sword stick and took off after him.

"Stop, thief!" she called out.

Mr. Bunyan glanced over his shoulder, made an expression of pure fear, then dashed between two trees in an obvious attempt to lose her.

He was taller and narrower and no doubt faster than Elizabeth, with his long legs unencumbered by petticoats. But the park was packed with people. Mr. Bunyan kept getting jostled and tripping over tree roots, which gave Elizabeth an opening to follow and the opportunity to regain lost ground.

As her shadow fell across Mr. Bunyan's fleeing feet, Elizabeth twisted the handle of her walking stick.

"No swords!" came her brother Jacob's distant shout.

Curse her brother's squeamishness! He must have tied the horses and followed in pursuit.

Elizabeth sighed and secured the handle guarding her blade. She leapt over a patch of geraniums. Arm and cane outstretched, she poked the fleeing Mr. Bunyan in the back of the knee with her sword stick.

He crumpled like a puppet with cut strings.

Elizabeth threw herself on top of him, flopping about bonelessly to pin him in place. Help would arrive soon. For her, not him.

Chloe was catching up to them, one arm stretched tight across her bodice.

"What the devil is going on?" asked a confused bystander.

Right on cue, Chloe pretended to trip over a yellow geranium and conveniently fell right on top of Mr. Bunyan. Elizabeth rolled out of the way just in time.

"*Oof*," emanated from Mr. Bunyan's lungs as the wind was knocked out of him. He did not seem to recognize Chloe.

"Can I help you, miss?" Elizabeth said loudly.

She pulled her sister up and off the villain. Chloe winked and melted into the crowd.

Mr. Bunyan scrambled to his feet and raced on, casting a triumphant look over his shoulder at Elizabeth, who trailed farther and farther behind as she pretended to chase him.

She gave up the act as soon as he disappeared from sight.

Overhead, a large brown hawk swooped down from the bright blue sky. The raptor had found them.

Chloe held up her palm as the bird dived toward her. The hawk's claws raked gently across her skin, scooping up a slender brass key. The trained raptor soared back into the sky, racing over the trees and across the road to a distant rooftop, where their brother Graham crouched, waiting.

He caught the key and bounded across the skyline, vanishing into the distance.

Elizabeth and her sister made their way toward Jacob's waiting carriage.

Chloe turned her head toward Elizabeth. "I must return to my baby. Come with me? We've got lemon ices."

Reflexively, Elizabeth took a cautionary step back. "Absolutely not. You know I'll have nothing to do with babies."

"Then you're letting the others have a head start at being 'favorite aunt,'" Chloe warned.

"Pah." Elizabeth smiled her cobra smile. "I'll be his favorite aunt once he's big enough to hold a sword."

2

*E*lizabeth startled awake in pitch blackness. Without making a sound, she kept perfectly still as she took careful inventory of her body.

First her toes. Her feet were sweltering. It was the beginning of May and she was draped with a blanket, but other than a bit hot, her feet were fine. Calves... would do. Knees... good. Thighs... normal. Hips...

Ah, there it was. The familiar ache she dreaded every time she was forced to give chase. Flinging herself into a full-blown tackle hadn't been the gentlest of maneuvers. It would have been easier to launch her sword through the thief's chest. If it weren't for a certain sibling's stuffy rules about not murdering ruffians in front of bystanders.

Elizabeth's back... Yes, her back definitely still felt that last tackle, but at least the muscles weren't spasming. Maybe her daily stretches had been helping, or maybe she'd just been lucky this time. There wasn't always a clear cause-and-effect to these things. Intermittent, debilitating flare-ups had plagued her since birth. Elizabeth's body would, on its own timetable and sometimes without warning, shut down for days or weeks at a time, and cause extraordinary pain.

She could trust her sword, and she could trust her siblings, but she couldn't trust her own damn body.

Elizabeth was never one hundred percent perfect, but today, she was all right. Her joints were swollen the way they always were. Her muscles ached the way they always did. This was a sixty-percent day. As usual, background pain was her constant companion, but at a level tolerable enough to allow for the swinging of blades and the vanquishing of enemies.

"Bad" days were terrible, and "good" days were...well, not terrific in terms of the discomfort that never went away, but *great* in terms of mobility. Eighty percent days were positively marvelous. Especially when there was a mission afoot.

Nonetheless, today she would make do with sixty and no mission. Elizabeth rolled out of bed gingerly and performed her customary hour of morning stretches with great care. She preferred to tempt fate on the battlefield, not by twisting the wrong way when dawn had barely broken.

"*Never* show weakness," she reminded her looking glass.

The message had been drummed into her as a child. Or shaken into her. And worse. She was no longer with that family, but she carried the hard lessons they'd taught her deep in her bones. It was one of the reasons she loved swords. A blade-wielding madwoman was visibly strong, capable of defending herself and others. And sometimes, first impressions were the only chance you got.

Flare-ups made her vulnerable. After a spate of heroics, her body required rest to fully recover. Only her immediate family had ever seen her in repose on a sofa. Clients and enemies alike believed her to be an indefatigable sword-wielding machine, which was how she liked it.

The other reason she liked swords was because they could be hidden inside sword *sticks*. Hers doubled as canes, which made them practical as well as deadly. Being underestimated was often a tactical advantage. And sometimes, her body simply needed support.

Elizabeth hurried down the stairs to breakfast. A swift speed made possible by the excellent craftsmanship of the even marble stairs and smooth wooden banister, and because the gods had blessed her with a greater-than-fifty-percent day.

She burst into the breakfast room with a smile. Not her attacking-cobra smile, but an *I'm-ready-for-kippers-and-eggs* smile. Which might have been the same smile.

"Good morning," said Marjorie, who was already at the table. She had a piece of buttered toast in one hand, and a splotch of blue paint on her nose.

Elizabeth cast her gaze toward Marjorie's husband to see if he, too, was speckled with paint. Answer: not yet. Adrian looked as though he had just woken up, and that his fondest wish was to go right back to bed—with his wife.

How the breakfast table had changed! Twenty-one years ago, an eccentric Balcovian nobleman called Baron Vanderbean had adopted six children between the ages of eight and eleven from various walks of life. They had called him Bean, and he became the father they'd never had.

In addition to Elizabeth and shy artist Marjorie, there was clever pickpocket Chloe, acrobatic spy Graham, sweet animal trainer Jacob, and fearless master of disguise Tommy. After Bean's death three years ago, the siblings' bond only grew stronger...and their family grew bigger. Chloe married the Duke of Faircliffe and moved out. Bluestocking Philippa fell in love with their sister Tommy and moved in. Next came Graham's wife, Balcovian warrioress Kuni—who was Elizabeth's fencing partner and was also teaching her how to throw knives. And then just last summer, Marjorie had married Lord Adrian, bringing the total number of justice-seeking Wynchesters up to ten. Eleven, if you counted the baby.

Elizabeth did not count the baby.

"We're all here," she said in surprise.

It had been weeks since the whole family had filled the dining room at the same time. They'd been busier than ever with clients and cases. More than that, four weddings in a row naturally meant that the newly married pairs would spend a fair portion of their time with their spouses rather than with their siblings. Chloe and Faircliffe only dropped by a few times per week to dine *en famille*.

Tommy piled a plate with kippers to share with Philippa. The lovebirds were always doing things like that. Little thoughtful, cozy gestures that Elizabeth would likely find deeply romantic if her heart weren't forged of steel like the blade of her sword.

Oh, very well. She would never admit it aloud, but Elizabeth longed for a partner, too. Not a flirtation, or even a temporary affaire, but the full, true, sonnets-will-be-written-about-this whirlwind of romantic love.

You wouldn't think a suitable companion would be this difficult to find. She was a woman of simple pleasures: scenic walks through pleasure gardens, wine-drenched candlelit dinners, impaling brigands through the gullet with a sharp blade. The usual.

She wasn't even finicky! Elizabeth was open to accepting love in any form. Man…Woman…A lethal warrior or two…No, *three*, each of them larger and deadlier than the last…All right, yes, Elizabeth was finicky. She would settle for nothing less than a fearless soldier in shining armor who wanted her fighting at their side forevermore.

And *no* babies! Nothing dampened an afternoon of light bloodshed quite like the squalling of a helpless infant. Elizabeth would happily skip up to the altar with anyone who swashbuckled. Proficiency with a blade was her one and only obligatory criterion.

And likely the reason she was still a spinster at the age of one-and-thirty.

"You'll never believe this," Graham said from behind a stiff broadsheet. Each morning without fail, he read every newspaper and gossip rag in London from cover to cover.

Elizabeth took her place at the long dining table and glanced over at him with interest. "Is it an advertisement from a dashing knight in search of a bride?"

"You do not want to marry *this* peacock." Graham lowered the paper, revealing mischievous light brown eyes the same shade as his skin. A riot of black curls tumbled over his forehead, and he shook them out of his face. "I swear, the more money some of these noblemen acquire, the fewer brains in their heads. You remember Richard Reddington, of course?"

Elizabeth perked up. "Did he assassinate someone again?"

"Those rumors have yet to be proven." Graham's disgruntled expression indicated that even his formidable network of spies had thus far been unable to confirm the whispered tales.

"Who is Richard Reddington?" asked Tommy.

"He's a viscount's son with dubious associates in and out of polite society," Graham answered. "He collects artifacts of war and struts around Dorset wearing replica military uniforms—despite the battles being long over and his never having fought in them."

"He loves to be the center of attention," Elizabeth explained. "When he's not waltzing and carousing, Reddington leads a troupe of men who perform military reenactments."

A troupe that wouldn't *have* to be exclusively comprised of male soldiers, if the men in question would accept the possibility of a woman wielding a weapon. Elizabeth would make just as good a leader as Reddington. Or at least a competent foot soldier.

Years ago, she'd applied to become part of his reenactment squadron—only to be laughed at for being a "useless jest." Reddington and his followers had called her *rotund* and *ridiculous* and *as frightening as a mouse*... despite refusing to take up arms against her in a nice, friendly duel to the death. Or at least until Elizabeth disproved their alleged male superiority.

With half a chance, she could also trounce him quite thoroughly in the enthusiastic debates on war strategies and past battles Reddington presided over in his various gentlemen's clubs. If women weren't barred from those, too.

Graham shook out the newspaper. "By day, Reddington parades through England with a flock of cronies flanking him, often in uniform. By night, he parades through ballrooms and humble homes alike, as the toast of the upwardly inclined."

Philippa cringed in agreement. "My mother would have wedded me to him without blinking. And she's far from the only society-adjacent hopeful for whom 'heir to a title' absolves any other sins."

"But we mean real sins?" Tommy asked. "Crimes against something other than fashion and good breeding?"

Elizabeth stretched out her arms. "Just murder."

Tommy swung her gaze toward Graham. "Is that true, or is Elizabeth being bloodthirsty again?"

"Again?" Elizabeth repeated in offense. "I never *stop* being bloodthirsty."

"You're very sweet to Tickletums," Jacob whispered, pointing to the hedgehog sleeping beneath her chair. "As you are to all my animals. As well as to everyone in this family. And our clients."

"Never repeat such slander again," Elizabeth whispered back. "You'll ruin my reputation."

Graham ignored them and lowered the paper to answer Tommy. "Possibly true. Reddington is not without enemies, a few of whom have conveniently vanished off the face of the earth after committing some perceived slight against him."

"And the courts have done nothing?" Tommy exclaimed. "Can an heir apparent claim 'right of privilege' to exempt himself from the law even before he's inherited his title?"

"There's no murder without a body and no crime without evidence,"

Graham explained. "All we have are unsubstantiated rumors. The truth is, he's lord of a large-enough sector of society that someone hoping to get on his good side might have acted without Reddington explicitly making the request. In any case, that's all old news."

"What's Reddington done now?" Philippa asked.

"He intends to host a mock battle of Waterloo."

Elizabeth stabbed a fork in her eggs. "Which is a battle he and his soldiers did not fight, in a country they've likely not been to. Or will they all be traveling to the Netherlands to put on the performance?"

Graham shook his head. "It'll be in Dorset, one hundred and forty miles southwest of London. Presumably at his vast country estate. For the first time, however, Reddington announced he'll be selling tickets."

Kuni's eyebrows shot up almost as high as her long black braids. She reached for the paper. "Charging admission, as though to a play?"

"It *is* a play," Elizabeth grumbled. "And for those who haven't noticed, women act in plays all the time. At least, they do when men let them. I hope no one buys a single ticket."

"I hope he trips and falls on his bayonet," said Jacob. "Reddington's family money comes from plantations in the West Indies. He's never worked a day in his life or earned any of his privilege. Yet he's treated as a god because he has a title."

"Never working a day in one's life *is* the dream, for mothers like mine who despair of their daughters marrying well," Philippa said.

"Reddington does put in considerable effort," Elizabeth admitted. "I may have witnessed him lead his troops through practice drills on a few occasions. Though the training would have gone more smoothly if he'd taken my advice. I swear, that's the last time I prepare an unsolicited two-hour strategy lecture for a faux war general."

"*You* spoke to Reddington?" Graham put down his newspaper. Rarely did any event occur in London without his knowledge. The fact that Elizabeth had successfully kept a secret caused his eyes to boggle. "When did you meet—"

"Pardon the interruption." Their butler, Mr. Randall, had appeared in the dining room doorway. "You've a guest." He held up a calling card. "Shall I show Miss Oak into the usual parlor?"

"Gracious, that's the third new client this week." Chloe looked up from her slobbering devil-child and exchanged exhausted glances with Faircliffe. "We've barely a moment to eat or sleep."

"I'll attend to the caller." Elizabeth leapt up. "Perhaps she needs an assassin-for-hire."

All of her siblings scrambled to their feet.

"Don't you dare greet the new client alone," Graham warned her.

"Or offer to murder anyone for money," Jacob added.

"Maybe she'll suggest it first," Elizabeth said eagerly. "I have room in my schedule to poke holes in a villain or two."

Swiftly, she and the others relocated to the front parlor, where their new caller awaited.

Miss Oak was an older woman with graying locks. She appeared slightly overwhelmed at the sight of ten-and-a-half Wynchesters streaming through the door. But the parlor was large enough to accommodate everyone. In no time, the introductions were completed and the Wynchesters were seated with their prospective client.

Elizabeth took the chair as far as possible from Chloe and her baby.

"I am in desperate need of your help," said Miss Oak. "There is no legal recourse I can take to right this wrong, and I've nowhere else to turn."

Elizabeth was unsurprised. Virtually all their clients' stories began with that same lament.

"Please," said Graham. "How may we assist you?"

Miss Oak gazed at them beseechingly. "Castle Harbrook is family land. My sister and I spent the past ten years planning to turn the property into an orphanage and school for the indigent. That castle is mine by rights, but my nephew, the Earl of Densmore, refuses to vacate the property or hand over the deed!"

Elizabeth bared her teeth in disgust at the heartless nephew.

The entire Wynchester clan held orphanages in the highest regard. Not only were most of the original Wynchester siblings orphans themselves, but also Chloe and Tommy had first met in an orphanage. Providing shelter to innocent children was a far worthier pursuit than whatever the Earl of Densmore intended to do with his appropriated castle.

"Whilst I sympathize greatly," said Chloe's husband, the Duke of Faircliffe, "property disputes are generally the domain of the courts and not something the Wynchester family can settle by hand. Have you considered hiring a lawyer?"

"I've considered everything. The lawyer is on my side, but can do nothing." Miss Oak rubbed her wan face. "The situation is not as simple as I've made it sound."

"Then, please," said Graham gently. "Start at the beginning. Explain in as much detail as you can. If it is possible for us to help you, then by all means, we will do so."

Miss Oak nodded and took a deep breath. "The property in question is a disused castle that has belonged to my family for centuries. That is, until forty years ago, when my parents decided to include it as part of my elder sister's dowry in order for her to secure an aristocratic husband."

Elizabeth whistled under her breath. "A castle would do the trick."

"You'd think so, but my sister was lucky enough to make a love match. The Earl of Densmore would have married Arminia if her dowry consisted of no more than a bag of dirt. He didn't want or need Castle Harbrook. But now that he had it, my brother-in-law discovered he liked it. Rather than implement the comprehensive orphanage plans my sister and I had devised, he remodeled the castle into a country home."

Of course he had. Elizabeth met her siblings' gazes. Why provide shelter and education for hundreds of homeless children, when you could use the space for port and billiards instead?

"Although the earl was disinclined to turn the castle into an orphanage or a school while he was alive, he had no quarrel with our philanthropic plans becoming the castle's eventual fate. He bequeathed the property to his wife in his will, and Arminia rewrote hers to ensure the property would come to me. And then they had a son."

"Figures," Elizabeth muttered. Babies were unpredictable little beasts.

Two maids entered the parlor with tea service. Chloe handed her devil-spawn to Faircliffe so she could perform duties as hostess.

"After the birth of their heir, your sister and brother-in-law wrote you out of their wills?" Elizabeth asked.

Miss Oak looked up from her tea. "No. The earl rewrote his to bequeath everything but the castle to his son, presuming the child would care for his own mother. Arminia's only property to speak of would be the castle, which remained bequeathed to me in her testament."

"Then what's the problem?" Tommy asked.

"No one has seen Arminia's will in years," Miss Oak replied grimly. "And without a document stating otherwise, the new Earl of Densmore is the de facto heir of both of his parents' holdings. Including Castle Harbrook."

Jacob frowned. "Didn't you mention a lawyer?"

Miss Oak nodded. "The same one oversaw the writing of both wills. He kept a copy in his office, and left the originals with my sister and brother-in-law. When the earl died, his testament was found in the top drawer of his desk, as one might imagine. When Arminia passed of the same illness the following morning…"

Philippa gasped. "Someone stole her will to keep the castle from becoming an orphanage?"

"Was it the nephew?" Elizabeth demanded. "I'll kill him for you."

"My nephew doesn't care about much of anything, save the gaming tables," Miss Oak said with a sigh. "I was his governess until he went to Eton. Densmore was unfocused and impulsive, but a good lad at heart. I trust that is still the case. The real problem, I fear, is my sister."

Tommy raised her brows. "Your... dearly departed sister?"

Miss Oak nodded. "Arminia has always been too clever for her own good, and an ardent devotee of puzzles. When we were children, she loved to devise elaborate riddles in which one could find a hidden treasure by following a series of cryptic clues. I never made it past the first step and quickly tired of such games, but the earl adored puzzles as much as he worshipped Arminia. Their favorite pastime was leaving each other complex riddles to solve."

"Oh no." Philippa winced. "You mean the countess hid her will decades ago, believing her husband could easily follow the clues to find it, only for him to die first and her immediately after, before she had the opportunity to ensure the document made its way to your hands."

"In fact," Marjorie said, "as far as Arminia knew, this puzzle for her husband was just a private game. She never expected anyone else to have to decipher it."

"That is exactly the situation." Miss Oak's eyes were bleak. "As you can see, it's hopeless."

"Not at all," said Tommy. "Philippa is brilliant with codes and puzzles of every kind. What are the clues? Perhaps we can solve it right now."

"That's just it," said Miss Oak. "I don't have any clues. And even if I did, they were meant for the earl to understand, not me."

"What do you have?" Elizabeth asked.

"Scores of letters from Arminia detailing our future plans," Miss Oak answered. "Castle Harbrook was to become a place for children to grow and learn and gain secure employment. We planned to employ underprivileged instructors who are just as worthy. And now none of it will come to pass. Worst of all—"

"You haven't told us the worst part?" Adrian said in disbelief.

"Every part is the worst part." Miss Oak's shoulders drooped. "The only will that surfaced was the prior earl's, which means everything now belongs to my nephew. And other than a brief glimpse of Densmore at the funeral, I've not laid eyes on him since."

"Dastardly," Elizabeth said with disgust.

Miss Oak's mouth tightened. "That lad is fully aware that his mother and I wished to turn the castle into a school and orphanage. Even if we haven't yet found Arminia's will, Densmore knows what it says. To then prevent me from fulfilling our dream...his mother's dream..." Her voice cracked.

"I imagine you sent your nephew correspondence?" Philippa asked gently.

"Enough to paper every wall in the castle," Miss Oak confirmed. "I didn't intend to open the school until after my year of mourning, but there was no reason to postpone possession of the deed and ensure all the pieces were in place. But without Arminia's testament, I have nothing. And her will is hidden somewhere in that castle."

"You mentioned a legal opinion being on your side?" Graham prompted.

Miss Oak set down her cup. "For as much good as it does. An accidental fire at the lawyer's office destroyed the only other copy. Densmore is my only hope. He responded to my inquiries only once, to say he had not come across his mother's will or any clues as to its location. Our year of mourning concluded last week. That very night, my nephew took it upon himself to go out drinking…and gambled away the castle in a card game."

Elizabeth gasped. "But it wasn't his to wager! He *knew* better."

"Perhaps why he wrote an IOU, but never handed over the deed," Miss Oak said.

Faircliffe inclined his head. "A debt of honor, like the letters from your sister, is not legally valid."

Chloe patted her baby's back. "Without a will, it could come down to possession of the title—and the castle."

Jacob placed the ferret he'd been holding on the floor. "Then we must talk Densmore into handing over that deed."

"Or steal it, if he refuses to cooperate," murmured Chloe.

Elizabeth smiled. "And then force him to leave the castle by sword-point."

"Has your nephew somewhere else to live?" Philippa asked.

Miss Oak nodded. "He owns several properties. Densmore does not need the castle for any practical reason and, indeed, has spent very little time there until after he lost that wager."

"The earl's there now?"

"He's not left the grounds since that night." Miss Oak's shoulders tightened in visible frustration. "I've a waiting list a mile long of bright young women eager to begin work as caretakers and tutors. I'd hoped to start interviewing instructors next week, but Densmore has barred the door and will let no one in."

"Wait." Marjorie turned toward Faircliffe. "Doesn't the earl attend the House of Lords?"

"I'm not sure I've ever seen him there," the duke replied. "I wouldn't recognize him if he were in this parlor."

"That's because he prefers gaming hells to Parliament," Miss Oak said. "The real question is how to stop him from giving the deed to Richard Reddington."

"*Reddington?*" said all ten Wynchesters at once.

"That's who won my land in that card game," Miss Oak explained. "At least, so he thinks. Without Arminia's will to say otherwise… Should I attempt to keep the castle, Reddington has the resources to make my life difficult."

"I'll run him through with my blade," Elizabeth said quickly.

Jacob kicked Elizabeth in the shins.

"And take off Densmore's head, too," she whispered unrepentantly. "Her wretched nephew is the one willfully refusing to hand the castle over to his aunt, as his mother wanted. Only a scoundrel would disregard his parent's dying wish."

Elizabeth had no tolerance for heartless, selfish, dishonorable knaves. In fact, she would be proud to wrest Miss Oak's legally inherited deed from the dastardly Earl of Densmore's cold, dead hands!

3

◈

The Earl of Densmore's very much alive hands . . . were nowhere near his mother's old castle.

Where, precisely, the earl's hands—and the rest of him—might be was a question Stephen Lenox would love to know the answer to. He'd run his lordship through with a blade himself for putting him in this damnable situation.

Cover for me, his favorite, if feckless, cousin had said. *I'll be gone for a few nights at the most. All you have to do is pretend to be me. It'll be easy! You're next in line to the title anyway. Just collect my correspondence, don't let anyone in the door, and I'll be back before you know it.*

The earl had not come back. Stephen was beginning to suspect he never would.

Castle Harbrook was now his prison.

Therefore, Stephen had taken it upon himself to fill the days with as many distractions as possible. This far from London, he did not have access to his workroom at home, but that did not prevent him from turning his cousin's castle into a makeshift temporary laboratory.

Stephen stood in the dungeon at the rear of the castle. An old trap-door, positioned above his head, hadn't been used in centuries. Over time, the door had been covered with soil and seedlings. Stephen had unearthed the portal out of boredom, his first week here. It was now wide open.

Sunlight streamed into the dungeon below. Footmen clamored around the opening, taking delivery of Stephen's latest purchases as rapidly as possible.

They had to be quick, because Stephen did not wish to be seen. Not because the ruse might fall apart. He and his cousin favored each other enough to easily be mistaken for brothers. Stephen was not worried about some Grand Unmasking. He worried about *passing* convincingly enough that someone would shoot an arrow through his heart.

Richard Reddington had threatened to do just that. And since more than one of his known prior enemies had disappeared without a trace...

"That's the last of the deliveries," said the butler, McCarthy.

Once the servants had gone, Stephen closed the trapdoor. After exiting the dungeon, he secured the interior door separating the underground chamber from the rest of the castle. This lock could only be opened from inside the residential part of the castle. Meaning anyone unlucky enough to sneak in through the trapdoor would find themselves trapped inside the dungeon for good. The last thing anyone needed was for one of the employees to be stuck inside.

Out in the passageway, the footmen did not tarry. They had already formed a queue and were passing Stephen's crates up the stairs to the medieval Great Hall, where Stephen had set up his work area.

He was not used to so many servants. Though in this old pile, he very much appreciated their assistance. Stephen helped carry the heavy objects upstairs, but taking on all that labor by himself would have caused an untenable delay in the current project underway.

On the main floor, Mrs. Hennessy, the housekeeper, arched her gray brows. "Have you considered receiving something *normal*?"

Like what? Mashed peas? New cravats? Visits from friends or paramours?

Stephen didn't know enough about fashion to mind that he didn't have any. The same went for other people. Romantic relationships lasting longer than one night weren't worth the bother. He was a recluse and liked it that way. In fact, he had spent decades keeping people *out*. Even at home, the only time he stepped out of doors was to receive a delivery like this one.

If only Stephen weren't so fond of his disarmingly charming, unabashedly useless cousin, he wouldn't be in this pickle.

Stephen did not understand other people, and other people tended not to understand him, but the Earl of Densmore... *There* was an easy fellow to fathom. Densmore liked exactly two things: fine wine and a good wager, not necessarily in that order. The probability that the earl had forgotten about his cousin entirely and was off in his cups in some gaming hell was approximately 0.9854, which was damn near mathematical certainty.

That was the sort of thing Stephen understood. Facts, figures, mathematics, science, machines. Things he could puzzle out with logic. Things he could put his hands on and touch.

The butler slapped the latest stack of correspondence into Stephen's hands.

"Are you certain you don't want me at the front door?" McCarthy asked, his eyes pleading.

"It's impossible to enter that way," Stephen reminded him.

"It wouldn't have to be," McCarthy grumbled, "if it weren't for your... renovations."

"And I have not finished my improvements," Stephen informed him. "I will continue until the rightful Earl of Densmore returns and my life is no longer at risk."

Stephen strode to the Great Hall. The enormous room could host a party fit for the Queen. Not that Stephen would ever host a party. He didn't even host tea. At home, he employed exactly one maid and exactly one manservant. Who, like Stephen, had expected him to return in a few days, not months.

"The new crates have been stacked next to the previous ones," reported a footman. "Will there be anything else, my lord?"

"I'm not your lord," Stephen reminded him.

"You said to pretend until the earl returns."

"I said to do so in the presence of witnesses who might otherwise—" Stephen cut himself off. The footman was apparently teasing him. At least the staff still had a sense of humor. "Thank you. That will be all."

The footmen filed out of the Great Hall. A few of them glanced askance at the mathematical equations scrawled over every inch of the gray stone walls in bright white chalk.

Yes, that was what Stephen needed. More chalk. It ought to be in one of the new crates.

He headed over to rummage through the boxes, tossing the stack of unread correspondence atop one of the piles while he searched.

The walls were covered in chalk equations, and the perimeter was lined with wooden crates. But the *interior* of the enormous salon— that was where the magic took place.

Not literally, of course. Magic did not exist. Only machines, which could be designed to perform tasks that seemed like magic.

Stephen's inventions, in various stages of completion, filled the castle. They were his companions, his friends, his family. Most of the time, he didn't need anything or anyone else. Machines were better than people. They could be counted upon to do exactly the thing you expected them to do, with no surprises or misunderstandings.

If Stephen did occasionally crave connection with others, he achieved it through science and mathematics. The farmers using the all-weather irrigator or the mechanical poultry feeder would never know their modern conveniences were thanks to Stephen Lenox. It didn't matter. He was useful, and his efforts were important in their lives whether they realized it or not.

"Aha!" Triumphant, Stephen pulled a fresh stick of chalk from a newly opened box. He tucked the white stick carefully into the lined inner pocket he'd had sewn into all his waistcoats for just this purpose.

Now he could attend to his cousin's latest correspondence.

Stephen carried the letters to the table he'd placed at the center of the four largest machines in the Great Hall. He supposed he could have commissioned a nice, heavy desk, but Stephen liked to keep things light and movable, when possible. He settled himself in the single, padded, high-back chair.

"I suppose some portion of these letters shall require a response of some type," he said aloud to the cavernous room. "Which means *I* shall require a plume."

He pulled the third of four levers attached to the table.

The slight action of having pulled the lever caused a slack rope to tighten. The rope stretched to the tall ceiling, slipped through a metal hoop screwed into the stone, and traveled several feet before terminating in a knot.

The knot was attached to the metal handle of a wooden pail. The sharp motion of the rope upset the balance of the full pail, and a gallon of water poured straight down into a basin perched atop a seesaw mechanism installed high above Stephen's head. As the basin filled with water, its side of the seesaw sank in a rush.

The opposite side of the seesaw therefore thrust upward—launching a fat red marble into the air, where it landed on the outermost edge of a long pipe cut in half lengthwise. The marble zigzagged along the floating metal track, until it shot out of the final opening and crashed into the back of a ragdoll.

The doll tumbled from its precarious perch and landed on a

battledore racket, the netting of which slapped down as the corresponding handle shot up. This handle was attached to a string that knocked a rubber mallet against the first in a long row of dangling glass vials.

Each of the transparent cylinders banged against the next in turn, the varying levels of water inside causing a recognizable melody to the sound. Stephen had chosen a popular reel for the tune. He was not one for dancing—such steps usually required a partner—but he did enjoy music, and thought a few bars of a Scottish reel added a sophisticated touch.

The final glass vial swung into a hook, which engaged a pulley, which pulled a wire, which activated a funnel, which released a sack of pebbles, which traveled down a tube, which led to a book, which fell against the rear of a small wooden horse on wheels, which rolled until its muzzle hit a button, which opened a hatch, from which tumbled a boot, which fell atop a cushion, which nudged a teacup, which spun into a domino...that had been placed in a long, snaking line of its brethren.

Each domino banged into its neighbor in quick succession, a rather melodious *rat-a-tat-tat* as the ivories clinked against each other faster and faster around a wide wheel suspended horizontally above Stephen's head. The fall of the final domino caused an infinitesimal gust of air, too small to be detected from where Stephen sat below, but just strong enough to knock a whisper-light feather free from its perch.

Thanks to a small weight attached to its nib, the feather fell slowly, lightly, tipping this way and that in its graceful descent until it landed at last in the center of Stephen's upturned palm.

"There," he said with satisfaction. "Much better. Now we can begin."

He retrieved a knife from his pocket and began shaping the tip of his new plume.

Yes, of course there was a simpler way to retrieve a feather. But who said simpler was better? Stephen abhorred being bored and prevented such an atrocity from ever occurring by applying himself to chalking theorems and resetting machines while he waited on deliveries of the materials needed for his next inventions.

And now, correspondence.

As usual, the majority of today's batch of correspondence was from Richard Reddington, Reddington's man of business, Reddington's lawyer, Reddington's other lawyer, and Reddington's *other* lawyer.

Stephen would not be putting in any Court of Chancery appearances in his cousin's name—he rarely stepped out of doors at all, except in the pursuit of pistachio ices—so he placed the legal inquiries to one side. Later, he would insert the documents in a machine that would raise them up to Densmore's study to be filed with the others.

He did, however, read the latest personal threat from Reddington.

The war enthusiast's vast country estate abutted the eastern border of Castle Harbrook. Only a strip of dense woods separated the two properties, half belonging to each of them. Well, it belonged to Reddington's father, anyway. But the viscount rarely left London, which put control of the country estate fully in Richard Reddington's hands.

This proximity to Castle Harbrook was the reason Reddington positively foamed at the mouth to take possession. He could not bear to live in the shadow of a castle that did not belong to him. And it would be the perfect site for Reddington's upcoming reenactment of the battle of Waterloo. He inundated the "earl" with missives alternatively demanding legal action, or felonious imprisonment, or demanding satisfaction at dawn in a duel to the death.

"I politely decline," Stephen murmured. "Yet again."

He had never shot a pistol, and did not intend to take a bullet for his cousin. Stephen *could* be talked into creating a remotely detonated projectile-firing machine, but it would most likely be too unwieldy to take to a clandestine clearing for a duel of honor.

What Stephen really wanted was to go home. He wished he hadn't given his word to guard the castle until Densmore returned. In an abundance of caution, Stephen had taken it upon himself to reinforce the security of the entrance to the castle.

"'Choose your seconds,'" he read aloud from the latest missive. "'This is not an invitation. It is a command. Hand over the castle as promised, or prepare your dueling pistol.'"

Stephen rolled his eyes. He didn't have a "second." He was a *recluse*. If he were forced to name a cohort, the only person he'd be able to come up with would be his cousin, the Earl of Densmore. And if Stephen knew where to find *that* roguish scamp, he wouldn't be in this position to begin with.

He tossed the letter onto the pile without responding. Reddington was Densmore's problem, not Stephen's.

For now.

4

There was a baby in the Planning Parlor.

Elizabeth went on full defense to stay clear, but the little devil's sparkling angel-blue gaze tracked her every move like the barrels of a pair of pistols.

"Dorian adores you!" exclaimed Chloe in delight.

"Keep it away from me," warned Elizabeth.

The rest of their siblings poured into the sound-dampened, second-floor room, their feet moving quickly across the black slate floor with its chalk remnants of maps and their plans for all of the other justice-seeking missions currently underway. Early morning sunshine streamed through narrow openings in the tall curtains.

For now, the Wynchester crew ignored the huge walnut-and-burl table with its myriad secret compartments in the center of the other half of the room. Instead, they settled in a large crescent of sofas and armchairs before an unlit fireplace.

"Let's get started," said Tommy, a cosmetics case in her lap, and a single bush of side-whiskers protruding from one of her cheeks. "I have to infiltrate a Cheapside tavern in less than two hours."

"And I must leave for St. James in forty-five minutes," said Kuni, a dagger in each hand.

The rest of the siblings chimed in with all the places they had to be and the tasks they had to perform before the day was through.

"Wait," said Chloe. "Lawrence isn't here yet."

"We can't wait for the duke," Graham told her, with a glance at his pocket watch. "I hereby call this meeting to order."

The door to the Planning Parlor swung open.

"Lawrence!" Chloe plopped the baby onto Elizabeth's lap. "Hold my son for me. I'll be back in a moment."

She ran to greet her husband before Elizabeth could object.

"*Help*," Elizabeth gulped. The chubby infant sagged forward and drooled on her stomach. "Somebody, *help* me."

Her family did not hear her. Their singular focus was intent on Graham.

"I was able to track down the lawyer who drafted the countess's will," he began. "Miss Oak was right. Due to the fire, he no longer has a copy of any item."

"But he corroborated its contents," added Jacob, with a four-foot snake draped about his shoulders like a winter scarf.

Faircliffe finally stopped nuzzling his wife. "A lawyer's memory is not the same as a physical document. Agreeing with Miss Oak isn't something that would hold up in court."

"Get over here," said Elizabeth. "Rescue me from your baby."

"Then we have to go to Dorset," said Tommy. "And search the castle from top to bottom until we find the original will and testament."

Marjorie frowned. "If the earl won't open his door to his aunt, he won't be an accommodating host to us."

"There are inns and hostelries," Adrian pointed out. "We can rent rooms nearby and pay as many calls as it takes to convince Densmore to do the right thing."

"I can't go," Chloe said with regret.

"You can come and collect your hell-spawn." Elizabeth poked at the baby's soft belly with her finger.

Dorian burped and chortled toothlessly. A white dribble of glistening milk appeared at the corner of his pink lips.

"Kuni and I can't go, either," said Graham. "We're handling the O'Sullivan affair."

"Philippa and I barely have time to don and doff disguises between missions," said Tommy. "If I don't finish applying my side-whiskers soon—"

"I'll go," said Adrian. "I love convincing people of things. It might be my single greatest talent."

"Second-greatest," Marjorie said with a rosy blush. "Unfortunately, you and I are promised to finish the restoration project for the Laurent case. And the first public showing for our newest crop of art students is on Saturday."

Elizabeth glared at the baby in her lap. Chloe had given birth shortly before Christmastide, which had kept her and the Duke of Faircliffe from joining the rest of the family on a holiday to Balcovia. Which meant this round ball of drool was now six months old.

Dorian fell forward, his still-bald head planting facedown in her lap.

"Oof," she said loudly. "This creature attacked me. Someone pass me a dagger. Self-defense is a perfectly reasonable reaction when under enemy fire."

No one looked her way.

"I could go," Jacob offered. "All you'll need to do in my absence is mind the hawks and raptors, collect rats to feed the snakes, ensure that the Highland tiger—"

"None of us are doing any of that," said Tommy. "No one but you can enter that barn and exit with their life."

Slowly, everyone turned to Elizabeth.

She paused in the act of trying to push the floppy, flailing baby back into a seated position. Dorian laughed as if he were having the time of his life. Elizabeth was ready to end her own.

"I'll feed the tigers," she said quickly. "I'll feed this baby *to* the tigers."

"Protect my baby with your life!" Chloe called out from across the room.

"It's a Highland tiger," Jacob assured her. "Too small to eat a baby."

"What if it shares the juiciest pieces with the snakes and raptors?" Elizabeth muttered under her breath. "This could be a team effort."

"You'll have to go to Dorset," said Graham.

"Elizabeth?" Marjorie said in disbelief. "She's better with children than she is at persuasion, and she just offered to feed a baby to a tiger."

"Rude," said Elizabeth. "Also true."

"Aren't you currently in the middle of a mission?" asked Philippa.

"Besides the one where I subtly divest myself of this baby?"

"She's not," said Graham. "Elizabeth finished her open cases yesterday, with the Bunyan recovery."

"And we're thinking of sending her…alone?" asked Tommy carefully.

"I'm never alone!" Elizabeth reached for her sword stick and almost dropped the baby. She had to wrap her arm protectively about the hell-beast in order to brandish her sheathed sword. "I always have a blade or two with me."

Marjorie cleared her throat. "Does anyone else think sending Elizabeth to gently persuade a haughty earl is like sending Attila the Hun to negotiate a peaceful ceasefire?"

"Attila the Hun is a personal hero," Elizabeth said contentedly. "I will make him proud."

The baby gummed a wet spot into the flesh of Elizabeth's upper arm.

"You might be able to do it," Kuni mused. "For a woman whose bedchamber could double as an armory, wheedling a simple piece of paper ought to be an easy task."

"I don't wheedle," said Elizabeth. "I *whack*." She demonstrated with several wild swipes of her sword stick.

The baby giggled and reached his pudgy hands toward the sword handle.

"You must play the diplomat," Graham warned her. "And if that doesn't work, you must use charm to manipulate him into handing over his late mother's will."

"I can be diplomatic and charming," she assured him. "I never murder people without justifiable provocation."

Truth be told, it wasn't the prospect of employing her as-yet-untried skills of diplomacy that worried her. Although Elizabeth had never attempted a calm, rational negotiation, she had read countless tomes on the art of warfare, all of which explained the ways in which logic and persuasion were as important as maintaining a sharp blade. Though she liked to pretend there was nothing rattling in her head besides swordplay, on the days she couldn't rise from bed, she often rehearsed the logistics of imaginary confrontations and peace treaties in her mind.

It was the not-always-able-to-rise-from-bed part that made her hesitant to undertake a mission without sufficient reinforcements.

If something went wrong—like, for example, her *body*, whose signature move was to rebel against her at the worst possible moments—Elizabeth would not have the luxury of nine other Wynchesters at her side to support her and pick up the charge.

She would be totally on her own.

"You can say no," Philippa said gently. "We'll find another way."

Elizabeth scoffed, far too determined to mask any lack of confidence and avoid showing weakness rather than actually voicing her fears. She would never let down her family. They believed in her. So did Miss Oak. Wherever a client needed Elizabeth, she would go. No matter how much panic boiled up inside.

"Maybe the mission will be a two-for-one," she said with forced cheerfulness. "I can poke holes in the Earl of Densmore *and* that strutting peacock Richard Reddington."

"We've been over this," Jacob reminded her. "No murdering. You can't run a fake general through with a real sword without ironclad justification."

Graham glanced up from his case notes. "Didn't you say Reddington's money comes from the slave trade? Ironclad justification."

"There we have it." Jacob plucked the baby from Elizabeth's lap and gestured toward her sword. "Run Reddington through as many times as you please. I'll loan you a few raptors to pick the bones clean."

"Recover the will and testament first," Tommy said quickly. "And *then* you can unleash Beth the Berserker."

"Done." Elizabeth smiled happily. Perhaps this trip would be fun after all.

5

The grueling two-day journey was absolute misery.

Elizabeth's body hated being cooped up in a carriage. She could manage a few jaunts across town, and could easily make the trip from central London to nearby Islington, where she lived with her siblings. Much farther than that, however...

The boat to Balcovia last winter had been glorious. One could stand up on a boat. One could stretch, one could walk, one could swing one's sword on the empty deck in the early dawn. One could even find oneself immediately surrounded by a dozen tall, strapping Balcovian warriors.

A tiny enclosed carriage was rubbish compared to that. She did not blame her body for rebelling. The Wynchester family's finest coach-and-four was still a rickety coffin, rattling along on iron wheels over rutted roads laced with jarring holes. She couldn't even read her newest book on war strategies.

By the time her carriage arrived in Dorset, Elizabeth wanted nothing more than to find an inn and bury herself in cushions and cheap gin until her body recovered.

Unfortunately, their benevolent client would not hear of her rescuer spending unnecessary coin on accommodations. Miss Oak possessed a perfectly fine cottage in town, with a perfectly fine guest room in which it would be perfectly fine for Elizabeth to stay as long as it took to gain entrance to the castle and find the hidden will.

"Perfectly dreadful," Elizabeth muttered, flat on her back in the unfamiliar bed.

"What's that, dear?" came the immediate response from the other side of the closed guest-chamber door.

Elizabeth covered her face with a cushion.

Nothing could be more embarrassing than convalescing in a client's guest quarters instead of charging out to right wrongs. Nothing, that was, except the client in question hovering right outside the guest-chamber door, querying about Elizabeth's well-being every five bloody minutes.

"Are you sure you're all right?" came Miss Oak's muffled voice.

Elizabeth added another pillow to the pile atop her face. Smothering herself to death was preferable to answering this query for the hundredth time this morning.

During a flare-up, her siblings knew better than to pepper her with such absurd questions, which called attention to the very thing Elizabeth was doing her damnedest to block out. The more she thought about her pain, the more it hurt.

The more she could distract herself, the faster time went. The faster time went, the more she relaxed. The more she relaxed, the quicker she healed.

"Miss Wynchester?" came her client's concerned voice again. "Do you need anything?"

"I'm fine!" Elizabeth shouted through her pillows.

She was angry at herself, and at her body. Frustrated that here she was, a stone's throw from the castle, unable to do a bloody thing about it. Elizabeth hated feeling helpless. She was only of value when she was out swashbuckling, and worthless when lying about motionless.

What could be worse than a worthless Wynchester?

"How is the temperature in the room?" Miss Oak queried. "Do you need help opening the windows? The sash sometimes sticks."

For the love of God, Elizabeth could open her own damn windows. Usually.

"The windows are fine!" she called back. *Please go away.*

Elizabeth had not told Miss Oak that the carriage had rattled her joints out of their sockets and set her stiff back to spasming as though her muscles had been replaced with pointy springs.

She didn't tell anyone. Not anymore. Her body was nobody's business but her own. When she was a child, the adults in her life hadn't believed her. Accused her of lying about the pain. Forced her to do more, rather than less, in punishment.

Years later, when she'd finally seen a doctor, they weren't much more helpful. Baron Vanderbean had taken her to as many specialists as he could find. The ones who actually listened to her had been sympathetic, but baffled. No one could fix a problem they didn't understand. The best the doctors could do was dose her with bitter laudanum until she was barely conscious. And if that was the best they could do, she'd rather drink something she enjoyed.

She reached for her flask, hesitated, then dropped it into her open valise beside the bed. She'd stopped drinking as soon as she'd fallen into a dreamless slumber the night before. Gin was tricky. She needed just enough to fall asleep, but not so much that she felt worse the next day instead of better.

"If you need anything . . ." came Miss Oak's tentative voice through the wall.

"I don't need anything!" Elizabeth yelled through the pillows.

She needed a new back, new hips, and new legs. These were not things one could order from a warehouse. Elizabeth was saddled with what she had. At least she was starting to feel better. If she could get decent rest, it would at least be a sixty percent day—which would feel miraculous after suffering through a fifteen percent night. Her fingers dug into the blanket.

Was it so terrible to want to be the heroine on her own terms? Her swords were right there, in their own trunk, waiting for her. And waiting. And waiting.

Go to Dorset, Graham had said.

It'll be fun, Tommy had said.

Maybe you'll meet someone, Marjorie had said.

And fill a nursery with babies, Chloe had said.

Ha! Comedians, all of them. A regular family of court jesters.

If Elizabeth could get out of this bed, then yes, she'd absolutely be willing to climb back up into it with the right partner. She was far from prudish—or even a virgin. She'd have followed any of the Balcovian warriors back into their cabin, if her family hadn't been aboard the same ship to tease her about it.

But as for stumbling into a real romance... Whom were they bamming?

The only people in her family not to have found the person they were meant to spend forever with were Elizabeth and Jacob. Her brother would no doubt be next to fall in love. He was handsome and warm and sweet and romantic and cuddly and poetic—none of which applied to Elizabeth.

Smitten women regularly threw themselves at her soulful brother. If he ever set down his snakes and raptors, he could find a match within seconds. Elizabeth secretly *wanted* a match and had had no luck.

Jacob was a poet. He was in tune with his feelings. Expressive. Eloquent.

Elizabeth was a lifelong curmudgeon who would rather hurl herself on the knife of despair than expose any vulnerability.

Perchance because she suspected the real problem was not that *she* hated other people so much as *Elizabeth* being the unlovable one. If she was a heroine, it was of the unlikeable variety. And so she reacted in the only way she could: by going on the attack before others could strike first.

"If you want tea…" Miss Oak began on the opposite side of the door.

Elizabeth dug her fists into the pile of pillows on her face to block out her scream.

"…there are biscuits in the oven," Miss Oak finished.

Biscuits. Elizabeth flung the pillows from her face and sniffed the air. The cottage indeed smelled like biscuits. Warm and sugary. Her stomach growled in anticipation.

With great care, she tested the suppleness of each joint and muscle one by one. Forcing her body into action before it was ready was the easiest way to exacerbate the problem. Contrarily, stretches and light exercise actually helped the recovery process.

Definitely at forty percent. Maybe even rising to forty-five.

It would have to be good enough.

Elizabeth eased out of bed. Her hips were stiff, but mobile. Her back sore, but not spasming. Her legs and knees, as good as new. This might even end up being a seventy percent day.

"Don't eat all the biscuits," she yelled. "I'm coming."

She cleaned up with the bowl of water at the side table, then slid on a fresh dress. Clothing sorted, she made a halfhearted pass with a hairbrush, then hurried to open her door.

Miss Oak was *right there*, beaming at her.

And in her hands was a tray of piping hot biscuits.

Elizabeth picked up a biscuit, tossing it from hand to hand between bites so that it would not burn her fingers. "When I finish these, I shall solve the puzzle and collect your sister's will. Maybe Densmore has already found it, and all I'll have to do is retrieve it from him."

Miss Oak brightened. "Do you want me to come with you? I'm rubbish at puzzles, but I've known my nephew all his life."

"It's better for you to stay here." Elizabeth selected a second biscuit. "If Densmore won't hand over the will or allow me in to search, I might have to do...diplomacy."

Miss Oak nodded. "My nephew can be hardheaded. I hope he'll listen to reason."

"He'll listen to"—*a sharp sword*—"my brand of persuasion, I am certain."

Elizabeth took another biscuit. These were exceptionally fine biscuits. Almost as good as the ones Cook made at home.

Her heart gave a pang at the thought. She'd scarcely been gone two days, and she missed her family already. But there would be no going home until she resolved the problem.

"What kind of clues did your sister leave when she made puzzles for you as children?" Elizabeth asked.

Miss Oak made a face. "Impossible ones. Oh, they were always logical in retrospect, but my brain doesn't work in double meanings. Which is partly how we came up with our institution. As a childless woman who has always longed for children to care for, an orphanage is the perfect vocation for me. Whereas my sister couldn't wait to instruct an entire school full of eager-eyed pupils in the art of puzzles and wordplay, amongst other topics."

Elizabeth shuddered. As a childless woman who prayed nightly for her unencumbered streak never to end, administering an orphanage sounded like hell on earth. She would rather do anything else. Such as tear a castle apart with her bare hands if that's what it took to find the will and help her client's dreams come true.

"You don't remember what any of her old clues were like?"

"That was decades ago, my dear. I can tell you the absurd question Arminia wanted to ask the potential instructors we interviewed: 'What we caught, we threw away. What we didn't catch, we kept. What did we keep?' Bizarre. I still don't know the answer."

"Lice," Elizabeth answered without hesitation. "Or fleas, perhaps, but in this case the answer is definitely lice."

Miss Oak blinked. "*Lice*? Who would guess that?"

"Anyone who's ever tried and failed to rid themselves of the itchy little pests. Or who recalls an ancient legend about the Greek poet Homer and a pair of fishermen on the isle of Ios."

"Naturally," Miss Oak murmured with a wondrous shake of her head. "My sister would have loved you. If we knew any of the clues she'd meant to leave behind, you probably *could* follow them to the hiding place."

"Are you absolutely certain we don't have any hint?"

"Arminia would have given the clues to her husband, not to me. And she died before she could do that much. Remember, they took ill at the same time."

"But are you certain she took all her clues to the grave? One cannot predict one's own death. An apoplexy, a carriage accident, an unfortunate batch of shellfish... There are any number of ways she might have died before her husband. Surely someone as clever as your sister would have accounted for such a circumstance."

Miss Oak looked impressed. "You're right. Arminia must have left the first clue long before she took ill. Something that wouldn't *look* like a clue to the average person but would make sense to her husband. Of course, we don't know what it was or where it might be, so I'm not sure how that helps."

Elizabeth considered. "You know what *would* help me search? A sense of the castle. Can you describe the layout of the rooms, as best you recall?"

Miss Oak brightened. "I can do better than that. Arminia and I refined countless sketches of how we planned to turn Castle Harbrook into an orphanage. I can give you maps of the castle's interior as it stands now, and how it will look once it becomes a school."

"Just a 'before' map, please. I'll see the renovations in person, once you've opened your school."

Elizabeth took one last biscuit as Miss Oak hurried to a portable escritoire and rifled through a large stack of papers.

At last, her client withdrew a document in triumph. "Here's your map. It may not be perfectly to scale, but it's as close as I can provide. Is there anything else you need?"

"Thank you." Elizabeth folded the map carefully and tucked it into a hidden pocket Tommy had sewn into her skirt. "One last item. Have you a conveyance I can borrow?"

"Didn't you come in a carriage?" Miss Oak asked with confusion. "You placed it in rented mews down the street."

Elizabeth shook her head. "I was hoping to arrive at the castle in something a little less extravagant. I don't want to tip my hand before I've had the opportunity to introduce myself."

"Well," Miss Oak said doubtfully, "I usually walk wherever I need to go, but we can borrow a simple pony cart, if that's something you think you could use."

"Oh, I can use it." Elizabeth smiled her cobra smile.

A pony cart was perfect. The earl would never see her coming.

6

Another day, another batch of correspondence. Stephen opened the newest missive from Reddington with a sigh. Did sons of viscounts truly have *nothing* else to do all day but scribble increasingly bloodthirsty threats to the earl next door?

Stephen skimmed the letter. Reddington was demanding immediate occupancy of Castle Harbrook grounds, so that he and his soldiers could practice their formations in time for a public spectacle next month on 18 June.

"'Consider this your official warning,'" Stephen read aloud. "'We're watching you. If you fail to hand over that deed...Mr. Reddington shall assume control by force, even if it means laying siege on his own castle.'"

Oh, for the love of God. Stephen wouldn't fall for that twaddle. No spoiled lordling was choleric enough to storm his own castle.

"'We're watching you,'" Stephen repeated in aristocratic accents. "Of all the idle, idiotic threats..."

Reddington's country estate did adjoin the castle property, but a dense strip of woods stretched between them. Reddington could station a man at every window of his resplendent manor, and at best all he would see was three acres of trees.

Nonetheless, the ominous tone was unsettling enough that Stephen peeked through a window to make certain Richard Reddington was not watching him.

No one was there.

"Don't let that man under your skin," he chided himself.

To prove he had no fear of Reddington's empty threats, Stephen donned a nice evening coat and a matching black top hat. After disabling most of the protective modifications he'd made to the castle's entryway, Stephen picked his way carefully to the front door and strode out onto the grass.

Whoosh.

An arrow immediately shot forth from the shadowed thicket of trees, spearing straight through the front of his hat with enough force to part his hair down the middle and send the black felt top hat flying backward.

With a yelp, Stephen dashed back inside the castle and slammed the enormous wooden door, grateful it was as thick as the length of his forearm. Penetrating this entrance would require a battering ram, not a bow and arrow.

Nonetheless, it was several moments before his frantic heartbeat returned to normal. And his arrow-punctured hat would never be waterproof again.

He scooped up the fallen hat and ripped the arrow from the felt, ruining both objects in the process. Curse his misguided attempt to help his cousin! Gritting his teeth, Stephen reentered the main quarters of the castle and stalked down the corridor toward the stairs leading up to his spy turret.

The butler intercepted him before Stephen could ascend the first step. "Did you have a nice breath of fresh air, my lord?"

"Did you *see* what happened?" Stephen exploded in disbelief. "That madman nearly took off my head!" He held up the two broken halves of the arrow.

McCarthy plucked the wooden pieces from Stephen's hand. "I'll add it to the kindling, my lord."

"We shouldn't have to worry about..." Stephen's chest tightened with anxiety. It was one thing for *him* to be inconvenienced due to yet another of his cousin's zany schemes. It was quite another for the innocent servants' lives to be in danger, all because their absentee employer promised their home to a madman. "Don't step outside. Tell the others. It isn't safe."

"The entryway hasn't been safe since the moment you arrived. No one can leave until you disarm the cobweb of—"

"No, not my machines. Richard Reddington *shot* at me. He may do the same to others. Please don't put yourself in harm's way."

"I just returned from out of doors an hour ago," McCarthy pointed out. "I delivered your correspondence."

Stephen stared at him. That was true. It was how Stephen had come into possession of Reddington's threatening letter to begin with. The scullery maids had also performed their early morning shopping at the market.

We're watching you was clearly meant for Stephen, not the servants. Or rather, the threat was against the Earl of Densmore, whom Reddington believed Stephen to be.

"I suppose that's as silver a lining as I'm likely to get," Stephen said. "Until Reddington controls the castle, he's prepared to shoot me on sight—but at least the rest of you are safe."

"Perhaps he hopes to keep us on staff," McCarthy said. "Finding good help can be difficult."

Finding Stephen's cousin was also vexingly difficult. Especially since Stephen couldn't admit he was looking for the earl, being as he was supposed to be pretending to *be* him.

"Shall I mend your hat?" asked McCarthy.

"More kindling," Stephen said with a sigh, and handed it over. "I shan't be venturing back outside until the real earl returns."

"A wise decision." McCarthy dropped the broken arrow into the ruined hat and strode away.

Stephen trudged up to the turret to reenable the castle's defenses.

Reddington wanted legal possession of the castle. The problem was, Stephen did not have the requested deed. Although the document had reportedly been stored with the late earl's will, Stephen had gone through every page of his cousin's accounts dozens of times without coming across any hint of it.

Even if Stephen were to stumble across the deed, Reddington wasn't the only one asking for it. Miss Oak, an older woman who lived in the main town, held an equally plausible yet legally unenforceable claim on the castle. Her sister had allegedly bequeathed it to her in her will.

Which was also inconveniently missing, making her claim impossible to verify.

Although he read every one of Miss Oak's pleading letters, Stephen hadn't allowed the older woman to enter on the many occasions she'd come to call. If she was telling the truth, any perception of a third party having a legitimate claim on the castle would draw Reddington's ire. Now that the man was shooting arrows at anyone claiming ownership of the property, Miss Oak was safest far away.

Therefore, the castle's deed must be in the possession of the absent Earl of Densmore. Who, at this point, *everyone* wanted to kill.

Perhaps that was why he'd thus far declined to return home.

Stephen dropped to the stone floor for a round of press-up exercises. His thoughts tended to ping and flail and spiral like the machines he put together. Concentrating on the flexing of his muscles and the breaths in his lungs calmed the noise and helped him to relax and to think.

He was angry, was the problem. Angry with his flighty cousin, to be sure, but also irritated with himself for being hoodwinked into this ruse to begin with.

Densmore knew there was nothing Stephen loved more than to be useful, and had taken advantage of that trait in the name of helping out family. Since they were children, the earl had long been the only soul who stood up for Stephen. Of course he would repay that unexpected kindness with the same loyalty.

And as long as Stephen was forced to play earl, he could not bear to leave any system unoptimized. The holdings desperately needed a keeper, and its current title holder was not up to the task.

Stephen was undeniably a better earl than the earl. In addition to settling accounts and making investments and overseeing improvements on the various entailed properties, Stephen had also gone ahead and given every member of staff a rise in wages.

Long before Densmore's father first took ill, Stephen had enacted a contingency plan to learn everything he could about the running of the earldom in case his cousin's careless behavior left the title without any heirs but Stephen.

Now that he'd literally taken his cousin's place, Stephen had also taken it upon himself to manage the rest of his cousin's affairs as well. All of the estates would be profitable this year for the first time since Densmore inherited the title.

Every aspect of the earldom might be running smoothly at the moment, but there was no guarantee that these conditions would remain in effect once Densmore returned. Stephen calculated those odds to be 0.00021, or next to impossible. If he didn't do something clever with his cousin's money while it still existed, the wastrel would simply wager it all away in a drunken haze.

Which was why Stephen had penned letters of recommendation for all his cousin's servants, from the butlers to the scullery maids, at every property. He had done so both as the earl and as himself, providing each employee with double the recommendation, should they find themselves in need of a new post.

The writing of so many letters, and the financial and practical restructuring of the entire earldom, had required an extraordinary amount of work. It had taken Stephen an entire *week* to accomplish it all.

After which, boredom had threatened. Which was when Stephen turned this castle into his laboratory away from home. He missed his books and his bed and his breakfast nook. Even though there was more staff in Castle Harbrook, the building somehow felt emptier and lonelier. A bold claim from a man so lonely, he spent every waking moment filling the emptiness in his life with machine after machine.

Nonetheless, Stephen would defend this castle to the best of his considerable ability. Richard Reddington would not cross Harbrook's threshold without Stephen's knowledge and authorization.

No one would.

Bells clanged overhead. Stephen jerked his head up to stare at them. Those bells were part of an early warning system he'd installed to ring when the property line had been crossed.

Had the hidden archer been followed by an even bolder attack?

Stephen kept telescopes in all four of the castle's corner turrets. Those bells specifically signaled that a vehicle had arrived on the northern side facing the street.

It wasn't a delivery. The most recent shipment had come in yesterday, and the next wouldn't arrive until tomorrow.

A cross breeze flowed through the large rectangular openings on all sides of the cylindrical turret. He hurried to the stone windows and dropped to his knees. Ducking to ensure he could not be seen, Stephen pressed one eye to the telescope.

A humble pony cart trudged into view.

It was an ordinary country gig. Simple. Mud-splattered. The pony lumbering up the private road was just as unassuming. Brown, short of stature, a general air of boredom with its task.

Inside the gig was a long, thin crate, and a woman whose visage was hidden beneath an enormous wide-brimmed bonnet. He could not guess her age without a glimpse of her face, but one daintily gloved hand clutched the handle of a stout wooden cane.

The beast drew to a stop. The woman climbed out of the gig with obvious gingerliness, as though the ride up the hill had been exactly as arduous an experience as the pony cart's appearance implied.

The wind whipped her dress against her body, revealing plump curves. Stephen changed his mind about being able to guess her age. The morning gown was of fine quality and tailored to flatter the woman's voluptuous shape. This was a young lady, walking like an old woman. Fashionable, but unchaperoned. Moneyed, but riding in an absolute turnip of a pony cart.

Stephen was certain of his conclusions. Yet they did not sum up to anything he could compute. The more he watched the woman, the less he understood. Was she here to sell him something? She'd left her crate in the gig—and the gig untethered.

The pony, for its part, seemed content to gnaw at the tall green grass, of which there was plenty. The grounds were covered in flowers and greenery.

Another gust of wind rose from the west, sending the brim of the woman's bonnet flying up away from her face. Just for a second. It was enough.

Stephen swallowed hard. He had no idea who this woman was, but she was extraordinarily beautiful. A missionary, perhaps. Here to chastise the earl for failing to attend church on Sunday. Again. Perhaps the crate was full of Bibles. He tilted his telescope to keep her in sight.

The woman glanced around the door for the knocker. Stephen had removed it months ago to make the entrance less welcoming.

She leaned on her cane, made a fist with her free gloved hand, and banged on the door.

He would never have heard it, were it not for another system he'd installed to carry sound up through narrow tunnels he'd bored into reinforced stone walls—surely Densmore wouldn't mind—in order to eavesdrop on any enemies who might approach. Stephen called it a whispering wall because it transmitted the slightest sound.

The visitor banged again, louder.

Stephen did not respond to her call. Neither did the servants. Before the earl abandoned his castle and its occupants, Densmore had instructed his staff just as firmly as he'd lectured Stephen: Let no one in.

Undaunted, the woman lifted her cane and used that to rap against the castle's thick oak door. *This* could be heard with or without the aid of any listening contraptions.

Its racket also went unanswered.

"I know you're in there!" she called up. "I can see smoke from your kitchen!"

Stephen fought the urge to yell back, *Your logic is unsound. Smoke from the kitchen means* someone *is at home, but it doesn't mean that* I *am.*

For one, this rejoinder would give away his position. For two, perhaps she *was* here to visit one of the scullery maids. He was 0.3523 certain this visitor wasn't here for the Earl of Densmore.

No man with half a brain would leave a woman this beautiful behind.

She rapped again with the heavy cane.

"*Please,*" she pleaded. "I've come from so far. Take pity on a weary traveler, I beg you."

Stephen could not help but feel sorry for her predicament. She seemed harmless and nice enough. But rules were rules for a reason. If he let her in just because she was pretty and carried a cane, who knew what would be next? An army of missionaries with five carts' worth of Bibles?

She rapped one last time, then heaved a breath.

Silence stretched around the castle. Even the wind stilled and the birds silenced. The tree leaves ceased to rustle. No one was answering her plea. Not even nature itself stirred.

"Have it your way," she muttered. Stephen heard the words as clearly as if the fetching visitor were whispering against the back of his neck. "Beth the Berserker it is."

He blinked. Perhaps he had *not* heard her clearly. It had sounded as though she'd said—

The woman marched toward the pony cart with her cane held high, like a field commander leading a platoon of marching soldiers into battle.

She handed a bit of carrot to the pony, then tossed her cane inside the gig and ripped off her dainty gloves. With her bare hands, she wrenched open the wooden crate. From its depths, she withdrew... two enormous battle-axes.

Stephen stared in disbelief as the woman raised each into the air. Beneath the feminine poofs at her shoulders, muscles visibly flexed in what had previously seemed to be deceptively soft flesh. Axes held high, she marched back to the front door without slowing her pace or panting for breath. She looked like a Valkyrie descending upon a battlefield.

Who *was* this woman? The latest intimidation tactic by Richard Reddington? Was the archer not enough?

"Tell Reddington I'm not to be bothered," Stephen called out through the window.

The woman jerked her gaze up to the turret, her previously pretty face a twisted mask of fury. "How dare you imply I hold any affiliation with that scoundrel!"

Interesting.

Before Stephen could apologize for his erroneous assumption, the

woman let out a primal scream—earsplitting enough to break glass—
then began striking at the ten-inch-thick oak door with enough force
to rattle the iron hinges.

There was no chance of anyone cutting through wood that impen-
etrable with an ordinary blade. Or perhaps, Stephen amended, there
was no chance of anyone *ordinary* doing so.

Beth the Berserker was anything but ordinary.

Five minutes later, neither the screaming nor the thrashing showed
any signs of slowing. As the woman struck at the door with her axes,
shards of wood flew up at all angles, spraying the air around her as
though she were caught inside a dust storm.

He either had to get rid of her, which seemed unlikely, or allow her
in—which was forbidden. Then again, at this rate, Stephen wouldn't
need to "allow" anything. It might take Miss Berserker three days of
frenzied chopping, but one way or another, this woman was slashing
and hacking her way in.

"Very well," Stephen murmured. "Have it *your* way."

He rose to his feet and pressed a lever.

7

⚜

*T*he door to the castle swung open.

Elizabeth lowered her twin battle-axes with a smile. "I knew I was good at diplomacy."

For the space of a heartbeat, she waited for a butler to appear, then hurried across the threshold before whoever had opened the door decided to close it in her face.

The heavy oak door clanged shut behind her.

Elizabeth stood still as she assessed her new environment. She was now in some sort of antechamber the size of a cozy parlor.

"Antechamber" was perhaps the wrong word. *Ante* meant before, implying that this room led somewhere else. But the only doorway in sight was the one she had stepped through.

There was also no butler. Nor *anyone* who might have been the person to open the door for her, then close it behind her.

She gazed about in bewilderment. "What the dickens *is* this?"

The center of the small stone room was empty. The walls and ceiling, on the other hand, were lined with ropes and pulleys and wheels and strange artifacts.

Hard as she looked, there was no other exit. The two windows on either side of the door were the narrow, slotted sort for firing arrows. Loop-hole embrasures, she believed those were called. A kitten couldn't squeeze through those narrow openings, much less

Elizabeth. And the exterior walls themselves were four feet thick. It made no sense. Why would the front door lead nowhere?

"One of the interior sections must be false," she murmured.

It's what a Wynchester would do. What the Wynchesters *had* done, on any number of occasions. At the Puss & Goose in London, they kept a secret room that was only accessible through the back of a wardrobe.

Not that there were any wardrobes in here. Just a spiderweb of rope and wires, with a staggering number of strange objects attached to or suspended from the peculiar net.

She took a step forward.

The stone beneath her feet immediately gave way, falling two inches without warning.

Elizabeth gasped and flailed her arms, which was difficult to do when carrying a battle-axe in each hand. A strange clicking sound echoed throughout the stone room as she windmilled for balance. Her back gave a vicious twinge of warning and slipped from a healthy seventy percent down to sixty-five.

"To the devil with you, Densmore," she shouted. "You can't keep me out."

All at once, the clicking sound stopped—and several gallons of ice-cold water dropped over her from the ceiling.

She gasped as the unexpected wave coursed down her back and between her breasts. The brim of her bonnet had protected her face but was now so sodden it hung limply, blocking her vision altogether.

With an axe protruding from each fist, she fumbled to untie the wet bow beneath her chin, then flung the waterlogged bonnet aside.

It slapped wetly against the bottom edge of the embrasure window—and sent a tall series of interlocking gears into motion. Elizabeth watched in fascination as the movement climbed up the stone wall, then activated an odd pulley, which tilted a metal pipe... which began shooting marbles directly at her face.

"Aaugh!" She leapt out of the way just in time, then wobbled for purchase on the uneven floor. This time, the stones hadn't moved beneath her boots. The danger was the old castle, worn in irregular patches from centuries of feet.

Elizabeth restored her equilibrium, arms outstretched, her blades like wings—or the talons of a raptor. But she did not feel like a bird of prey. She felt like a popinjay trapped in a birdcage.

Puffs of smoke shot out from the walls at either side of her head. No, not smoke—clouds of colored chalk, coloring her blond hair pink on one side and blue on the other. The suffocating dust filled her lungs, and she let out an involuntary hacking cough.

"You will not best me!" she rasped.

This was the most dangerous terrain she'd ever attempted to cross. Not only was the gray stone floor uneven and rigged against her, it was also now wet and littered with marbles. Carefully, she took another step, adjusting her weight in slow increments.

She fervently wished one of the battle-axes was her cane.

Elizabeth inched forward despite the increasing risks to her person. What else could she do? No one was coming to rescue her. She was the one meant to do the rescuing. Miss Oak had legally inherited this godforsaken pile, and by all that was holy, Elizabeth was determined not to leave without clutching the will and deed in her hand.

A Wynchester didn't give up. A Wynchester won the fight.

"Densmore, you blackguard!" she called out. "Afraid of a girl, are you? Show yourself!"

Her voice echoed against the stones. No earl appeared, recalcitrant or otherwise.

"I'm not afraid of your puzzle room," she shouted. "But you'd better be scared of *me*!"

Nothing.

She glanced over her shoulder at the external door she'd come through. It was still shut tight. Perhaps it was locked, and perhaps it wasn't. But she didn't want out. She wanted in. She was going to force a meeting with that court jester of an earl if it was the last thing she—

A tiny breeze whispered across the base of her cold, wet neck.

She spun back around.

There were still no other visible entrances or exits. The room was a solid mass of stone from floor to ceiling.

But there, before her, stood...the strangest man she'd ever seen in her life.

The Earl of Densmore's clothes were ordinary enough, if abominably wrinkled. He appeared to be of average height and average build. His chin was freshly shaved, as was the fashion. But atop his head was a strange leather helmet. It completely hid his hair from view, as well as most of his face. His left eye appeared thrice as large as it ought to be, due to a large monocle attachment that magnified the blinking orb threefold. His right eye was hidden altogether behind some sort miniature telescoping lens that appeared to move and whir of its own accord.

"Shoddy hospitality," Elizabeth informed him. "I am cold and wet and those marbles could have killed me."

"Improbable. Those particular traps are calculated merely to bruise skin and break limbs," Densmore responded, his voice smooth as fresh cream and his words absolutely infuriating.

"Is that right?" Elizabeth lashed out with her axe. "See how *you* like being under attack!"

In one quick stroke, she sliced open all three layers of his plum coat, jade waistcoat, and white cambric shirt—without breaking the skin below. A piece of chalk fell from a cut pocket and shattered on the stone floor. Only his cravat remained untouched.

The earl's tattered garments fell away to reveal...a surprisingly chiseled chest and abdomen.

Elizabeth tried not to look.

All right, so she looked. How could she not? She rarely saw muscles that defined outside of a marble statue in a museum.

"Quite the introduction," he said dryly. "How do you do?"

"Charmed, I'm sure," she managed, forcing her gaze back to that enormous light-gray eye with its long curling eyelashes. "Take off your helmet. It's ridiculous."

The earl considered her for a moment, then removed the helmet.

Had she thought his *abdomen* chiseled? Good God, that *face*. Densmore could cut glass with that jaw and those cheekbones. A mass of soft, wavy brown hair only called more attention to the angular beauty of his absurdly handsome visage.

"I changed my mind," she said hoarsely. "Put the helmet back on."

He did not.

"Look," she said. "I'm sorry about the door. I'm supposed to avoid unnecessary property damage, because I promised my siblings I'd only use my weapons to kill people."

He took a hasty step back. "What?"

"Listen closely." She edged toward him. "This is your final opportunity."

The earl retreated another step. "Final? I've never seen you before."

"And if you play your cards right this time, you'll never see me again. Just hand over that deed."

He held up his palms. "I haven't any deed."

"Don't waste my time." She angled her deadly battle-axes toward each side of his neck. "You saw me cut down that door. Do not annoy me any further, Densmore, or I shall cut you down, too."

8

Stephen cleared his throat. The one boxed in by sharp blades.

"Just one small detail," he said politely. "I'm not the Earl of Densmore."

It was not what he was supposed to say. Stephen would do almost anything for his cousin, but he drew the line at decapitation.

Beth the Berserker scoffed at his claim. Hers was not a coquettish scoff—more of an *I hold you in eternal disdain* sort of scoff—but Stephen could not help but notice how much more attractive she was in front of his face than the pretty picture she'd made through his telescope. Taking off his helmet to see her clearly was the best decision he'd made all day.

It did not hurt that the trough of water had drenched her ample bosom, plastering her wet bodice to the contours of her chest. Since the berserker's blades were at his throat and she obviously knew how to use them, Stephen did his best to keep his eyes on her suspicious green gaze and not on her enticing décolletage.

There was also the chopped door to consider, and the fact that the shirt, coat, and waistcoat he'd donned that morning were now rent in two, and hanging from his shoulders in tatters.

"Not the earl? A likely story," sneered the berserker, with a curl of one of her plump, pink lips. "Am I supposed to believe you to be a butler?"

"If you know anything at all about the Earl of Densmore," Stephen replied calmly, "then I needn't convince you that his lordship is not the sort of person to answer his own door. Or care why it is that you have come to call."

The berserker considered this, then inclined her head. "He's about to care. Take me to him."

"I cannot."

"Why not?"

"He's not here."

"Where is he?"

"I don't know," Stephen admitted.

She harrumphed. "When will he return?"

"I don't know."

Her green eyes flashed. "Do you know anything?"

Stephen knew he had to get this lady off his property and attend to shoring up the castle's defenses. Already, the water had drained from the floor. The marbles had followed each other down specially designed cracks between the stones to a neat queue against the wall, for ease of restocking the traps.

Easier to do, when one wasn't being held at sword-point.

Stephen sighed. "I know that there's a 0.000152 probability of you finding the earl before he intends to be found. Indeed, I am three hundred and eighty-nine percent more likely than you to divine his whereabouts. Yet despite my having collated and analyzed all the—"

She nudged a battle-axe into his cravat. "Stop flirting with me."

His eyes widened with interest. "You interpret my use of logical reasoning as . . . flirtation?"

"Everyone shows off when they're flirting. If you don't mean for it to be arousing, then cease doing so."

He closed his mouth obediently. Arousing, did she say? A torrent of theorems and equations was suddenly bursting to pour out.

"If you're not the earl," said the berserker, "then who are you? And why do you have such a phenomenal physique?"

"I . . . What?"

"Your abdomen. Why does it have so many muscles?"

"I possess the same quantity of muscles as everyone else."

"I don't think you do," she muttered. "Stop it. It's distracting."

"It's my anxiety," he admitted. "When the world presses down on me, I drop to the floor and press *up* instead. It's my solution to stressful situations."

Her gaze lowered, and she licked her lips. "I shall endeavor to be more stressful."

"You're doing a wonderful job," he assured her. "If it weren't for the razor-edged blades at my throat, I'd be doing press-ups at this very moment."

She looked tempted to lower the battle-axes. "I shall take that into consideration, Mr. . . . ."

The berserker trailed off and looked at him expectantly.

He smiled without responding. It was one thing to avoid an inconvenient beheading, and another to take a berserker into one's confidence. Then again, her blades were still at Stephen's throat.

Which was perhaps *her* idea of flirting.

"I'm waiting for your name," she said.

"I know," he answered.

He also now knew several facts about her. She was clever and determined and dotty as a ladybug. She had also come closer to breaching the castle in the space of an hour than anyone else had managed since his arrival. Perhaps even centuries.

Other traits he observed were less important at the moment. Such as the soft smoothness of her skin, and the fetching curl to her blond hair. Or the wet flower petal from her bonnet that now clung becomingly to her round cheek, just begging to be plucked by Stephen's fingers.

He was not going to touch her, he reminded himself firmly. He was not the sort to touch anyone. He was a turtle who liked his shell. There was safety in solitude and science. Interaction with others led to confusion and risk. He was better off alone than accompanied.

Yet here he found himself.

With her.

"I'm still waiting," she reminded him.

"I know," he answered.

He had always liked taking time to think things out. Preferred being methodical, deliberate, careful. None of his inventions would work properly if Stephen comported himself willy-nilly. His life had always been a constant, and he was unprepared for this new variable.

There. That was where he could start.

"Before I answer any more questions," he said politely, "might I inquire who *you* are?"

"Elizabeth Wynchester," she answered without hesitation.

"Oh, for the love of..." He winced and closed his eyes. "Anything but a Wynchester!"

The battle-axes scraped at his throat. By now, his poor cravat was in ribbons.

"How is being a member of my family possibly worse than whatever you thought was happening?" the berserker demanded. "What's wrong with Wynchesters?"

"Rumor has it, you're a pack of relentless madmen with no scruples about operating outside the law." He opened his eyes and tilted his gaze toward the closest blade. "The gossip seems credible."

"Take note: We're the pack of lawless madmen you want working on your side, not against you. I will ask you one last time. If you're not the Earl of Densmore, who are you?"

"Stephen Lenox," he said with a sigh. "Scientist, mathematician, inventor...and first cousin to the earl."

"Cousin as in…" She tilted her head, as if mentally scanning *Debrett's Peerage.* "You're heir presumptive to the earldom?"

"To my eternal consternation. Come to think of it, perhaps you *should* impale me with your blades. I'd rather die an honorable death than present myself in the House of Lords."

Miss Wynchester leaned forward and glared deep into Stephen's eyes, as though determining the veracity of his introduction by staring into his soul. Her lips were almost close enough to kiss. Temptingly close.

With a sigh of frustration, she yanked the battle-axes down to her sides. "I no longer wish to impale you."

Stephen's inexplicably aroused body wouldn't be opposed to having a thrust or two.

"Are we finished here, then?" he asked, instead of pursuing a flirtation. "I have a pot of tea I ought to get back to."

"Good idea. I'll take mine with brandy." She passed both axes to one hand and curved the other about his arm. "Whilst you explain the whole tale from the beginning."

9

⚜

Elizabeth had not sliced open the sleeves covering Mr. Lenox's arms—a lack of forethought she was highly tempted to correct—but the taut bicep currently flexing beneath the curve of her fingers felt every bit as toned as the muscular chest and abdomen constantly winking at her in the gap between the cut edges of his clothing.

"One moment, if you please." Mr. Lenox was exceedingly polite for a hostage. "I ought to bring along our bonnets."

He stepped away from her...Leapt away from her...Did some strange, twisting dance, clearly meant to avoid placing his boot down on several specific stones in the floor, despite there being no difference between them to Elizabeth's eye. She memorized each step anyway.

Mr. Lenox caught her gaze and gave her a winning smile. "Best to avoid the blanket of needles, wouldn't you say?"

Blanket of needles. She now wished she had brought more supplies than her trusty battle-axes. She needed her chain mail and a proper helmet. One considerably hardier than the gear-and-monocle-adorned leather hat in Mr. Lenox's hand.

He scooped up her soaking bonnet gingerly, then made his hopping, twisting way back to her side. "Shall we?"

Elizabeth realized she had no idea how they were going to go anywhere. The room was still devoid of exits, save for the exterior door through which she'd entered.

Mr. Lenox slid on his leather helmet and adjusted the pair of lenses before his eye.

"The spot to press is only visible when viewed through glass of a specific hue and polarity," he explained, as though such an explanation made any sense at all.

He was flirting again, she was sure of it.

"Ah, here we are." Mr. Lenox reached out and tapped lightly on a small section of uneven gray stone that looked exactly like all the other uneven gray stones. A rectangular section of the wall swiveled ninety degrees on a center hinge, leaving an opening on either side just big enough for someone Elizabeth's size to squeeze through.

Mr. Lenox did not wait to see if she followed, but ducked through the doorway with the hurried air of a man hoping to find his teapot was still warm. Elizabeth placed each foot exactly where Mr. Lenox's boots had fallen, turning to her side to slip through the opening after him.

The rotating door swung closed behind them. They were now standing in a long corridor made of the same large gray stones as the rest of the castle. From this side, there was likewise no indication of how to turn a solid wall back into a doorway.

"Am I going to need to borrow one of those bonnets in order to leave the castle?"

"Bothersome, isn't it," droned a voice behind her.

She spun, axes at the ready, to discover an older man with white hair, thick jowls, and impeccable, if simple, dark blue attire. He raised his eyebrows at her stance and sighed heavily, as if she were the least alarming disturbance in a long succession of vexing inconveniences.

Mr. Lenox handed the disgruntled man her wet headpiece. "McCarthy, I need you to dry Miss Wynchester's bonnet, if you would, please."

"You're the butler?" Elizabeth guessed.

McCarthy glared at Mr. Lenox. "See? Our guests would not suffer this unnecessary confusion if you allowed me to assume my proper station at the front door."

"We've not admitted any guests until now," Mr. Lenox reminded him. "The entryway is designed to repel them."

Elizabeth nodded in approval. "By killing them, sight unseen."

"A disgraceful practice." McCarthy held his nose in the air and Elizabeth's dripping bonnet pinched between two outstretched fingers. He spun on his heels and stalked off down the corridor, muttering all the while. "Unseemly lack of manners. The indignity!"

"I'm not the earl," Mr. Lenox called after him. "Reclusive curmudgeons don't need manners."

Elizabeth agreed wholeheartedly.

A loud sniff was the butler's only response before McCarthy disappeared from sight.

"Where were we?" asked Mr. Lenox.

"Forget the tea," said Elizabeth. "Just pour me a glass of brandy."

Mr. Lenox tucked his helmet under his arm. "That'll be over this way."

Soon they were ensconced in what might have been an ordinary study, were it not for five hundred years of nicks and scars in the tall stone walls, and the inexplicable network of bits and bobs strung about from floor to ceiling.

"Is this another murder room designed to kill me?" she inquired.

"Strongly deter," he corrected firmly. "I hope never to kill anyone."

"Then what *is* all this?" She pointed at the walls and ceiling.

He glanced around, as though he had forgotten they'd walked into a human-size crow's nest. "It's for adding milk to one's tea."

Of course it was.

He stoked a small fire, then dropped into an armchair and motioned for her to do the same. "I apologize for activating the entryway's defense mechanisms."

She perched on the edge of her seat with interest. "It's not always a murder room? Then how did you know to deploy the weapons?"

He arched a brow. "Have you heard of a telescope?"

"Ah." She leaned back in her chair with satisfaction. "You saw me knock upon your door. Energetically. With a pair of battle-axes."

"You also invoked the word 'berserker,' which I've calculated to have a 0.9879 probability of imminent trouble."

"Are any other doors guarded in such a manner?"

"There are no other doors."

"Then how do *you* leave?"

"I never go anywhere if I can help it. Except to satisfy the occasional craving for pistachio ices. That is, back home when I am not under fire."

Elizabeth could not argue with her host's priorities. Pistachio ice was far preferable to most people, armed or not. "Might I scoot my chair closer to the fire?"

"Be my guest."

"Thank you." She tried to relax her tense muscles. With luck, the fire would dry her dress in short order and return her bedraggled appearance to some semblance of normalcy.

Mr. Lenox, for his part, showed no indication of changing his shirt. The act of flinging himself into the armchair had likewise flung open both sides of the shorn material, leaving most of his chest and one hundred percent of his rock-hard abdomen exposed to Elizabeth's hungry gaze. Her fingers itched to touch those positively lickable sharp planes.

Damn him.

Mr. Lenox had taught her so many things already. Until today, she'd believed herself solely capable of admiring sword-wielding, warrior-and-warrioress types.

Who would've guessed that an equations-quoting tinker wearing a hat with a monocle would be capable of turning her head? Or that such an attractive knight could defend a castle without sword or shield?

"Could you have a footman bring in my crate from the pony cart?" she asked.

"Of course." He rose to tug the bellpull.

"And my cane," she added.

Elizabeth was prepared to deflect any comment he might have about a young woman who used a cane, but Mr. Lenox didn't seem to find the request any more peculiar than a desire for brandy. Come to think of it, he hadn't even inquired why a nice woman like her happened to travel with a pair of battle-axes.

While on his feet, Mr. Lenox retrieved a fancy bottle and two snifters from the sideboard. Before retaking his seat, he poured for them both, then handed her a glass. "Will 1811 cognac do?"

"Nicely." She clinked her snifter against his, then took a sip. Delicious, syrupy heat traveled down her throat.

She sighed happily. Fine brandy was ever so much better than cheap gin. Which was the primary reason she never kept any on hand. She could scarcely blame the Earl of Densmore for being a shameless wastrel when his sideboard was stocked with quality liquor like this.

"You really don't know where your cousin is?"

"Trust me," Mr. Lenox said wryly. "If I had the slightest clue, I would hand the incorrigible wretch over to you myself."

Something about his story didn't make sense. "Why did you come to visit him, if he wasn't here? I thought you didn't go anywhere, save for pistachio ice."

"My good-for-nothing cousin is my only other weakness, I'm afraid. Densmore has been my closest thing to a friend since we were young. At school and university, he was always trying to drag me to gatherings and parties, but I was too involved in my inventions to waste time with social niceties."

"There's nothing nice about social niceties," Elizabeth concurred. "If someone tried to separate me from my sword, I'd stab them with it."

He nodded, as if this were a reasonable position to take.

"Except," she was forced to admit, "if it was family."

"Precisely the situation I find myself in," Mr. Lenox agreed with feeling. "Densmore told me he was dealing with an urgent matter and required my immediate aid. I was to take up residence here in Harbrook, bar the castle door, and pretend to be him until he returned to relieve me."

Elizabeth slid her axes out of the way beneath her chair. "That didn't sound...suspicious?"

"Frankly, every plot my cousin has ever dreamt up sounds suspicious. My talent is machines, and his forte is making trouble. Until now, the only person he'd ever put in a pickle was himself. Picnics and soirées cannot entice me from my laboratory, but saving Densmore from his own schemes...Shall we say, we've been in a bit of a pattern since childhood."

Elizabeth understood that much. Each of her siblings had their own role in her family as well. "Did the earl provide a date for his reappearance?"

"He did indeed." Mr. Lenox lounged back in the chair, his shirt gaping wider. "Densmore was to return three months and fourteen days ago."

Three and a half *months*? Family or not, the murder room was starting to sound like an excellent place to drop the earl.

"You've heard nothing from him since?" she asked in affront.

Mr. Lenox took a sip of cognac. "From him, no."

Elizabeth frowned. "Who have you heard from?"

"First, a Miss Oak, Densmore's aunt on his mother's side. She purports to have legal claim over this castle."

"She does have legal ownership."

"Does she? Her letters indicated the 'proof' was in a will no one has seen."

"We'd have a spare copy, if a fire at the lawyer's office hadn't destroyed his records."

"Convenient. You're certain the document existed and reads as she claims?"

"To the letter. My brother spoke to the lawyer himself."

"I see." Mr. Lenox drummed his fingers on his sculpted abdomen. "Miss Oak is your client, then, I take it?"

"Yes. Her late sister, Arminia, loved puzzles, and hid the original copy of her will here in the castle for her husband to find."

Mr. Lenox blinked. " 'Hid'?"

"As if the pages were buried pirate treasure, attainable only by following a series of coded clues...which I unfortunately do not have access to. To solve the puzzle, I'll have to rely on brute force."

"You intend to solve a treasure hunt without any clues?"

Elizabeth nodded. "I shall uncover the missing will and present it to Miss Oak this very day. With luck, the late countess hid a copy of the deed with her testament, and you and I will both be gone from this pile by nightfall."

"Hmm," Mr. Lenox said noncommittally. "How do you know Densmore didn't find the will already, and take the testament and the deed with him?"

"Is Densmore the sort of conscientious lord who packs important business documents in his knapsack before fleeing to parts unknown?"

"How certain are you a secret will really exists at all?" Mr. Lenox countered as he swirled his glass. "In my one hundred and four days of debilitating boredom, at no point in my desperate search for distraction did I come across anything resembling clues to a treasure hunt."

"The will is definitely here somewhere," Elizabeth said with absolute confidence. "The countess assured her sister of the fact in writing. Arminia *wanted* the testament to be found and her wishes to be fulfilled. She just did so a bit...unconventionally."

"Hmm" was all Mr. Lenox said. The fingers of his free hand idly brushed the flaps of what had once been a waistcoat pocket.

She bit her lip. "I'm sorry about your stick of chalk. I didn't mean to destroy it."

"I have an entire box of chalk," he assured her, then arched his brows. "You're not going to apologize for slicing open my clothes?"

She smiled. "I'm not sorry about that."

"Ill-mannered wench. I'm sorry about drenching you."

She snorted. "No, you're not."

He grinned. "No, I'm not."

She fought the urge to lean forward and plump up her wet bosom. "You mentioned someone other than Miss Oak has come to call?"

Mr. Lenox let out an aggrieved sigh. "Richard Reddington's cronies. First, it was lawyer after lawyer. Because I refuse to answer the door or his letters, Reddington has apparently placed a marksman in the strip of woods separating the two properties. Although they ignore the servants, the one time *I* stepped outside, I took an arrow to the hat."

She gasped. "Not your fancy leather monocle helmet!"

"I fear I was wearing an ordinary top hat at the time."

"It's still poor sportsmanship," she huffed.

"Thank you. I felt much the same way."

"An interesting wrinkle," she mused. "I didn't expect Reddington to use real artillery in his mock battles."

Stephen arched a brow. "So now what?"

"Now," she said, "I need to find the deed, the will, and the earl."

"Is that all?" Mr. Lenox asked mildly.

No, Elizabeth supposed it was not all. This had become a Situation that needed to be resolved. Handsome Mr. Lenox had been brave in the face of being taken hostage because he was *already* hostage.

And Elizabeth was a Wynchester—protector to those who needed it. Which meant she now had two clients. Blast. She had so looked forward to returning home soon. She supposed Mr. Lenox felt the same way.

"Very well. You've convinced me." She set down her cognac. "I shall station myself as your bodyguard until I am able to safely extract you from danger."

"You're stationing yourself as my…bodyguard?" he repeated carefully. "Here?"

"In a one hundred percent professional capacity," she warned him with a shake of her finger. "No more dampening my bodice with buckets of water, or slicing open your clothing to show off your rippling muscles."

"You're the one who sliced open my clothing!"

"I'm advising myself not to do it again, no matter how you tempt me. We'll see how that goes. As you mentioned, Wynchesters aren't used to following rules."

"Including the prohibition against an unmarried woman spending the night unchaperoned beneath the same roof as an unmarried man, so as to protect her reputation?"

"Oh, I haven't any reputation to protect," Elizabeth said proudly. "All the rumors are true."

Mr. Lenox narrowed his eyes. "Is there any gossip about you successfully acting as a bodyguard?"

"I've years of experience," she assured him. "The only thing I love more than a good offensive strike is defending someone else from harm. I shall be honored to personally oversee the protection of the castle and your person."

"Until you find the papers you're looking for."

She nodded. "Which will secure your freedom and Miss Oak's future."

Silence stretched between them. They both took another sip of cognac.

"Well," said Mr. Lenox. "It's certainly a big enough castle for two. If you're determined to stay and search for a hidden will, I shan't prevent you."

"You couldn't stop me if you tried."

"I did a very good job of stopping you," he pointed out. "You'd still be chopping at the door if I hadn't let you in."

"You created a semi-efficient temporary roadblock," she allowed. "I would've come through the wall one way or another eventually. And your secret panel, too."

"Hm." He considered her. "I suppose if anyone were capable of such a feat, it just might be you."

She beamed at him.

After Miss Oak's suffocating attempts to coddle her, it was a relief to be treated as competent again. Elizabeth decided not to mention her throbbing hip and aching back from the encounter with the murder room. Or how daunting she found the prospect of her new temporary residence.

Even without Mr. Lenox's devilish modifications, medieval castles were not designed for someone like Elizabeth. A warren of dark, narrow corridors with slippery stone floors, steps of uneven height, every staircase narrow and curving and dangerous with nothing to hold on to or to break one's fall...

She kept her voice brisk. "Could you please have a footman return the pony cart to Miss Oak and retrieve my belongings from her guest room?"

"Of course. It shall be my honor to host you."

Elizabeth hoped so. Because until they found the hidden testament or turned up the real Earl of Densmore...

She and Mr. Lenox were stuck with each other.

10

When her trunks arrived, the castle staff settled Elizabeth and her belongings in a southern-facing guest chamber overlooking Castle Harbrook's rear garden.

After ridding herself of pink-and-blue chalk residue, she dashed off a quick message apprising her family of the change in plans, then painstakingly copied the map Miss Oak had loaned her in order to send a duplicate home to her siblings. If some discrepancy might indicate a secret hiding place, cartographer Tommy would be the one to spot it.

After dispatching her correspondence, Elizabeth took a much longer time going through her full stretching routine. Her newly clean body seemed to be holding steady at sixty-five percent, but there was no sense getting cocky and tempting fate. Who knew when she might have to take up arms again?

With luck, the answer was: soon. Elizabeth *loved* taking up arms. Defending a castle was the mission she was born for. She just had to be ready.

Once her joints were as limber and supple as they were likely to be for the day, she began her search for the will—or at least a helpful clue—in the long corridor spanning the guest quarters. She tested every stone for cracks that might contain a slip of paper, felt behind every sconce, and inspected every looking glass.

Which was how she managed to trigger a hidden lever that dropped a hook that activated a pulley that lifted a chute that dispensed a row of iron balls that crashed into a miniature weighted wagon whose spinning wheels yanked a wire...that dislodged the carpet from under her feet.

Elizabeth flailed her arms for balance, cursing not beneath her breath but at the top of her lungs, in the hopes that Mr. Lenox would hear it wherever he was hiding. She managed to save herself from falling onto the stone floor, but the sudden twisting motions jarred her joints and hips enough to ensure she'd be limping for hours.

She gritted her teeth in fury and renewed determination. She would not let this case best her, or this castle, or its deranged temporary owner. A future orphanage of children were counting on her. Limping or not, she would find that damned will if it was the last thing she did.

By the time Elizabeth made her way back to the earl's study, her fresh new morning gown was streaked with dust and her never-particularly-impressive patience was wearing thin.

"What the devil have you been doing?" Mr. Lenox asked, sliding partially out from beneath a hotchpotch of planks and tubes and wires.

"What I've been hired to do," she snapped crossly. "Which shouldn't include fending for my life against your utterly unnecessary contraptions. What the double-devil are *you* doing?"

He launched into a lively explanation about wood grains and counterbalances and geometry.

She blocked it out. Her attractive host had changed his clothes and put his abdominal muscles away. The rest of the details were superfluous.

The gist of his situation was obvious enough: He was an inveterate tinker who had rigged the entire castle with devices designed to entrap and confound enemies...and, apparently, the bodyguard stationed to protect him. As if medieval architecture wasn't perilous enough.

The tinker was clearly spending the earl's money on materials for his inventions. Which, to be fair, was arguably a better use of Densmore's funds than losing all of the earldom's resources at the gaming table.

Elizabeth crossed her arms and glared at him. She was trying to do things that would make a difference for her client, whilst Mr. Lenox was devoting his time to... *this*, whatever "this" was.

"Finding the will would be easier if you showed me how to avoid bumbling into traps meant for our enemies," she groused uncharitably.

He paused with a nail in his mouth and a hammer in his fist. "You need my help?"

She lifted her chin. "I don't need anything from anyone, especially you."

He set down the hammer and craned his head to give her his full attention. "On my best day, I am dreadful at navigating interactions with other humans. But in our case, I believe you are objectively giving conflicting signals."

"I'm vexed you changed shirts," she muttered. "And that I've not solved the puzzle yet."

"It's been"—he checked his pocket watch—"three hours."

"And yet, there's been no sign of the will!" She threw her hands wide.

"All right." Mr. Lenox spat the nail out from the corner of his mouth. He slid out from under his machine and brushed off his trousers. "I'll help for a little bit. Not because you need assistance, but because two heads are more efficient, and it sounds like we both appreciate efficiency."

"And both hate other people," Elizabeth added. "That's the best thing we have in common."

"I said I can't *understand* other people."

She nodded. "That's exactly what I hate about them."

Living with her birth family had been awful. Everything about Elizabeth displeased them. If she asked for help, she was ridiculed as weak. If she attempted to do more than her body allowed, she would wind up on the floor gasping in pain, so she was disparaged as worthless. If she tried to explain her physical limitations, she was called a liar and assigned even more grueling tasks in retaliation. Which of course she could not complete in the short time allotted, causing the cycle to start all over again. Things only got worse when they rejected her altogether and sent her to live with even harsher guardians.

Many years later, once Elizabeth had found the kindhearted, multi-talented Wynchesters, she learned that the mere presence of a sword was often more than enough deterrent to attacks, whether physical or verbal. Was it any wonder she'd vowed never to lower her defenses to outsiders again?

Of course, she was now playing bodyguard inside a stranger's home, where the building itself was out to get her. As if that was not enough, the handsome inventor she was protecting was armed with delectable muscles and a roguish smile, proving him dangerous even without his machines.

Mr. Lenox smoothed the wrinkles from his fully buttoned waistcoat. "I must warn you that I don't believe there is any treasure hunt to follow. In order to put Densmore's affairs in order, I walked through every room in this castle. Nothing was out of place until I made it that way."

"But you weren't looking for a missing will."

"True. I was looking for a clue to finding my cousin." He held Elizabeth's gaze. "My attention is on you now."

Her cheeks heated.

Mr. Lenox was staring at her with enough heat in his eyes to warm this entire drafty castle. His pupils had dilated, his lips parted, his torso tilted forward ever so slightly . . . It didn't take a mathematician to read these signs. He wanted to kiss her.

And she was absolutely going to let him. Particularly if his kisses came with unfettered access to those phenomenal abdominal muscles. Elizabeth hadn't *planned* on a torrid temporary affaire—but she wasn't foolish enough to turn down the opportunity.

She fluttered her lashes and gave her best non-cobra, come-hither smile.

Mr. Lenox blinked and took a step backward. All hint of his previous attraction vanished.

"Well, I'm sure you're in a hurry to be done with this task," he said briskly. "It'll go faster, now that both of us are searching. Where shall we start?"

Elizabeth didn't bother to hide her disappointment, but she made no further attempt at flirtation...at least for the moment. He was, after all, correct. She was here for her client, not for kisses. Keeping their interactions professional was the most efficient choice.

If a boring one.

"Well, the countess created the clues and the testament. Why don't we try her rooms?" she suggested.

"They've been cleared of personal effects."

"No one would toss out a will."

"Not knowingly," he agreed. "But if it were stuffed inside some other item that got disposed of...Besides, we're looking for a clue to a puzzle, and we haven't a clue what the clue looks like. If such a thing was ever here, it's almost certainly been discarded by now."

Elizabeth narrowed her eyes. "Are you always this full of sunshine and light?"

"This is my standard base level, yes. Pessimism is a critical component of my work. If I assume that everything that could go wrong, will do so, then I can prepare for those eventualities before they occur."

"I'm the same way," said Elizabeth. "I assume everything will go wrong...and that my swords can put it right."

"Like the castle door?" he said wryly. "How long would it have taken you to chip through ten inches of wood?"

"That wasn't my aim," she reminded him. "I wanted inside, which I achieved, thanks to my blades. See how that works?"

He shook his head. "That's not 'working.' That's luck. You couldn't know that would happen. The smartest path is to wait until you have calculated every variable from every angle and determined the surest course with the least variance of probability."

She placed her hands on her hips. "That's not a 'path.' Your way sounds like standing still. Swords are faster. Making things happen is better than just ruminating about them ad infinitum."

He stepped closer. "Recklessness leads to mistakes."

She leaned in. "I like mistakes."

His nose was an inch from hers. "You're looking for four-leaf clovers by stampeding over them astride an elephant."

"And carrying a sword," she snapped. "A big one."

He snorted. "What did you say we had in common again?"

"Congenital grumpiness," she retorted.

And perhaps a fondness for pistachios. Though Elizabeth was not ready to suggest she might enjoy such an outing with Mr. Lenox.

She licked her lips despite herself.

His gaze snapped to her mouth at once, his own lips parting. The world seemed to stand still. She could feel the blood rushing in her veins, and hear every heartbeat in her ears. Was he finally about to—

Mr. Lenox straightened. "We'll have to suffer through each other's company until we find that missing will and can be rid of each other at last."

Damn it. Elizabeth inclined her head. "To the countess's chambers?"

"Very well."

They spent the next four hours going over every inch of Arminia's apartments. Fortunately, Mr. Lenox had not set up traps in this area.

As an investigator, he was even more thorough than Elizabeth could have hoped. He took down finishings and dismantled furniture and tested the mortar between every stone for tampering.

"I don't believe there's anything to find," Mr. Lenox said for the thousandth time.

"I cannot believe the earl left a wet blanket like *you* here in his place," Elizabeth groused.

"Can you not? Densmore says I don't do anything important anyway. Of course, a useless tinker would do any small favor for an earl."

"What poppycock!" Elizabeth was suddenly furious on Mr. Lenox's behalf. "Why didn't you stab him?"

"I can't find him," he reminded her.

She searched along the hem of a curtain. "Do you mind if *I* stab him?"

"You don't know where he is, either."

"My brother Graham will find him," she said with confidence. "At which point I'll behead Densmore for you, at no extra charge."

Mr. Lenox crawled inside the empty fireplace. "Could you leave him a little bit alive? I don't want to be an earl."

"I suppose," she agreed reluctantly. "But let me know if you change your mind."

He appeared to consider this. "What I would really like is some way to prevent Reddington from breathing down my neck."

"Blech." She rolled her eyes in agreement. "Rich people."

Mr. Lenox cocked his head at her from under the mantel. "Forgive me, but aren't you reasonably well off yourself?"

"Not like Reddington," she protested. "If I had his mountain of gold, I'd use it to help people, not to stage self-aggrandizing, war-themed pantomimes." She thought it over. "All right, I'd do both."

"I would expect no less." Mr. Lenox ran his hands inside the flue. "I also think we've exhausted every potential hiding spot in my aunt's private quarters. Wherever the clues to the will might be, they're not in here."

Elizabeth was forced to agree. She brushed off her skirts. "Thank you for helping me search."

He crouch-walked out of the fireplace and stretched up to his full height. "My pleasure."

"I doubt crawling around a hard stone floor on your hands and knees is anyone's pleasure."

"You might recall that I was going to be on the floor anyway," he reminded her. A hint of soot accented one of his cheekbones. "That's what I was in the midst of when you interrupted."

She stiffened. "Don't let me stop you from getting back to your precious machines."

"I shan't." He paused. "Let me know if you need me again."

He was close enough to touch. Lord, how she wanted to. Elizabeth had thought of little else from the moment he had removed his helmet and revealed those sharp cheekbones and soft brown hair. For some unfathomable reason, she didn't even care that he wasn't a sword-wielding warrior. Her unquenchable desire to reach for him had grown when she'd cut open his clothing and accidentally treated herself to the finest chiseled torso outside of the British Museum.

Thinking was different from doing, of course. Particularly when she wasn't meant to be drooling *or* touching. She'd left her sword stick in her room, specifically so that its sharp blade would not lead her into temptation.

Elizabeth had a will to find, and a deed to deliver. Such an important task required...

Forty percent of her focus. She smiled.

Rolling up carpets and tapping for hollow stones did not require genius-level concentration. The rest of her brain was free to concoct fully operatic fantasies in which she reprised her attack on

Mr. Lenox's clothing—all of it, this time—then abducted him at sword-point, and spirited him away on a black stallion, upon which he would then make love to her with uncontrolled passion.

Unprofessional, of course. And more than a little improbable. Logistics aside, she wasn't certain her body could withstand a vigorous *anything* atop a galloping horse.

Then again, she and Mr. Lenox were arm's reach from a bed. Elizabeth was very good at lying on beds. Cushioned surfaces of any kind, really. Parlor sofas, chaises longues, a carpet in the middle of the floor...

He brushed her elbow briefly. "Where are you off to now?"

To the bed. With him. Where he could touch her arm again, if he promised not to stop there. Perhaps there were still a few things left to explore in this room after all.

"Er," she managed. Where was a bucket of cold water when you needed one?

"We should eat something." His gaze had not left hers. "I was going to ask you to join me for supper tonight, if that's something you—"

"Yes. I want." Her stomach growled in anticipation. Possibly unrelated to the menu.

He lifted his hand again but paused before touching her this time. "Do you mind if I—"

Do it. Push me against the wall and have your wicked way with me. Do it now.

But before she could voice her enthusiastic consent to whatever sinful pleasures Mr. Lenox wished to acquire permission for, the corridor filled with what sounded like...church bells?

"Subtle," she told him. "And a little preemptive. I prefer to dabble in sin before making permanent vows."

"It's the early warning system." Mr. Lenox dropped his hand, and his gaze flicked over her shoulder. "The perimeter has been breached."

"By whom?" Her battle-axes were back in her room. She patted her bosom for concealed knives and found two. Twice as many as she needed. "Is it Reddington?"

Mr. Lenox watched her hands with interest, then visibly collected himself. "Shall we go and find out?"

11

Stephen hurried down the spiral steps, his boots sliding over the worn stone. He was halfway to the ground floor before he remembered he usually went *up* instead of down. His best telescopes were in the corner turrets. But he had been thinking about kissing, not logic.

Ever since Elizabeth Wynchester had arrived, he'd been at sixes and sevens, his normally orderly mind a jumble. As though his brain were one of his careful, complex machines, and she'd come and taken an axe to it.

There was no sense turning around. McCarthy was striding up the primary corridor toward the staircase, a peevish expression on his wizened face. Most likely because the older man preferred greeting visitors with a warm welcome, and Stephen was spoiling his fun.

"Technically, everything you're vexed about is Densmore's fault," Stephen reminded the butler for the dozenth time. "The door is barred to callers because his lordship ordered it so. I am here in his stead for the same reason."

McCarthy let out a long-suffering sigh, as though everything that had ever been wrong in the world had always been his lordship's fault.

"Miss Oak has come to call," he announced. "*Again.* Shall I have her thrown in the dungeon?"

"Please don't," said Stephen. "I'm expecting another shipment tomorrow, and caring for a hostage would disrupt the smoothness of the delivery. Just ignore her, as you've been doing."

"No," said Miss Wynchester. "Let her in."

At this impertinent interruption, regal McCarthy looked torn between delight and disdain. Though the butler was appalled to hear a visitor countermand the orders of her host, Miss Wynchester had voted for the exact outcome McCarthy himself wished.

"Granting an audience is pointless," Stephen told Miss Wynchester. "There's no information to impart. We don't have the deed. We didn't find the will. There's no sign of any clues to any puzzle. I could sum up our progress on a single sheet of paper by leaving both sides blank."

"She makes biscuits," said Miss Wynchester. "And she's my client. As soon as she gets what she needs, *you* get to go home, too. Miss Oak doesn't even know you're here! She thinks her nephew has been ignoring her calls. Can we not spare a quarter hour?"

Stephen never wished to entertain other humans for a single moment, much less fifteen minutes. But Miss Wynchester had proven surprisingly tolerable. She somehow tempted him to act against his better judgment.

"Oh, very well. Just this once." Stephen turned to the butler. "Please escort our guest to the western parlor via the trapdoor, as the dungeon is currently safer than the modified entranceway. The footmen will help you with the rolling staircase."

McCarthy murmured something unintelligible while casting Stephen a disapproving glare, then hurried down the corridor to retrieve the new guest.

Miss Wynchester arched her brows. "How many trapdoors are there? They're not on my map."

"Just one," he answered. "The original owners of medieval castles were serious about fortification. The only entrances are the front door, which leads to what you call the murder room, and a hidden trapdoor on the ground behind the castle, which leads down to the dungeon. Reddington does not appear to know about the latter. The rear of the castle must not be under surveillance."

"Amateur," Miss Wynchester murmured.

"And yet more than dangerous enough." Stephen held out his elbow. "If you'll come with me..."

Miss Wynchester started to take his arm, then hesitated and touched her hip. The slightest wince flickered across her face.

He frowned. "Is everything all right?"

Her guilty gaze sprang to his and she grabbed his elbow firmly. "I was just noticing that I'm not carrying a sword."

"I thought you trusted Miss Oak. Have we invited her in despite misgivings?"

"One can never be too careful." Miss Wynchester's voice held an ominous tone. "Perhaps my blade is meant for you."

"Hmm. Well, if you think it necessary, I can send someone up to your rooms to fetch a weapon."

She brightened. "Would you? Have them bring the sword stick lying on the bed."

"Not the battle-axes?" he asked in surprise.

"Sometimes it's better to carry what looks like a cane."

"Ah." He put it together. "Miss Oak doesn't *know* you're a sword-wielding berserker."

"That's right," Miss Wynchester said quickly. "Which way to the parlor?"

"Down this corridor." Stephen murmured instructions to a footman, then led Miss Wynchester to a small enclave outfitted with a circular Axminster carpet, bookshelves covered in colorful figurines, an ornate desk and matching tea cabinet with gold-filigree-covered drawers, four bright tangerine armchairs, and a small yellow sofa lined with daffodil-embroidered pillows. The rest of the ceiling and walls were covered in Stephen's contraptions.

Miss Wynchester took the sofa, which was farthest from the machines.

Before Stephen could seat himself in the armchair closest to her, McCarthy swept back into the room with a pink-cheeked, salt-and-pepper-haired woman at his side.

"You must be Miss Oak," Stephen said, as though he had not seen her through his telescope on multiple occasions. "I am Stephen Lenox."

"Densmore's cousin?" she said in obvious surprise, then peered at him closely. "Why, I might have thought you *were* my nephew! You could almost be twins."

"Aren't I lucky," Stephen murmured. He waited for Miss Oak to take a seat before settling into his own chair.

She folded her hands over a cloth satchel in her lap and sighed with obvious frustration. "I'm sorry to bother you. I know that if Miss Wynchester had uncovered the will, she would already have informed me. I was just so hurt to think my nephew opened his door to a stranger and not to his own aunt."

"No one opened it for me, either," said Miss Wynchester. "I had to chop my way in."

Miss Oak looked startled. "You mean that metaphorically?"

"I promise to repair the damage before the children arrive," Elizabeth assured her.

Stephen raised his brows. "Children?"

Miss Oak leaned forward. "I don't know if my nephew or Miss Wynchester already told you, but my sister and I spent decades planning to turn Harbrook into a school and orphanage. Arminia didn't live to see its completion. I don't want to die before realizing our dream, too."

Stephen nodded his understanding. It was not an enemy attack that Miss Oak feared, but time itself. She was more likely to be felled by a bad case of the ague than the blade of a sword.

"When I open the orphanage we planned together," Miss Oak said with determination, "I shall christen the school in my late sister's honor."

"I already adore it," said Miss Wynchester, "and I never adore anything."

"You'll like it much better once Harbrook looks like a proper home and less like..." Miss Oak gestured at the panoply of bits and bobs strung across the parlor. She turned to Stephen. "How long would it take you to clear all these contraptions out?"

"You may keep them," he said magnanimously.

Miss Oak looked horrified.

Miss Wynchester leaned forward to whisper into his ear. "Orphans don't need murder rooms."

"I'll take it with me," he amended. "You'll be able to enter freely through the front door."

"Thank you," Miss Oak said with feeling. A moment passed. She looked at him expectantly.

Damn it. Stephen was dreadful with small talk. Much better not to allow anyone in than to sit in awkward silence.

When he was a child, his school years had been torture. His parents had been glad to be rid of their peculiar little goblin who preferred to lock himself in his nursery with hammers and wires rather than interact with family and neighbors who openly castigated him for not sharing the same interests and behaviors as a "normal" boy.

His schoolmates' scathing opinions had been a hundred times worse. What began as constant insults escalated into physical bullying and the gleeful destruction of whatever Stephen was working on. He'd learned to hide his true self in order to make himself more

palatable to others, and when that failed, he'd learned to shutter himself away altogether and never allow anyone in.

His cousin, the Earl of Densmore, was the only exception. The one
person who didn't look at Stephen as though he belonged in a circus.
Gregarious Densmore was happy to deflect attention away from his
awkward cousin.

But Densmore was not here now, and Stephen had absolutely no
idea what he was meant to do with the people in his parlor.

Forester, a footman, arrived with Miss Wynchester's sword stick,
taking some of the pressure off Stephen. After the cane was delivered, however, Forester melted back against the far wall rather than
leave the room.

Stephen wished he could drop to the floor and do some press-ups
to relieve his anxiety.

To his relief, both women ignored him completely. Miss Wynchester turned her chair toward her client and asked, "Did you think
of something that might aid in the search?"

"I'm not certain." Miss Oak opened her satchel and pulled out a
thick pile of correspondence tied with string. "Here is every letter my
sister wrote me that includes any mention of the will. If she did leave
me a clue . . . perhaps it's somewhere in there."

Miss Wynchester took possession of the letters eagerly and began
to scan their contents at a truly impressive speed.

"Is she really reading that fast?" Stephen whispered to Miss Oak.

"Maybe she can't make out Arminia's horrendous handwriting,"
Miss Oak whispered back.

"Bah," said Miss Wynchester. "This is high art after having to
decipher my brothers' horrid scrawls. I'm delighted to report that I
have good news."

Miss Oak's mouth dropped open. "You *do*?"

"And bad news," Miss Wynchester added. "The good news is that your sister did indeed leave behind a clue for you."

"But that's wonderful!" Miss Oak exclaimed.

"The bad news . . . is that I have no idea what it means."

"You *must* know," Miss Oak insisted, her eyes shining. "Think about your lice."

Stephen edged his chair away from them both. "Lice?"

"Not mine. Homer's. See what you think." Miss Wynchester handed Stephen the stack of letters. "Blazes! It steams me that I cannot fathom it out. Absolutely boils my brain. Simmering saffron, I thought I was hot on the trail, only for smoke to rise from my ears. This is one hell of a puzzle. Really bakes my breeches."

Stephen blinked slowly. "Are you making heat references on purpose?"

"Yes. So did the countess, in every one of these letters. I haven't the least notion why."

"Surely Arminia wouldn't have stored an important paper document in an oven," Miss Oak fretted. "Or a fireplace. Or inside a teakettle."

"Or on the sun, or between a pair of curling tongs," Stephen agreed. "The references must mean something else."

"Obviously this means something else. It's a *clue*, not the answer." Miss Wynchester drummed her fingers on her sword stick. "Can I keep these letters?"

"Yes, of course. Whatever you need. I just know you'll find my sister's will." Miss Oak's voice shook. "You *must*. It's not just me counting upon it, but all the children, too."

"I understand," Miss Wynchester said with surprising gentleness. "I promise we are working to that aim as quickly as we are able. In the meantime, I must beg of you to remain at home for your own safety. Reddington has made credible threats against the castle."

Miss Oak gasped. "You cannot let him harm a single stone!"

"We won't." Miss Wynchester plucked the letters from Stephen's hands and retied the stack with string. "Now, promise me you'll stay safe at home until you hear from me. I won't stop searching, no matter how long it takes. And my family is hunting for your nephew as we speak."

Miss Oak gave a grateful smile and rose to her feet. "Thank you, Miss Wynchester. I knew I was right to come to you."

Stephen instructed Forester to accompany Miss Oak. Once they left, Stephen turned toward Miss Wynchester. Both her hands gripped the handle of her cane, and her brow was furrowed.

"Is something amiss?"

She glanced up with an odd little smile. "Besides all the things that are quite obviously amiss? No. Just my impatience, I'm afraid. It's easy to vow to hold strong 'as long as it takes'...and much harder to actually wait that long. At this rate, my brother will find Densmore before I follow the clues to the will."

Stephen doubted it. "You're looking for Densmore where, might I ask? I've sent missives to every inn and gaming hell in England—"

"Bah, *missives*. Try sending spies. What makes you think he'll pause his gameplay to read a letter from his cousin? Particularly when you're doing exactly what he wanted you to do."

Stephen cleared his throat. "Did you just say...I should have sent *spies*?"

"Or messenger crows. Those usually get a second glance. Didn't you promise supper? Let's move this conversation to the dining table, shall we?"

"Of course. Our meal should be ready at any moment. If you'll come with me?"

She hauled herself up from the sofa with her sword stick and gave him a winning smile. "I'll follow you anywhere that leads to good food."

"Don't tell Reddington that. He'll know how to lure you from the castle."

"I said follow *you*, not toddle after any old ordinary scoundrel." She took Stephen's arm. "You, sir, are an extraordinary scoundrel, which happens to be my favorite type of rogue."

"I've never been more bewitched by a berserker," he found himself replying.

What *was* this inane conversation they were having? Had Miss Wynchester been right from the beginning, and they had been flirting all along? Or was this something new? A corner turned from where they'd been before?

It wouldn't do, Stephen told himself. At the very least, this nonsense couldn't progress beyond idle flirtation. His goal was to resume his cherished, solitary life. Not invite someone else into it.

Besides, once they found Densmore or the will, whichever came first, Miss Wynchester and Stephen would go their separate curmudgeonly ways.

Good. It was better that way. Wasn't it?

12

*O*ver the course of the meal, Miss Wynchester peppered Stephen with a steady stream of inquiries about his cousin. Stephen forced himself to respond as pleasantly as he could, but the questions kept coming. It was one thing for Densmore to deflect unwanted attention from strangers when he was actually there, and quite another for the earl to be distracting Miss Wynchester from any thought of Stephen while they were alone together in the same room.

When the last dish had been served and the topic had not changed, he groused, "Are you writing a biography about the man?"

"Not me," she replied. "My brother."

Stephen paused with his fork halfway to his mouth. "Your brother is writing a biography about the Earl of Densmore?"

"Graham keeps extensive journals on everyone in London and its periphery. His notes on your cousin are light only because Densmore is rarely *in* London, seeing as his lordship has never bothered to take his seat in the House of Lords. I want to be certain to pass on any information that might aid my family. These details give me something to include in my daily summaries."

"You send home daily summaries?"

"I'd report hourly, if there was anything useful to relay."

Hourly. Stephen could not fathom communicating that frequently with other human beings. "Are your missions always like this?"

"Not at all. Usually I undertake cases alongside my siblings." She popped a strawberry into her mouth. "This time, it's you and me."

He nodded in comprehension. Miss Wynchester hadn't simply barged into his territory uninvited. She hadn't expected to find Stephen here, either. And now they were both saddled with each other, for better or for worse.

For the first time in possibly *ever*, Stephen was part of a team. It had never happened before, for a variety of reasons. His preference for solitude, other people's preference for... anything but Stephen.

The arrangement hadn't bothered him because he kept his life too full to have space for anyone else. If anything, he had dedicated a fair bit of his energy to keeping people out at all costs. Miss Wynchester had forced her way in.

To his surprise, he kind of liked her there.

One could argue that their initial impressions of the other had not been under ideal circumstances. But from the very first, Miss Wynchester had beheld Stephen at full tinker, and accepted him that way without hesitation. By word or gesture, she had given no indication of perceiving his idiosyncrasies as flaws. Her only questions had been how she could best navigate the world he'd created, rather than insist he become someone other than the person he was.

Maybe because she, too, knew what it was like not to fit others' expectations. She'd certainly defied all of his, in the best possible ways.

There was no choice but to accept the beautiful berserker as a new variable in the formula of his life. The equation had changed, if temporarily. For a short while, it would be two against the world.

"It's late," he said as the last of the plates had cleared. "I'll leave you to relax in your quarters."

"What are you going to do?"

Think about her. Polish his monocle. Take a cold bath.

"Reset my machines," he answered. "I'm working on a new one up on the roof."

"A murder machine?" she asked eagerly.

"Not all my machines are murder machines."

"Well, that's disappointing."

He could not help but smile. Stephen invented systems to keep boredom at bay, but since Miss Wynchester's arrival, he had not been bored once.

"If you ask me nicely, there's a 0.8912 probability that I might turn my rooftop device into a murder machine just for you."

"That is the sweetest thing anyone has ever said to me. If you did so, I would swoon on the spot." She gave a happy sigh. "I love percentages. I'm at fifty-five at the moment."

He waited.

That appeared to be the end of the explanation.

"Fifty-five what?" he asked politely.

"Fifty-five percent Elizabeth," she answered as she rose to her feet.

He joined her. "What does that mean? Aren't you always one hundred percent Elizabeth?"

"The percentages are an agility thermometer. It measures current capabilities compared to maximum strength."

"What were you this morning, when you attacked the castle with battle-axes?"

"Sixty-five and falling."

" 'Beth the Berserker' is Elizabeth Wynchester at sixty-five percent power?" he said in disbelief. "What must you be like at full capacity?"

Her eyes glinted deviously. "The world has yet to find out."

"I'm not sure anyone is *ready* to find out. The universe might come apart at the seams."

"Destroyer of Worlds," she said dreamily. "It does have a nice ring to it."

She was certainly turning Stephen's orderly world upside down.

She was also standing only a few inches away from him, and in no apparent hurry to hie off to her private quarters.

Standing there, within arm's reach. Touching distance. Kissing distance. He longed to scoop her into his arms and find out if she tasted half as good as she looked . . . and he suspected she knew it.

He couldn't prevent his body from reacting to her, try as he might. Even with bits of blue and pink chalk dust still clinging to her hair, she was an impossibly tempting, voluptuous siren. Stephen had never seen a prettier picture.

But pictures were for looking at, not touching. And this was his guest, not his lover. The last thing a gentleman of any moral substance ought to attempt was—

"Well, are you going to do it or not?" she demanded.

He stared at her. "Going to do what?"

"Good God, I always have to do everything," she muttered, and hooked her cane over the back of the closest chair. "*This.*"

She grabbed his lapels with both hands and lifted her lips to his.

13

All day, Elizabeth had hesitated before making the first move. Before making *any* move. Although Mr. Lenox appeared to enjoy her as much as she enjoyed him, thus far he had showed no hint of planning to do anything about it. If anything, every time he seemed on the verge of kissing her, he visibly collected himself and pulled back.

Shoring up defenses was *her* move, damn it!

If she slashed through his walls and got roundly rejected for her troubles, they would still be stuck with each other. The mortification would be extreme. But *not* as torturous as the unbearable wondering of where this tangible awareness and gut-wrenching anticipation between them might go if they let it run wild.

So she did the only thing a fearless warrior could do: She hung up her cane and kissed him.

He froze for only the briefest of seconds. Then he answered Elizabeth's kiss as though he'd hungered for her throughout the entire meal.

His hands skated up her sides, pulling her to him. There were half a dozen layers of clothing between them, but she knew what lay beneath his. She had seen the rock-hard slabs of his chest and counted the tiled muscles of his taut abdomen with her own eyes. She hoped to do it again. Perhaps now was a good time. She reached behind her back for her sword stick.

Before her fingers could make contact, he grabbed both of her hands and placed them around his neck.

"You think I want to touch you, tinker?" she murmured against his lips.

"I know you do," he murmured back, then captured her mouth with his.

Arrogant. She liked that.

Heat emanated from him in waves. Or perhaps that was the manifestation of her own sexual desires. Her body craved him as though kisses weren't performed only by mouths, and she could consume him with her hands, her hips, her breasts.

She pressed against him without shame or shyness. After all, it was he who had locked her arms about his neck. He wanted her close. She was happy to oblige.

His legs felt as thickly muscled as his torso. Happily, there were far fewer layers of clothing between his thighs and hers. A light spring gown over a whisper-thin chemise on her end, and on his, skintight pantaloons that left no doubt as to what his strong legs might feel like, tangled up with hers.

Forget cutting open his clothes. She was going to use her sword stick to knock the remaining supper items off the table and see what kind of trouble they could get into right here in the dining room. Normally she preferred a soft mattress, or at least a few pillows, but she saw no reason why she couldn't recline on a linen tablecloth, just this once.

His kisses were ravenous, his tongue demanding. Yet his hands cupped her face as though she were precious. A dish to be savored, not devoured whole... if only he could maintain the self-control required.

Elizabeth had never put much stock in self-control. She'd always believed she would have made a formidable pirate, what with her love of pillaging and plunder. But it turned out, being the one pillaged was every bit as much fun. She welcomed his plundering. Reveled in it. Rubbed herself against him to keep it coming.

After all, he was not really conquering her. She was an unconquerable bulwark, allowing him across the threshold because this sensual onslaught pleased her. Her walls were on the inside, guarding not her body but her heart. The one treasure she would allow no one to touch.

Pleasures of the flesh were so much simpler. There was nothing complicated at all about the ways two bodies could fit together. First there was need, then release. She liked drawing it out, making the battle last longer so that the surrender was sweeter. She also liked rushing in, no holds barred, barreling straight toward the goal.

But she was getting ahead of herself. This was just a kiss, nothing more. They could both walk away, unscathed, whenever they pleased.

She was sure of it.

14

*H*ad Stephen thought he no longer hungered for human contact? That was because it wasn't *people* he needed. His hunger was for one specific person. The strawberry-flavored, sword-wielding berserker in his arms.

It had been hard not to turn into a berserker himself, the moment Miss Wynchester had grabbed and kissed him. He burned to hold her, squeeze her, devour her. Rend her garments asunder. Toss the table aside. Make love in the middle of the floor.

He liked her strength and adored her decisiveness. There was no wondering whether a kiss would be welcomed. A kiss was demanded. Five kisses, ten, a hundred. She did nothing by half measures. Not when knocking on a door, and certainly not when letting her desires be known.

Stephen had thought he could conceal his own desire. Had *tried* to hide. He'd spent a lifetime crafting a shell around himself, so deep and so safe that he'd believed no one would ever penetrate his defenses without his invitation.

Miss Wynchester had come swashbuckling in, and she was anything but safe. Everything about this kiss was dangerous. Their bodies were powder kegs, and each stroke of their tongues another spark of flint.

He cupped her face, then slid his fingers into her hair. Her skin was soft and her blond curls silken, but that was not why he did so. He was desperate to keep his hands in somewhat safe territory. A kiss was not permission to explore her curves as he yearned to.

But even her ringlets were not safe. His fingers twisted in the soft curls, his palms holding her head in place as though to prevent even a single kiss from escaping. As though each brush of her mouth was precious as rubies and ephemeral as bubbles rising to the surface of the sea to disappear into the sky overhead.

A passing fancy, he told himself firmly. Of course he wanted to kiss her—who wouldn't want to kiss her?—but that was all this was. Just lips against lips, tongue against tongue. Pieces and parts that would not amount to emotions he need fear.

Miss Wynchester had not penetrated his defenses at all. His heart was still tucked safely behind its shield. He'd merely taken a step outside into the light to breathe in the fresh air.

That he was happier in this moment than he'd felt in ages was not to be examined. Of course she made him feel more alive. *She* was unabashedly, overwhelmingly, gloriously alive. Kissing her was like wrapping his arms around the molten sun. He melted more with every touch.

Like the sun, radiant Miss Wynchester was a fiery ball of energy Stephen should not allow himself too close to. He was Icarus, with wings made of wax. He could only hope the shell around his heart was made of sterner stuff. If he allowed feelings to become involved, later, when Miss Wynchester eventually left, the shields protecting him would be as chipped and scarred as the castle's front door.

Then again, if he kept his wings fully intact…if he reinforced them, grew them, strengthened them, flew far away…then he would not be able to experience kisses like this one. He would not know the taste of her mouth, the scent of her hair, the feel of her skin. The terrifying euphoria of soaring far too high.

It was the landing he feared. The knowledge that what flew up…
inevitably came crashing back down to earth.

With regret, Stephen forced himself to break the kiss before he fell
too far.

* * *

The next morning before dawn, Stephen successfully avoided the
threat of romance by busying himself managing his cousin's affairs,
rather than risk being present in the dining room the same time Miss
Wynchester descended to break her fast.

It wasn't that he didn't wish to kiss her again. It was that he *did*.

He was not proud to admit that when he'd finally lifted his lips
from hers, he'd fled into the safety of his murderous machines rather
than risk another moment in the charming company of Elizabeth
Wynchester. Returning her to his arms was the last thing he needed
and the only thing he wanted.

The memory of how her mouth had felt, and the thought of tasting
it again, had kept him tossing and turning all night without his imagination allowing a single respite. At dawn, he'd thrown himself into
his press-ups and other vigorous exercises in the hopes of burning off
the residual tension.

What he needed was to concentrate on something else, anything
else, besides the tantalizing prospect of kissing Miss Wynchester
anew. They were puzzle-solving treasure hunters, not fated lovers.
Embraces would lead nowhere. He had no interest in changing his
ways. Any hope of romance was doomed before it began. Therefore
it was much more logical to turn his brain to tasks upon which the
future really did depend.

Bells tinkled overhead, startling him from thoughts about Elizabeth

Wynchester. He hurried up to his turret, where telescopes faced in every direction. It didn't take long to find the source of the alarm.

Reddington's men were down below, crawling around the exterior of the castle like ants.

Today, the soldiers weren't in their usual red uniforms but dressed in browns and grays. Whether they thought this would fool Stephen or help them to blend into the early morning light, he couldn't say. Their efforts at disguise were wasted. He could clearly see each of their faces through his magnifying lens.

This must be some sort of scouting mission. The front door was devoid of a knocker—or a handle—making it a poor choice of entry, so the soldiers were understandably searching for an alternative way in.

They wouldn't find one.

Stephen watched in amusement as they surrounded the castle, feeling the cold gray walls and tapping softly on ancient stones. The only other entrance was through the exterior trapdoor in the rear of the property above the dungeon.

Several of Reddington's men were standing on the precise patch of moveable grass right now, though they did not realize it. Lucky for them. The hinges could only be unlocked from inside the castle, when triggered via a lever Stephen had installed up here in the turret.

As diverting as it would be to surprise them with a twelve-foot fall, he did not wish to give away his secrets so easily. To be honest, Stephen was hoping to avoid a physical confrontation altogether. He had no doubt he could handle Reddington in a bout of one-on-one fisticuffs, but only a fool would pit himself against an entire army.

Especially when it wasn't even him they were after. Whenever the real earl deigned to return, Stephen wasn't sure whether he would hug him in relief or throttle him for putting Stephen in this position to begin with. Possibly both, in that order.

Far below, Reddington's men were making their third round about the perimeter of the castle. The sun began to rise. They shot each other startled glances, then scurried off into the woods like fleeing vermin.

Before disappearing into the trees that separated the two properties, Reddington sent a smug look over his shoulder at Castle Harbrook, confident that he'd pulled one over on the Earl of Densmore. Trespassing without anyone in the castle ever being the wiser.

Stephen set down the telescope. Reddington wasn't nearly the infallible war general he believed himself to be—a fact that did not make him any less dangerous. Men like Reddington would kill to keep their beliefs intact and their high status unchallenged.

Stephen left the turret and made his way down to the study to return to the tasks of running the estate. After almost four months in Stephen's hands, the earldom had more than emerged from the muck and bloomed into profit. But with great success came added responsibilities. There was farmland to maintain, properties to buy, stocks to sell, and business ventures to manage.

Columns of stark black figures on a crisp white page were exactly what Stephen needed to corral his focus. Whenever he concentrated on mathematics or tinkering, the world around him disappeared. He did not notice his hunger or the passage of time. An entire herd of horses could thunder right past him, and he would not be distracted. Stephen wouldn't even notice if—

A soft footfall sounded in the corridor. His head jerked up from his accounts so fast he got a crick in his neck. It was Miss Wynchester. Or the butler. Or a ghost.

But possibly Miss Wynchester.

He ran a hand over his hair, straightening his spine and squaring his shoulders before he recalled that it was six-thirty in the morning. Young ladies from London tended to keep town hours, meaning breakfast came shortly before noon. Even those who attempted country hours tended to break their fasts between nine and ten of the clock.

The sound Stephen had heard was nothing more than a gust of wind in a creaky old castle. There was an infinitesimal 0.0001 probability that an ordinary town miss would be awake at this hour, much less dressed and heading toward Densmore's study. Toward Stephen.

Er, make that an absolute certainty.

There she was. Lounging against the doorway with a buttery soft periwinkle morning dress clinging to her curves and a dashing sword stick in one hand.

Stephen could not quite credit his eyes. For as long as he could remember, he had always been up hours before any of his peers. He was an unfashionably early riser who had lived through thousands of lonely mornings, even when housed in a crowded building bursting with other students.

But Miss Wynchester was bright-eyed, armed, and dangerous, before the sun had even properly risen.

"Good morning, Mr. Lenox." She swung the tip of her sword stick to and fro above the stone floor. "I trust you slept well?"

"Like a hibernating bear," Stephen lied.

Her blond brows lifted. "Did you know that hibernating bears do not sleep the entire winter? They exit their caves for any number of reasons. And may not even hibernate inside of a cave to begin with."

"I...did not know that. Why do *you* know that?"

"I'm Jacob Wynchester's sister." She shrugged as if this were a full and cogent explanation.

Because of her position leaning against the side of the doorway, only half of her body was visible. He wished he could see all of it. He wished he could run his *hands* over all of it.

"I'm very busy," he said instead.

"Busy plotting your next tender assault on my petal-pink lips?"

Yes. "No."

She looked skeptical. "Not even constructing a few plans for a minor, brief bout of ravishing?"

Now he certainly was.

"I'm afraid I haven't the time to engage in frivolous deviations to my schedule. I've accounts to balance, a delivery to prepare for, a series of mechanical and pneumatic devices whose gears and levers shan't calibrate themselves—"

"Balderdash."

He blinked. "You've seen my contraptions. They're everywhere. At this very moment, I'm seated at a desk piled high with—"

"—someone else's responsibilities," she finished. "You *are* a bear, and this castle your cave. You think you can hibernate behind a big warm den of mathematics and miscellaneous earl duties that aren't even yours—"

"What makes you think—"

"Because I have mastered that maneuver. I'm the bear when winter is over and spring comes. When it's not safe anymore and I must venture outside, I hide behind a sharp tongue, and sharp claws, and a sharp sword."

"Please don't tell me bears have swords," he murmured.

"Be a bear if you want to be a bear," she replied. "But be honest with yourself about your motives, and be honest with me, too."

"I—"

"Those kisses last night felt honest. Can you truthfully say you're not tempted to have another?"

"Tempted?" he burst out. "I am the bear in summertime. Hot and sweaty and grumpy and ravenous. I wish I could say that you are the tasty little morsel that wandered into my cave by accident, but no. You're the dangerous huntsman. If I don't watch my step, I'll be the bear carcass decorating your parlor."

She shook her head. "My brother would murder me if I harmed a bear."

"This is a metaphor," he reminded her. "Not real life."

"It's very real," she said. "I *am* a huntress by nature. And I would very much like to lie with you on the floor in my parlor. But is that any reason to hide yourself away—"

"Literally every animal does their best not to get caught by hunters. It's natural. It's *logical*. Protecting oneself from hurt is a mathematically sound practice that has ensured the survival of species for centuries."

"I was never really going to stab you." She paused. "Unless you deserved it."

"I can survive a flesh wound. But there's no sense in inviting injury unnecessarily. You and I may be experiencing a temporary overlap of proximity, but as soon as we find the testament and the deed... We'll both be gone. Disappear from each other's lives." He snapped his fingers. "Just like that."

She didn't look impressed. "Is that a valid reason not to spend what little time we do have together, kissing?"

"It's every reason," he said firmly. "Besides, aren't you on a mission?"

"You would apparently be very surprised to learn the sorts of extracurricular activities that can take place when one is on a mission. My family increases in size every year due to unexpected distractions whilst undertaking professional missions."

"Well, I neither have nor want a family, so what yours does is irrelevant. I have my machines to consider, and a den of solitude to return to."

"Bor-ing," she sang under her breath.

"To you. Not to me. I spent all night puzzling the matter, and shan't be budged. Maintaining physical and emotional distance from you is the only logical solution."

She sniffed. "I thought you spent all night sleeping like a hibernating bear."

"Hibernating bears don't sleep the whole time," he muttered. "They can leave their possibly-not-caves for any number of reasons. Learn some science."

They glared at each other for a moment, then burst out laughing.

"All right," she said. "Have it your way."

Was that it? He'd conveyed his reasons for hesitation, and she'd accepted them? Could communication really be that easy?

"Why do you keep leaning against the wall like that?" he asked. "Are you hiding half of your body from view on purpose?"

"Yes." She stepped into the center of the doorframe. Her free hand held a plate piled with breads and fruits and cheese. "I brought you breakfast. You don't deserve it."

"Bring it here anyway." He made room atop the desk. "I'll share it with you."

She set the plate on the table, hooked her cane over the side of an armchair, and settled onto the cushion. "The marmalade is for me. And the bread rolls. And the apple slices."

"I thought this was my breakfast."

"You lost ten percent of it every time you annoyed me," she informed him.

"I'm surprised I still have a right to any of it," he admitted.

"You don't. I am being incredibly generous just by allowing you to see and smell this delicious repast whilst I consume it right in front of you."

"You are all that is kindhearted and benevolent," he murmured.

"Oh, go on then, Mr. Logical Lenox. I'll allow you to share my spoils just this once."

"Stephen," he corrected her. "Anyone fearless enough to upbraid me for failure to ravish her shall earn the right to call me by my given name."

"Elizabeth," she answered, then waggled her brows. "What other liberties have I earned?"

"Half of the marmalade," he responded. "And only half. I'm watching you."

She broke off a piece of bread and dipped it into the marmalade with exaggerated daintiness. The twinkle in her eye indicated the next time he looked away, the rest might disappear altogether.

"If only the countess had left her clues somewhere obvious," she said with a wistful expression. "Like a bright yellow box, helpfully painted with big black letters: WILL AND TESTAMENT INSIDE."

"That would certainly have been more convenient," he agreed. "Then again, deuced little about this experience has been particularly convenient, from the hidden will to the missing deed. A miracle would be nice, but one cannot summon documents out of thin air."

She lowered her apple slice. "Maybe we can."

He raised his brows. "You're a soldier... *and* a sorcerer?"

"My sister Marjorie essentially is. A sorcerer, I mean. She and her husband, Adrian, can forge anything under the sun. They can create copies of wills and deeds in their sleep. Documents indistinguishable from the originals."

"I'm sure they would be, if we *had* originals to copy. We don't know what other items might have been mentioned in that will. Are you willing to inadvertently cut other persons out of their legal inheritance?"

She sighed. "No, of course not. Ugh. We must find the real will."

He piled cheese on bread and added a dollop of marmalade. "Can your sister really forge anything?"

Elizabeth smiled fondly. "Anything and everything. Books, portraits, sovereigns... She met Adrian when he was under the thumb of a corrupt moneylender. Adrian is an artist, too. His specialties are sculpture and pottery, whereas Marjorie's specialties are pen and paint."

"Have they considered producing original works?" he asked politely.

"They produce loads of original work," she protested. "They are both respected and established artists in their own right. They have a studio where they tutor students and regularly host art exhibitions in their public salon. In certain circles, Marjorie is more famous for her paintings than she is infamous for being a Wynchester."

"Fame *and* infamy." He leaned back in his chair, impressed. "Is there anything the Wynchesters cannot do?"

"Individually? Quite a bit," she answered honestly. "But together, as a team? We're unstoppable."

The words were positive and uplifting, but her lively expression had turned somber.

He put down his cheese. "What is it?"

"Nothing." She dipped her bread in marmalade and sighed. "Oh, all right, it's this mission. The Wynchesters *are* undefeatable as a team. But they're not here. *I* am."

"Where are the rest of your siblings?"

"Handling other cases. Our notoriety has increased over the past few years, and we now have more clients than we can attend to as a group."

"So, you're not the only one who's tackling missions alone. The others might have the same worries you do."

Elizabeth looked startled. "I suppose that's true. It hadn't occurred to me. I'm so used to thinking of the others as bold and unconquerable."

"I would be surprised if anyone doubted that you embody those very same qualities yourself."

She fluttered her eyelashes at him. "And to think, so far you've only seen me at my *least* swashbuckling."

"Good God." He gave an exaggerated shiver. "I shudder to imagine the carnage."

"Stay in my good graces," she advised. "You'll lose fewer appendages that way."

"So noted. Might I inquire which finishing school you attended, that instructed docile misses in the fine art of violent combat?"

"The school of Bean. Not him directly; there was a tutor. A series of tutors. I was precocious."

"Does that mean you kept stabbing them?"

"It doesn't *not* mean that."

A throat cleared in the corridor. "Er... Forgive me, my lord."

Stephen glanced up to see one of the footmen. "Yes, Forester?"

"Your delivery is in progress."

"Marvelous." Stephen rose to his feet. "Elizabeth, do come with me, if you like. Or please forgive my momentary absence if you prefer to stay behind."

She tossed what was left of her bread onto the plate and snatched up her sword stick. "I *never* prefer to be left behind."

15

꽃

*D*eliveries are made through the hidden trapdoor in the rear of the castle," Stephen explained as he and his beautiful house-guest followed the footman down a series of corridors to a winding stone staircase.

"Deliveries of what, exactly?" Elizabeth asked.

"Of whatever I need for my inventions. Or whatever I think I might need. Or whatever I want, because it caught my fancy."

"That sounds like...quite an eclectic list."

He rubbed his hands in anticipation. "The only way to construct eclectic machines."

"I presume you have even more contraptions at home?"

"My home *is* an eclectic contraption. Filled with other eclectic contraptions. It is truly the most splendid place on earth."

She considered this. "You must miss it terribly."

"Every minute of every day. I do what I can to re-create the convenience of my usual laboratory here in the castle, but these small, intermittent deliveries cannot rival London's easy accessibility to shipping and suppliers. As soon as my cousin comes home..." His voice trailed off.

"You'll be able to go home, too," she finished with obvious sympathy. "Do you still believe your cousin intends to return?"

"Don't say that. Densmore may be a self-indulgent wastrel, but he's fond of me. And is a lord with numerous responsibilities. He wouldn't abdicate an earldom."

"Not to poke holes in your logic, but... Isn't abdicating an earldom exactly what Densmore did?"

He glared at her. "I said *not* to say it."

"His defection won't last much longer," she assured him as they descended the stone steps. "My brother Graham could find a specific grain of sand in the desert. He'll find your cousin, too."

"And use his powers of persuasion to talk Densmore into returning?"

"Pah," said Elizabeth. "Who needs to waste words, when my sister-in-law Kuni will be there to throw knives?"

"Not to poke holes in your logic," said Stephen. "But if anyone murders the earl..."

"I promised we'd leave him a little bit alive, and I meant it. A few daggers to the chest never hurt anyone."

Stephen raised his brows at this pronouncement. "Where do you derive your information?"

"The people I stab *rarely* die," she protested. "Easily eighty-five percent of them go on to live long and full lives."

That was... a disturbing statistic. "Fifteen percent of your victims are murdered in cold blood?"

"I wish I could take credit," she said with a sigh. "One of my stabbing victims recovered fully, only to be hit by a carriage. Two recipients of my sharp blades mended handsomely, only to be felled by a virulent—" She ran past him into the dungeon. "What in the world is *this*?"

"A dungeon," he replied helpfully.

"I can see the dungeon. I adore the dungeon. I was referring to *that*." She jabbed her sword stick in the direction of the many footmen taking possession of the half-dozen wooden crates being lowered through the trapdoor overhead.

"My delivery," he told her, then raised his voice to the footmen. "Carry it all up to the Great Hall, if you would, please."

"Wait!" She flung her arms out to block Stephen's forward progress. "Have you never heard of the Trojan Horse?"

"Who's going to hide a horse inside a five-pound crate of nails?"

"They didn't hide the *horse*. They hid *inside* the horse."

"I didn't order a horse," he pointed out.

"You ordered whatever is in those crates. If *I* were attempting to lay siege to your castle, the first thing I would do is intercept your deliveries and fill the crates with bombs, or poison, or distempered hamsters."

"Distempered...hamsters?"

"My brother Jacob would think of a way to make the little beasts more dangerous than shrapnel. Stay back, for your own safety." She rushed forward to address the footmen. "You, there. Set those crates down. No one is moving anything anywhere until I've had an opportunity to inspect the contents."

The footmen glanced over her head at Stephen.

He shrugged. If there were any angry hamsters hiding inside, he wanted to see them.

Elizabeth stepped as far back as she could before slowly easing open the first crate.

"Well?" Stephen asked. "How furry is it?"

She dug through the contents with the tip of her blade. "It seems to be...a five-pound box of nails."

"Devious," said Stephen. "Exactly as I'd ordered. Perhaps Reddington is hoping I'll spill the nails and tread upon them with my bare feet."

"That sounds more like something *you'd* be hoping." She glanced up at him suspiciously. "These nails aren't meant for carpentry at all, are they?"

"It's for a minor entryway modification I call The Maelstrom of

Terror," he confirmed. "Reddington's arrow could have taken out my eye. Turnabout is fair play. Now that he fired the first shot, I think increasing the quantity of flying metal projectiles will add a certain flair to the usual water and marbles."

"It has potential," she admitted. "I would love to see how Reddington reacts to being turned into a porcupine."

"I'll let you press the lever," he promised.

"That is the most romantic thing anyone has ever said to me. I accept your proposition. Now stay there." She turned to inspect the other crates.

He leaned back and watched her. "I mistrust Reddington because he shot at me. Why do *you* mistrust him so much?"

"Because he's a man. And an aristocrat. And I mistrust everyone. Particularly those with power they enjoy wielding over others."

Stephen raised his brows. "Is Reddington particularly powerful?"

"Let's just say, you and I are perhaps the only known people to naysay him...and live."

Stephen ran his fingers over his arrow-tousled hair. "For now."

"Hence the importance of looking for Trojan horses," she reminded him. "Reddington is always up to something. People try to stay on his good side to climb up the social rungs, but he's slippery as a greased grape."

Stephen started to inquire whether she'd actually ever greased a grape, then decided he was better off not knowing. "Why does anyone put up with him?"

"Because he *is* powerful. A viscount's heir is an excellent marriage prospect for a woman looking to secure her future. And for others in his influence, he can grant entrée into social circles, memberships to gentlemen's clubs, invitations to exclusive investment schemes..."

Stephen tilted his head. "Much of that is only attainable for those with money."

She nodded. "Reddington gives men of the lower classes the appearance of status and power. Those who can't afford an officer's conscription in the army—or whose families cannot afford lost income due to a dead family member—get to wear officer's uniforms in faux battles as a lark, without any of the risk. For many, being a known associate of a future viscount is currency enough to raise their own stations, whatever they might be."

Stephen was grateful not to need someone like Reddington to establish his worth.

Elizabeth straightened in disgust. "Very well, you were right. It appears Reddington has missed this opportunity to cause mayhem. Have fun with your bits and bobs."

"I will, thank you."

She tossed the lids back onto the crates. "May I ask what the laudanum is for?"

Stephen frowned. "The what?"

"The bottle of laudanum. As far as murder weapons go, a common sleeping draught seems a little underwhelming. Your style leans more toward the unexpected and showy."

He stared at her. "What are you talking about?"

She returned to the crates and lifted one of the wooden lids she'd dislodged. "This laudanum. You're the one who ordered it."

"I did no such thing." He joined her side and gazed at the contents of the crate. "That's a wine bottle."

"An unmarked wine bottle. Containing laudanum."

"It sure looks like wine. What makes you think it isn't?"

"When you've ingested as much laudanum in your life as I have... Look carefully. Red wine is, well, red. This liquid is more of a brown."

"It could be the bottle."

"It's not the bottle. Measure the viscosity." She tilted the bottom of the container. "Not the right consistency at all, is it? And if you sniff the cork..." She placed the stopper just beneath his nose.

Stephen did not sniff the cork. He dropped his voice to a whisper so that the footmen wouldn't overhear. "Did you just say 'measure the viscosity'? I have never heard a phrase more erotic. Prepare to lose your virginity."

"I don't have any. Pay attention." She tapped the unopened bottle against his chest. "If you didn't order a liter of laudanum... Who sent it?"

They looked at the crate, looked at each other, then said at the same time, "*Reddington.*"

"I told you not to accept deliveries willy-nilly!" Elizabeth scolded Stephen. "See what can happen?"

He plucked the bottle from her hands and dropped it back inside the crate. "Reddington was expecting me to serve us a tall glass of poison tonight at dinner?"

"Or just pour a finger or two for yourself."

"And then what was his plan? To sneak in and steal the deed to the castle?" Perhaps *that* was why Reddington's men had been crawling around outside the castle.

"It wouldn't work," she agreed. "He can't get inside, and even if he could, he has no better idea where to find the deed than we do."

"Not to mention the entire household of servants would still be awake, even if I were knocked unconscious."

"Or dead," clarified Elizabeth. "Maybe the trick would have worked, even if Reddington couldn't breach the castle. Laudanum is fatal in high doses, and your cousin has no other heirs to fight Reddington's claims of ownership."

"Everyone knows my cousin is a drunk," Stephen agreed. "The sort who wouldn't remember if he'd ordered any wine or not, much less wonder why the bottle was missing a label."

Between this and the arrow through his top hat, Stephen could no longer deny Reddington's threat to take the castle by force.

"My cousin should be back soon," said Stephen. "Maybe Densmore knows what the heat and fire references his mother left behind mean. Perhaps he can solve the puzzle."

"Will he be back in time to try?" Elizabeth said doubtfully. "It doesn't look like Reddington intends to wait patiently. At least he didn't poison the well and kill us all. Yet."

"He's not *that* evil," Stephen said. "Or if he is, he's at least intelligent enough not to commit a mass murder easily traced back to him. A sleeping-draught overdose could be explained away as a tragic accident."

"Humph. I'll show him a tragic accident." Elizabeth snatched the bottle up from the crate and pulled the stopper free.

Stephen grappled for it. "What the devil are you doing?"

"Dumping this into a chamber pot before it finds its way into the stomach of an innocent bystander."

"No chamber pots in the dungeon. But there are drainage troughs running through every cell."

"Disgusting," Elizabeth muttered. "And a perfect ending to Reddington's assassination attempt."

As she emerged from the closest cell, one of the servants divested her of the empty bottle. The other footmen collected the rest of the crates to carry them up to the Great Hall with Stephen's other tinkering supplies.

When they weren't looking, Stephen kissed her on the cheek. "Thank you for saving me from certain doom."

She shook her finger at him. "Check your crates every time, even when I'm not here to be your bodyguard."

"I'll build a crate-checking device that tests all incoming deliveries for poison, explosives, and concealed assassins," he promised.

She bit her lip. "As much as I appreciate the absolute anarchy of your contraptions, have you ever considered inventing something that *other* people might find useful?"

"I frequently do just that," he said as he led her up the stairs, behind the footmen. "Last year, I perfected a mechanical poultry feeder. The summer before, an all-weather irrigation device. The year before that, a rolling hinge."

Elizabeth stared at him. "A what now?"

"I can show you my sketches and the sales logs. Making absurdly overcomplicated devices is merely my favorite pastime to fill the spaces between the paying projects." He offered her his arm. "Just a little quirk of mine to stave off boredom."

They exited the dungeon and made their way up the stairs.

"What did you do with the irrigator and the poultry feeder? Do you have a store?"

"No. For boring things, I license the patents."

"But not to your overcomplicated devices?"

He wished he could. "For some reason, my quotidian inventions appear to have more commercial appeal than my large-scale complex devices. I cannot understand it. Who amongst us couldn't use a nice murder room?"

"I want one," Elizabeth said fervently. "In the unlikely event that I were ever to move from home, I would be first in line to install multiple murder rooms in my humble cottage."

"If only the world were made up of practical people like you."

She beamed. "I could kiss you. But I shan't, don't worry. You voiced your disinclination to pursue physical pleasures at this time, and I shall respect your wishes."

He arched an eyebrow. "I thought you said you were the plundering type."

"Willing plunder is the only plunder I undertake. If the mood should strike you for a consensual co-ravishing, you know where to find me. In the meantime, I've a castle to search."

He paused outside the corridor leading to the Great Hall. "You don't need my help?"

"Your abdominal muscles are a constant distraction."

"They're hidden beneath three layers of fabric."

"*And yet*," she said with feeling. "Besides, you're not a Wynchester. This is my case and my client, and it is therefore up to me to fulfill my promises. You're free to tinker in privacy, just as you wished."

That *was* what he wished. Or at least, it had been so, every previous moment of his life...up until Elizabeth Wynchester chopped down his door. Now he wasn't so certain.

For years, Stephen had made an art form out of keeping people out. He did not know what to do with the idea of letting someone in. The very specter was more terrifying than wandering into a maelstrom of sharp nails.

But perhaps this was his chance to try something different. To *be* someone different. To pause the relentless rise of his fortified stone walls and look for a trapdoor instead. Take a risk.

Just this once.

"Would you..." He shifted his weight. There was a 0.0001 possibility that she would be interested. No one ever was. What was the point in asking? But he could not stop himself. "That is...Would you like..."

Her eyes lit up. "Is it ices? Have you got pistachio ices?"

"I do not have ices, pistachio or otherwise. I have five pounds of nails and two thousand yards of string, both of which are significantly less tasty." He cleared his throat. "But...If you're not terribly busy, that is...You could come into my laboratory. For a minute."

Her lips parted. "And see what you're working on?"

He inclined his head.

She clapped her hands. "Marjorie *never* lets me see what she's working on! She has an entire wall of easels covered in canvas to keep us from peeking. Yes! I'm honored. I would love to see what you're up to."

He could scarcely believe it. "You would?"

"You must know how exceptional your machines are. Didn't your logical brain ever realize that your talent makes *you* exceptional, too?"

"Exceptions aren't always good things."

"Well, you're a splendid one. I had no idea buttering bread could be both time-consuming and deadly until I met you."

Stephen ducked his head to hide his pleasure. Smiling, he led her into the Great Hall.

Hesitantly at first, then with growing loquaciousness, he began to explain each of the machines-in-progress. Their ostensible functions, their hidden defensive traps, the reasoning behind each element.

Elizabeth's unrestrained enthusiasm was both infectious and flattering.

When he finally finished his tour, she turned to him in wonder. "How could you dream of keeping all these magical devices secret from me?"

"Decades of experience," he replied. "No one else has ever shown interest. The lads at school tore down my machines whenever they caught me tinkering, and followed that up with their fists for daring to be different. My parents despaired at having birthed such an inane embarrassment. They threatened to destroy every stick if I did not give up my unseemly hobby."

"Tell me you did not give up," she breathed.

"I had to," he said simply. "Densmore used to help me repair my machines after others broke them, but between the threats of bullies and Bedlam, I had no choice but to box it all away. Densmore and I couldn't take on the world. In the end, we stopped trying. That is, until I was of age to be my own man and live alone, free to tinker as I pleased. No more beatings from bullies, or impending incarceration from my own parents."

"But that's horrible," she exclaimed. "Families are meant to be *supportive*. It shouldn't even matter whether your machines work or not. The fact that your devices bring you joy should be reason enough for people who love you to accept them."

"Maybe in the Wynchester family," he said. "Whereas, in the Lenox family...But that was long ago. It's been twenty years since I last had to face their disapproval."

Her eyes flashed. "I know a thing or two about disapproving parents. If you weren't an orphan, I'd slice your parents into pieces for being so dreadful at their primary role."

"I'm not an orphan."

She frowned. "But you said..."

"I'm a castoff," he explained bitterly. "My father died a few years ago. My mother still lives. Neither of them has spoken to me since the day I left home. Not that they spoke to me *that* day, either. I got the distinct impression they feared paying me the slightest attention might tempt me to stay."

Elizabeth looked as though she was going to cry. "I will find your father's grave and stab my sword through his shriveled heart."

"It's a bit late for that, though I appreciate the sentiment. Please don't kill my mother, though. I wish her no ill will. I don't need her anymore."

"I wish her a trough of ice water to the bonnet! You're fine just as you are, Stephen Lenox. Better than fine. You're phenomenal. You have a big brain, and you're not afraid to use it. In any manner you see fit. What could be more attractive than that?"

"And yet," he said dryly, "the first decades of my life would indicate few others share your opinion."

"Of course there are plenty of people who do. There is always someone for everyone. The trick is to go out there and find them. You can't hibernate forever. Winter has to end sometime. Seize the summer. Find the pack who likes you exactly as you are."

"Easy for you to say," he muttered.

"Oh, I never said it was easy. But stepping out of the den and glancing about the forest is not any more difficult than"—she gestured wildly at the web of machines surrounding them—"*this*."

His stomach fluttered as he gazed at her. She had him all twisted up inside. His normally orderly brain churned with smoke as it attempted to make sense out of his reaction to her.

She made him feel like...he didn't know quite what. No, it was simpler than that. She made him *feel*. She made him hope, and she made him want. She made him yearn to believe in possibilities he'd given up on long ago. Futures he'd never dared imagine.

"I adore your machines," she said firmly. "In case it was unclear."

"I'll design you one," he blurted out. "I'll...I'll fashion a sword-sharpening device."

Elizabeth visibly recoiled. "No one touches my blades, thank you. I'm one hundred percent self-sufficient."

Heat rushed up his neck and cheeks at the unequivocal rejection. He shouldn't have hoped for otherwise. "Of course you don't need my aid. My apologies. I didn't mean to imply—"

"But do you know what would make the most marvelous keepsake ever?" she continued, green eyes shining with excitement. "Could you create a souvenir for one of my siblings?"

"I could create something for each of your siblings," he offered.

"Huzzah!" She made a little dance with her sword stick. "I am going to be the favorite of my family. Your machines will be the best thing that's happened to them all year."

She was the best thing that had happened to him all year.

He kissed her. He couldn't help it.

Maybe he was wrong to have pushed her away in the beginning. Maybe what he ought to have done was pull her close. Maybe a five-foot-tall berserker was exactly who should be tinkering with his shields.

A veritable tempest of energy and self-confidence, who somehow thought *he* was the amazing one. She not only delighted in the very things that made him peculiar, but even wished to share his oddity with others, so convinced was she that they would deem his inventions worthy. And, furthermore, that Stephen himself was worthy.

He did not want to drown in this exquisite kiss. She made him want to *thrive*. To build a life that was bigger than the cave he'd been closing off and closing in, making the space he took up in the world smaller and smaller so as not to risk coming face-to-face with his loved ones' disapproval time and again.

Elizabeth was the opposite of disappointed in him. She looked as elated to experience his inventions as Stephen was while he created them.

Yet even that emotion did not compare to how he felt when her mouth was locked on his. It was as though all the disparate levers inside his body had been pressed at the same time, releasing a cacophony of chaos and clouding his well-worn path with new possibilities.

But like all the best moments in life, this was only temporary.

16

The next morning after breaking her fast, Elizabeth carefully ascended the slippery, uneven stairs to the rooms Miss Oak's map indicated had been used as the nursery. She decided to begin by taking inventory of all the rooms young children were likely to have utilized. She didn't know much about babies, but young ones had to be kept warm, right?

Today was an eighty percent day—practically peak Elizabeth!—but there was no sense risking her cherished limberness on a careless misstep. Castles were already designed for maximum inconvenience. Narrow, slippery stairs of differing heights in dark spirals wasn't a flaw, but a defense mechanism against invading warriors.

And Elizabeth Wynchester.

Since her arrival, Stephen had blown hot and cold. Vexingly inconsistent about what, if anything, he wanted from her. As much as she wouldn't mind a torrid affaire, neither the current case nor Reddington's patience would last forever. She needed to find the will before he harmed the property. Which meant concentrating on the task at hand, not on the rock-hard chest she *wished* was under her hands.

As Elizabeth wandered through what had once been the current earl's nursery, she kept detailed notes in a journal. She recounted each day's search in her nightly reports home via messenger hawk, in case one of her clever siblings saw something she might have overlooked.

Thus far, their praise of her methods meant she was being depressingly thorough. How much easier it would be if someone would say, "Ah, but did you tap your toes three times on the third stone from the left?" and up would pop framed copies of the will and the deed, for her convenience.

Elizabeth rarely even managed to find a speck of dust. The servants in Castle Harbrook were *good*.

Impatiently, she moved an apple-embroidered fireplace screen out of the way in order to crouch down and peer up the empty flue. No reasonable person would store an important slip of paper in a place where a fire was likely to be lit, but if life had taught Elizabeth anything, it was never to assume that other people were reasonable.

She felt around for nooks, crannies, or loose stones—but there were none. Just as there hadn't been in any of the other chimneys she'd doggedly checked.

With a sigh, she backed away from the unlit grate. After pushing the embroidered fire screen back where she'd found it, Elizabeth reopened her journal to mark off yet another fruitless fireplace. Her pencil paused in the act of drawing a tick mark next to the current room on the list. She froze in place.

Fruitless. Fruit. *Apples.*

Every fireplace in the castle had an embroidered fire screen. And every design was decorated with a different fruit. This one was apples, but the others were... She flipped through her journal, heart beating rapidly. Blackberries, cherries, dates, elderberries, figs. Was that another hint? Almost every letter of the alphabet seemed to be represented, and there was otherwise no indication of what these disparate fruits had in common.

She glared at the beautifully embroidered fire screen. Maybe its design wasn't a clue after all. Maybe embroidery was just embroidery, and there was so damn much of it because embroidery was one of the few things gently bred women were allowed to do with their time. Not that Arminia was particularly skilled at it.

Despite the impressive quantity, the still life scenes themselves didn't make much sense. The fruits were recognizable enough, but the embroideries in the bedchambers also contained baby animals completely out of perspective compared to the relative size of the fruits. There was a sheep half the size of a pear in Arminia's old room, and a little lamb no bigger than a bowl of gooseberries in the one belonging to her husband.

"It's a good thing you were a countess," Elizabeth grumbled. "If you'd tried to make your mark as a serious artist, they would've taken one look at your pear and berries... Pair of berries... Sheepskin... Baby lamb..." She burst out laughing. "Why, you delightfully saucy wench!"

She'd solved the first clue!

Fire, like the heat generated between passionate lovers. Fruit, as in the fruit of their loins. Pair of berries, as in male genitalia. Sheepskin, like the "French letters" some men wore for protection during lovemaking.

This wasn't a hint. It was the giant, red-letter sign Elizabeth had been searching for. Directing her to... wherever the earl and the countess were most likely to make love?

"I hope this compass is pointing to a bed here in the castle and not some random log in the middle of the forest," she muttered as she rushed out of the nursery and into the countess's old bedchamber.

With a sinking feeling, she remembered that she and Stephen had already searched every inch of Arminia's private quarters and come up empty. Any erstwhile clues had either been cleared away by over-zealous servants or had never been present in this room to begin with.

Elizabeth hurried to the earl's private chambers and began her search anew. Bedclothes, pillows, mattress. All unadulterated, just like the countess's room.

But she would not give up. She tossed her sword stick onto the prior earl's mattress and climbed up onto the bed. She ran her fingers up the wood of all four bedposts. Nothing. Then she checked each hem of the blue silk canopy, inch by inch.

One of the edges was lumpier than the other.

"Either that's a dead mouse, or you've hidden something in the hem," Elizabeth murmured. "Please don't have hidden a dead mouse. I'd rather that wasn't the next clue."

She pulled the tiny throwing knife her sister-in-law had given her out from its secret compartment in her stays and carefully sliced open the hem.

A scrap of embroidery no larger than a playing card fell into her palm.

"I did it!" She spun in delight. "I made it to the next clue!"

Once she'd twirled herself out of breath, she stumbled over to the wall and rested her shoulders against the cold stone so she could inspect her prize. The square of cloth contained an embroidered unicorn.

"A *baby* unicorn, so at least we're still on theme," Elizabeth said out loud.

Now that she thought about it, maybe all the baby references weren't referring to the fruits of the countess and the earl's personal loins—after all, nothing seemed to specifically point toward their runaway offspring. The child motif might rather be indicating the *raison d'être* at the end of the treasure hunt: a school and home for orphans.

"Brilliant," Elizabeth muttered. "But what the devil does this bit of needlework *mean*?"

The soft tap of leather boots sounded just outside the earl's bedchamber.

Elizabeth jerked upright, then wished she hadn't. The sudden motion dropped her from eighty percent down to seventy-five. Still high enough for swashbuckling, which meant it was also high enough to straighten her wrinkled skirts and adjust her knifeless bodice and throw back her shoulders and plump up her—

Stephen stepped into the room.

"Oh, good day," said Elizabeth. "I didn't hear you coming. I was just…"

"…casually assuming a deliberately provocative pose, with one hand on your curvaceous hip and your head thrown back just so to catch the sunlight in your blond curls? Ah, yes, that makes perfect sense. I carry out searches in exactly the same pose."

She didn't change position. "Provocative, you say? Is it working?"

"It's not helping you find the missing will." His gaze heated. "But, yes. It's working."

She grinned at him and gave her bosom a little wiggle.

"Have mercy," he begged. "I am but a poor foot soldier, bearing an offering of sandwiches."

"Sandwiches! Why didn't you lead with that?" Elizabeth took a seat in the middle of the carpet, picnic-style, and motioned for Stephen to do the same. She placed the small needlework on the floor beside her.

"Did you find something?" he asked with curiosity as he settled across from her.

"Oh, this?" She held up the tiny embroidery. "It's my lucky fictional avatar. A security totem I like to carry when I don't have claymore swords or battle-axes handy."

"It's a *clue*?" He set down the plates of sandwiches and held out his hand. "Let me see it."

She handed him the scrap of cloth.

"A baby unicorn?" He handed back the embroidery in mystification. "What does it mean?"

"I have no idea." She tucked the needlework into her bosom for safety.

He watched with interest, then shook his head. "Do you have time for nuncheon?"

Unfortunately, now that she and Stephen were *on* the carpet, Elizabeth wasn't thinking about sandwiches at all. She was thinking about yesterday, when he had grabbed her and kissed her. He'd seemed as though he had been trying with all his strength to resist temptation, only for overwhelming desire to break down his defenses and unleash the warrior he kept hidden beneath his tinker shell. She wouldn't mind doing that again.

Many people found Elizabeth to be a little...*much*, but Stephen took everything in due course, from his cousin's original deception through to Beth the Berserker. He had never made her feel as though she were Too Much Elizabeth. On the contrary, here he was, seeking out her company for no reason except to enjoy it.

He handed her a sandwich and bit into his own. For a long moment, they chewed in companionable silence.

"Is going around solving cases always this difficult?" he asked at last.

"Maybe when I'm on my own," Elizabeth said. "I suppose I should get used to it, now that there are more cases than Wynchesters."

He looked skeptical. "Really? How many of you are there?"

Elizabeth took a bite rather than answer right away.

The number of siblings in her family was a perfectly reasonable question. The precise number was speculated about endlessly in the papers. Tommy alone had played the role of dozens of Wynchesters. Family was also a normal getting-to-know-you topic between new friends.

It was just that...Elizabeth never made new friends, if she could help it. She had her family, and they were enough. Opening herself up to potential rejection when she'd first met them over twenty years ago had been traumatic enough to last a lifetime.

She was a berserker. Berserkers weren't friendly. Extreme and unapologetic unfriendliness was a berserker's very essence. No one expected a berserker to sit down with a plate of tea cakes and tell charming stories about their berserker family.

No one except Stephen Lenox, apparently. He was smiling at her encouragingly, as if whatever tale she might impart would be a totally normal response.

There was nothing totally normal about Elizabeth. She doubted she was even fifteen percent normal. She was fine with that. She *nurtured* her oddness. But she wasn't certain she was ready to share her full self with anyone else. Peeling personal details out of her throat felt like trying to remove a suit of armor that had rusted shut.

But she could not sit here forever, poking at her bread crumbs. A berserker did not dither, and neither did a Wynchester.

They faced all challenges head-on, no matter the peril it placed them in.

17

*E*lizabeth straightened her spine with determination. Sharing personal details with someone outside the family was only slightly more terrifying than teetering on a wet floor covered in marbles.

"How many Wynchesters? Ten and a half."

Stephen's eyes widened. He lowered his voice to a whisper. "Which one did you chop in half?"

"Two halves would still sum up to eleven," she pointed out. "The half-Wynchester is my nephew, who is six months old. He won't count as a whole person until he can hold a sword."

"I assume that's your rule?"

"It should be everyone's rule."

"The others all fight with swords, too?"

"All right, no. You make a solid point. Until Kuni, I was the only blade-wielding Wynchester. She prefers knives."

"As one does," he murmured. "Much more ladylike."

"She would kill you if she heard you say so. She's a warrioress from a long line of Balcovian soldiers. If you want ladylike, that would be Philippa. At any given moment, she's swathed in enough lace to make a tablecloth the size of a cricket pitch."

"That sounds...frightening."

Elizabeth nodded. "There's more than one way to construct a shield."

He seemed to consider this. "Who else in your family uses a shield?"

She answered without hesitation. "Tommy."

"Tommy is ... ?"

"Everything. Everyone. A boatman, an old woman, a barrister, a lady's maid. Whatever she needs to be to achieve the mission. We despaired of Philippa ever falling in love with the real her, if Tommy insisted on always pretending to be someone else."

"Philippa fell in love with ... her," he repeated, blinking twice.

"It was inevitable," Elizabeth said with a romantic sigh. "As soon as Tommy peeled off those side-whiskers, Philippa didn't stand a chance. It was love at three hundred and seventy-fifth sight."

"And now Philippa is a Wynchester?"

"Yes. Well, not legally, marriage laws being as shortsighted as they are. But who cares about legalities? I personally inducted her into the family in our official Wynchester knighting ceremony."

He looked wistful. "There's an official ceremony to become part of your family?"

"I'm still working on it," she hedged. "Philippa was the first to get a ceremony. I've added a little more flair with each new Wynchester, but I still think the proceedings lack a certain *je ne sais quoi*. Which Jacob thinks means 'wild badgers.'"

"Your brother thinks *'Je ne sais quoi'* means ... 'wild badgers'?"

"Oh, he speaks French better than I do. Jacob just thinks *any* situation could be improved with badgers. Especially if they have been trained to execute maximum destruction."

"Utterly reasonable," Stephen murmured. "I should have thought of it myself."

"I can ask him to send you some," Elizabeth offered. "I'm sure he'd be delighted to put together a gift basket."

"Perhaps when I return home," Stephen said quickly. "It's bad form to set feral badgers free in someone else's home."

"Is it? We do it all the time." She raised her sandwich, then paused. "Oh! I almost forgot to tell you. A messenger crow arrived an hour ago with good news. My brother tracked down your cousin!"

"He *did*?" Stephen's tone was filled with wonder, disbelief, and... something else Elizabeth couldn't quite identify. "Where was the scoundrel? Is he on his way back?"

"Not exactly. Densmore took a boat to France."

"Of course he did," Stephen muttered. "I'm here getting the hat shot off my head, and he's off drinking champagne in Paris with Beau Brummell. Probably gambling themselves into entirely new scrapes we cannot even fathom."

"We aren't privy to the earl's precise plans, but his boat departed a fortnight ago, days before I met Miss Oak. Densmore *could* be gallivanting around Paris with pinks of the ton. With luck, however, he's still in a port town and can return quickly. Most of Graham's spies are in London, and all of them are in England, so as you can imagine, it's been a bit of a challenge."

"Oh, I don't have to imagine," Stephen said dryly. "Densmore has always been a challenge."

"The best of us are." Elizabeth finished the last bite of her sandwich. "Thank you for nuncheon."

He collected the empty plates. "Back to the search, is it?"

She waggled her brows. "Unless you can think of a better way to pass the time?"

"Well..." He looked charmingly bashful. "I did complete the first draft of one of the souvenirs, if you'd like to see how it's coming."

Her eyes widened. "Machines come in drafts, like parliamentary speeches?"

"Do you... write many parliamentary speeches?"

"My sister Chloe does. I often practice with her. I can do the voices of all the lords." She affected the Duke of Wellington's accents. " 'Whilst marching from Portugal to a position which commands the approach to Madrid and the French forces, my officers have been diligently complying with—' "

Stephen applauded her impression, laughing as she threw her voice to different corners of the room. "Don't let Reddington know you can emulate his hero. He'll try to recruit you over to his side."

"No, he won't," Elizabeth said darkly. "He had his chance. Now he will pay."

Stephen glanced at her askance. "What chance? Reddington was one of your suitors?"

She pretended to vomit. "A love interest? Hardly. He wouldn't offer me a cup of water if I were on fire. Now that makes both of us."

"Then…"

"Oh, very well." Her cheeks heated. "Years ago, before I realized Reddington's true nature, I was captivated by the idea of participating in a reenactment. The real military would never allow a female soldier on the front lines, but ordinary civilians engaged in communal make-believe? That had the potential to be much more equitable."

"I'm guessing it was not," Stephen said dryly.

"I'd have had better luck applying to be Napoleon Bonaparte's first-in-command," she said bitterly, twirling her throwing knife.

"Reddington wouldn't let you audition?"

"He was laughing too hard to even take the request seriously. I've never been good at backing down, so I persisted. When I finally convinced him I was serious, he called me several choice insults that proved there was nothing I could do to make him view me as a fellow human, much less a military equal."

"His loss," Stephen said firmly. "For what it's worth, even if he had taken you aboard, it would not have worked out well for him. Within the week, his men would have been following *you*, rather than Reddington. And he would have deserved the defection."

She smiled at the thought. "Then we both got lucky. I haven't the time to be general of an army. Though the extra manpower once in a while might have aided our missions." She brushed away the old memories and held out her hand. "Shall we go and see that souvenir?"

Stephen pulled her to her feet with ease, the bashfulness in his expression back in full force.

"This version of the machine is just a rough draft," he warned her.

"You said so," she agreed. "Yet my expectations are still high."

"Don't say that. It's unnerving."

"Sky high. Constellation high. Pearly gates high."

"Good God."

They bickered all the way to the Great Hall, where he led her to a tall wooden contraption...that looked remarkably like an unusually intricate guillotine.

"And which one of my siblings is this beauty custom designed for?" she inquired.

"It's two for one. Marjorie and Adrian." His cheeks pinked. "I hope it's all right that I've first-named them *in absentia*. I wasn't certain if Marjorie was still a Wynchester, or if Adrian had become one himself—"

Elizabeth waved this away. "Wynchesters are Wynchesters, regardless of their surnames. Besides, they're not present to be taken aback by your impertinence, and wouldn't be offended even if they were here. Tell me about your invention. What does it do?"

"You said they were artists, yes? Both of them? And that your sister in particular is prone to covering up her paintings until she's ready for others to see them?"

"That's right." Elizabeth squinted at the guillotine. "I don't remember mentioning a penchant for beheadings, but Marjorie can be surprisingly feisty when crossed."

"Behead...Oh, no, it's not a guillotine. Though the pulleys perform a similar function. Watch this." He placed a framed canvas on a thin horizontal shelf and mimed painting a picture.

"You invented...an easel?"

"*Oh no,*" Stephen said in a loud falsetto. "My sister Elizabeth is here, and I cannot let her see this portrait."

He pressed a lever.

Gears whirred, releasing a series of heavy weights on long ropes, which in turn dropped a thick sheet of metal that absolutely *could* cut off someone's head...but instead, sliced down into a pre-constructed groove at the front of the easel, blocking the canvas from view. A series of wooden slats tumbled down on all four sides, encasing the entirety of the structure until it appeared a solid wooden crate.

Stephen flung out an arm dramatically. "*Voilà!*"

Elizabeth lifted one of the slats with her finger. Or tried to. It didn't move. She retrieved a crowbar from a pile of tools, slid the chisel edge between two of the horizontal boards, then raised an eyebrow at Stephen.

He gestured his permission. "By all means."

She leaned heavily on the iron bar to force the slats apart.

They didn't budge.

"Marjorie will love it," she said, impressed.

"The un-display case fits pottery as well as paintings," he said quickly. "I wasn't certain if Adrian was as private as Marjorie, but I didn't want him to feel left out. Three of the sides serve as work stations, so they can be working on sensitive projects simultaneously."

"They'll both love it," she promised.

He bent and twisted a series of marked knobs at the rear of the

unit. The wooden slats rose with a series of clacks, nestling themselves back into place at the top like a decorative mechanical clock
whose figurines were hiding themselves until the next time to chime
the hour.

He pointed at two small openings inside the framework. "See that?"

She peered closer. "Is there something inside?"

"Automatic brush cleaners," he said with satisfaction. "Left side for
water-based paints, right side for oil-based. This button activates the
cleaning process. The brushes then deposit over here." He pointed at
a series of pockets.

"It's magnificent." She reached for a bright red lever. "What does
this do?"

"Don't touch it!" He grabbed her wrist before she could make contact. "That launches the emergency detonation sequence."

She paused. "Really?"

"Really," he confirmed with satisfaction.

"You thought of everything," she breathed. "This will make the
best gift ever."

"I hope so. It folds down to fit inside a standard traveling trunk," he
added. "For maximum mobility."

"Tell me I can kiss you," she begged.

He gave her a slow smile. "I earned a kiss?"

He'd already chipped away enough at her armor. It was becoming
harder and harder to pretend she didn't care if he kissed her or not.

"You earned *two* kisses," she informed him, and made good on her
promise.

She wrapped her arms about his neck, careful to keep her hip clear
of the cherry-red emergency detonation lever.

This was nothing more than a lark, she reminded herself. A holiday
to enjoy while it lasted. When she went home, she would take her

fully intact heart with her...as well as the flashiest, deadliest easel in all of England. This would be just a memory.

"*Densmooore*," came a distant male voice.

Stephen lifted his lips from hers, their eyes locking.

"I shall not be ignored!" the voice insisted.

They ran to the nearest window. A man stood on the edge of the green grass, ten yards out from the tree line, wearing a blatant copy of the Duke of Wellington's red regimental uniform. Black boots, white pantaloons, crimson-and-gold coat, black bicorn hat—even the exact insignia on the shoulders, earned by the duke and not by the impostor below.

"His Grace, Richard Reddington, grows impatient," Reddington yelled up.

"Is he talking about himself in the third person?" Stephen whispered.

"And using an honorific as though he were a duke," Elizabeth confirmed. "This is a new development. I expect he thinks it'll help sell his reenactment, starring himself as England's hero."

Stephen inclined his head. "Maybe he's hoping to position himself in his peers' minds as a god on par with Wellington, or at least in the same category."

"His wiles won't work on me." She glared at the red-uniformed lord on the lawn.

Reddington held up a square of parchment. Presumably, the IOU Stephen's cousin had signed when he'd lost the castle in a wager. "Densmore! This castle belongs to His Grace and you know it."

"You can't have it," Elizabeth shouted down.

"With all due respect, miss, His Grace is hardly afraid of a *woman*." Reddington chuckled in obvious amusement. Just as he'd done the day she'd tried to join his squadron.

She reared back from the window with a huff. "All due respect? I hold absolutely none for him whatsoever. Can I please borrow the guillotine?"

"I've been advised to ignore bullies," Stephen advised.

"And let him think he's managed to cow us? Over my dead body."

"Send down that deed," Reddington shouted, "or His Grace will come in there and take it from you."

Elizabeth leaned out of the window. "You, and whose army?"

Reddington grinned and snapped his fingers.

One hundred infantrymen emerged from the forest. Each in matching uniforms...and carrying long black muskets, all equipped with bayonets.

Stephen looked aghast. "Er...*that* army."

Elizabeth bounced on her toes. Reddington really had shown up with every scrap of ammunition he could find...to even the odds in a fight against Elizabeth and one other person. "This is the best thing that's ever happened to me!"

"Do not go charging out there," Stephen warned.

"I can't behead them all from in here," she pointed out reasonably.

He tugged on her elbow. "Stay back from the window. He has arrows. I don't think his animosity extends to anyone other than my cousin, but it's better to be safe."

"Reddington's men aren't armed with arrows now," she assured him. "His soldiers are carrying muskets."

"Which means bullets," Stephen enunciated. "Objectively as inconvenient to find in one's chest as arrows."

She unsheathed her sword. "I'll deal with this."

"You can't take a sword to a gunfight!"

"Reddington is as much a war hero as my left shoe," she reminded him. "They're just ordinary men *playing* at soldiers."

He arched his brows. "That arrow didn't play its way into my hat."

"A lucky shot. I wager their muskets aren't even loaded."

"Their bayonets sure look pointy."

"That's what chain mail is for."

He snorted. "Do you know how heavy chain mail is?"

"I know exactly how heavy chain mail is. Tommy made me a chain mail petticoat. I go on long walks with it beneath my dress at least once per week."

He blinked. "You take your chain mail...for walks?"

"It gets the heart pumping," she explained. "Now then, if you'll allow me to negotiate?"

"Wait." He stared at her. "Are you wearing chain mail right now?"

She fluttered her eyelashes at him. "Wouldn't *you* like to know."

"I want to know why I'm aroused by this," he muttered.

Elizabeth poked her head out the window and shouted, "Don't be a bully, Reddington! Leave us alone!"

"If you wish to be left alone, then vacate His Grace's castle," Reddington yelled back. "I won this land fair and square, in front of witnesses, and have the vowels to prove it. Send Densmore down with the deed at once, and I shall grant you twenty-four hours to collect your things and be gone."

Stephen snorted. "Twenty-four hours to pack up a medieval castle and sort through the belongings of two recently departed parents? So generous."

Elizabeth called down, "At the time of your wager, the castle was no longer Densmore's to give. He regrets the error and any inconvenience it may have caused. Good day!"

"Liar," Reddington roared. "Either show me proof, or bring me the deed to this castle!"

"As I said, it's not yours or his," Elizabeth shouted back. "Densmore mistakenly—"

"Lost his castle to *me*. Listen closely, both of you. His Grace is done being patient."

Stephen's eyes widened. "Arrows and bottles of poison was him being patient?"

"Can we buy him out?" Elizabeth whispered. "How much is this land worth?"

Stephen named an eye-watering sum. It wasn't how Elizabeth had intended to spend her inheritance, but...

"We'll pay you the difference," she shouted down. "You'll have a bank draft by morning."

"No substitutions," Reddington yelled back. "This is *my* castle. I *will* take possession."

"Double the value," Elizabeth tried again. "Huge bank draft. Enormous."

"Tell Densmore it's too late to change the deal. My men and I will hold our scheduled Waterloo reenactment right here one month hence as advertised to the entire country. And I shall install my men in this castle *now*, in order to prepare the grounds for my glory."

"It is not and never will be your castle," Elizabeth called down. "We can show you legal proof, but we need more time."

Stephen whispered, "How much time do we need?"

"Enough to find the missing will," Elizabeth whispered back. "Or for Graham to bring home the real earl, so he can face his own consequences."

"Two weeks," yelled Reddington. "I shall grant you no later than the first of June. If this land isn't in my possession by that morning, my army shall storm the castle and take it from you by force!"

"We would really rather—"

"I have spoken," Reddington roared. "Mark my words, if you value your hide. You have until dawn on the first of June to surrender."

Elizabeth unsheathed her sword stick. "We shall never bow to the likes of you."

Reddington sent his men a smug expression, as if her retort was proof that he held the upper hand. "Then prepare to meet your fate. Your only choices are to surrender or be sieged. I will not rest until this castle is mine or my blade has tasted your blood."

"You can try your best." She shook her sword and smiled her cobra smile. "I'll be waiting."

18

Early the next afternoon, Stephen swung his helmet's telescopic lens away from his eyes and blinked at all the devices in their varying stages filling up the Great Hall. When his eyes adjusted, he removed his leather tinker's helmet and placed it and his tools in a compartment he'd devised for safekeeping. Absently, he ran his hand over his hair in a halfhearted attempt to fluff the matted locks out of their helmet shape.

What time was it? Normally, he would have pressed a lever to trigger an outdoor machine he'd created that, after an intricate series of cause-and-effect reactions, terminated in the display of a sundial. But that sequence took forty minutes to reset. The position of the sun and his pocket watch confirmed it was midafternoon. He smiled. For the first time in years, Stephen wasn't looking for ways to fill up his empty days. He knew exactly how he wanted to spend his time:

With Elizabeth.

He dusted off his trousers and glanced out of the open window. The empty grass indicated the castle was not yet under siege. Reddington and his men might be lurking in the forest, but as long as they weren't actively charging the castle, Stephen planned to continue ignoring the threats.

Elizabeth, on the other hand, was constitutionally incapable of ignoring any potential violent skirmish. The only thing stopping her from charging out into the woods with her sword raised high was her commitment to making her client's case her top priority. After breaking her fast with Stephen, she immediately resumed her quest to solve the puzzle and find the hidden will.

But even a Wynchester ought to pause intermittently for sustenance. This seemed as good a time as any for a bit of company and a hearty tea.

Stephen placed his request with a footman, then hurried through the stone corridors in search of Elizabeth.

He found her in the library.

A twinge of sympathy twisted in Stephen's chest. Both Elizabeth and Miss Oak were trying their hardest to accomplish a worthy mission...that they might never be able to realize. For both their sakes, Stephen hoped his cousin would walk through the door at any moment, will and deed in hand.

Even if Stephen put the probability at 0.0013.

He stepped into the room. "How is it going?"

Elizabeth glanced up from the tome in her hand, green eyes shining. "Philippa would *adore* this library. She loves bookshelves with ladders."

The walls stretched twelve feet tall, and every inch of them was covered with shelves of books. A track around the ceiling allowed for the hooking of a stationary ladder. Stephen would have added wheels to the ladder, but he supposed the current system was satisfactory enough. He could imagine his aunt Arminia seated in one of the flowery chairs, paging through a novel.

"The unicorn led you here?"

"It didn't lead me anywhere," she admitted. "I thought maybe it was a literary reference. Her favorite book, or one she loved to listen to as a child."

"Clever. How many of these books were her favorites?"

"I haven't the least notion...but there are one thousand, six hundred and fifty-two volumes. It took all day, but I flipped through every last one of them, hoping the next clue would be written in plain English on a piece of paper hidden inside."

"Was it?"

Her shoulders slumped. "No."

"I'm sorry you didn't find anything." Somewhat sorry. If she did manage a miracle, their interlude would end all the sooner.

"I found five volumes referencing unicorns and a recipe book for biscuits, including Scotch petticoat tails." She gestured with her sword at a pile lying on one of the ornamental tables. "The books I intend to borrow are over there, if you're interested."

"I'm always interested in shortbread. In fact, when I was a child, I dreamt of meals in which every course was a different, delicious dessert."

Her eyes brightened. "Me too."

He grinned. "I was hoping you might have time to take tea with me. It's being delivered to the study."

"Tea sounds perfect." She twirled her sword. "I can come back to this later."

"Is that a new sword?" he inquired as she fell into step beside him.

"It's a very old sword. Or at least, modeled after one. Many of my heroines were medieval knights."

"Really? I didn't think *any* women were medieval knights."

"Well...They weren't given that exact title," Elizabeth admitted. "But that's a matter of semantics. Are you familiar with the Order of the Hatchet?"

"I am not," he replied. "Nor am I surprised to learn that you *would* be familiar with it."

"One hundred and fifty years ago, a Spanish count founded the

Order in honor of the women of Tortosa. The women dressed like soldiers—and battled like soldiers—to defend their town from attack whilst the men were off fighting elsewhere."

"They used hatchets?"

"Hatchets, swords, farming tools...anything they could get their hands on. These ladies shared the same jaunty *anything-can-be-a-murder-weapon* outlook as your machines. I would have been honored to fight alongside them."

"Your sword is modeled after one of theirs?"

She shook her head. "Those blades are at home. This one is in honor of Nicolaa de la Haye, an Englishwoman from Lincolnshire."

"Who was also a knight?"

"Even better. Seven hundred years ago, she commanded hundreds of knights, men-at-arms, and infantrymen to successfully defend her castle from siege. More than once! Given the current situation, I felt following her precedent to be the most appropriate." Her voice turned dreamy. "How many warriors do you think I'll need to kill before I'm immortalized in history, too?"

Was it strange to wish she felt as warm toward him as she did about hatchet-wielding farm maidens?

"I don't think you need to worry about engineering a legacy," he told her. "You seem destined to be discussed in reverent tones centuries from now."

Just then, maids arrived with the tea service.

"Allow me to pour." Stephen placed her cup in the milk-dispensing device and pressed the lever.

As the machine worked, Elizabeth said, "The tea cakes look delicious. Perhaps tomorrow we can try the Scotch petticoat tails."

"I'll pass the recipe to the kitchen."

He also could not help but note that planning for tomorrow implied two things: One, that Elizabeth also doubted she would solve the treasure hunt between now and then, and two...that she looked forward to their meals together as much as Stephen did.

When it came to Elizabeth, he never knew what to expect with their conversations. She was the most brilliant berserker he had ever met. While his head was full of mathematics, her brain was practically bursting with esoteric facts on subjects that had never even crossed his mind.

Sometimes she acted as though this knowledge was a by-product of being a Wynchester. Of course she knew the mating habits of the great crested newt—she was Jacob's sister. Of course she knew the precise accents and linguistic quirks of every member of the House of Lords—she was Chloe's sister.

Other times, the random details she casually spouted were so quintessentially Elizabeth that it was impossible to pass her cleverness off as anyone else's influence. She somehow made her bloodlust seem charming.

"Do you read anything besides lurid accounts of war?" he asked.

She glanced over both shoulders and lowered her voice. "Sir Gareth Jallow. But don't tell my brother."

"I shall take your secret to my grave," said Stephen. "Is Sir Gareth also a medieval knight?"

Her eyes brightened. "I wish. No, all of Sir Gareth's jousts are performed with words. He's a renowned poet."

"And which of your brothers takes exception to renowned poets?"

"Jacob," she replied fondly. "Who is a poet of no acclaim whatsoever, primarily because he refuses to allow anyone to read his poems. Then again, what are you and I famous for?"

"You are unequivocally infamous," Stephen reminded her. "Whereas I have been forgotten completely, even in the town where I was born and raised. My own mother doesn't tell stories about me. I learned about my father passing because I still receive the local papers. My mother did not see fit to write."

"But that's horrible!" Elizabeth placed her hand over his and squeezed.

He shook his head. "It's all right."

"It's not all right," she said firmly. "And it is all right for you to admit when it's not all right."

He swallowed hard. "I don't miss my old life anymore. It never felt like home, and I've no desire to go back."

"I've a desire to go berserker on everyone who has ever hurt you," she muttered. "Out of respect, I'll spare your mother my sword . . . but she won't escape receiving a piece of my mind."

"She's old now. It's been decades. We're strangers to each other." He shrugged.

"Is that why you live alone, and pretend to enjoy the seclusion?" Elizabeth asked softly. "Because loneliness is easier than being rejected by someone you care about?"

19

Stephen stared at Elizabeth, his throat thick. How could she guess—

"Please," he managed. "Let's talk about something else."

She gazed at him for a long moment, then nodded. "More tea."

Briskly, she plucked his cup from its saucer and placed it back into the machine, then set about arranging all the pulleys and wheels and trapdoors and dominoes and other paraphernalia until the device was once again ready to dispense milk.

She pressed the correct lever, then settled into her seat with a smile. "Where were we?"

"You reset the tea machine?" he asked in disbelief.

"You always do it. I thought it was time I did my part."

"But...how did you *know* your part? No one has ever been able to reset any of my machines. Not even when I was a child, and still learning how to make them."

"I watched you do it," she replied. "Isn't that what I just said? I've witnessed you put your devices in order dozens of time. Including a few minutes ago."

"Yes, of course I saw you were here, but..."

But I didn't know you were watching. Not like that. Paying attention to how his creations worked. To how *he* worked. Figuring him out. Putting things in order. Even if that order was messy and chaotic and absurd.

"I would have taken over sooner, but I was afraid I'd get it wrong," she admitted. "Accidentally put whiskey into your tea, or launch a firestorm of grenades. Keeping up with someone so clever isn't always simple, but I do enjoy a challenge."

He stared at her in wonder. She didn't think him a peculiar, mathematics-obsessed tinker. Well, maybe she did, but she didn't view it as a *bad* thing. The opposite. She played along with him. Wanted him to be one hundred percent Stephen. The idea was dizzying.

"Come with me," he said, and put down his tea.

She rose from her chair at once. "Where are we going?"

"My laboratory. I was going to wait to show you what I've been working on for your next family members, but...Maybe you would like to help me design the mechanism?"

Her eyes shone. "I would be honored."

He gave her a quick kiss on the lips because he couldn't help himself, then wrapped her fingers about his arm and led her to the Great Hall, where a new multi-levered wooden pyramid reached toward the sky.

She took in the new machine with interest. "Does this one also break down to fit inside a single trunk?"

"All of the keepsake devices will," he confirmed.

"Who is this one for?"

"I'll give you a clue. This side has a lever that will raise up to four illuminated manuscripts for reading, then automatically store them back inside, away from dust and sunlight. There's also a mechanical arm for reaching books on high shelves, and a pistol that fires marbles."

Elizabeth clapped her hands. "Philippa! What else does it do?"

"This side sorts and retrieves wigs and associated accessories in predetermined patterns. For example, if your sibling typically requires A, B, and C for a certain disguise, and C, D, and E for another, each button can be programmed to select the relevant items, which will be delivered on this tray."

"Tommy will adore it." She feigned a swoon. "Are you certain you need me for anything?"

"Well, there are two more sides. I was thinking metal tubes that squirt hot oil at intruders, but it's been done before—"

"Passé," she agreed. "So last century."

"—and I really wanted something that meshed more with their particular skills and personalities."

"An action that causes chaos," she said slowly, "in the most Tommy-and-Philippa way possible."

He nodded. "Any ideas?"

"Well..." She walked around the machine in a slow circle. "They both wear disguises. My favorite is when they pretend to be Great-Aunt and Great-Uncle Wynchester. They have caused a *lot* of chaos that way, and they look about as frightening as wrinkly old ancestors in some nob's Hall of Portraits."

"That's it!" He grinned at her. "I'll make living portraits. It'll only work in dim lighting, but there are always plenty of shadows."

"Living...portraits?"

He gestured at one of the empty sides. "Imagine this has a trapdoor that allows Tommy to slip inside. And a canvas comes down, appearing to be a life-size portrait of Great...Which 'great' is she?"

"Great-Aunt."

"...Great-Aunt Wynchester. Unnervingly lifelike. Because it's not a painting at all. At least, only the background is. The rest is colored gauze. It's really Tommy, *disguised* as a painting, which she can step out of at the moment it would most inconvenience whoever is passing in front of her."

"I love it," Elizabeth breathed. "I want an entire hall of portraits that aren't portraits. It'd be like your murder room, except I'd get to leap out of a painting and do the murdering myself!"

He pulled her into his arms and kissed her.

Not just for helping him put the perfect touch of anarchy on the souvenir he was making. Not even for caring about his machines—caring about *him*—enough to teach herself how to reset his absurdly complicated devices.

But because she had achieved the impossible. Instead of trying to prevent someone else from entering his life, Stephen was trying unsuccessfully to avoid thinking about the day he'd return home to a life without Elizabeth in it.

So he kissed her as though that day would never come. As though if they kept their bodies pressed together and their mouths locked in—

"Densmooore," boomed a distant male voice.

"You must be bamming me," Stephen murmured against Elizabeth's parted lips. "Is that blackguard going to interrupt *every* time I kiss you?"

Her eyes sparkled. "Let's see what he wants."

She bounded over to the closest window without hesitation. Stephen followed, mortifyingly cognizant that whilst *he* would rather keep wooing his houseguest, Elizabeth was already back on the case.

He should do the same, he reminded himself. It was illogical to make room for her in his life when they both knew she would soon leave it. Their arrangement was temporary and could end at any moment. Just as soon as they found the will or the deed.

Or until the rumors about Reddington's murderousness turned all too real.

"Well," Elizabeth said, leaning her head out of the window. "He brought his army again."

Stephen looked out over her shoulder. There on the grass below was Reddington in his Duke of Wellington costume, along with the same squadron of foot soldiers as before.

At least, Stephen assumed these were the same players. Elizabeth had probably memorized their precise formation and written down descriptions of each individual visage in her journal.

"It's an intimidation campaign," she whispered to Stephen. "It's not working."

"Speak for yourself," he murmured back.

A hundred or so armed soldiers, whether a properly trained regiment or not, could certainly do a significant amount of damage.

"Mere days remain until the battle royal," Reddington announced through a long brass speaking trumpet.

Stephen's heart skipped. "Until the *what*?"

"Battle royal." Reddington fired a musket into the air. Birds squawked and fled. Reddington smiled.

Stephen did not. That had been a real bullet.

"If you do not surrender this castle by the first of June," Reddington continued, "lawyers will be the least of your concerns. His Grace and his men will storm these grounds and take possession of this land by force. Your tongue may be sharp, but your castle will crumble."

Elizabeth snorted under her breath. "I'm not afraid of a battle royal."

"*I* am," Stephen whispered. "Have you noticed which side has an army?"

"If you wish to avoid total annihilation, bring me the deed," Reddington's voice shouted up. "We can settle this now, like men."

"Then you will die," Elizabeth called back. "I settle things like a woman. Are you afraid to be as honorable? I did not peg you as cowardly, *Your Grace*."

Reddington jerked backward. "What did you just say?"

"I asked for a fair fight," she called down. "No more long-distance attacks on the earl with your poison and arrows."

"In your opinion," Stephen whispered. "One hundred to one is a fair fight? As long as it's up close?"

"You want fair?" Reddington roared. "This castle is mine and you are keeping it from me. His Grace shall retaliate as he sees fit!"

"He hasn't agreed to a thing we've said," Stephen pointed out. "He answers without answering. Or implies something different from what he means."

Elizabeth nodded. "Reddington is tricky. We won't let him get away with misdirection."

"Or murder," Stephen added.

"I thought we both *liked* murdering," she whispered back.

"I dislike being hanged for it," he specified. "Or being on the wrong end."

"You're one hundred percent safe. Reddington could never beat me."

"Are we talking about the man who arranged to have his enemies killed and successfully avoided legal repercussions? Then attempted the same trick on me?"

"His mock soldiers could never beat me in *combat*," she clarified. "Not one at a time."

"What makes you think he wouldn't send all his men in at once? We have to stop this battle royal. It's not a fight we can win."

Elizabeth made a face, then leaned out the window. "Reddington, we understand your position. Please understand ours. If we can prove that you've no claim over this castle, you must never step foot on this property again. Do we have your word as a man of honor?"

Reddington's head looked ready to explode. He shook his IOU at them in defiance. "You do not. What about Densmore's word as a man of honor?"

"At least negotiate terms with us like a true general," she tried again. "We can set a future date for a calm, rational meeting. If you like, you can bring a lawyer, and we'll settle the matter like gentlemen."

"After reneging on a debt of honor, you dare accuse His Grace of not being a gentleman?" Reddington shook his musket. "You go too far, girl. I am the honorable one. Therefore, I shall negotiate battle terms with you on one condition."

"Don't do it," Stephen said. "It's a trick."

"It doesn't matter," Elizabeth said with frustration. "We need him to agree to negotiate, or he'll keep attacking the castle. I doubt implementing war strategies is part of Miss Oak's planned curriculum for the orphanage. If Reddington will agree to sit down for a peaceful conversation on one condition—"

"We don't know the condition," Stephen reminded her.

"Well, whatever it may be is better than what we have now." She leaned out the window. "What is your condition, Reddington?"

"His Grace shall grant Densmore an audience for negotiation if— and only if—Densmore wins a duel against one of His Grace's men."

"*No*," said Stephen. "I'm not my cousin, and I don't intend to die for him."

"No problem," said Elizabeth. "I'll do the battling." She poked her head back out the window. "We accept on a condition of our own. No dueling pistols. Each side shall contribute exactly one representative, who will be armed with the sword of his choice."

"We'll cut off your head!" called out one of the soldiers.

"Then tomorrow afternoon, at five o'clock—" Reddington began.

"Tomorrow?" Stephen choked. "We don't even get a few days to prepare?"

"—Densmore will bleed," Reddington finished. "When he loses the duel, the castle is mine."

"Not Densmore," Elizabeth shouted back. "His representative: me."

"You?" Reddington sputtered. "A woman cannot possibly hold her own against—"

"Then you should have no objection to an easy win. *I'll* be ready. Send your best contender."

"You haven't a chance in hell," Reddington said with a confident smirk. He shot another musket ball into the air. "Tomorrow, your head will roll!"

Stephen winced at the musket blast. Those were definitely real guns. Which meant, tomorrow, Elizabeth would face down a real soldier, with a real sword.

A delegate who might really believe it his duty to divest her of her head.

Elizabeth grinned at him. "I can't wait."

"Did you not hear the part about your impending decapitation?"

She snorted. "They'll never get close enough."

"I won't risk your neck." Stephen turned to the open window and yelled, "One more condition: The duel is to the disarming, not to the death!"

It was not until he awoke at midnight in a cold sweat that Stephen realized Reddington had not given his word.

20

⚱

The next morning, Elizabeth continued her hunt for clues by poring through the books she'd borrowed from the castle library. In less than an hour, she finished the children's books without gaining any useful insight. She was left with a collection of legends and an illustrated volume of medieval art. After breaking her fast with toast and marmalade, she decided to start with the compendium of art. Illustrations were faster to skim than text.

Nonetheless, she almost missed it.

There in the final third of the book, on the bottom left-hand corner of the page, was a unicorn. Not just any unicorn, but an ugly, furry beast so grotesque that it would be easy to miss the short, spiraling horn protruding from its hairy forehead.

In fact, Elizabeth *had* missed the horn the first time she saw the creature: on a fading tapestry somewhere here in this castle.

"Shite. Where did I see this beast before?" She tossed the book aside and reached for her journal, frantically flipping through the pages. "Was it the nursery? No, that would be too easy."

Unlike Adrian and Marjorie, Elizabeth was no artist, so she hadn't sketched the interiors of the rooms she'd searched, much less drawn replicas of associated wall hangings. She had, however, taken pains to jot down anything of note, and a wooly half-bison, half-goat hybrid certainly made the cut.

She couldn't believe she hadn't noticed its horn the first time. Then again, why would she have thought the faded dye on an eight-hundred-year-old tapestry had anything to do with Miss Oak's future orphanage?

"Here!" She jabbed her finger at a scribble on the page, then hurried out of her room to find the wall hanging.

The room was empty now, save for the hideous old tapestry. After a second glance at the legend Arminia had made on Miss Oak's map—

"Ha!" Elizabeth chortled in understanding. "I had to read the 'legend'! I *knew* you would have given your sister extra clues."

This room, one floor below what had once been the current earl's nursery, had once been used as Densmore's schoolroom, before he'd been sent off to Eton.

She strode up to the enormous, floor-to-ceiling tapestry but did not touch it. As decrepit as the thing was, it was liable to crumble on contact, and then there would be no clue to follow. In fact, artist or not, she'd be better off sketching what she could before the sun bleached the dyes away completely. Philippa probably had ten copies of medieval art books in her personal library and would be able to compare the illustrations for clues.

Once Elizabeth completed her sketch, she sent up a small prayer to whoever might listen. "Please don't fall apart in my hands," she whispered as she slid a tentative finger between the cold stone wall and the edge of the tapestry.

A breeze tickled her fingertips. Something was most certainly back there.

With delight, Elizabeth glanced around for something to stand on to unhook the tapestry from the high wall. There was no furniture in sight. She hurried out of the room and down the corridor, peeking into every chamber she passed until she found a tall wooden chair, which she dragged back to the schoolroom, next to the wall hanging.

"With apologies, ancient tapestry, you're coming down. Try to hold yourself together."

As carefully as she could, she unfastened the first corner from the wall. The tapestry didn't fall apart, but it did immediately tumble to the floor in an ignominious, dusty heap.

Revealing a large, light-filled window—and an ancient wooden door.

Elizabeth frowned. An exterior door up on the third story of a castle? She kept a careful distance from the threshold as she gripped the chilly iron handle and gave the old wooden door a tug.

It swung open easily, as if its hinges had been recently oiled. On the other side was a cramped stone protrusion a little wider than she was and about as deep as her arm.

The bottom half was a stone ledge, at the right height for a bench. But rather than a smooth seating surface, the center of the ledge contained a hole large enough to drop a pumpkin through.

"A medieval water closet!" she exclaimed, then wracked her brain for the right term. Back then, it would've been called a *garderobe*, because clothes would have hung here so that the stench of human waste would keep moths from invading and destroying expensive cloth.

"But what does it mean?" she asked in frustration.

The countess's clue had clearly led to this. Was there some private personal hygiene jest to which only she and her husband would understand the reference? Or was the garderobe irrelevant, and the window was the important part?

Elizabeth stepped away from the medieval toilet and took another look out the window. It was the same view as could be had from any of the adjacent chambers: the forest. On the other side of which Richard Reddington lurked like a snake, coiled in the darkness and ready to pounce.

Perhaps it was not the view but the windowsill itself that held the clue. She retrieved a throwing dagger from its secret compartment in her bodice and used its sharp edge to poke at the mortar between the stones in the hopes of finding a hidden cubby or lever.

Nothing. The construction was solid as...well, solid as a rock.

Elizabeth swung her gaze back to the garderobe. The clue must be in the water closet after all. Heart pounding, she checked every stone from the ceiling to the floor, eager to know where the puzzle had led.

Nothing. Again. Yet another dead end. Unless...

She stared dubiously at the gaping stone hole which for centuries had served as a disposal chute for unknown quantities of human waste. Ugh, better not to think about it. Surely the countess would not have hid the next clue in there. *Surely.*

"Of course she did," Elizabeth said grimly. "*I* would have."

She held her breath, made a pained expression, and plunged her arm inside the stone canal. To her intense relief, her straining fingers did not scrape against anything disgusting. Either this particular garderobe had never been used for its intended purpose...or, like the hinges of its wooden door, the stone chute had been just as meticulously cleaned and prepared for a future intrepid treasure hunter.

What was she meant to find? Elizabeth wasn't thrilled about the idea of blindly digging around the chute with her dagger. One careless movement, and the blade would fall three stories to the ground below—or be trapped in some medieval waste receptacle, depending on how the disposal system had been constructed.

But before she was forced to make a decision, her fingers touched... nothing at all. A large stone had been removed from the inner chute! She patted inside, walking her fingers around the smooth surface, until her fingernails brushed against something metallic. Odd-shaped and fist-size.

Carefully, she withdrew the object from the stone chute, then stared at it in wonder. It was a small tin bird, complete with movable wings. Likely almost as old as the castle.

Elizabeth hadn't the foggiest notion what this object meant, but she'd worry about that later. The important part was that she was finally closer to solving the puzzle.

She ran to show her peculiar find to Stephen, who immediately rang for a basket of food so they could pause for a picnic on the castle roof to celebrate.

As she explained how the search had unfolded, Stephen didn't seem the least bit missish about digging around inside a garderobe. He was fascinated by the tin bird, with its cunning movable parts.

"You can't keep it," she reminded him. "Or use it in one of your machines. I have to decipher its secret message first."

"Based on the other clues, the bird must symbolize something." He turned it over, again and again. "Flight? Song? Eggs? Spring? Nesting?" He brightened. "Feather pillows? A love of worms?"

"How about a love of sandwiches?" Elizabeth plucked the tin bird out of his hands and tucked it away safe in her reticule. "I'm hungry."

Stephen opened the basket. "Help me with the blanket?"

Together, they unfurled the thick woolen square atop the flat castle roof. They placed sturdy rocks at each corner to keep the breeze from whipping the cloth into their faces.

"Cold?" he asked as they settled onto the wool blanket.

"No," she answered, but snuggled into him anyway.

His expression turned serious. "I hope Reddington doesn't send his dueling envoy until after we've finished our repast."

She knew he wasn't worried about interruptions to their picnic.

"It'll be fine," she assured him. "*I'll* be fine." Mostly fine. She was currently at sixty percent. Climbing on chairs and leaning into toilets was rarely a good idea.

Stephen's forehead lined with concern. "There's a 0.8683 probability that Reddington's men—"

"—have not trained with swords as long and as obsessively as I have," Elizabeth finished firmly. "I won the fight the moment he agreed to put down his rifles and pick up a blade."

"I'm building you a sword-throwing machine," he muttered.

"Build it for yourself," she retorted. "I don't need it."

She had already told him she was one hundred percent self-sufficient. When it came to swords, that number rose to one hundred and ten. She had dozens of skilled fencing partners, including her sister-in-law Kuni. But as long as Elizabeth was in top form, no one— not even the Balcovian warrioress—had bested her in years.

"I'm fully confident," she promised him.

"You're sure you're not overconfident?"

"I've never shot a pistol, and my ability to aim daggers is middling at best. But I live and breathe swords. I sleep with them. As a child, I was raised by a wild pack of deadly Claymores. They recognize me as their own. I speak their sword language. I'm their sword princess."

"All right, all right." Stephen chuckled despite himself. "I'll stop worrying."

Elizabeth knew better than to think *that* would happen, but at least they could move on to other subjects. Once Stephen had seen her fight, he would understand. Swords were *her* devices. Each swipe of her blade as precise as any mathematical equation.

As the sun crested high over the castle, Elizabeth and Stephen sat on the roof, looking out over picturesque Dorset. They turned to face each other at the same time.

"It's a gorgeous view," she said softly.

"Isn't it?" he murmured back.

They were no longer looking out over the square stone crenellations at the low clay valley, or the steep limestone ridges, or the distant chalk downs. They were gazing into each other's eyes, her hands in his, her sword stick lying on the gray stone next to the forgotten picnic basket.

Elizabeth hadn't even tried to see if she could glimpse any of Reddington's red-uniformed men in the woods. Once upon a time, the sight of so many soldiers in one spot would have looked like a veritable feast of delicious morsels. But since coming to Castle Harbrook, she'd had eyes for no one but Stephen.

Smiling, he pulled out a bottle of chilled Veuve Clicquot champagne.

She arched her brows at the notoriously expensive vineyard. "Depleting your cousin's reserves of the good stuff, I see?"

"I ordered a few crates from Madame Clicquot last week."

"A few crates," she repeated. "Let me rephrase. Depleting your cousin's coffers of gold, are we? All of these deliveries must add up to—"

"—a fraction of what I earn any given month," he finished. "I pay for all my expenses myself. I could purchase this castle outright, if it weren't already promised to two other people. I had to plump up Densmore's finances with my own funds in order to settle his accounts and devise more logical investments."

She stared at him. "Your cousin manipulated you into becoming a sitting duck for a literal army and your response was to give him money?"

"Not him," Stephen said. "The estate, which you'll recall at this moment is headed for me anyway. And I am indebted to Densmore for all the times he tried to help me at school. Once I realized the earldom needed *my* help, I temporarily loaned it sixty thousand pounds. Which I then transferred back into my own accounts with interest once the first investments proved profitable."

Elizabeth choked on her expensive champagne. "Did you say *sixty thousand* pounds? What exactly is it that you do, again?"

"I told you." He shrugged. "I'm a tinker. I invent things, and sometimes other people want them. When they do, I either sell the invention outright or lease the patents to multiple parties. In England alone, my rolling hinge is part of tens of thousands of wagons and carriages."

"You're as rich as Reddington," she breathed.

"Impossible to say," Stephen demurred. "He has not offered public access to his financial information."

Elizabeth snorted. "The fact that it's close enough that you'd have to compare ledgers to determine a winner... Reddington knows not with whom he has picked a fight. He should've held out for three times the castle's worth."

"I'd prefer nobody knew my financial state," Stephen said. "London is not the town in which to be an independently wealthy bachelor, unless you want every matchmaking mama in Christendom knocking upon your door."

"With axes?"

"Battering rams, more like. I would not know a single moment's peace."

"Then why are you telling *me*? Are you attempting to lure me into the parson's mousetrap? Because I must warn you that I am an heiress in my own right, and do not require the financial aid of any man. When Bean passed away, he left each of us a considerable sum. It is the reason we rarely accept payment from our clients. All my siblings are self-sufficient."

"I'm telling you because you asked," Stephen replied simply. "You're not 'most people.' You're Elizabeth Wynchester, full-time sword princess and part-time berserker. We're friends. You can ask me anything."

"Is that what we are?" she asked. "Friends?"

Stephen plucked her champagne from her hands. He set both glasses a safe distance from the blanket, then pulled her into his arms and crushed his mouth to hers.

He tasted like expensive champagne. Like a man who could have literally anything he wanted. A man who had looked around and decided what he wanted was Elizabeth. If only until they turned up the missing will. Part of her wanted to never solve the riddle. That way, she could stay right here in Stephen's arms indefinitely.

Once the case concluded, so would these kisses. The holiday would be over.

Stephen would return to his laboratory, and Elizabeth would go wherever the next case took her. There would be no more machines, no more taking meals together, no more castle to defend. No more moments like these, locked in each other's arms. No more softness of his lips, or warmth of his embrace. No more Stephen.

So she kissed him now with all she had. A kiss for every moment they had enjoyed together. Another kiss for every moment they soon would live apart. A kiss for every marble and playing card and domino in his contraptions. Another kiss for every stone in the castle, whose strong ramparts kept them together, instead of forcing them apart.

Stephen's hands slid up her sides, exploring all the dips and valleys of her curves. So she ran her own fingers over his shoulders, his arms, his chest, his mouthwatering abdomen...which, come to think of it, really ought not to be covered up by so many restrictive layers. Muscles like these deserved to be set free.

Still kissing, she unbuttoned his coat and pushed the flaps aside. She did the same with his waistcoat. The soft cambric beneath was so thin she could feel every hard plane of his taut abdomen, but it still wasn't good enough. Even linen was too great a barrier to have between her palms and his skin.

She tugged the hem of his shirt up from his waistband. The wind caught it, fluttering the fabric against his chest. She slid her hands beneath and splayed her fingers against the heat of his flesh. He wasted no time exploring her as well.

She gasped as Stephen's hand cupped the front of her breast, trapping her nipple between two of his fingers. That was it. She was absolutely going to make love to this man straight away, here on top of this castle. Who cared about the bloody picnic? They were friends who did naked things like *this*.

All right, sure, Stephen might not currently be considering full-on consummation. But she would unsheathe her dagger and slice her own garments from her body just to be closer to his. The tryst needn't lead to *marriage*, so long as it led to pleasure. She would kiss him, stroke him... anything and everything so long as he responded in kind.

Elizabeth sucked his tongue. The next battle she fought was the one called Win Stephen. It might not happen today, but by all that was holy, before she left this castle—

"Densmooore," came a distant yell.

Oh, very well. The next battle would be with the nodcock screaming at the foot of the castle. But before this mission was over, she and Stephen would find pleasure in each other's arms. This she swore.

"Unbelievable," Stephen murmured against her lips. "Every time I kiss you."

She waggled her brows. "Next time, we can jump straight to the good stuff."

"Kissing is good stuff," he protested. "It's all good stuff. We can—wait. Did you just suggest that you'd like to—"

"Densmooore!"

"I'm *coming*," Elizabeth yelled. At least, she might have been coming, if Reddington's men had left her and Stephen alone for a few more minutes. She lumbered carefully to her feet, minding her hips and joints, then straightened her bodice. "I must retrieve my sword."

He handed her the cane with confusion. "Isn't there a blade hidden in here?"

"Yes, but not the right kind. I need one of my dueling swords."

"You have multiple dueling swords?"

"I have a collection of hundreds. I only brought a handful, because I hadn't dared to hope... And now look what's happened. From now on, whenever I leave the house, I'll be traveling with the whole set."

21

⚜

*E*lizabeth left the picnic on the blanket. There was a duel to fight. Time was wasting.

Stephen held open the rooftop door for her and she stepped into the darkness. She kept one hand firmly around the handle of her cane and the other palm skating the cold stone wall as she descended the narrow, uneven spiral steps. Each wedge seemed to fit only half her foot, and be of vastly different height than the one before or after.

When she reached the landing outside the corridor that led to her private quarters, she picked up her sword stick and jogged the short distance to her bedchamber. In no time, she'd exchanged her cane for an appropriate sword.

All right, it wasn't *no* time. There had been decisions to make. Length, girth, weight, how the handle gripped. She was leaving nothing to chance.

She also had to do her stretches. Her body still hadn't fully recovered from the toll of the strange contortions she'd had to assume during her search of the castle. She was operating well below peak competency levels.

"Densmooore," came the muffled cry outside of the castle.

"For the love of God," she muttered. "I will come and kill you in a second. Have patience!"

As soon as she was ready, she burst back into the corridor.

"Do not kill anyone," Stephen reminded her.

"You sound just like Jacob. Were you listening to me talk to myself?"

"One needn't eavesdrop to reach an obvious conclusion. I know you. Please convince Reddington to duel to the disarming, not to the death. That'll be more than enough. The mortification of being bested by a woman will send him scurrying off into the night." Stephen paused. "I hope."

"Humph." Elizabeth pushed past him. "We'll see what happens."

She made it to the stairs and hurried down the triangular spiral steps faster than she ought. In her eagerness to spar with her enemy, her foot failed to gain purchase on a thin sliver of stone, and shot forward into nothingness.

She flung out her free hand to grasp the banister—but of course there was none.

A strong hand grabbed her flailing wrist, righting her before her foot's terrifying skid sent her over the edge of the staircase, and tumbling into an early grave.

"Slow down, Berserker. Are you all right?"

"I'm fine," she said quickly, and gave what she hoped passed as a carefree laugh. "Just eager to cut off heads."

She wasn't fine. Not completely. After being jarred like that, her left hip spasmed every time she put weight on that side, causing her to walk out of rhythm and out of balance. She took each step gingerly, determined not to make a permanent mistake on the staircase.

"I thought you said you were in a hurry," Stephen said with a chuckle. "Now what are you doing?"

Trying not to die.

"Making him sweat," she answered lightly. "I decided he doesn't deserve unnecessary promptness. I'll slice through his throat when I'm good and ready."

Stephen touched her side. "You're limping."

"I'm not."

"You're *limping*. If you're already in pain, we need to call off the duel—"

"I'm *fine*." She put her full weight on her leg to prove it, and regretted it immediately. "Once I best him, we can negotiate for more time."

Stephen frowned, but seemed to take her at her word. "And a cease fire. No killing, unless he tries to kill you first."

She brightened. "You're saying . . . I *can* kill him? If he deserves it?"

"Of course. If he tries to murder you and you let him live, I'll kill him myself."

She kissed him. "You are a prince amongst men."

Stephen swung open the rotating door to the entryway. "We exit through here. I'll show you where to step."

"I remember which stones." She scanned the floor for stray marbles, then strode through the antechamber.

"Densmooo—"

Elizabeth opened the front door. Sunlight streamed into the castle, and she stood blinking for a moment before her eyes found their focus on the source of all the yelling.

Next to Reddington was a man approximately the size of a full-grown oak, with arms and legs each as wide as tree trunks. He stood twenty yards before her, a heavy sword in his enormous, cabbage-size hand.

"Get back in here," hissed Stephen.

Elizabeth stepped out into the sunlight. "I am Elizabeth Wynchester, first in command of the Earl of Densmore's ad hoc army, here to defend Castle Harbrook. And you are?"

"They call me Crump," said the giant. "Reddington appointed me to win this fight."

Motion rustled in the trees. The rest of the army lurked in the forest, watching.

Reddington smirked. "His Grace hopes your earl is standing by with deed in hand."

"Tell him I'm not Densmore," Stephen murmured into the back of Elizabeth's neck as he came up behind her.

She held up a finger to Crump, then turned around to whisper to Stephen. "When the cat's away, the mice will storm the castle in full force. We can't tell them who you are until we find the will, and can prove Reddington doesn't own this land."

She turned back around. Too quickly. Her hip gave a twinge that almost made her stumble. She gritted her teeth and smiled her coldest smile at Crump.

"Very well, good sir. Prepare to die."

He laughed. "You won't get near me, girl. The 'fight' will be over in seconds."

"No one dies," Stephen said loudly. "The duel is to the disarming. Understood?"

Elizabeth curtseyed obediently.

"'Disarming' doesn't mean 'cut off his arm,'" Stephen reminded her.

She waved this away. Words were open to interpretation.

Reddington glared at them both. "Make haste. I want my castle."

"You agreed to negotiate about that," she reminded him. "After I win this duel, we cease all interaction until we reconvene a week from today to discuss the matter calmly and reach an amicable solution."

Elizabeth hadn't the least faith in Reddington's ability to be calm or amicable, much less that he possessed any willingness to accept her refusal to hand over the castle. What she really wanted was a full week's reprieve from external distractions. With luck, she could follow the clues and find the hidden will long before Reddington returned with his lawyer—or an army.

"*If* you win," he corrected with a smirk. "Which you won't. Let the duel begin!"

Crump hefted his huge sword. "Ready to lose, little girl?"

Elizabeth lifted her own blade, swinging it in figure eights, faster and faster, then tossing it from hand to hand with a swirl to the side or over her head in between.

Reddington took several steps back.

Elizabeth grinned. Was she showing off? Absolutely. Intimidation was often the first step toward victory. That was why Reddington had appointed Crump. And it was why Castle Harbrook had Elizabeth.

Crump's eyes watched her flashing sword first with annoyance, then with awe, then with an unmistakable flicker of hesitation.

Perfect.

"Ready when you are," she called out, without slowing her blade.

Crump visibly collected himself, then lifted his sword and charged, hollering like a wild boar.

Elizabeth waited until he was almost on her, then stepped aside and flicked out her blade, flipping his own sword up and out at such an angle that it flew from his hands and soared across the grass to land at Stephen's feet.

"Why, Crump," said Stephen. "It looks like you dropped something."

The big man was skidding across the grass, trying to catch his balance before he fell face-first into the solid stone wall of the castle. He righted himself just in time, then spun around, his wide face bright red with anger.

"Well," said Stephen. "That's that, then. Au revoir. Come back in a week prepared to negotiate like gentlemen. I assume you dropped enough bread crumbs to find your way home through the forest?"

Crump stalked over to Stephen, bared his teeth in a humorless grimace, then swiped up his fallen sword.

"Please don't take your defeat personally," said Elizabeth. "You are not the first inadequate man to face me, nor shall you be the last. Many discover much too late that the skills he thought he possessed—"

Crump lifted his sword high, showing no sign of surrender.

"The duel is over," Stephen shouted. "Elizabeth won! You can't keep—"

"Stay back, *Densmore*," Elizabeth yelled back pointedly. "I'll deal with this knave."

Crump sneered, not appearing the least bit susceptible to being dealt with.

Stephen appealed to Reddington. "Did you not claim to be a man of honor? We agreed to duel to the disarming—"

"That was your suggestion," interrupted Reddington. "His Grace decided Crump shall fight to the second disarming."

"The second... *Obviously* we meant the first disarming," Stephen exclaimed in exasperation.

"Then you should have said so," Reddington replied, unimpressed.

"Who the devil ever heard of—"

Elizabeth held up her free hand to shush Stephen. Crump had crouched into fighting position, and there was no time to waste on words of outrage that would wash off Reddington like rain.

A man of honor? More like a fairy-tale trickster. If Reddington kept his word, it would be on technicalities. If they did sit down for a negotiation, Elizabeth would have to take uncommon care with her phrasing if she wished to come out ahead.

"All right, Your Grace," she said carefully, measuring each syllable. Such caution was foreign to her. Usually she spoke without thinking and worried about the consequences later. This new twist could prove more dangerous than the armed giant before her. "To the second disarming. But after I do so, we shall have a full week's cease fire before reconvening for a calm, good-faith conversa—"

Crump charged at her.

She leapt from his path just in time, flashing out with her sword to bend his blade—and his wrist—backward. The sword shot from his grasp as Crump stumbled forward out of balance.

Elizabeth landed in a light crouch, her own sword holding fast in her hand.

All right, she landed in a mostly light crouch. A somewhat light crouch. A much-heavier-than-usual crouch, in which one hip was stiffer than the other. Her knee wobbled with warning.

"Not now," she muttered to her flaring joints. "This is *not* the time."

The other knee gave a twinge of its own. If she held this crouch much longer, her legs would collapse out from under her.

Never show weakness.

"It's over," Stephen shouted. "Elizabeth bested you twice!"

Crump scooped up his sword with obvious fury. He spun to face her, then charged forward with a roar.

This time, he got her.

Not with his blade—that would require competent swordsmanship— but with a full-body tackle, like a raging bull taking down a bunny rabbit.

When Elizabeth's back hit the ground, every bone cried out in protest...and the sword handle slipped from her suddenly sweaty palm.

She plummeted to thirty percent. If she was lucky.

Crump sprang to his feet and beat his fists against his barrel chest. "You dropped your sword! I won!"

"You dropped yours, too," Elizabeth groaned as she forced her flattened limbs into a crawling position. Make that twenty-five percent.

"*You* didn't make me lose anything," Crump said. "I let go of my weapon because I won."

He scooped up his sword and swung it carelessly, pleased with himself.

She wiped her palms on her skirts, then wrapped her hand around her sword handle and hauled herself to her feet. Twenty percent.

"You didn't win," she spat. "Not only is this supposed to be a *sword*fight—"

"It's not my fault if you can't lose gracefully."

"—you also insisted on ending the fight after the *second* disarming. Which I accomplished and you did not. The duel is over, Crump. You lost."

Rather than admit defeat, the giant let out a deafening roar and charged at her all over again.

Elizabeth barely got out of the way in time. Her hip locked and her knees buckled and her sword arm thrust out toward his gracelessly in a last-ditch attempt to—

The blade flew from the giant's hands for a third time. She followed through by slamming the hilt of her sword into Crump's chest, causing him to flail backward.

Pain radiated throughout Elizabeth's body at the impact. Somehow, she remained on her feet. Barely.

Never show weakness.

"There. That's it," she yelled out to the fallen Crump, gasping through the pain. "You lost!"

Red-faced, the giant rose, snatched up his weapon, and stalked away from her without a single polite syllable of goodbye.

It was a good thing. She was a woman teetering on unstable joints and grimacing with repressed agony. A puff of air could disarm her at this point.

She turned toward the castle and concentrated on keeping her feet moving.

"Get back here, young lady," Reddington blared through his speaking trumpet. "You might have bested my soldier, but you shan't best me!"

"Because we're done," she called without turning around. "As a man of honor, *Your Grace*, you must grant the promised seven days' cease fire, followed by the agreed-upon peaceful negotiation. If you show your face beforehand, I shall interpret it as full capitulation to our complete ownership of this castle."

As Reddington sputtered and shouted new threats behind her, Elizabeth lurched her way back into the castle out of sheer force of will. Reddington's fury faded to nothing.

"He's leaving!" she heard Stephen say as he intercepted her just inside the murder room. "You did it, Elizabeth. I've an entire crate of champagne we can celebrate with. I might even be able to find us a nice—"

She pushed past him, the muscle spasms in her lower back so intense that she could barely keep from vomiting.

"Elizabeth?" he said hesitantly.

"I'm fine," she choked out without stopping.

She wasn't fine. She was at fifteen percent and falling.

"Where are you go—"

She ignored him. All her focus was on putting one leg in front of the other, again and again, until she reached the blessed softness of her mattress.

The floor conspired against her. Every stone was lumpy, every surface too slippery. The stairs looked dark and infinite.

Ten percent and falling.

One foot at a time. Grit your teeth through the pain. Grind them into dust if you must. Showing weakness is how you get tossed aside as worthless. Now the right foot. And then the left. Careful. Don't let the spasms tumble you down the stairs. Hold the wall. It's your hand that's slippery, not the stone. You're drenched in sweat. Cold sweat. And tears. Don't let him see. You're almost there.

Five percent and falling.

"Elizabeth?"

"I said I'm fine," she choked out. "Just tired. I need to rest. I'll see you in the morning. Don't wait for me for breakfast. I might sleep past noon."

Her stomach gurgled. She was definitely going to vomit. She lurched down the corridor, each excruciating step less stable than the one before.

There it was. Her bedchamber. She pushed open her door and banged it shut behind her, locking it with one hand as the sword fell limply from the other and clanged to the stone floor.

Zero percent.

Lights out.

22

⚜

*E*lizabeth awoke with a gasp. She kept her eyes shut tight. Slowly, carefully, gingerly, she began the inch-by-inch inventory ritual. She started with her toes. Not a full wiggle—a slight, experimental flex.

Her knees twitched in response, which caused her hip to jerk, which caused her lower back to grip her in the sharp talons of a vicious muscle spasm.

Perfect. Splendid.

She didn't bother checking the rest of her body. She just lay there, concentrating on evening out her breaths, in through her mouth, out through her nose, slow, steady. There. Like that. She would get through this. She always did.

She cracked open one eye. Early morning sun streamed through the windows. She'd survived the night. Somehow.

Her fingers flopped at her sides, then found something light and smooth and sticky. Her flask of gin. Empty. She'd probably guzzled its contents in one swallow.

Now there was nothing to take the edge off. Her head was pounding, her mouth thick, and her body ached as though she'd spent the night being beaten with a mallet.

It was tomorrow, then. Twelve or more hours of semi-consciousness had slipped away. The bedchamber door was locked tight. She vaguely recalled several knocks at it, intermittently. And a voice. Probably Stephen's. She'd called out that she was fine. Unless she'd dreamed the interactions.

She forced open the other eye. The high stone ceiling greeted her. Relentless gray. Cold. Pitted. Unfeeling. God, she hated this castle. Why had she ever thought she liked castles?

A few minutes passed. Or an hour.

She tried her toes again, slower this time. Her knees tensed, but didn't flinch. Which meant her hips stayed stable, and the muscles of her back didn't rebel against her.

Good. An excellent sign. Moving her toes meant she was at fifteen percent Elizabeth. Sure, it sounded like a lot less than fifteen percent, until you factored in that she'd moved her toes *without pain*. That was the key. If she took it slow, she might get up to twenty percent today, or twenty-five. Maybe even thirty.

The problem was, holding still only tempted her muscles to stiffen. The more she babied her limbs, the more vehemently they reacted when she tried to use them. On the other hand, doing too much too fast was the quickest way to drop back to zero. The trick was to do the gentlest of stretches. As constant of motion as she could stand, without pushing her body too far. Coaxing it back to life. Limbering one joint, one muscle at a time.

It was a good plan in theory. Backed by years of firsthand experience. It was also boring as bloody hell. Lying here, doing nothing. Stretching her toes, testing her wrists.

Usually her upper body was all right. But not her lower back. Her hips were often a mess, and the knees not so great, but the rest of her often returned to form within a day or so of the first onset of a flare-up.

She tested the theory by moving one arm, then the other, then raising them toward the ceiling. Everything was fine until she lifted her shoulders a little bit. Her back decided to take umbrage with the movement. She sucked in a sharp breath and let her arms fall back to her sides.

Bloody hell. She was helpful when swashbuckling and worthless when convalescing. There was nothing Elizabeth hated more than waking up like this.

Ordinarily, she could go reasonably long stretches between flareups, but the castle was physically challenging. It had only been a matter of time. There were countless stairs, low overhangs, crooked steps, uneven floors. Stretching, crouching, crawling, hammering, twisting. A bloody swordfight.

And now she couldn't do any of it. She was letting Miss Oak down. Letting the whole family down.

Letting Stephen down.

She definitely wasn't going to open that door and show him just how bad things really were. How bad *she* really was. What if she lost his interest, or his esteem lowered?

She'd rather him think her a rude, moody curmudgeon than to know her body was broken and she was lying here, helpless as a baby, unable to do the simplest of tasks.

Hiding the truth was always better. Never show weakness. *Never.* It had been her mantra for as long as she could remember. Long before Bean or becoming a Wynchester. This was nothing new. Elizabeth had learned to grit her teeth and hide before she was three feet tall. Maybe younger.

It was difficult to remember those days. Or rather, she'd tried so determinedly to forget them, to refuse to succumb to the memories, that it was all now a blur of pain and tears and the sharp crack of the back of a hand.

I don't see anything wrong with you. You're lying. I'll give you something to cry about.

And then, when they finally *had* believed her... That day had been so much worse.

She shook her head to clear it. Concentrate on the ceiling. That was safer. Make your mind cold and gray and blank, just like the slabs of stone all around you. Don't think about the past. Don't think about the pain. Worry about your stretches. You know they help. Try it again. You can do this.

Horse hooves thundered outside the castle. Her head pounded along with it.

She turned her head toward the window, then squeezed her eyes shut. Reddington. Six days sooner than agreed. He was relentless.

And she couldn't do a bloody thing about it.

Wetness coursed down her cheek. She really had let everyone down. Sweet Miss Oak and all the children who could have been living in comfort right now, if Elizabeth could get off her arse and find the will. She'd even abandoned Stephen, who had no experience at all with duels or defending himself against an army of Crumps.

In short, she was ruining everything for everyone. Reddington would win. And it would be all Elizabeth's fault.

Loud knocks banged at her door. Each strike caused her splitting head to blare with pounding pain.

"Go away," she whispered, her jaw clenched tight. She wished she'd had a chance to finish her new book on war strategies. A good offense could help in moments like this.

The pounding grew louder.

"Elizabeth?" came Stephen's voice. "Answer me!"

"Go away," she gasped, then rallied her strength to say it loud enough for her voice to carry. "Go away!"

A key turned in the lock and the door flew open.

Stephen burst into the room in obvious panic, face pale, eyes wild. "Elizabeth! What happened?"

She struggled up onto her elbows, and earned a horrific muscle spasm for her labor.

"Get out!" she screamed. "I didn't invite you in! This is a gross invasion of privacy."

"Are you injured?" He ran to her bedside and began patting her body, each touch setting off new paroxysms of excruciating agony.

"*Go. Away.*" Her vision blurred, half from pain, and half from involuntary tears caused by him witnessing her fragility like this. "You're hurting me."

"But what's wrong with you?" he asked plaintively, clearly at a loss.

What's wrong with you?

Wrong with you.

Wrong.

Her body occasionally failed her. Yes. No sense denying the obvious. But she didn't want to be *defined* by her disability. For *her* to be the problem, rather than the flare-up. For Stephen to stop looking at her like a goddess and treat her like an invalid. For eyes that had heated with sexual intent to fill instead with pity.

Just like he was doing now.

23

Stephen raked a hand through his hair. He was desperate to help Elizabeth, but absolutely clueless as to what the problem was. The way she was lying there, pale, clammy, unmoving...Had he *ever* seen Elizabeth not moving? She was constantly in motion. A cyclone of energy. Unstoppable. Un*slow*able. And here she was, still as a corpse, as though this was her deathbed.

"Please," he begged, sinking to his knees beside the bed. "Just tell me what's happening. Maybe I can—"

"You can go away! You can't break down someone's door because you feel like it."

"You were literally doing just that when I met you."

"I thought you were the enemy. I was trying to *destroy* you. Is that what you want?"

"No! I want to help." Had she twisted an ankle? Broken a leg? He reached out his hand to determine the source of the problem.

"*Do not touch me,*" she bit out through gritted teeth. "I...This happens, all right? Sometimes for good reason, sometimes for no reason. My body just...gives up. Are you happy now?"

He'd be happy when he fixed it.

"I'll make splints," he offered. "Do you need splints? I can also make crutches. Or add wheels to a chair. Do you need medicines? There's an apothecary in town. I can also summon a surgeon. I'll do all the things: splints, crutches, wheels, poultices, surgeons. I'm making a list."

"Stop it." Her green eyes were glassy. "Do not fuss over me. I am not your baby, and you are not my nanny. Stop treating me like a problem to solve or a contraption to fix."

"But clearly..." He gestured at her prone in bed.

She closed her eyes. "Please go away, Stephen. *Please*."

"Oh, I know what will help!" He jumped to his feet and rang the bellpull.

"What are you doing?" Elizabeth said in horror. "If I wanted other people to see me like this, I would have rung for the maids myself."

"I'll be quick," he promised. "Here's a footman now. Forester, could you please bring me the oak crate currently on the left side of the desk in the Great Hall? Miss Wynchester is feeling under the weather, and—"

Elizabeth moaned. "Get out! Both of you!"

Forester looked startled, but nodded at Stephen before hurrying off.

Stephen turned back to Elizabeth and readjusted his variables. The berserker wasn't infallible after all. Her own body sometimes betrayed her, and she had tried to hide it. He wondered if half of her bluster was an attempt to make up for this perceived failing.

"You don't have to be invincible to be extraordinary," he told her. "You're already so far past extraordinary, the numbers of probability cannot encompass your magnificence. You're 0.999—"

She glared at him. "What is the probability that I can get you to leave me bloody well alone?"

"I've just summoned a crate," he explained. "Once I've set it up—"

"Go to hell," she spat. "I didn't ask for a crate. I didn't ask for *you*. I didn't ask for any of this. I definitely didn't ask for you to stand around gawping at my weakness—"

Anger flared within him. There was no reason to lash out like that. He was trying to fix the problem!

"*I* don't think you're weak. *You* think you're weak." His voice rose. "I think you're the strongest woman I've ever met. The strongest *person*."

"So strong and powerful, I can't even get you to leave me alone?" She gestured at the window. "Don't you have Reddington to deal with? I heard the horses, but I cannot fight."

"What? Oh, no, I didn't need you. That was a hackney bringing a potential orphanage instructor who wanted to see the castle—presuming we find the will. McCarthy is giving her an external tour of the grounds from the safety of her carriage. Apparently, Miss Oak told several applicants that as long as they—oh, look, here's Forester with that crate."

"Shove the crate up your arse," Elizabeth said with a ragged breath, "and close the door behind you."

Stephen glanced around her bedchamber until he glimpsed a washing table. He placed the pitcher and basin onto the floor, then swung the small table over to the bedside. Working quickly, he assembled the pieces inside the crate until the device was fully functional.

"It's a perpetual tea machine," he explained. "I intended to give it to you later, but...Tea isn't *really* infinite. The reservoir only stores a gallon of water at a time. But for tea purposes, that quantity should do. Just press this lever, which will engage that flint, and so on, setting off a series of reactions that last precisely three minutes, at which point the pot will tip forward, pouring a single portion into the teacup. I've not yet figured out a sensor to let the teapot know—"

"Who cares what the teapot knows! I can't even get through *your* thick skull." Elizabeth slapped a pillow over her face and let out a bloodcurdling scream.

"Er," said Stephen.

She flung the pillow aside and glared at him. "Listen to me carefully. I am not a system to observe and optimize. I don't need to be tinkered. I do not need *you*."

"I just want—"

"It's not about what you want. You are not helping. Your presence is hurting me. You. Are. Hurting me." Her green eyes glistened with unshed tears. "If you care about me at all, then go . . . the hell . . . away."

"I . . ." He faltered, his heart tripping. Or perhaps it was Elizabeth's words, finally catching up to him. He replayed them, slower. She was right. Her lack of consent was the variable he ought to have been paying attention to.

Whenever there was a problem, Stephen immediately wanted to remedy the matter. But this wasn't about him, or what he wished. It wasn't even his problem.

If Elizabeth wanted him to know what she was struggling with, she would have told him. On her own terms. On her own time. When she was ready to do so. When she felt *safe* to do so.

Safety he'd taken from her, by barging in and *fixing*.

Instead of his fussing making her feel cared for, he'd made her feel diminished. Less than. Useless. Hurt.

He'd made a stoic berserker cry, for God's sake. Broken the fragile bond of trust between himself and the woman he was starting to fall for. Who might one day have loved *him* . . . if he had bothered to treat her like the capable woman she was. All she'd needed was for him to listen to her.

"I'm sorry," he choked out, backing away from the machine, from the bed, from her. "You're right. I should've left when you . . . I should never have entered. I won't come back unless you ask for me. And if you never ask for me, if you never want to see me again . . . That's your right, too. As it always should have been. I'm sorry."

He shut the door and leaned against it, his heart pounding. Or maybe breaking. If he'd just ruined his chances with the one person he cared about more than any other...

Oh, what was this "if"? Of course he had. She'd told him so, plainly: *Get out. I don't need you.*

He finally listened. A little too late.

24

Elizabeth gazed up at the ceiling and did her best to calm her breath and racing heart. It wasn't working.

Stephen had finally left her alone, just as she wanted. He had also now seen her at her worst. A cringing, pathetic lump. Exactly as she *didn't* want. Not only had she been incapable of ejecting him from her bedchamber by force, but she had also appeared so feeble and worthless that even her repeated commands packed no more punch than a gnat.

Now that he'd seen the truth, he would no longer view her as strong. The image of her helpless and weak would be forever burned into his brain, just like the expression of pity on his face would be forever burned into hers.

Her eyes welled up with tears. She glared at the ceiling, refusing to blink until the disgraceful wetness went away. A warrior did not cry. A warrior showed no weakness. A warrior *had* no weakness.

Which meant Elizabeth...

She turned her head toward the window. The perpetual tea machine came into view instead. Another sign that Stephen found her helpless and weak. He hadn't asked if she'd *wanted* tea. He had decided what she needed and presumed with a single glance that she was incapable of performing even the most basic functions for herself.

It wasn't a romantic gift. It was a baby bottle.

Things would never again be the same as before. How could they be? The illusion of invincibility had been shattered.

God, she wished her family were here. She missed them with every aching cell of her body. The castle felt like a mausoleum, not a mission. She was so isolated and alone. Her family would know how to make her feel like a worthy human. They understood that fifteen percent could be as normal as sixty-five. To them, she was never too much or too little. They took in stride whatever percentage Elizabeth happened to be on any given day, and loved her back one hundred percent, regardless.

Her fingers dug into the blanket at her sides as her heart struggled to find its rhythm. The idea that Stephen might never admire her the same way again was too gut-wrenching to contemplate.

Elizabeth knew she wasn't broken or helpless or useless. There were times when she could take on an army, and times when she couldn't win a fight with a flea. But nobody in the world was constantly vanquishing something, twenty-four hours a day.

Others could think what they wanted, but they couldn't make her feel ashamed of her body. Elizabeth chose to take pride in all the things it *could* do. She was proud of her whole self. Not just when she was swashbuckling, but always. Including here and now.

She propped herself up on her elbows, gingerly. Her muscles were tight, but did not immediately contract in agonizing pain. She was almost at twenty percent. Maybe soon to be twenty-five, if this perpetual tea machine worked as claimed.

Three levers protruded from the right-hand side. She stared at them. Which one had Stephen said to press? She decided to begin with the first one and see what happened.

The machine whirred and clacked as pieces began to move. The wick beneath the teapot did not light. Rather than boil water, at the end of a series of movements, a trapdoor sprang open, and a wooden arm punched through.

In its grip was a single red rose.

A startled laugh escaped her throat. Gently, she plucked the stem free from the wooden clamp. As soon as she did so, the machine whirred again. A slender ceramic vase appeared. The pitcher suspended at the top of the device poured a dollop of water into the vase instead of the teapot. A tiny bell gave a little clang, as if signaling that this particular sequence was through.

Elizabeth brought the rose to her nose to inhale its sweet aroma. How very Stephen. She lowered the vase to the floor beside her bed and slid the stem into the ceramic column. There. She could look at her flower whenever she liked.

She gathered strength and pressed the second lever. Sparks lit the tinder, which lit a wick connected to an oil reservoir. The resulting flames were just tall enough to lick the bottom of the teapot.

It would take a few minutes for even a teacup-size portion of water to boil. She propped herself up with pillows to wait and to watch. The cup itself was already in place, from when Stephen had given his explanation of how the device worked.

He *had* been trying to help.

"No—be fair," she murmured. "He did help. Tea is always a good idea."

She was begrudgingly glad he'd done all this. Which forced her to consider the possibility that him offering help was not the same as calling her useless. It was unfair to ascribe to him any intention of making her feel incapable of taking care of herself, when it was clear that Stephen simply wished to feel useful, too.

While Elizabeth was being charitable, she was forced to admit that Miss Oak had also offered tea—and biscuits—without receiving this much of Elizabeth's wrath. But there had been some important differences.

For one, Elizabeth had been *ready* to leave her room when she'd accepted Miss Oak's offer of tea and biscuits. Here in her strange bed at Castle Harbrook, with her joints still flaring with pain, Elizabeth was far from prepared to mingle with others.

For two, Miss Oak was a relative stranger and could not be expected to know the first thing about Elizabeth. Their limited relationship was one of service provider and client.

Stephen had spent most of his waking moments with Elizabeth for weeks. Talking with her, kissing her, learning her. But the one thing he hadn't done when she'd needed his understanding the most was to stop and *listen* to her.

He hadn't just hurt her feelings. She *cared* about Stephen's opinion of her. Viscerally.

She did not want him to think her weak or lesser, or worst of all, a broken thing unable to be fixed.

Elizabeth didn't just want him to see her as worthy and strong. She wanted him to understand that she was the same Elizabeth she always was, no matter what percentage she was currently operating at. Which was why she had reacted to his poking and prodding by lashing out like a wild creature. By rejecting him before he could reject her.

They would both have to figure out where to go from here.

25

The tea was better than Elizabeth had dared to hope. The water supply indeed lasted all night, then all of the following day and subsequent morning. By then, she was able to collect the pile of hawk-delivered missives that had accumulated on the floor inside her window.

Her brother Graham had tracked down three different associates of the missing earl on the coast of France and was close to finding Densmore himself.

When Elizabeth rose to forty percent, she rang for food. When she reached forty-five percent, she cleaned herself up in the basin. When she reached fifty percent, she could have made tea and biscuits on her own. When she reached fifty-five percent, she brushed her hair and dressed in clean clothing.

When she reached sixty percent... it was time to face the world.

And Stephen.

She selected her sturdiest cane and made her way out of her bedchamber in search of him. Her heart pounded. Stephen wasn't in the dining room, and he wasn't in the earl's study. He was in the Great Hall, tinkering with one of his machines.

He looked as handsome as ever. That much hadn't changed. The casual deshabille of shirtsleeves, the molded-to-his-muscular-thighs pantaloons, the ridiculous leather helmet with its monocle and miniature telescope.

He must have heard her approach. His head swung toward the open doorway, and then he jerked himself upright. He yanked the hat from his head, pressing it against his chest with one hand while the other fingers raked through his brown, helmet-matted hair.

"Elizabeth," he said hoarsely. "Come in."

She stayed where she was. "Good afternoon."

"It isn't a good afternoon. It's a terrible afternoon. At least, it was, until I looked up and saw you. Now it's a great afternoon. Or it would be, if *I* didn't feel terrible. Let me start over." He flung the hat aside and strode up to her, his gray eyes soulful. "I'm sorry. That's what I meant to say. I'm sorry I wasn't what you needed."

This was it. Her chance to tell the truth.

"You could have easily been what I needed," she said quietly. "All I asked of you was to respect my privacy."

"I know." He raked his hand through his hair again. "You did tell me. Clearly and repeatedly. You're right. I just wanted to do more. *Be* more. I wanted to help."

"I know how bad it looked. How dreadful *I* looked."

"What are you talking about?" He rubbed at his face, which bore the markings of his telescope. "You didn't turn into a werewolf. Nothing I've seen has made you less desirable to me."

"I wish I could say the same," she said softly. "*You* turned into a werewolf. You clawed your way through and started pawing at me."

"I thought you were hurt!"

"*You* were hurting me."

"I stopped as soon as you said so. Almost as soon." He looked stricken. "If you'd warned me earlier..."

"It's *my* body. It's up to me what I share with others."

"That's true. And this is my body. It can't read minds. If there's

something you want me to know, or a way that you want me to act...
You're going to have to tell me so. Out loud. With words."

Stephen...was right. Elizabeth couldn't expect him to intuit what
she needed from thin air. He couldn't think her thoughts or feel her
pain levels, much less guess her preferences or emotional state.

It wasn't just a matter of communicating competently. She had
learned young that her best advocate—for years, her only advocate—
was herself. She'd explained her wishes to her adoptive family two
decades ago. So long past that she'd forgotten her siblings hadn't
materialized already knowing what she needed. Especially since
Elizabeth had done such a good job of keeping everyone else at arm's
length.

If she was going to let Stephen in—if she was going to expect him
to act as though he knew her as well as her siblings did—then she
would have to lower her shields and expose who she truly was.

"All right. Here are some words." She leaned on her cane. "If you
feel you absolutely must intervene, please ask for permission before
you meddle where you're not wanted. Then fully and immediately
respect the answer. If the reply is 'stay away' or 'stop asking'...then
you must *stay away* and *stop asking*. It's not 'help' if it goes against
the person's direct wishes. And for the love of God, please don't
attempt to 'fix' someone without an explicit invitation."

"I wasn't trying to fix you...exactly. I was fussing because...I
wanted to show you I was on your side. That I cared. That I was fighting alongside you."

"You have to be invited to fight at someone's side. Teams aren't
teams because one person decides something is wrong with the other
person."

He let out a long breath. "You're right. Teams become a cohesive
unit when they choose each other and decide what and how to fight
together."

"Yes." She bit her lip. "Do you remember when I said I was fifty-five percent Elizabeth?"

"I remember." The corner of his mouth quirked. "I still cannot fathom how much *more* Elizabeth you could become."

"Today, I'm at sixty percent. Yesterday, a high in the forties. The night before that, after the duel...Essentially nothing. By the time I crawled into my bedchamber, there was no Elizabeth left. Zero percent remaining." She tried to smile and couldn't. "Bean abhorred my percentages."

Stephen's eyebrows lifted. "He did? Why?"

"He said I was always 'optimal Elizabeth' because I was always me. Never lesser than anything or anyone." She swallowed. "When he first found me, I judged myself a zero, no matter what my body was currently doing."

Stephen looked outraged.

"The swords were my way of proving to Bean that I was as valuable and strong as any warrior. That I was of worth, every single day. One hundred percent. Bean said the swords didn't matter. He accepted all parts of me, just as they were. All he wanted was to nurture me to grow into myself." Her voice cracked. "I had never experienced anything like it."

"Your birth family was less understanding?"

"They couldn't find any visible injuries. So they didn't believe I was in pain, and they punished me for lying." New pain meted on top of existing pain...How she had tried to block out those memories. "Eventually, they did believe me."

"Did that make them accept you more...or less?"

"They didn't want me at all. If I couldn't perform the tasks assigned, then I became an unnecessary mouth to feed. They told me I was weak, and worthless. They sent me to live with my grandparents, who sent me to live with an aunt and uncle I did not know, who traded me to a merchant and his wife in exchange for an old dog cart. To them, the cart was the better investment. At least it was useful."

He winced.

"None of my relatives ever came back around to check on me. One day, when I felt an astonishing seventy-five percent, I ran away from the merchant. I doubted anyone would come for me. Who would pick up rubbish from the side of the road?"

"How far did you go?"

"All the way to London. I walked twenty miles in two days. On the edge of the main thoroughfare. No one came looking. By the time I reached Islington, I could barely crawl. I collapsed not far from Baron Vanderbean's new home, though I didn't know it at the time. He was driving past and stopped his coach and asked me if I needed a place to spend the night."

"So you climbed into his carriage?"

"I thought it over. He was a stranger, but even at ten years old, I had been bouncing from stranger to stranger for years. I wasn't afraid of new faces. Or corporal punishment. I had run away once, and knew I could do it again. But one thing convinced me above all others."

"The fact that this particular adult had bothered to ask a child what she wanted?"

"That he wasn't alone," she said softly. "There were five other children in that coach. Happy ones, with smiling faces. Waiting patiently, maybe even a little anxiously, to see if I would be willing to join them. Not judging me as lacking. The opposite. Fearful of being rejected themselves. So, yes. I got in. They helped me up that day, and every day after. We help each other up, just by being there. By letting each other have their power."

"I do think you're powerful."

"It didn't feel like it yesterday."

"That was a poor reflection of me, not of you." He sighed. "You accused me of treating you like a tinker with a faulty machine, rather than as one friend to another. Maybe you're right. But it was not because I thought you weak or useless. In my machines, every element is important. No matter how small or stiff or silly or abrasive. Every bit is an integral, irreplaceable part of the whole. So is everything about you."

"You're saying you still think of me as a broken machine?"

"No! I'm saying the sharp, prickly thorns of a rose don't outweigh the soft, delicate petals. They both make up one thing of beauty. You are the most gorgeous, fascinating, perfect equation I've ever had the fortune to try and decipher. You need all your pieces and variables in order to add up to Elizabeth."

"I can see the charm of Beth the Berserker's thorns. But what about the days when . . ." She held up her cane.

He took her free hand in both of his. "Elizabeth, I don't like you in *spite* of any given characteristic. I like all of you because it's who you are."

She cocked her head and held her silence.

"I more than like you," he said in a rush. "I am an utter fool for you. I like you so much that it shuts down my logic and makes me react with emotion, which is not a thing I believed myself capable of, until you battle-axed your way inside the castle."

She made a self-deprecating smile. "I'd do it again."

His expression was earnest. "For you, my door is always open."

She bit her lip. "I apologize, too. When it comes to how others view my disability, I've learned to fear the worst. I lash out when I'm angry or scared or in pain. Or embarrassed. And yesterday I was all those things at once. I accused you of overreacting, but the truth is, so did I. You're right that I cannot expect you to guess what I'm thinking. I purposefully did not communicate the full truth, and then blamed you for not reacting appropriately."

"We can both communicate better." His eyes beseeched hers. "I want to prove to you that I can be a safe place, that I respect you more than any other person I know. And then, I will *ask* you where, if anywhere, you'd like to go from there. Please let me spend the days we have left showing you how it could be, going forward."

"I am not much of a prize," she warned him.

"Because of your disability? I told you—"

"No, not that. I'm not a prize because I'm a prickly, off-putting berserker. You now know that my base personality is to attack first with claws, teeth, and swords, and apologize for the carnage later."

"I'm not afraid of your sharp edges. As it happens, I appear to have a fondness for prickly, off-putting berserkers," he assured her. "One in particular, anyway. You're not the only one willing to battle for what you want."

"All right, then." She took a deep breath. "I know I'm not easy to get close to. But if you really want to fight this war, then go ahead. Try your best to win."

26

Elizabeth was up to seventy percent the next day—a high percentage indeed. This was a very good day—but whenever she crossed paths with Stephen, she could not help but *feel* like a zero all over again.

He insisted he thought no less of her, but how could she be certain it was true? Elizabeth was here to guard the castle and she couldn't even defend her own bedchamber from invasion. How could anyone believe in her ability to save the day, if she couldn't even help herself?

For his part, Stephen had now taken it upon himself to forgo words entirely, and tempt her back into his arms using the most devious weapons in his arsenal: his abdominal muscles.

Every time Elizabeth turned a corner, Stephen was there. Inexplicably shirtless.

He wore a waistcoat as some sort of inane nod to modesty...or perhaps because he suspected the peekaboo glimpses of muscled chest and abdomen between the unbuttoned flaps of his waistcoat would drive her absolutely mad with the desire to rip the flimsy sapphire silk from his half-naked body and feast her eyes on the toned panorama beneath. His theory wasn't entirely inaccurate.

Stephen caught her looking again and smiled.

Elizabeth glared at him.

He smiled wider.

They were in the Great Hall. He was ostensibly working on his machines—in skintight buckskins and a sleeveless blue waistcoat, with no other coat or shirt to clothe him. He somehow always managed to be lifting a hammer or a piece of wood or some other task that required him to flex his arm muscles whenever she happened to glance in his direction.

Elizabeth was in the center of the room lying on a chaise longue she'd allowed him to provide for her. The tin bird sat on the stone floor within arm's reach. She was paging through tome after tome she'd pilfered from the library. Unfortunately, this time, the number of literary volumes that mentioned birds created a stack as tall as her hip.

A loud yawn that could rival the roar of a lion sounded from just two feet behind her.

She turned her head to send Stephen a dismissive glare. He was engaged in the most outrageous display of ostentatious stretching, ensuring every nude muscle rippled for her benefit.

"Oh, drat, is my presence distracting?" he asked with faux innocence.

"Have you *nothing* else to do?" she demanded.

"You're absolutely right. It *does* look like a hot, summery day. I think I'll go toil in the garden." He whipped his blue waistcoat from his absurdly wide and muscular shoulders and tossed the garment to the floor.

Elizabeth tried to ignore him, truly she did. But the unobstructed view of Stephen's chest and abdomen had frozen her as efficiently as Medusa turned her beholders into stone.

Luckily, Elizabeth had not solidified into granite. Unluckily, she feared she was now drooling like a rabid dog.

"What the devil do you think you're doing?" she managed.

"Mustn't dirty my tailor's fine silk." Stephen made a production of swinging his arse in her direction as he bent over to pick up his fallen waistcoat.

"Do not forget that I carry a sword," she warned him.

"I have one, too." He waggled his eyebrows over his shoulder. "Figuratively speaking."

"Oh, for the love of..." She burst out laughing despite herself.

"*There* you are." His gray eyes sparkled as he loped up to her. "I feared I'd never see you smile again."

"I'm laughing *at* you," she informed him. "You're incorrigible."

"I've missed you." He reached for her free hand, then paused. "May I touch you?"

Elizabeth's entire body caught fire at the thought of his skin against hers.

"You may...touch my hand," she allowed. Brief contact. Then she would toss him through the closest window so he could toil in the garden at his leisure, well out of her view.

He drew her to her feet, then placed her hand on his naked chest and covered her fingers with his own. "Do you feel that?"

"Your extremely boring, totally ordinary, not-interesting-in-any-way bare skin beneath my palm?" She sniffed. "I hardly notice it."

"Not that." His voice turned gruff. "The irregular beating of my heart beneath. It skips every time I see you. I never want to look away. Unless the reason is because I have closed my eyes to kiss you."

She swallowed hard.

They had not touched in days. Not since he had clumsily prodded her prone body in search of injuries. Elizabeth had thought that she could not bear for him to ever come close to her again. Not if it made her think of that awful memory instead of pleasure.

Breaking the cycle by having her reach for him instead of the reverse was clever indeed. She couldn't keep holding on to the vortex of anger and hurt and mortification she'd felt in that moment. Not when it was long past, and her greedy fingers were touching his bare muscles at last.

In this position, she wasn't thinking about all the reasons to stay away from him. She was thinking about giving that strong chest a little squeeze. Maybe tossing her sword aside like he'd done with his waistcoat so that she could splay both hands across the heat of his chest. Maybe dribble him with a bit of warm oil and rub it in herself.

"You don't fight fair," she said hoarsely.

He widened his eyes. "Is it the clothes?"

"You know it's the clothes."

"Am I wearing too many? I can take off my buckskins. Or rather, I *can't* take them off without the aid of a valet, so if you would slide your hands into the waistband and give them a little tug..."

"I will brain you with this sword and knock you unconscious."

"I hope you don't." His eyes held hers. "Because then how will I kiss you?"

"Who says you're going to kiss me?"

"Only *you* can say." His smoky gaze lowered to her mouth, then lifted back to her eyes. "May I?"

"Just one," she allowed. "Make it quick."

He slanted his head down until his parted lips just barely grazed hers, then pulled back a fraction of an inch and waited.

"That was no kiss," she whispered. "Do it properly."

"As you command." This time, his mouth covered hers with hunger, plundering, claiming, demanding she do the same.

She swung her sword atop the closest flat surface, knocking over the carefully piled stack of books. Neither of them paid any attention.

Now both of her hands were free to roam over his abdomen, his chest, his shoulders. Every inch of him was hard and hot and incredibly arousing. She could only imagine what it would feel like to climb atop his entirely naked body and—

She pulled her mouth from his with a gasp. "That's enough. Goodbye."

"Did I fail to kiss you properly?"

Too properly. Her entire body was covered in gooseflesh in eager anticipation of what it would feel like to have his mouth explore all the rest of her.

"I thought I wanted...an affaire," she told him. "Initially. Now I'm not sure."

His heart skipped beneath her palm. "Because of what happened?"

"Because of what's going to happen next. If you would stop distracting me, I could follow the clues to the will, and then we'll both go home. After which we'll never see each other again."

"That's a likely outcome," he agreed, "but not the only possibility. We both live in London—"

"You never leave your house," she reminded him. "And I'm rarely in mine, because I'm always off on missions like this one."

His chest muscles twitched beneath her palms. "Exactly like this one?"

"Usually with ninety percent less nudity," she admitted. "And considerably fewer kisses."

"Do you object to more kisses? With me?"

"I object..." *To being hurt. To missing you. To letting myself be vulnerable. Never show weakness.* "Let's not make promises, shall we? What happens, happens."

He gazed at her in silence for a long moment, then took a half step back.

Her hands fell away from his chest. She missed him immediately.

"I did make one promise I'd like to keep." He gave a crooked smile. "And I swear it doesn't involve nudity or kisses."

Worst promise ever.

"What is it?" she asked suspiciously.

"The keepsakes for your family. There's just one left."

Her breath caught in excitement. "Jacob's?"

"Do you want to see it?"

"Show me." She retrieved her sword. "And put some clothes on."

He shrugged into his completely useless waistcoat with an unapologetic grin. "Follow me to the kitten dispenser."

She looped her free arm through his. "You made a *kitten* dispenser?"

"It's actually a vertical animal playground that doubles as an automatic petting device." He led her to a tall wooden structure. "Kittens—or badgers, or weasels, or ferrets, or whatever your brother would next like to unleash upon the world—can climb the various towers and scratching posts, or position themselves on the petting shelf, where a cloth-covered clockwork hand will stroke their fur every time they rub a certain panel."

"Like a mechanical nanny," she breathed. "Your invention can give the animals attention and entertainment even when Jacob isn't there to snuggle them. But you said it served another function?"

"That's right. When he *is* nearby, he need only press this button, and a door will lift next to the petting station, allowing adventurous kittens to slide down a curving chute to land right in Jacob's arms."

"He's going to adore it," she promised. "If the rest of us let him near it. I suspect we will install this contraption in the sibling sitting room, where we can all take turns dispensing ourselves puppies or kittens or hedgehogs."

Stephen smiled. "I'm glad you like it."

"Though I must admit it seems…less murderous than the other machines."

"Oh, I haven't finished explaining the best features. There's also a hawk-launching pad, a bat cage, and a lever that when pressed deploys—" He launched into a dizzying description of sufficiently murder-y flourishes.

Elizabeth grinned. "I'll have to rent two extra carriages to cart all these devices home, but it will absolutely be worth it to see the looks on my siblings' faces."

"Maybe I can invent a flying machine to deliver correspondence," Stephen suggested. "Inspired by your tin bird. I can even add song. To know when the package is arriving, all you'll have to do is listen for—"

He broke off, wearing an expression of stupefaction.

"Listen for…a minuet?" Elizabeth guessed. "Perhaps something from Bach or Beethoven?"

He grabbed her arm. "We could listen for invading armies."

She blinked. "You *might* be able to devise a way for a machine to play a recognizable melody, but how on earth could you possibly replicate the sound of—"

"Not me. My aunt Arminia. She wants us to listen for invading armies."

"She does? How do you know? Did she tell you somehow?"

"She told both of us. Birds are known for their song, yes? An obvious association. But the mechanical toy was only half of the clue. The other half of the clue was where you found it."

"In a toilet? Are we listening for a particularly flatulent invasion?"

"A secret compartment in the wall," Stephen corrected, his eyes shining. "You remember how I outfitted all four sides of the castle with whispering walls so that I can hear what's happening outside on the ground from all the way up in my turret?"

"A very Stephen-y thing for you to do. Medieval kings *wish* they'd thought of it."

"They did think of it. I got the idea from them. Castles like these often feature hidden 'listening galleries.' Exterior walls can be six to twelve feet thick. Perfect for keeping enemies out, but ironically just as competent at muffling the enemies' approach. So medieval architects would hollow out sections, creating secret tunnels to conduit any unusual noise to guards listening for tunneling or digging."

"And you think Castle Harbrook might have a listening gallery?"

"I know it does. Lined with wood, to amplify sound. I used some of the passages as a base for my own whispering walls. And in the process of designing my own defensive measures, I discovered something strange: an *interior* tunnel."

"But...that couldn't have helped detect the approach of enemy soldiers."

"Precisely. I discounted the modification as useless to my endeavors and forgot about it completely. But there's a way to access the tunnel from a storage pantry on the floor just above the nursery."

"That has to be it!" Elizabeth grabbed his hands. "Take me now!"

"I have been dying for you to say that," Stephen told her. "But in a slightly different context."

She waggled her brows. "Your chances will improve dramatically if you just solved the next clue."

They were out of the Great Hall in a flash, ascending the spiral stair and racing down the corridor to the storage pantry. The room was small and cramped, and contained two large pieces of tall, heavy furniture. Stephen tilted the farthest one and dragged it out of the way. Behind it was a waist-high crawl space not much wider than Elizabeth's hips.

"You didn't think to tell me this was here?" she demanded.

"I did tell you," he objected. "Sort of. I told you about my whispering walls. You knew there were listening tunnels all over the castle."

"But I thought *you* put them in." She gestured around them. "How did you even find this place? Do you have a storage pantry obsession? Why would you run around turning the furniture upside down?"

"I was bored," he protested. "When I'm bored, I turn everything around me upside down. You're lucky I didn't turn this into a murder room."

"We don't know that it *isn't* a murder room," she told him haughtily, and immediately crouched to poke her head inside.

It didn't murder her. The tunnel was definitely a clue, and Stephen had been the one to find it. Elizabeth was both grateful and vexed.

"Stay here," she said. "I'm going in."

Had she thought the width was larger than her hips? Not by much. Her thighs squashed against the wall as she duck-walked through the tunnel, hunching her shoulders and crouching her head to avoid concussing herself on the uneven stone ceiling.

After six feet of waddling and three minutes of cursing, she emerged on the other side and stood to find herself in the middle of a room smaller than the pantry she had just exited.

Smaller and considerably darker. No windows in a secret room after all.

"What did you find?" came Stephen's disembodied voice.

"No idea," she called back. "Can you bring a candle?"

"One moment."

"A real candle," she added quickly. "Not some two-hour contraption that eventually lights a small flame."

He either ignored this, or was already gone.

She reached out in the darkness to touch the walls of her new enclosure. The area was large enough to fit a two-person sofa, though there did not appear to be any furnishings inside. The walls were bare of shelves or framed artwork, and the floor held no rug.

If there was a clue here, it wasn't anywhere obvious. She sighed and pulled out her trusty dagger. At least she wasn't exploring another latrine.

An orange glow flickered inside the tunnel, followed by the shuffling of Stephen's feet. Soon, he emerged holding an oil lamp—significantly brighter and more resilient than the candle Elizabeth had requested.

She kissed his cheek. "Thank you."

He held the lamp higher and let out a low whistle. "Well…this certainly isn't the Louvre."

Every surface of the secret room had been whitewashed, and then painted over with untrained hands. The two longer sections of the rectangular pantry contained murals of some sort of beach scene, both signed by the countess.

The narrower two walls were painted by an artist who didn't even attempt a realistic landscape. Instead, asymmetrical spiral seashells in fantastical colors swirled over the whitewashed surface in an array as random as snowflakes. This masterpiece was signed by none other than the prior Earl of Densmore himself.

"Finding this clue would apparently not have been nearly as hard for the earl as it was for us," said Elizabeth. "He helped to make it."

"What do these designs mean?" asked Stephen.

"I don't know," she said in bafflement. "I don't think the earl knew, either. Maybe their secret seaside watercolors didn't become a clue until later? I suppose I'll have to sleep on it."

"Before you do…" Stephen's gaze latched on to hers with intensity. "Are you free after supper?"

She narrowed her eyes. "Why?"

"I have one more surprise for you. Something else you haven't seen yet, that I'd sure like to show you."

She pursed her lips and smirked. "I bet you do."

He made an unabashedly rakish grin. "Is that a yes?"

27

An hour later, Stephen gazed at Elizabeth across the supper table. Rather than settle at opposite ends of the ridiculously long table, they sat at one corner, as though it were a table meant for two and not for twenty.

He'd dressed in his formal best for the occasion, with a shirt under his waistcoat and all, though he was not certain if this sartorial choice helped or hurt his cause. Elizabeth's war might be against Reddington, but Stephen's struggle was for a fighting chance with Elizabeth. He suspected it would prove to be the most important battle of his life.

All he could do was try to show her what a relationship with him *could* be like, if she were willing to allow him to woo her. When she wanted him close, he would be there for her. And if she needed room for her thorns and her swords, he would give her the space and time she needed.

Thus far, she had consented to supper and a surprise. Stephen was anxious by nature—the sheer quantity of press-up exercises he performed to relieve the pressure were proof of that—but he was more nervous tonight than he could recall ever experiencing.

Elizabeth had made a salient point when she'd reminded him that any clue could lead them to the will at any moment, and bring this holiday to a close. Tonight's supper and a surprise might well be Stephen's final opportunity to prove himself a viable romantic partner and show her how much she meant to him.

"Thank you again for the keepsakes." Her green eyes sparkled over her glass of wine. "I cannot wait to take them home to my family."

Stephen could wait indefinitely for that dark day's arrival.

"It was my pleasure," he said aloud, because this was the proper response to *thank you.*

Yes, he'd built the contraptions, and yes, they were meant to be gifts for her family. But handing them over meant Elizabeth going away, and he was not ready for goodbye.

Not that he blamed her for missing her family. They sounded sweet and clever and unpredictable and ludicrously fun. Meals with Elizabeth were often spent with her recounting various exploits and misadventures, and Stephen laughing until his cheeks hurt. He adored her eccentric siblings without ever having met them, and was wildly jealous that her life was so full of meaning and family and love.

Elizabeth didn't *need* Stephen. She might still see him as a temporary amusement. Yes, she'd agreed he could try his best, but the very wording indicated she expected any romance between them to dissipate once they left these walls. Their interactions today would be an amusing future anecdote about that one time in Dorset, when she'd defended a castle with an improbably athletic tinker inside.

Stephen would soon be nothing more than an old memory... unless he could change her mind. Then again, maybe the future he could provide wasn't the sort she was hoping to have.

"Do you want children?" he asked cautiously.

She set down her knife. "Do I want children to exist in the world? Maybe. Do I want to birth them and raise them? Not in the least. Luckily, there will be plenty of baby Wynchesters without me having to contribute any."

She told him about the multiple nurseries at home, and Graham and Kuni's plans to provide a cousin for Chloe's baby.

The description sounded charming. It also sounded like there would not be room in the house for any of his painstakingly crafted gifts. Oh, who cared about the gifts? It sounded like there wasn't room in Elizabeth's life for *Stephen*.

His laboratory barely fit inside his own house. He'd build 105 more rooms with pleasure to make space for Elizabeth and her armory, but the effort was unnecessary. There was no hope of tempting her away from the home and the family she loved so much.

Elizabeth paused with her wineglass halfway to her lips. "Do *you* want children?"

He thought it over. "To be honest, I have lived my entire life assuming that was not part of my future. Between a childhood plagued with bullies, and parents who were not particularly pleased with the offspring they produced..." He shook his head. "Whilst *I* would never rebuff a child due to their nature, at this point in my life, I cannot imagine myself raising one at all."

She made a commiserative expression. "Too much drooling and screaming."

"That, and I enjoy being a recluse. I like to shutter myself in my laboratory for weeks at a time, working on contraptions that could save mankind or blow it up. I'm no authority, but I suspect filling a house with devices that could kill you is not the ideal environment to raise a child."

She raised her wineglass. "But it does sound like a party."

"Only you would think so." He clinked her glass and took a sip of wine.

"My only regret with the new brood of future Wynchesters is that they will never know Bean." She gazed pensively into her glass, then lifted soulful eyes. "He was everything a father should be."

Stephen shared her wistfulness. It must have been utterly magical to encounter a new family that welcomed her with open arms and loved her with their whole hearts, exactly as she was. Who thought it perfectly reasonable to have a dressing room that doubled as an armory. Who were a veritable beehive of togetherness and liveliness and jolly escapades. Who always said and did exactly the right thing whenever Elizabeth dipped below fifty percent.

How was he supposed to woo her away from *that*?

Stephen gulped down the rest of his wine. The truth was, no one could compete with her family. There was no sense trying. If he had any prayer of becoming a permanent part of Elizabeth's life, it would be by convincing her he was worth making a little bit of room for. If not in her home, then in her heart.

Which meant Stephen could not shutter himself up in his make-shift laboratory with his goggles and his algebra. He would have to woo her the only way he knew how: with something unnecessarily complicated and more than a little gruesome.

"Are you up for a trip downstairs?" he asked.

Her brows lifted. "I'm up for anything you wish to show me."

He pushed to his feet and held out his hand. "Then come with me. It's time for the surprise."

She placed her hand in his. He squeezed it gently. He would rather have tugged her forward into his chest and wrapped his arms around her and kissed her with all the emotion lodged in his heart, but he didn't want to push things before she was ready. He'd done enough of that already. If he was lucky, there would be plenty of time for torrid embraces and passionate kisses in the future.

"Over here." He led her down the corridor toward the spiral stone stairs that descended into the dungeon.

At the mouth of the stone opening, a sconce hung on one side. Below this, Stephen had placed two unlit torches. He let go of Eliza-beth's hand to light the tips in the flame of the sconce. He handed her the first one before attending to his own.

"Are you giving me a tour of the dungeon?" Elizabeth asked.

"I can. But there's something I think you'll like even more."

They crept down the stairs carefully. The subterranean cavern was black as pitch. The orange flames of their sputtering torches lit their faces with an unnatural yellow glow and sent shadows dancing and skittering along the dark crevices of the dungeon.

Her eyes sparkled in the torchlight. "How delightfully ominous."

He motioned for her to follow him past the rows of stone caves with their rusted iron bars on crooked hinges. At the farthest point from the only exit, the ceiling dipped low and the walls grew narrow. A pile of large gray boulders lined the squat far wall like a dam to block the flow of water—or rivers of blood.

"Did they flood this place?" She glanced over her shoulder toward the cells. "To drown the prisoners?"

"Maybe. The stones have another use now."

"Wall art?" she said doubtfully.

"Misdirection. It's not a solid wall at all." He handed her his torch.

She leaned closer. "What are we doing?"

"You'll see." He rolled up his sleeves and pushed a waist-high boulder with all his might.

At first, it refused to budge. Then it scooted a few inches across the dust and dirt of the stone floor. And then it rolled, gathering steam and momentum until it knocked into another pile of rocks two feet from where Stephen had started pushing.

A gaping black hole as high as his hips lurked just behind where the boulder had stood.

"What is that?" Elizabeth stepped forward. "An animal's warren?"

Stephen grinned at her. "The den where I go to hibernate."

"You went *in* there? Why?" She rethought her question, then handed him his torch. "Why not?"

Stephen's chest thumped. How could he not fall in love with this woman and her bravery? He adored that her natural response to being led to a gaping hole in a gothic dungeon in the dark of night was to surge forward and see what else she could find.

"Tilt your torch at an angle," he cautioned. "If it scrapes the top of the tunnel, the flames could extinguish."

She nodded her understanding, orange light dancing over her animated face.

He dropped to his knees and began crawling through the narrow opening, sending up a silent apology to his tailor for ruining yet more of the man's handiwork.

Elizabeth crouched behind him without hesitation. When he glanced back, she was hiking up her skirts with her free hand as she edged her way forward a few inches at a time.

Ten feet later, they neared a dark, dank cavern. The air smelled musty and stale, as though the dust had been untouched for years until their intrusion.

"Not very beachy," she ventured. "This has nothing to do with the clue?"

He shook his head. "No. This is for you."

As they emerged into greater darkness, he helped her to her feet, then hooked his torch into a notch in the wall.

She frowned. "Where are we going now?"

"Nowhere." He stepped out of the way. "We're here. Look around."

She lifted her torch. Orange flames sent murky golden light shimmering along a spiderweb of tall, narrow tunnels, branching forth in all angles from where they now stood.

Eyeless skulls grinned down at them from every surface. Here, the walls were not made of stone, but rather row after row of interlocking bones.

Elizabeth gasped. "*Catacombs.*"

She ran forward to inspect the closest wall, passing the torches from one side to another to display skulls in strange patterns amongst the thousands of stacked femurs and ulnas and rib cages.

Off she went down one of the tunnels, leaving Stephen to hurry behind her lest he be left in the darkness surrounded by the remains of the long dead.

When they reached another opening like the first one, piled high with bones like a beaver's dam of sticks, she spun to face him, mouth agape.

"Do you like it?" he asked quietly.

"This is the most romantic evening I have ever experienced," she answered, her eyes shining. "You are the cleverest suitor in the world."

"It isn't difficult," he demurred. "If I see something one hundred percent Elizabeth, I give it to you."

She slotted her torch into the wall, then threw her arms about his neck. "Let me give you one hundred percent of *this*."

She kissed him. Passionately. Of her own free will.

He held her tight. For the moment, there was nowhere he'd rather be than here, in the darkness. Kissing Elizabeth.

Relinquishing another previously guarded part of his heart.

28

A few days later, Elizabeth paged through the library's many books referencing beaches, oceans, and seaside resorts in the hopes of inspiration. Her eyes were on the hunt for the next clue, but her mind was filled with memories of Stephen. The catacombs. The kiss.

Though she sometimes still worried he viewed her disability as weakness, Elizabeth loved that Stephen not only accepted the more bloodthirsty aspects of her personality, but actively indulged that side of her, without any missish shudders or prudish recriminations for her to act like a proper lady.

Who decided what was proper? She was happy how she was. Stephen was happy how *he* was. Why should they dampen their true natures because polite society frowned on berserkers and tinkers? As long as they were comfortable with and as themselves, she didn't give a damn about anyone else's opinions on the matter.

Which she supposed made them rather similar to the late earl and countess, who hadn't let a little detail like complete lack of artistic talent stop them from covering four walls in painted seascapes.

Well, two walls in seascapes. The other two contained a riot of shell-like color blobs, recognizable only by their classic spiral shape. Elizabeth paused with her finger in the middle of a treatise about the English Channel. The earl had drawn the colorful shell-blobs, and the clue was for him. Which perhaps meant the sea was irrelevant, and the blobs were the important bit.

Or were the strange colors the key? She tossed her tome aside and reached for her journal, where she'd listed as many details as could potentially be useful. The quantity of shells per wall, the list of associated colors, as well as how many examples of each.

As to which colors were used, the answer appeared to be: all. Unless Elizabeth was on the hunt for a rainbow, the answer didn't seem to lie in the hues. There were twenty-five shells on the northern wall, and only twenty-two on the southern face...but if that was meant to imply some great meaning, she couldn't guess what it might be.

Which left the shells themselves. The least remarkable aspect, given that they were all the same spiral shape. Rather than varying the assortment with any number of shell types commonly found at any given seaside from Brighton to—

All the exact same spiral shape.

Her heart leapt. The classic spiral *was* the clue. And what else in a medieval castle shared a classic spiral form?

"The stairs," she breathed, and shut her journal in triumph.

Possibly preemptive triumph. All the stairways were spiral, and there were nearly a dozen of them, stretching from down in the dungeon all the way up to Stephen's topmost turret.

Her joints were going to love this.

After trading her sword stick for her sturdiest cane, Elizabeth approached the problem methodically, starting with the staircase closest to the nursery and working her way around the castle clockwise from there.

"Probably this would be easy for the earl," she grumbled as she searched. "He would have bounded through the castle on spry legs, knowing at once that the code referred to a specific spiral staircase tucked away behind—"

She stopped so suddenly she had to fight for balance. She'd made it through half the staircases in the castle and was currently ascending the narrowest and most uneven of all: the one on the south side of the servants' quarters. Toward the south, like Brighton, one of the most popular seaside resorts in England. The one likely depicted in the countess's murals.

There, on the cylindrical center stone column just above the next step, was a tiny sliver of graffiti. A double "W" had been etched into the cold gray stone, its notched crevices filled with whitewash. Maybe the double "W" *stood* for WhiteWash, and had been carved there by one of whitewash's most ardent fans.

Or maybe it symbolized the waves of the sea, as a child might draw them.

Elizabeth lowered herself to a seating position—no more crouching for *these* knees until they'd had a full night's rest—and ran her finger over the tiny ocean wave.

The stone fell inward with a thud.

She jerked back in surprise. Not a brick at all, but merely a thin façade, thick enough to stand upright when wedged properly into place, and light enough to give if someone poked at it at just the right angle.

Carefully, she lifted the inch-thick stone slab out of the hole and peered into the opening.

Nothing. Not even dust.

Was she too late? Might some unsuspecting servant have cleaned out whatever had once been in this cubby, after knocking the covering off with a broom or mop?

"*Damn* it." Urgently, she pressed her hand all through the interior, digging at it with her blade, her fingernails, anything that might reveal the secret.

There was none.

With a sigh, she lifted the stone slab to place it back where she'd found it—and discovered the step it had been resting upon now glittered in the sunlight.

Quickly, Elizabeth flipped over the slab, facing the "WW" side down toward her lap.

The rear of the stone slab was covered in a thick layer of…solid gold? Who the devil would gild the unseen inner side of a secret panel?

"The countess would," she muttered. "Probably another breathtakingly easy clue. If I were her husband."

Elizabeth suddenly realized she took the innumerable inside jests she shared with her siblings for granted, and wondered what it must be like to share that sort of history and closeness with a romantic partner. The thought made her wistful.

"How is it going?" came a low, familiar voice.

Stephen! Elizabeth jerked her head over her shoulder to glance down at him and couldn't help but grin.

He was up to his old tricks. A pair of molded buckskins clung to Stephen's muscled thighs, and nothing but the flimsy panels of a purple silk waistcoat fluttered uselessly on either side of his wide, chiseled chest.

"Lose your shirt again?" she asked.

He snapped his fingers. "I knew I forgot something."

"You forgot to take off your goggle helmet."

He slapped his hand to his head in alarm, then glowered at her when his grasping fingers encountered only tousled brown hair.

She cackled unapologetically. "I thought that only worked on my sister Marjorie! She's covered in paint so often that she believes us even on the rare occasions when she's clean. Do you sleep in that helmet?"

"No." He crossed his arms, hiding his chest from view to punish her for her jest. "And you just lost your opportunity to find out in person."

"Liar." She shook her dagger at him. "I don't even need to threaten you with this blade for you to drag me upstairs to your bedchamber if I should wish it."

"I would carry you gently, not drag you," he protested.

She snorted. "I'm too heavy to carry up the stairs."

"Want to make a wager?" He waggled his eyebrows. "Loser has to slice off the other person's clothing."

"You're barely wearing any," she pointed out. "Half my work is done."

"I'll have you know, installing banisters is hard, sweaty labor." He pretended to have a sudden idea. "Mmm, do you know what *else* is hard, sweaty labor?"

She frowned. "Did you say banisters?"

He made a dismissive gesture behind him. "On the stairs. Don't worry, I waited until you were done with each before making my adjustments."

Mortification and fury warred within her veins. "If I needed your help—"

"—you would ask for it," he finished calmly. "I didn't say I was coming home with you to install handrails everywhere you go. But this castle is soon to house many small children, is it not? Not to mention at least one woman of advanced age. *You* might be athletic enough to manage any terrain, but I doubt Miss Oak wants the entire castle to be made up of accidental murder rooms."

"That...is a good point," Elizabeth grumbled. And, in fact, hadn't she wished for banisters from the beginning? Perhaps if she'd been less obsessed with appearances and more concerned about advocating for herself and the conditions she needed to be safe, she wouldn't have nearly tumbled down the stone steps to start with. "Very well. Carry on with your modifications."

"As my lady wishes. How are *you* doing?"

She held up the small stone slab, "WW" side out, then flipped it over to reveal its gilded backside.

Stephen made an impressed expression. "Just when I thought my aunt and uncle couldn't get any more peculiar. Any clue what it means?"

"That I have to think faster. Reddington will be here at any moment to negotiate. He wants to take possession of the castle on the first of June—which is in four days. Without the will, Miss Oak has no proof that she is the legal owner of this property. Densmore's wager with Reddington may not be legally binding either, but your cousin made that 'gift' in front of witnesses and signed a paper promising ownership."

Stephen drummed his fingers on the stone stairwell. "Reddington has more than enough money, time, and power to make trouble for Miss Oak indefinitely. She won't be able to run any kind of school with the son of a viscount stomping about with an armed militia."

"Nor is Reddington willing to wait indefinitely. He threatened a siege if we fail to deliver the deed in time to stop him. There's no doubt he fully intends to storm the castle and take possession by any means necessary." She rose from the stairstep and winced.

Stephen started forward, then corrected course, and visibly forced himself to resume lounging against the stone wall.

"What percentage are you today?" he asked quietly, his gaze intense.

Elizabeth clenched her teeth reflexively, then reminded herself not to assume the worst. He'd asked a fair question, not branded her a worthless weakling. And she *had* been hobbling around the castle all day.

This was new territory. No one outside of the family had ever asked her about her percentages before. No one outside of the family knew her well enough to know what the numbers meant. But if Elizabeth wouldn't be cross with her siblings for making the same inquiry, she could hardly take exception with Stephen for caring about how she was doing.

He was safe. She could trust him.

"Sixty-five," Elizabeth said at last. "Fifty and above is good."

"I have more than a passing acquaintance with mathematics. Fifty percent is the definition of middling." His gaze softened. "Is there anything I can do?"

She shook her head. "It's one of my legs. Probably from crawling to the catacombs. Though I wouldn't change a moment of it."

"Would you like me to rub your muscles? And before you take umbrage with my presumption, let me state for the record that I am happy to rub anything of yours at any time, regardless of its current percentage. This is not me taking pity. It's me taking advantage. I'm purely driven by lust."

"Well..." She considered him. "I suppose I could allow you to *lustfully* rub my sore leg. Just for a minute."

He brightened and made an expansive gesture. "Sit back down, my sweet."

She eased back onto the stone step, her legs askew before her.

"This one." She indicated the left side.

He knelt between her knees and lifted the hem of her skirts. "Do you know what *else* I could do for you in this position?"

"Rub," she commanded. "My *leg*."

Stephen gently lifted her left foot onto his lap and tossed her slipper aside. He started there, with the arch of her foot, kneading slowly, firmly. Long straight lines exactly where she needed it. He hadn't even touched her leg yet, and already the muscles were relaxing.

Eventually, he moved up to her ankle. Then made his way up her calf. Lazily, leisurely. As if there was nothing else he would rather do than sit on a stone floor and massage her tight muscles into pudding.

To her surprise, it seemed to be working. Her entire body was now a limp lump of treacle. The soreness was gone. She was back up to seventy percent. Maybe seventy-five. If he kept working magic like this—

Dun dun-dun. A loud bugle blared outside the thin arrow-slit windows.

"What in the devil?" Elizabeth glanced over her shoulder.

"I'll look." Stephen lowered her leg and pushed to his feet. He hurried down to the closest embrasure window, then grimaced. "It's Reddington, in full uniform, atop a white stallion. He appears to have brought a dozen foot soldiers, a bugler, and some sort of page boy carrying a large sword."

Elizabeth slid her foot back into her slipper. "This I have to see."

"Densmooore," came Reddington's grating cry through a speaking trumpet.

Elizabeth peered down through the embrasure window. The spectacle was exactly as Stephen had described. Elizabeth was surprised Reddington didn't have a portraitist on hand to capture him in his full, faux-Wellington glory.

"Are you here to negotiate peacefully as promised?" she called down. "As a man of honor? The sort who keeps his word?"

Reddington looked offended. "Densmore is the one who has failed to keep his word. He and I are nothing alike. Now let me in."

"He does have a fair point about your cousin," Elizabeth whispered to Stephen. "None of us would be in this mess if Densmore hadn't gambled away property that didn't belong to him."

"You have my permission to lock the earl in the dungeon as soon as your brother finds him."

She made a face. "Ugh, we've been so busy, I didn't have a chance to tell you."

Stephen tensed. "Tell me what?"

"Densmore isn't in France."

"He's back already? Isn't that good news?"

She shook her head. "He was never on the boat to begin with. He bought the ticket, then missed the sailing. We do believe he fled somewhere by boat. If your cousin were still in England, Graham's spies would have found him by now. They still will. This is only a temporary setback."

"What do we do in the meantime?"

"We certainly can't admit Reddington into the castle. He might have come here to negotiate, but the moment we let him through the door, he'll never leave. We have to meet him outside."

"No dueling this time," Stephen said quickly.

"You don't get to determine whom and when I do or don't duel," she snapped, then winced. She was trying to be less volatile. At least with Stephen. "You're right. No dueling today."

Together, they headed down the stairs, through the murder room, and out the front door, where Reddington and his men waited.

On cue, a page boy ran up and showered Reddington with pink rose petals, while another lad launched into *God Save the King* on his bugle.

"*This* suffocating saffron," Elizabeth muttered.

Stephen sent her a sharp look. "This what?"

"Something Kuni says." She waved her hand. "Not important."

Reddington slid down from his comically large white stallion with surprising grace, and accepted his sword from a page boy whilst another dusted him with more rose petals. "Now then. At what time today will you be handing over the deed to the castle?"

"*Peaceful* negotiation," Elizabeth reminded him. "Put down your sword."

Reddington hesitated, then handed his sword back to his page boy. "I don't need a weapon to handle the likes of you."

"Spoken like a man who's never attempted to 'handle' Beth the Berserker," Stephen murmured.

Elizabeth could have kissed him.

She forced herself to concentrate on Reddington instead. "We've run into difficulty procuring the will and testament we mentioned at our last encounter. If you could please grant us a few more weeks—"

"Denied," Reddington said flatly. "This castle belongs to me, with or without your little papers. I have the signed proof in my hand." He brandished the IOU.

"As I told you, this land wasn't the earl's to gamble—"

"As I told *you*, Castle Harbrook becomes mine on the first of June. I recommend you be gone by that date if you don't wish to die for your cause."

"No dying," Stephen interjected. "No one is to do any murdering."

"You said I could if he deserved it," Elizabeth whispered.

"*Peaceful* negotiation," Stephen murmured back.

"What's that?" asked Reddington. "I couldn't quite hear you surrender."

"We will not be relinquishing this castle," Elizabeth informed him firmly.

"Then there is nothing to discuss. Prepare to be besieged in four days hence." He turned his back on her and stalked toward his horse.

"Wait." She hurried forward. "We need to determine the rules of battle."

Reddington spun around, stray pink petals falling from his shoulders. "Here is what shall happen: We fight. I win. You lose."

Elizabeth took a deep breath. "As the Earl of Densmore's interim battle general, I must inform you—"

He snorted. "If you're Densmore's general, Castle Harbrook is already lost. You couldn't cut down a dandelion with a pair of shears." Reddington frowned and took a few steps closer to squint at her. "Wait a minute. You do look familiar. My suspicions were correct. Aren't you…"

"No," Elizabeth said.

"You are! You're that woman who wanted to be part of His Grace's army," he exclaimed in recognition. "You were so upset when I wouldn't let you join us."

"Guess what." She swung her sword in a circle. "I'm not playing now. This fight is real, and I'm going to take you down."

"Spare me the hysterics." Reddington scoffed. "You might have bested Crump, but you won't best His Grace. The castle is as good as mine. You may think yourself clever against one man, but let's see you defend this castle against hundreds."

Elizabeth curled her hands into fists. "If you're so superior to me, then certainly you cannot object to a fair fight. To start with, we have no guns. Therefore, you cannot unfairly use bullets, either."

"Not just 'unfairly,'" Stephen said hastily. "You cannot arm your muskets with bullets or projectiles of any type."

Good catch. Elizabeth sent him a nod of appreciation.

Reddington's men watched on with avid interest, forcing him to respond audibly to the new demands.

"Fine," he bit out with obvious ill will. "No bullets. Are we done here?"

"We're ensuring the battle royal is a fair fight," Elizabeth reminded him. "Which means both sides should have the same number of representatives. Agreed?"

Reddington's men watched him carefully.

His face grew florid. "The same number of active fighters on both sides. Very well. You'll still lose."

"And no further skirmishes before or after June first," Elizabeth added, ensuring her voice projected. "No matter who surrenders during the battle, at the end of that day, the matter is to be considered resolved by all sides. Most importantly, if we can produce legal proof that the castle is not yours, you will respect the law, as decreed by the king your soldiers fight for."

Reddington's jaw worked with anger at her less-than-subtle appeal to his men's patriotism over any loyalty to their leader. "Prepare to fail."

Elizabeth's mind whirred. Had she missed anything? "The battle royal shall take place at ten o'clock in the morning, before an impartial witness, who is to be informed of the entirety of the agreed-upon conditions as stated here today."

"Is that all, princess?" Reddington asked sarcastically.

Everyone was watching her.

She tried to think. "One last thing. Regardless of any given soldier's statements or actions, if either general yields to his opponent at any time, that is to be considered a forfeit. The battle is over then and there."

"The battle is already over," snarled Reddington. "You've lost. Pack your valises."

"Does that mean you agree to these terms, as stated, and witnessed by your men?"

Reddington glared at her, clearly thinking over her demands as he remounted his steed. A sudden wolflike smile took over his face. "Agreed."

A sinking sensation roiled in Elizabeth's stomach. She must not have worded her position as carefully as she'd thought she had. Was it too late to add—

Reddington raised his fist and shouted, "Until the first of June!"

The bugle sounded and he rode off into the forest, rose petals flying. His soldiers raced behind him on foot. Any chance to continue the discussion was lost.

The moment the invaders were out of sight, Stephen swung Elizabeth in an elated circle. "You did it! You negotiated terms!"

Elizabeth chose not to mention her misgivings. It was probably nothing. Nerves, which wasn't something she was used to having. In fact, she'd already all but forgotten Reddington, in the giddy rush of Stephen swinging her in circles as though she were light as a feather.

"Mother of God." She squeezed Stephen's arm muscles in fascination, her feet dangling several inches from the ground. "You really could carry me up five flights of stairs."

He grinned at her and held her tighter. "Want to find out?"

She kissed his lips, then wiggled back to the ground. *Yes*, she wanted to find out, damn him. She wanted to see and kiss and explore every glorious inch of him, and have him do the same to her.

But an affaire with him would not be as meaningless and easy as others in the past. Elizabeth liked Stephen more than she cared to admit. And it turned out that baring herself to someone who knew her this well took more bravery than she was ready for.

Fighting to the death was easier than lowering her defenses. The wisest thing to do would be to maintain firm borders and stay safely on her side of the battlement for the rest of her stay.

Then again, Elizabeth had never backed down from a challenge.

Even one guaranteed to end in tears.

29

Late afternoon sun streamed through the square stone windows of the earl's study. Stephen's knee bobbed beneath his cousin's desk as he tried to concentrate on the documents before him.

Difficult, when they were three days away from the forewarned battle royal.

Stephen's mind kept replaying Elizabeth's negotiation with Reddington, and the duel she'd fought with Crump. She absolutely had the upper hand on the self-proclaimed warlord and every soldier in his army, but there was always risk in battle. The only way to ensure no harm befell Elizabeth was to find that will.

Stephen also wanted to protect Miss Oak. He researched alternate locales for an orphanage in the vicinity as a contingency plan, and found several that looked promising. He would not purchase any land without her consent—Stephen had learned his lesson about assuming he knew best what someone else wanted or needed. Nonetheless, creating a trust for the earl's aunt was the least he and Densmore could do for all the hassle and heartache the earl's careless wager had caused her. The funds would empower Miss Oak to make decisions for herself.

Besides, the reason there was excess money in the earl's accounts was because Stephen had managed the earldom's finances these past sixteen weeks. Setting a bit aside to staff a school and provide housing for children was certainly as worthy an investment as any of the others Stephen had made in Densmore's name. It wasn't charity, but an apology for Densmore wagering what wasn't his to begin with.

The clock on the mantel showed a quarter past five in the afternoon. This morning Elizabeth had mysteriously announced it was *her* turn to plan a romantic evening. She hadn't given a time, but Stephen hoped it would start soon.

Quickly, he signed and franked the required papers for the formation of the trust, then rang for a footman to send the documents to Stephen's lawyer.

Forester appeared at the door. "Yes, my lord?"

"Post these, if you would, please."

"At once." The footman hurried off, documents in hand.

Miss Oak and her orphanage thus sorted, Stephen returned to his cousin's accounts and correspondence. Little was urgent, but Stephen had discovered he was extraordinarily efficient with the promise of a rendezvous with a beautiful woman pending. He made quick work of the matters that remained.

The next time he lifted his head, it was six of the clock. The sun would not fully set for another two and a half hours, but already a chill breeze had rolled in over the chalk downs and limestone ridges.

Or perhaps Stephen was especially sensitive because his chest and arms were naked beneath his waistcoat.

He rose from the desk to go and close the windows. When Stephen turned around, he was no longer alone in the study.

Elizabeth stood in the doorway, a sword stick in hand and a mischievous expression on her face.

"Our rendezvous begins now?" he asked.

She inclined her head. "This very moment. Unless you are too busy?"

"I would walk away from being crowned King of England to spend one more minute with you."

The corner of her mouth quirked. "We'll see if you say the same thing after you've seen your surprise."

Intrigued, he joined her in the corridor. "Should I put on more clothes?"

The look she sent him was withering.

"Should I...remove all my clothes?"

"We'll see," she replied loftily.

His cock twitched in anticipation. But it grew three sizes the moment Stephen realized where Elizabeth was leading him.

"Your bedchamber?" he asked hoarsely.

She arched an eyebrow outside the door. "This time, I'm inviting you. Don't make me regret it."

He shook his head earnestly. "Never."

She opened the door and pulled him inside, then waggled her brows. "Tonight, I'm at seventy-five percent."

A low fire burned behind the grate. Several cushions and pillows were strewn artistically before it. The bed was made, the entire chamber impeccably clean and orderly...Except for a horrifically lopsided tower of miscellaneous rubbish nailed together in listing, slapdash fashion in the center of the room.

"And what," Stephen asked as politely as he could, "is that wooden abomination?"

She dug an elbow into his ribs. "Behave, or you don't get your surprise."

"It's beautiful," he said at once. "Excellent craftsmanship. You should design all my devices." He considered the monstrosity from all angles. "Just one small question."

She rested her sword stick against the wall. "Ask."

"Um." He would have loosened his cravat if he were wearing one. "What is it?"

"A custom contraption," she said brightly. "It's your gift. I made it for you."

"You shouldn't have." He stared at it even more dubiously. "Thank you?"

She curtsied. "It was my pleasure."

"Er...What does it do?"

She pointed with a finger. "Press that lever and find out."

"That's a lever? It looks more like..." He cleared his throat. "Yes, of course. Here I go. Pressing the lever now."

It *was* a lever, in the sense that, when Stephen pressed it, it moved.

Every other piece of the—machine?—also moved with it. Not in any identifiable pattern, but in absolute chaos. The entire haphazard structure disintegrated before his eyes, clattering to the stone floor in an inelegant heap of broken wood and bent nails.

He didn't move.

Neither did she.

And neither did the broken machine.

"What was it...*supposed* to do?" he inquired in a low voice.

She grinned at him. "It delivers a kiss."

Before he could respond, she wrapped her arms about his neck and kissed him.

Stephen kissed her back for several minutes until the absurdity of her creation overtook him. He burst out laughing despite himself.

She placed a hand to her bosom in faux offense. "You wouldn't be laughing at my first tinkering attempt, would you?"

"I loved your first tinkering attempt." He returned his mouth to hers without delay.

They were thus engaged when a knock sounded outside the chamber door.

"Ah." She broke away with obvious reluctance. "That will be Martha with our evening repast."

It was indeed Martha, and three other maids besides. They carried in several trays laden with covered dishes and silver pots, as well as little tables, which they placed on either side of the sea of pillows and cushions.

"This came, too, ma'am." Martha handed Elizabeth a missive.

"Thank you. That'll be all. We're not to be disturbed unless I ring for you."

"Understood." The maids bobbed, then hurried from the room with wide grins. They shut the door behind them.

Elizabeth kicked a path through the detritus of the obliterated machine, and led Stephen to join her in relaxing before the fire.

"I intended to pour our chocolate whilst it was hot, but I recognize Graham's handwriting on this letter. Do you mind?"

"I'll pour. You read."

She broke the seal and skimmed the contents, a smile growing on her face.

"Good news?" he could not help but ask.

"Wonderful news." She pressed the letter to her chest, her green eyes shining. "My brother has uncovered Densmore's true whereabouts."

"Eyewitness confirmation?"

She nodded. "Your cousin was spotted by two different sources disembarking in Ireland. Graham's men are closing in. They should have the precise location of the earl in a matter of days, at the most."

The news did not fill Stephen's chest with as much joy as he might have predicted four months ago. While he was glad to know his cousin was hale and hearty, the return of the Earl of Densmore meant the respective departures of both Elizabeth and Stephen.

"That's great," he managed. "Truly splendid."

"I know." She bounced a little as she handed him the letter. "Densmore will be a great help. As his mother's son, he'll have a better understanding of the clues she left behind. In fact, he may have found the will already and be carrying it with him. This will all be over before you know it."

"Yes," Stephen said. "It does sound as though a conclusion is impending."

Looming over them, if you will. A multi-headed hydra, casting unwanted shadows over an evening meant to be light and happy. He set the letter aside.

Elizabeth sipped her chocolate, eyes twinkling. "I do hope you enjoy the nutritious menu I've selected for our supper. Take a look."

He lifted the first lid, then the second, then the third. Every single dish contained cakes or biscuits or bonbons or candied fruit.

"It's everything my nine-year-old heart ever dreamt of," he answered honestly. "I cannot wait to gorge myself sick."

"Not too sick." She shook a finger at him. "There's a real supper later. But before we get there, if you're very lucky, there might be one...more...present to unwrap."

"I will consume a respectable, but non-gluttonous number of delicious desserts," he assured her. "Thereby, I shall be in optimal condition to unwrap anything you please at any moment you wish it."

They sampled all the various tea cakes and sweetmeats, then settled into a comfortable snuggle before the fire. Elizabeth kicked off her slippers, so Stephen removed his shoes as well. Their legs were now gently intertwined, and her cheek lying against his chest.

"The floor isn't as comfortable as a sofa, is it," she murmured.

"Well," he said. "Cushions cannot compare to a bed, but I would happily hold you like this anywhere we happen to be. Grass, sand, stone staircase, river of nails..."

"Lake of marbles from one of your machines..."

He nodded and kissed her forehead. "I'll make a new one that spits out a carpet of goose down."

"How long will that take to build?"

He considered. "Two hours? Well, two hours after we take delivery of a large enough shipment of goose down. With luck, that could happen in the next few days."

"Too long to wait," she answered, rolling off his chest and to her feet with impressive agility.

Stephen could not help but admire her. If this was Elizabeth at seventy-five percent, Elizabeth at one hundred percent would eclipse her brother the acrobat.

She held out her hand to him.

He took it, not because he needed help up from the pillows, but because he had no intention of wasting an opportunity to pull her back into his arms for another kiss.

Without taking her lips from his, she tugged him backward toward the bed—and promptly tripped over the loose fragments of the erstwhile contraption that now littered the floor.

"Ow." She hopped on one foot, trying to stay clear of the jumble of broken parts.

"Here." Stephen helped forge a safe path to the bed. "May I rub your foot?"

She made a regal expression. "I suppose I'll allow it."

As she climbed onto the bed, he tossed some of the pillows from the floor back onto the mattress, then seated himself at the opposite side and pulled her feet into his lap.

He adored touching her. She was strong and soft and curvy, but it was more than that. He liked being helpful, and he loved bringing her pleasure. He would happily build her a foot rubbing machine that was really a wooden box with Stephen hiding inside.

"You can rub higher," she said softly.

His eyes cut to hers. "How much higher?"

"My legs."

"Through your gown or beneath it?"

She hesitated. "Through."

He set about massaging her legs at once. It was not as easy, with the skirts tangling up every few moments, but any manner in which he could touch her was heaven indeed.

"You...can rub a little higher."

He glanced up at her with interest. She made a gesture that might have indicated her bosom. He pretended not to understand. His hands were already on her outer thighs. He placed them on her hips instead. "Here?"

"Higher."

He slid his palms up her hips to the curves at her midsection. "Here?"

"Higher."

His hands skated lightly up her sides until the tips of his fingers grazed the underside of her bosom. "Here?"

Her voice was no louder than a breath. "Higher."

He cupped his hands over her bosom, each plump breast larger than could fit in his hand. His fingers found her erect nipples beneath the soft muslin and gave them a light squeeze. He lowered his mouth until his lips brushed hers. "Here?"

"There," she said, and kissed him.

Stephen needed no further invitation.

30

※

*E*lizabeth wrapped her arms around Stephen's neck as they kissed, then immediately untwined her wrists. His mostly naked arms and chest were right above her, and there was no sense wasting a golden opportunity to run her hands over all those taut, flexing muscles.

Her back arched toward him as he stroked her breasts and teased her nipples. Her blood pulsed with desire. She yearned to wrap herself around him, to feel him surging inside of her.

And yet, when he'd offered something so simple as to rub her legs without the protective covering of her skirts, she had hesitated.

Removing her gown would feel like charging into battle without a shield.

Elizabeth had sought out and enjoyed sexual escapades before. Those had just happened to be with people she had no intention of seeing again. The hurried couplings rarely involved the removal of many items of clothing, and had never transpired with anyone who had ever glimpsed her at any less than full strength.

The only part of that description that matched Stephen was the unlikelihood of seeing each other again after this mission concluded— a detail that Elizabeth was trying dashed hard to forget. She didn't want to think about future goodbyes. She wanted to lose herself in the moment here and now, while he was still with her.

If this was to be one of her only opportunities to be intimate with

Stephen, she did not wish to have any barriers between them. If his ridiculous waistcoat was an affront to her senses and she longed to fling it from his otherwise bare torso every time she glimpsed it, then she could not hide beneath layers of chemise and gown.

"Take off your waistcoat," she murmured against his lips.

"Without delay." He shrugged the purple silk from his wide shoulders and tossed the garment over the side of the bed.

"Now remove..."

He lowered his hand to his waistband.

"...my dress," she finished, and held her breath.

His eyes lit up as though she'd just offered him a special delivery of all the best tinkering supplies in the world. As he eased her gown up to her waist, Stephen kissed her with hunger. He pulled them both into a sitting position so that he could untie the cords at her back and lift the gown from her body.

Unlike the waistcoat, which had been tossed ignominiously atop a pile of machinery detritus, Stephen folded her gown with care before placing it on the floor beside the bed.

"Next?" he asked huskily.

"Maybe I'm done for the night," she teased. "Maybe you can go back to your room now."

"And maybe I'll give you one guess as to what I would do with my hand and my body if I were to return to my bedchamber at this moment."

"I don't want to guess." Heat flushed her cheeks. "Show me."

His eyes widened slightly at her challenge, then he leaned back and unfastened his trousers, one button at a time. The panel of his fall tumbled forward, and his shaft rose tall, tapping against the tight muscles of his lower abdomen.

Without taking his gaze from Elizabeth, Stephen curled his fingers about his shaft and began stroking it with light tugging motions that made it grow even larger.

She wrapped her hand about his, learning the pressure, the rhythm. "May I?"

He released his grip at once.

Her fingers closed about his hot, hard flesh as she did her best to match his motions exactly.

A guttural sound escaped his throat. He reached for her, cupping the sides of her face and pressing his lips to hers, consuming her in a ferocious kiss.

"If there's more to unwrap," he gasped against her mouth, "we should do it soon."

He was right. She swallowed her fears, then released his shaft from her grasp. "My chemise, if you would, please?"

Did she sound hesitant? She never sounded hesitant. But her voice had wobbled the tiniest bit. This was the first time she hoped a passionate encounter would be the start of many more just like it. That she would meet or exceed his expectations, causing him to not only devour her now, but hunger for more.

Stephen began at her ankles, lifting her shift a fraction at a time and kissing each new inch of flesh he bared. By the time he reached her thighs, she was ready to rend the garment from her body with her bare hands or forgo its removal altogether. But the hem crept ever higher, over her hips, up over her abdomen. The kisses never ceased, continuing over every hill and crease with the same lazy savoring.

By the time his mouth reached her breasts, she'd forgotten she'd ever been self-conscious at all. She grabbed his hair and held him to her bosom as he licked and suckled and teased.

He sat up to tug her chemise over her head, dislodging her hand from his hair. This time, he forgot about folding the garment carefully. Instead, the chemise fell to the floor atop his fallen waistcoat, to be equally forgotten, as he returned his mouth to her breast.

She propped herself up and fumbled for his trousers. Already unbuttoned, they hung loose on his hips, and took no persuasion at all to slide down his muscular legs and join the other garments on the floor.

Stephen pressed hot, urgent kisses all the way up her chest, along her throat, to her mouth. "Now what?"

She widened her legs so that his hips fell between her thighs. "Now I want you inside me."

He kissed her. "With pleasure."

She arched a brow. "You're not going to ask if I'm certain? Or give the traditional sanctimonious speech about my future husband's expectations of a virginal bride?"

"And risk a beheading? When has Beth the Berserker ever *not* been certain about what she wants? Or at all concerned about how self-important men think women ought to behave?"

"What about what *you* think?"

"If I haven't been clear, I think you should have anything you want. And if what you want is my cock inside of you"—Stephen affected a pious expression—"then, as a personal favor, from one friend to another…"

She pinched his nipple. "Too much talking."

"Let me fix that." He lowered his mouth to hers and positioned himself between her legs.

She was already damp and slick and very eager. In a single thrust, he was in. She held on tight and gripped his hips with her thighs, their kisses frantic as their bodies met again and again. Soon, she was so close—but not quite there.

"I want to be on top," she breathed against his jaw.

Without hesitation, they rolled over so that he was on his back.

She bent her legs into a comfortable seated position where she could easily control the speed of their rhythm, and the depth of penetration. She was also no longer partially concealed by the blanket of his body. Now, all of her was completely on full display to him. They could both watch as their bodies merged, retreated, and merged again.

She met his eyes. "I'll give you one guess what *I* would have done with my hand and my body, had you left when I suggested it."

A smile lit his handsome face. "I don't want to guess. Show me."

She slid her hand to where their bodies joined and rubbed the slick, sensitive spot she knew would tilt her over the edge. Her hips rocked as her fingers circled.

His hands gripped her hips, digging into the soft flesh as his shaft surged within her. "Do you like this?"

"I'm at one hundred and ten percent and climbing," she gasped. "Don't stop."

There it was; the peak she had been searching for. One hundred and fifty, one hundred and eighty, two hundred percent and bursting into a thousand fragments of pure pleasure.

She sagged forward and he spun her onto her back, breathing hard. With a final thrust, he shuddered and jerked out of her, spending into his hand with an expression of utter abandon. He fumbled over the side of the bed to clean his hand with his crumpled waistcoat, then drew her back into his arms, her head on his chiseled chest, where she could hear the rapid pounding of his heart.

Elizabeth wrapped her arm around her brawny tinker and held on tight. This felt...right. Maybe she hadn't spent her life searching for a warrior after all. Maybe what she needed was someone just like Stephen.

One short night together was not nearly long enough.

31

⚜

The next twenty-four hours passed in a whirlwind of lovemaking. Stephen and Elizabeth could not walk within three yards of each other without finding themselves atop a sofa or against a wall or on a chair, with frequent breaks for rest or stretching or cuddles. He had never felt giddier.

At the moment, they were up in the topmost room of the northern turret, ostensibly so he could show her how the whispering walls worked, as well as the views from the various telescopes.

They'd done all of that and more. They were now collapsed in a naked heap in the center of a soft, thick rug Stephen *might* have had sent up to the turret just in case they tumbled into each other's arms.

As splendid as he found their encounters, Stephen could not shake the constant fear that each time would be the last.

It wasn't simply a matter of not yet having made promises of a shared future. There weren't any promises to make. Elizabeth had been clear from the beginning that she viewed her relationship with him as nothing more than a brief holiday from her real life. She still talked about returning home to her family and what sort of mission she might be sent on next.

If there was another prince in a castle to save, Stephen hoped the bastard kept his shirt on.

Uncharitable? Yes. Hypocritical? So be it. He didn't want to be a forgotten domino in the middle of a long line. He wanted to be the domino left standing, instead of brushed aside or packed away.

But pushing Elizabeth was not the path forward. She would have to choose him of her own free will, or not at all.

"I'll miss this," she murmured in his arms. "Nothing will top this mission."

Stephen's exposed skin felt colder than ever. She wouldn't *have* to miss this. No, they couldn't keep the castle, but that didn't mean they had to give up on each other.

Except it sounded as though Elizabeth had already done just that. She was relegating him to a memory before he was even gone from sight.

"You are aware," he said softly, "that since both of us live in—"

"The battle royal is imminent," the telescope in the corner said in a perfect imitation of Reddington's voice. A discarded shoe answered in the real Duke of Wellington's voice, "Then prepare to die!"

Throwing voices again. Elizabeth turned into a regular court jester whenever Stephen brought up topics she didn't wish to discuss. Things like what might or might not happen when their forced proximity ended and the future was up to them.

Very well. If she wanted to keep their focus on the problem at hand for now, he supposed he couldn't blame her. He just hoped to have enough time to convince her to give him a chance before the case ended, and their relationship terminated right along with it.

Stephen pushed himself up on one elbow to gaze over at her. "Pomp and arrogance aside, Reddington should not be underestimated. There's nothing he hates more than looking foolish. He has an army. He will employ any trick he can to get what he wants."

"Let him try his best," Elizabeth replied. "Remember my request for equal numbers? After our last negotiations, I called in reinforcements."

He raised his brows. "King George's army, I hope?"

"Even better," she assured him. "My siblings."

Stephen's stomach gave a little lurch. "Your family is on their way here?"

Marvelous. They wouldn't just fight on their sister's side. They'd take Elizabeth away.

If his life had been lonely before he'd understood what—and whom—he was missing, it would be unbearably drab without encounters with Elizabeth to look forward to.

She nodded distractedly. "Well, most of my siblings are coming. Chloe and Faircliffe cannot leave London because of Parliament and the baby. But the other seven should arrive the day before the siege. Which should give us plenty of time to prepare our counterattack."

"The day before the siege? That's today." He fumbled in his discarded trousers for his pocket watch. "It's half seven in the morning. Are you saying your family could arrive at any moment?"

"Mm-hm." Elizabeth propped herself up on her elbows. "Do you think Reddington will storm the castle at ten o'clock sharp tomorrow? Or do you think he'll camp out the night before, to be outside our walls at the break of dawn, trumpets blaring?"

"I don't know."

There was a lot Stephen didn't know. Now that the arrival of Elizabeth's family was imminent, his chest felt hollow. He could no longer concentrate on the previously relaxing warmth of their tangled naked bodies.

Her intimidating family might sense their involvement and disapprove of the match. Temporary or otherwise. With his luck, her siblings would size him up in a single glance and decide a reclusive tinker was the exact opposite of what their gregarious, swashbuckling sister needed.

The Wynchester family's disapproval would have the same effect as a trough of cold water to the face. And if they did not accept him, it was unlikely Elizabeth would wish to prolong the "holiday" either.

She would awaken from this fairy-tale dream and discover Stephen to be an ordinary man.

The kisses would end, and goodbye would soon follow.

"Any minute now," he said. "I can't wait."

Her eyes flicked toward the horizon. "As much as I'm looking forward to you and my siblings meeting each other, followed by a nice, old-fashioned battle to the death—"

"To the yield," he reminded her firmly. "I was very clear about neither side doing any murdering."

"Spoilsport. The thing is . . . bloody aftermath or not, I still feel like I'm letting Miss Oak down. She hired me to find her sister's will, not to chop down our enemies."

"I respectfully contend that 'chopping down' another human definitely counts as defending your client's rights."

"That stupid gilded stone." She groaned, and flopped over onto her back. "What could it mean? Why would anyone gild a stone? And hide it? Back in London, the Mayfair town homes are fairly dripping with gold, but Castle Harbrook is delightfully gray through and through. The only other—"

She let out a garbled sound and grabbed his wrist.

"What's wrong?" he asked in alarm. "Do you need breakfast?"

"I know where the next clue is," she gasped. Frantic, she scrambled up from the floor and started pulling on clothes.

Stephen hurried to do the same. By the time he shoved his feet into his shoes, Elizabeth was already down the first flight of stairs. He tore after her, catching up just as she reached the parlor where Stephen had welcomed Miss Oak.

"The next clue is in here?" he asked.

"It has to be. This is the fussiest, frilliest room in the entire castle. Even more so than the countess's private quarters. *Suspiciously* fussy."

The furniture looked exactly as it had before: delicate and expensive.

Arranged atop a gorgeous Axminster carpet stood four tangerine-colored armchairs, a plush yellow sofa...and the ostentatious desk with matching ornate tea cabinet. A glass-paneled gilded cube protected the expensive tea china, along with three slender, gold-filigree-covered drawers beneath.

"Gold," he breathed.

She grinned at him. "Exactly."

They made their way over to the tea cabinet and lifted the protective glass covering. Inside were four gilded porcelain teacups atop four gilded porcelain saucers.

"We appear to have come to the right place," Stephen admitted. "Should we pour ourselves a cup?"

"A nice tall glass of brandy, if we find the next clue. But first we have to solve this one."

Elizabeth hooked her sword stick against the back of an armchair and tugged open the first of the gold-filigreed drawers.

Empty.

She made a frustrated sound. "Here's a riddle for you: Why is the vital thing you're desperately trying to find always in the last place you look?"

He shrugged. "Why?"

"Because when you find it, you stop looking." Elizabeth opened the second drawer. Also empty. "We won't stop until we find what we're looking for."

She slid open the third and final drawer—or tried to. It stuck halfway and had to be coaxed out of its cubby.

"The next clue has to be here somewhere." She handed all three drawers to Stephen to be placed atop the sofa for safety, while Elizabeth sank to her knees to peer inside the compartments. "Thank God for soft carpet, or I'd never rise from this position."

"I can ravish you down there," Stephen promised her.

She fluttered her eyes at him. "I'll remember that promise. Check those drawers for loose panels, please. I'll do the same here."

All of the drawers and cubbies were of the same sizes and dimensions. The construction was solid. There was no hidden compartment.

"It was a good idea," Elizabeth said, dejected. "I was so sure I was right."

"Maybe you *are* right," said Stephen. He pulled a magnifying glass from his pocket and began to walk around the tea cabinet slowly, hunching and squinting in concentration. "We need to find a button. A lever. A spring-release valve."

"This is a tea cabinet, not one of your contraptions."

"Not one of mine, no. But that doesn't mean—"

"The china!" Carefully, Elizabeth placed all four cups and saucers aside, revealing an intricately carved, three-panel surface beneath, styled like vines and flowers. "Why hide a shelf this beautiful behind rows of cups and saucers?"

"Because it's a shelf. In a tea cabinet." He felt less brilliant by the second. "Perhaps you're right. This is ordinary furniture, not one of my contraptions."

"Don't give up. If you saw something that made you pause…" Elizabeth ran her finger across the raised dips and whorls that made up the leaves and petals of the stunning display. "Look! Only one flower thorns, and it possesses exactly one. Strange, no?"

She touched it with the tip of her finger—and the mahogany thorn immediately sank into the background. She jerked her finger away.

As soon as the pressure was gone, the center panel sprang open, flying away from the thorn on two hinges and revealing a narrow hidden compartment beneath. It was just large enough to slide a book into—or an important document.

"I told you all we needed was a spring-release valve," Stephen chortled.

Elizabeth eased two fingers into the cubbyhole. "I feel... *parchment.*"

"Is it another clue?"

"It's tied with string. Give me a minute." Elizabeth snapped the thread with her dagger, then carefully opened the hidden document. After checking the date at the top of the page, Elizabeth read aloud, " 'I, Arminia Southridge, Countess of Densmore, possessed of sound mind and body—' "

"You found the will and testament!" Stephen gaped at her. "I can't believe it's really over. No battle royal. No Reddington. Castle Harbrook finally belongs to Miss Oak."

Elizabeth turned the paper over with a frown. "I found the will, but no deed. I suppose it doesn't matter. We have the proof we were looking for. Reddington is owed nothing." She handed Stephen the document and let out a long-suffering sigh. "How I wanted to beat him at his own game. We would have emerged victorious."

"We *did* emerge victorious." Stephen scanned the testament with a mixture of pride and dread. "My aunt's will could not be clearer. Miss Oak is the full, sole, and legal owner."

"And we didn't even need your useless cousin."

Stomach sinking, he gave a wan smile. He'd been afraid every night would be their last night together. He was finally right.

Elizabeth had achieved the impossible. Stephen had failed to do the same. Their courtship was over as abruptly as it had begun.

Stephen handed her the will. "Congratulations. Shall we give His Grace the devastating news?"

She brightened. "Ooh, let's do it on paper. Then I can shoot it at him with an arrow. That might be the only way to get through to his black heart."

Horse hooves and carriage wheels sounded outside the castle.

Every muscle in Stephen's body tensed. "Good Lord, that was impeccable timing. Do you have your arrows ready? Reddington's cold black heart is waiting."

Elizabeth rushed over to the closest window and let out a whoop of joy. "It's my family!"

Oh. Stephen had been afraid of that. He joined her at the window. Hawks circled ominously overhead. He had never seen so many in one place. It felt like a harbinger.

By the time they arrived on the front lawn, the Wynchesters had descended from their trio of carriages. He recognized each of them from Elizabeth's descriptions of their appearances and personalities.

There were Tommy and Philippa, each easily identifiable. Philippa, a pale white cloud wrapped in a storm of lace, and Tommy, fair and lanky with short brown hair and men's trousers.

Next were athletic Graham, with his golden-brown skin and floppy black curls, and his wife, Kuni, with her long black braids, dark brown skin, and bright pink pelisse that presumably hid a collection of daggers.

After them came Marjorie and Lord Adrian. Contrary to expectations, neither appeared to be a white canvas covered in colorful paint splotches. Marjorie was a tiny little blond wisp of a woman, and Lord Adrian a mischievous rogue disguised as a fine gentleman.

Last came Jacob, with his gentle poet's air, dark brown skin, and what appeared to be some sort of mink or ferret draped about his neck like a particularly furry scarf.

The siblings took turns hugging Elizabeth and kissing her cheeks in familial joy, barely sparing a glance at the towering medieval castle or its picturesque backdrop of chalk downs and limestone ridges.

Stephen didn't want to interrupt their happy reunion. Nor was he making his intrusion any less awkward by hanging back, halfway between the castle and their carriages.

"Darling tinker!" Elizabeth made an exaggerated *get over here* motion with her arm.

As Stephen approached, one of the circling hawks shot from the sky, streaking toward him like a poisoned arrow. He squeaked and jumped backward out of the way.

The bird ignored him and aimed its deadly claws toward Jacob Wynchester...who lifted his arm in welcome. None of the siblings blinked as the hawk landed on the leather gauntlet at Jacob's wrist as docile as a dove.

Stephen wasn't certain his heartbeat would *ever* return to normal.

"Family," Elizabeth began as if there had been no interruption, "please allow me to present Mr. Stephen Lenox. Stephen, these are my siblings, Tommy, Graham, Marjorie, and Jacob, my sisters-in-law Philippa and Kuni, and my brother-in-law Adrian. These are the Wynchesters. Most of them."

Stephen bowed. "The pleasure is mine."

When he straightened, Graham shook his hand. "So *you're* the famous Stephen. It's so good to put a face to the name after hearing so much about you."

Stephen stared at him blankly. "I'm...famous?"

"In Elizabeth's daily reports," Tommy explained. "We've read them a hundred times. There's usually a line about Reddington, two lines about the castle, three sentences about Miss Oak's future orphanage, and then four pages about you."

Stephen looked at Elizabeth.

Her cheeks turned pink. "On the days when there wasn't much progress to report, I had to fill my reports with *something*."

"You made him sound a little less"—Kuni waved her hand toward Stephen's midsection—"clothed."

Stephen closed his eyes and cringed. "Tell me you didn't write home about the state of my abdomen."

"It's on my mind a lot," Elizabeth protested. "You've a very nice abdomen."

"And, apparently, you also possess a very big—" Marjorie began.

Jacob coughed into his fist.

"—brain," Philippa finished. "The vast majority of her letters detail how clever you are. I can't wait to see your machines for myself."

Stephen rubbed the back of his neck. "I make them to stave off boredom, mostly."

"Well, if that's true, you'll never be bored again," said Graham. "On our trip up, we compiled an entire list of fantastical devices we would love to own. If you can make a device even half as fanciful, we'd pay you handsomely."

Stephen cut a glance toward Elizabeth.

Her eyes twinkled as she whispered, "I've not told them yet."

"Secrets!" Tommy held up a fistful of reports. "After *this* stack of intelligence?"

Elizabeth smiled. "You'll find out soon enough."

Jacob shook Stephen's hand. "It really is good to meet you. After a month of letters, we all feel like we know you. We're glad to make it official."

"I feel like I know you all, too," Stephen admitted. "Elizabeth has told me a few stories—"

"A few!" Tommy's brown eyes were fond. "I imagine she trotted out the wildest of our adventures, complete with throwing voices to imitate each of us perfectly."

"Several times a day," Stephen said with a grin.

A low rumble thundered in the distance. The Wynchesters glanced up at the blue sky overhead in surprise.

"Is that a storm?" Philippa asked.

"Worse," said Stephen grimly. "It's Reddington and his troops."

32

The distant rumble grew louder.

Stephen grimaced. "Rather than sneak up on his enemies, Reddington likes to make his soldiers sound as threatening as possible."

"*Are* we his enemies?" Philippa asked.

"Mortal enemies," Elizabeth answered. "He has declared war against us, and I accepted the challenge."

"You would," Tommy said with obvious affection. The other siblings grinned.

Philippa didn't look as lighthearted. "We had better get inside before they burst through the trees and attack us."

Kuni held up a dagger. "A Wynchester doesn't retreat."

"It's not retreat," Graham assured her. "It's a stratagem. A Wynchester never acts rashly. We always have a plan."

"Er..." Stephen slid a skeptical glance toward Elizabeth.

"No need to tell them I always act rashly," she whispered behind her hand. "They know."

"There's something very important that they *don't* know yet." Stephen gave Elizabeth a meaningful look.

"Oh!" Elizabeth grinned and pulled out the freshly discovered document. "We found the will! The castle unequivocally belongs to Miss Oak."

The siblings cheered and hugged her.

Tommy sent a doubtful glance over her shoulder. "Does Redding-ton know?"

"Not yet," Elizabeth admitted. "We haven't had a chance to make a plan, and a Wynchester never acts rashly."

Stephen snorted, then motioned her family toward the castle. "Please come in. The front lawn is a dangerous place to be with Red-dington about."

The siblings hurried to do just that.

As the castle footmen took care of the horses and carriages, Ste-phen escorted the Wynchesters and their servants safely through the murder room and around the rotating door to the interior of the castle.

"Those...are a lot of trunks," he observed as the contents of their carriages quickly filled an entire wall of the main corridor.

Elizabeth arched an eyebrow. "Says the man who receives daily deliveries of lumber, piping, and gears of all shapes and sizes?"

"I wasn't criticizing," he protested. "I'm taking notes."

"I brought paints and canvases." Marjorie straightened her pink hair ribbon. "Just in case."

"And I have my supplies." Adrian gestured at a portable forge. "Just in case."

Unexpected delight fired through Stephen's veins. The portable forge currently standing in the corridor was one of Stephen's earliest inventions! He received payments on the patent every quarter, but this was the first time Stephen had encountered an active user. He was dying to ask Adrian a thousand questions, but Stephen did not want to make the conversation about himself and his inventions rather than the real reason they were all here: to stop Reddington and save the school.

A bugle sounded outside, followed by muffled shouting.

The Wynchesters exchanged glances.

"Reddington, I presume?" asked Philippa. "Bleating orders to his men?"

Elizabeth nodded.

"What is he saying?" Kuni whispered. "It sounds like..." She made incoherent mumbling sounds through her fingers.

"He does sound like that," Tommy agreed. "Should we stand near a window to hear better?"

"No need," Elizabeth said. "Reddington's tirades are all the same, although there's a new twist. His latest posturing involves him referring to himself in the third person, as 'His Grace.' "

"Let him do all the posturing he wants," said Graham. "We have news, too. I located Densmore."

Stephen's heart skipped a beat. "Where was he?"

"Dublin. A gambling house. I'm working on extricating him from his latest scrape."

"Of course he's in another scrape," Stephen muttered.

"We're still in ours," Elizabeth reminded then. "Come look."

She led her family into a large parlor whose embrasure overlooked the side garden, where the castle's eastern perimeter abutted the thicket of trees.

Soldiers in red uniforms emerged from the wall of forest separating Reddington's property from Castle Harbrook. Reddington was atop his white stallion again, in full regimentals. At his booted heel was a young lad with a bugle to his lips.

Dozens of armed soldiers stood at the ready, flanking Reddington on both sides. To the left and the right, men in red uniforms erected tall canvas tents.

Stephen whistled under his breath. "The tents are new."

Graham jotted notes in a small journal. "I count ten of them."

"Camping over here is completely unnecessary." Tommy held up a hand-drawn aerial map. "Reddington owns the adjacent property.

Even following the least hospitable trail, it cannot have taken them more than half an hour to tramp through the woods from his land to ours."

"Disturbing the peace of countless woodland creatures in the process," Jacob added.

"Wait until he starts with the drums," said Elizabeth. "Then no one sleeps. I keep hoping a bear will attack him."

Jacob shook his head. "There are no bears in these woods."

"I hoped you'd bring one for luck," she replied.

Stephen raised his brows at her. "Who would pack a good-luck bear?" he asked.

"I brought twelve raptors, fifteen ferrets, and a python," Jacob offered.

"See?" Elizabeth smiled at Stephen in satisfaction. "Wynchesters make their own luck."

From atop his white stallion, Reddington handed a long brass speaking trumpet down to a soldier standing by his side. The soldier lifted the narrow, conical metal tube to his lips and pointed the flared end toward Castle Harbrook.

"Hear ye, hear ye," the soldier boomed.

"Is *that* new?" asked Jacob.

"Sadly, no." Elizabeth mimed banging her forehead against the stone wall.

The soldier continued, "We announce the arrival of His Grace—"

"He really does make his followers use a false honorific!" Kuni exclaimed.

"Should you fail to surrender Castle Harbrook before ten o'clock tomorrow morning," the soldier continued, "you leave His Grace no choice but to take possession by force."

Elizabeth harrumphed. "I'd like to see him try."

"He is going to try," Adrian pointed out. "Look."

The backdrop of uniformed soldiers parted as a pair of horses emerged from the wall of forest...this time, pulling a cannon behind them.

"You're bamming me." Elizabeth groaned. "I *knew* he capitulated too quickly."

Philippa frowned. "Capitulated to what?"

"Reddington agreed the muskets would not be armed with bullets or projectiles," Stephen explained.

"The guns aren't loaded?" Kuni clapped a hand to her face. "Of all the frothing cork-feathers...Does he *want* to lose?"

"Which side are you on?" Philippa hissed.

"How did you convince Reddington to make any concessions at all?" Adrian asked Stephen.

"It wasn't me. Elizabeth negotiated with him," he answered with pride.

"Elizabeth negotiated?" her siblings chorused in disbelief.

"I can be charming," she protested.

They stared at her.

"But I didn't know he had cannons," she admitted. "Those are probably loaded."

Marjorie stepped back from the window. "How are we supposed to defend against cannon fire?"

"We don't have to," said Philippa. "We have the will. That means there's no war. Right?"

Stephen and the other Wynchesters exchanged skeptical looks.

"What if Reddington ignores the legal proof and attacks anyway?" asked Adrian.

Graham put down his pencil. "I don't suppose this creaky old castle holds a Planning Parlor?"

Elizabeth glanced at Stephen and smiled. "It has something even better."

33

*E*lizabeth couldn't wait to see her siblings' faces when they saw the Great Hall. It was leagues larger than any room in the family home back in Islington.

Tommy was the first to stride into the spacious chamber. She reached for Philippa's hand to point out one of the machines. The other siblings carried baskets or small parcels. Everyone's eyes widened as they filed into the room.

Graham let out a low whistle at the chalk equations wallpapering the gray stones on all four sides of the Great Hall.

Kuni's jaw dropped at the sight of the enormous machines. "Are these the famous contraptions?"

"I can't imagine what these do," said Jacob.

"Of course we know what they do." Graham consulted the notes he'd made from Elizabeth's reports. "That one franks the post, this one shines boots, the one over there—"

"I'd be happy to demonstrate," Stephen offered.

Marjorie clapped her hands. "We'd *adore* that."

"But first," said Elizabeth, simultaneously delighted that she was the one to bring her siblings to order for the first time in her life . . . and that the reason for their distraction was the impressive imagination of her lover. "We have a battle to plan."

"No, dear sister," said Jacob as he settled himself and his gerbil into one of the chairs. "Actual physical combat is a contingency to a contingency to a contingency."

"There are three other plans already?"

"Not yet," he admitted. "But that's why we've assembled."

"Is this how your family normally operates?" Stephen asked as he joined Elizabeth on a sofa.

"Close." Her heart suddenly ached for home. "We have the most cunning Planning Parlor perfectly designed to devise schemes of every flavor. Tommy draws maps on the slate floor, and the cabinets are filled with—oh, I wish you could see it!"

Her siblings exchanged intrigued glances.

Elizabeth's cheeks warmed. The only non-Wynchesters to ever step foot inside the siblings' Planning Parlor...had themselves later become Wynchesters. Part of the team, and part of the family. By wishing Stephen amongst them, she'd as good as declared herself publicly.

It was a good thing Stephen didn't realize she'd done so.

Admitting how she felt was terrifying. Being vulnerable meant being weak. Elizabeth never showed weakness. Not if she could help it.

"Creating so many surprising and useful things *is* very Wynchester-y of Stephen," Marjorie said meaningfully.

Elizabeth shushed her and assumed a nonchalant expression. "Let's concentrate on our task, shall we?"

"We have the will," said Jacob. "Our first step should be to tell Reddington."

Stephen nodded. "That might be all it takes. Elizabeth explicitly stipulated that if we provided sufficient proof, Reddington must follow the law."

"He agreed?" Tommy asked. "Out loud? In those words?"

Elizabeth sent Stephen a leery expression. "He didn't *dis*agree. Out loud. Using words."

Stephen lifted a shoulder. "We have to try."

"Ooh," said Marjorie, "we can use the new speaking trumpet that Adrian created."

He held up a long brass cone.

"Reddington does seem to find amplified shouting quite compelling." Tommy tossed the speaking trumpet to Graham. "Let's go yell at him."

"Hide the will and testament, just to be safe," Jacob cautioned. "Once it's tucked back where you found it, I'll lock Apophis in the parlor as guard until we can get the good news to Miss Oak."

Stephen lowered his mouth to Elizabeth's ear. "Is Apophis the Highland tiger?"

"Python," she murmured back.

"That should do the trick," he agreed.

"Off to resolve the problem straight away. Here I go." Elizabeth held out her hand. "Trumpet, please."

"Voluntarily allow my least charismatic sister to oversee negotiations?" Graham muttered as he slapped the speaking trumpet into her palm. "I never thought I'd see the day."

Jacob and Philippa stayed behind to secure the papers while Elizabeth hurried to the closest window.

She stuck the flared tip of her speaking trumpet through the crack. "Hold your fire! Hold your fire! Please confirm cease fire! You promised not to attack before ten o'clock tomorrow morning!"

She yanked the trumpet back into the room while they awaited Reddington's reply.

After a long moment, his voice sounded through his own trumpet. "Cease fire confirmed. Now awaiting your surrender."

Elizabeth hurried from the parlor at a run.

Stephen stopped her just before she reached the murder room and grabbed her by the elbow. "Do you really trust him? His soldiers have *arrows*."

"It's a cease fire. I want to see his face when I give him the news."

Stephen didn't look convinced. "I like your pretty eyes too much to want some overzealous archer sending off a wayward arrow and inadvertently giving you a new nickname."

Elizabeth sighed. "Oh, very well, spoilsport. Give me your safety helmet."

She held perfectly still while Stephen settled the leather helmet onto her head and strapped the thick goggles over her eyes.

"That's better."

"I'm waiting!" came Reddington's impatient voice through his speaking trumpet.

"Your patience is about to be rewarded," Elizabeth murmured.

Stephen lifted the heavy wooden drawbar securing the door.

She pushed the door open and stepped out into the bright sunlight.

The army seemed significantly closer now than they had when she'd first spied them an hour ago. The huge glass lenses over her eyes were magnifying the enemy. Reddington had wasted no time encroaching farther on Castle Harbrook territory. Elizabeth could probably speak in her normal voice from this distance and still be heard.

She put the speaking trumpet to her lips anyway. She wanted to be certain every single soldier heard the news.

"You are not the owner of Castle Harbrook," she bellowed into the trumpet. Her voice shook the trees. Yelling into a speaking trumpet was surprisingly satisfying. "We have the late countess's will in our possession. The castle was bequeathed to the countess's sister. It never belonged to her son. You cannot have won it in a game of cards. It wasn't the earl's to wager."

Reddington's men exchanged hesitant glances.

"Go home, all of you," Elizabeth forced herself to say. "You have vowed to follow the law. Ownership is clear. There is no war to be waged."

"His Grace will decide that!" shouted Reddington, aiming his speaking trumpet at his men, rather than at Elizabeth. "If you really do have such a will and testament, then produce it at once. His Grace wishes to inspect the document for himself."

"No way in hell," came Graham's voice behind her. "He'll rip up the will and storm the castle anyway."

Elizabeth nodded and raised the trumpet. "For now, you'll have to trust us. We can arrange a meeting in the coming days with our client and her lawyer—"

"Trust the enemy? I'm afraid that's not how wars are won, wench. You have my castle. I'm coming to get it. Cease fire over."

"You gave your word to—"

Stephen yanked her back inside seconds before the first arrow struck the wooden door right where Elizabeth had been standing.

"But we found the will," Philippa protested weakly. "The case is over. We saved the day."

A swarm of arrows rained against the door and the stone walls.

Elizabeth straightened her spine with determination. "It's not over until we win the war."

34

✿

*A*ll right, everyone." Graham held up his palms. "Let's distract ourselves with something else for a while until we calm down enough to think."

"Like what?" Philippa asked.

Elizabeth's eyes shone. "Stephen has gifts!"

"Gifts?" The siblings looked at one another.

Stephen swallowed his nervousness.

Elizabeth beamed at him. "They were meant to be a surprise, but... What better souvenir than to take home the very weapons used to defeat an obnoxious enemy?"

"Again," Philippa murmured. "The idea is to settle the matter of property ownership *without* the grounds coming under enemy fire."

"Bah." Elizabeth shooed this objection away and hooked her arm through Stephen's. "Where's the fun in that?"

Tommy jumped to her feet. "I want to see the devices."

"Follow me." Stephen led them to the converted parlor that now contained several fully assembled machines.

"Ooh," said Tommy. "That one looks like... a complicated guillotine?"

"That's for Marjorie and Adrian," Elizabeth said with obvious pride.

Stephen's heart warmed.

"And this one looks like..." Tommy stroked her chin, then squinted. "It seems to be..."

"It's for Jacob," Elizabeth blurted out before Stephen could explain the machine. "It's a kitten dispensary!"

"A *what*?" All the siblings gathered round at once.

Stephen cleared his throat. "Actually, it's more like a mechanical nanny."

After Stephen explained how the machine worked, Jacob placed Tickletums on the petting platform and pressed the button. The hedgehog immediately slid down a chute, out of the machine, and into his waiting arms.

Jacob grinned. "I adore it and cannot wait to test every feature."

"You might not have to wait long," Adrian said. "Reddington seems the sort of chap who deserves a snake to the thigh or a hawk to the head."

"Somewhere other than the head," Marjorie told him. "Our guillotine will take care of his neck."

"It's not a guillotine." Stephen motioned them over to the next machine. Marjorie watched him closely. "This one is for you and your husband both. It's a three-sided easel—"

"But there are four sides," said Adrian.

"Only three of which are easels," Marjorie retorted. "The fourth is probably a tiger launcher. Pay attention."

"If you're working on a piece that is not yet ready for public consumption, you simply press this lever, and…"

He pointed.

Marjorie grinned and pushed the lever. The machine instantly whirred into motion, gears spurring weights that moved pulleys that released a thick sheet of metal, fully obstructing the sketchbook from view in a matter of seconds.

Wooden slats tumbled into place along all four sides, hiding not just the canvas, but the machine itself. It now appeared as innocuous as a simple wooden crate.

"That shield isn't going anywhere," Elizabeth told Marjorie. "It looks ordinary, but I couldn't move those slats even using a crowbar as leverage."

"Your machines are a true marvel," Adrian said. "What does the fourth side do?"

"Protects you." Stephen reset the machine to its original presentation. "This lever launches the emergency detonation sequence."

Marjorie's eyes widened. "What gets detonated?"

"Everything," Elizabeth said with satisfaction. "The machine self-destructs, sending its pieces flinging off in all directions like the world's largest grenade."

"Almost all directions," Stephen corrected her. "The fourth side is reinforced with metal for safety, and is not in the line of fire. It is the other three directions which are showered with shrapnel."

"Oh, Mr. Red-ding-ton," Marjorie sang. "Do come out to play. I have a lovely painting to show you."

Adrian mimed holding up a large speaking trumpet. "That's 'His Grace' to you, missy."

Marjorie pretended to press the lever. "And...*boom*."

"No murdering," Jacob scolded them all.

"Only as a contingency," Elizabeth and Kuni chorused in unison.

"What about Tommy and me?" Philippa asked, forgetting her earlier hesitation. "Is ours just as practical and deadly?"

"If practical-and-deadly is the game, I think you will be pleased." Stephen led her to the next machine. "If you'll take a look over here..."

The Wynchesters followed him eagerly.

Stephen could not quite name the warm feeling spreading throughout his chest. For his entire childhood and youth, his machines had been a guilty secret. He'd been punished, berated, mocked, snubbed. Until he no longer attempted to share that part of him at all. Not publicly, at least. When he reached adulthood, he began to sell his lesser inventions—a rolling valve here, a life raft there—and built his machines in solitude. Did everything in solitude. Day after day, year after year.

Until Elizabeth.

He had been terrified to show her this part of himself. And couldn't quite believe his fortune when she not only accepted his passion without hesitation, but also seemed to think his unusual quirks were the best thing about him. And now, she was not the only person in his life who looked at his machines—looked at *him*—and saw someone worthy, rather than worthless.

The Wynchesters were indeed special. Individually unique, yet part of a cohesive whole capable of seeing potential and intrinsic value where others did not. No wonder they were such a force to be reckoned with. Hope filled Stephen's chest.

If anyone stood a fighting chance against an army, it was the group of tight-knit siblings right here in this room.

35

All right," said Graham once everyone had finished fawning over their new machines. "Back to the planning."

Elizabeth led the way. "Time to devise our offensive attack."

"You mean our defense," Jacob corrected her.

"She's right," said Philippa. "George Washington opined two decades ago that 'offensive operations' are the surest means of defense. And look what he's managed to accomplish."

"He had an entire army at his disposal," Adrian pointed out.

"We have…things," said Marjorie. "In addition to our new devices."

Tommy opened the basket at her feet and pulled out a handsome black-and-gold military coat. "I created Wynchester regimentals based on the family coat of arms. We may not be a real army either, but there's no reason we cannot look like one." She grinned at Kuni. "Yours is absolutely riddled with hiding spots for daggers, of course."

Kuni blew her a kiss.

"The uniforms are gorgeous." Elizabeth held out her hand. "May I?"

Tommy passed her the coat. "I made yours a size too big, in case you wished to wear chain mail beneath."

"How did you know we would be attacked by arrows?" Stephen asked.

"I didn't know," Tommy answered. "But I do know Elizabeth. I'd wager a meat pie she's wearing chain mail at this very moment."

Elizabeth's cheeks heated further, though not for the reason her siblings likely assumed. She *would* have been wearing chain mail... if she hadn't spent the morning making love to Stephen. There had been little time to do more than throw on a wrinkled gown.

Then again, that might be *exactly* what most of her siblings imagined.

"This is excellent craftsmanship," said Stephen, clearly impressed. "Though I am not familiar with the Wynchester coat of arms."

Marjorie flipped through her sketchbook and tilted one of the pages in his direction. Two animals rose rampant on their hind legs on either side of the imposing black shield.

"You intimidate your enemies with...a kitten...and a hedgehog?" Stephen asked.

"We took a few artistic liberties with the original medieval design," Marjorie said proudly.

"Wynchester animals are the cleverest and fiercest in England," Jacob added. He leaned forward to drum his fingers on the stone floor while making clicking noises with his tongue.

Tiglet, a three-year-old calico cat, scampered into the Great Hall in a blur of tricolor fur. Coming right behind waddled the adorable, if less agile, Tickletums—Elizabeth's personal favorite.

"You really do bring a kitten and a hedgehog everywhere you go?" Stephen said in surprise.

"They would follow us anyway, even if we didn't," Elizabeth explained. "That's a homing cat and a homing hedgehog. They've been trained to consider Jacob's current whereabouts as home." She lowered her voice. "One of them is significantly better at the task than the other, but I would never leave Tickletums behind."

"Is that the..."

"Hedgehog. The homing cat is Tiglet."

Philippa scooped up the cat. "Tommy loaned this kitten to me once, and he kept escaping. But now he treats me like a real Wynchester."

Tommy kissed her cheek. "You *are* a real Wynchester."

"What props did you bring?" Stephen asked Philippa.

"Wait, I haven't finished." Tommy pulled a second army coat from her basket.

Stephen leaned forward. "That looks just like Reddington's!"

And Stephen would look handsomer than their enemy wearing it. Or wearing nothing at all. Elizabeth waggled her brows at him meaningfully.

"It matches on purpose," Tommy agreed. "One never knows when one might need to infiltrate the enemy's ranks and cause confusion amongst his soldiers."

"I adore causing confusion," said Adrian.

"I'd rather charge straight ahead and poke holes in them," said Elizabeth.

"Seconded," said Kuni.

"Are we *sure* we shouldn't just stay inside the castle where it's safe?" Philippa asked.

"It's not a sustainable defense. Not with Reddington," Elizabeth explained. "The battle won't end until someone surrenders, and Reddington won't surrender unless forced to do so at sword-point. We have no other choice but to fight back before he can cause irreversible structural damage."

A deafening boom sounded outside the castle, vibrating through the stone floor.

"Is he *firing* at us?" Philippa's jaw dropped in disbelief. "We're supposed to have peace until ten o'clock tomorrow morning!"

Marjorie ran to the closest window. "It looks like they're practicing. I'll wager that's the loophole. The cannonball landed twenty feet short of the castle."

"Small comfort," said Philippa. "He dragged that cannon through a forest. He can push it twenty feet closer."

"Let me at him," said Elizabeth. "I'll solve this problem with hand-to-hand combat."

Jacob stopped her. "No you won't. You have a sword. Reddington has a cannon."

"He's overcompensating," she muttered.

"He's calibrating," said Stephen. "First shots are often to establish range."

Kuni leaned forward. "About the battle royal. What's royal about it?"

"Nothing." Elizabeth explained, "It's a term that means a fight to the finish. Unlimited combatants against unlimited combatants, with the victory going to the last man standing." She winked at her sister-in-law. "Or women."

"For now, at least, we're protected by a castle," said Adrian.

"*Are* we?" Jacob asked. "Harbrook is very old."

"Which works to our advantage," Tommy told him. "With only one visible entrance and all the ground-floor windows angled into embrasure arrow slits, Reddington has limited ways to breach the castle."

"The upper floors have regular windows," Graham pointed out.

"Only you could scale a sheer wall to access them," Tommy said fondly.

Jacob frowned. "Only Graham could climb up with his bare hands. Reddington certainly has access to ladders and ropes."

"And we have Stephen," Elizabeth said. "He can turn every wall and window into a death trap."

Marjorie grinned. "I cannot wait to paint a commemorative portrait of Reddington's ignominious defeat."

36

The next morning was bright and sunny, much like the mood inside the castle. The Wynchesters were simply so confident they could resolve the unresolvable that Stephen could not help but be swept along in their buoyant optimism.

Elizabeth and Kuni were fencing in one of the castle's many rooms. Meanwhile, Stephen threw himself into his press-up exercises between tinkering with telescopes and pulleys.

Jacob had been absent from sight since the night before, introducing his animals to the castle environment and teaching the homing creatures to return to new locations.

Stephen had expected to spend the morning setting up the Wynchester siblings' new machines wherever so instructed, but Marjorie and Adrian had quickly proved more than capable of dismantling and reassembling them without issue. They were such a well-matched pair that Stephen found himself a fifth wheel, even amongst his own inventions. When he'd stepped out of their way, they hadn't even noted his absence.

He tried not to mind that they didn't need him. No one ever did, a sorry fact that never made the not-being-needed any easier to bear. He was useful only whilst inventing. After that, it was his creations which were useful, not Stephen.

Yet he kept trying.

"Is there anything I can do to help you?" he asked Philippa.

She looked up from the stack of open books on the dining room table with the thinly concealed annoyance of someone who had been concentrating very hard on something exceedingly important, until she was so rudely interrupted.

She forced a smile.

He could not help but grimace. "I'm sorry."

"No, *I'm* sorry." She placed a ribbon between the pages of her book and closed the tome. "Believe me, I know exactly what it's like to feel like the least Wynchester-y Wynchester of the group."

"I *am* the least Wynchester-y, by definition. I'm the only non-Wynchester amongst us."

"Yes, well, one never knows how long that particular condition will last. The others aren't ignoring you, in case that was your fear. When they have a client, the case often commands their full concentration, to the exclusion of all else. And with less than ninety-five minutes until Reddington's siege begins in earnest—"

"You're counting down the minutes?"

"Aren't you?"

"I don't have to. I built a machine that will lower an hourglass to mete out the right amount of sand sixty minutes before the battle is to begin. When the glass empties, the machine will sound out a warning."

"Of course you did." Philippa chuckled. "Honestly, I might *still* be the least Wynchester-y Wynchester. Whilst you are all off doing remarkable things, I sit in a chair surrounded by books."

"What are you reading?"

"Items from Elizabeth's collection. Military histories...Biographies of war generals...Journals from the front lines...Copies of letters Wellington sent home from the battlefield." She patted each stack in turn, then held up the volume she'd been studying when he interrupted. "I wish I could make heads or tails of this one."

He peered closer. "Is that...Chinese?"

She nodded. "*The Art of War* by Sun Tzu. I don't speak the language, but a scholarly friend of Elizabeth's does. She's left translations of important points in the margins."

Stephen took a second look at the additional stacks of books before her. "French...Italian...Greek...Scholarly friends left translation notes in all of these?"

"Oh, no. All the other books are part of our personal library. I read those for sport."

For sport. Stephen gave her a crooked smile. "I think you are a very Wynchester-y Wynchester."

"Except in one way," came a voice from behind him. "She and Jacob are pacifists."

Stephen turned to see Tommy approach.

She arched her brows. "Shouldn't you be off tinkering on one of your...tinklings?"

"Stephen is no mere tinker," said Philippa.

Tommy looked at him with interest. "Oh?"

Stephen was just as baffled as Tommy was. "I don't know what she means."

"False modesty, if I've ever heard it," scoffed Philippa. "Our Mr. Stephen Lenox has registered no fewer than one hundred and forty-seven patents in just over a decade, several of which have revolutionized industries, and many of which are important components of conveniences you take for granted."

He stared at her. "You know how many patents I've registered?"

"My reading circle devoted an entire summer to studying inventors and their inventions, and your works took up a disproportionately large segment of our time."

"Wait. You knew who I was *before* you took this case?"

"Patent sixty-five: an automatic cutlery cleaner. Patent one hundred and four: an apparatus for automatically raising and lowering chandeliers. You are arguably England's most important living inventor!"

"Never test a bluestocking," whispered Tommy.

Stephen's skin warmed. To Philippa's reading circle, he wasn't some anonymous inventor of obscure creations. He was Mr. Stephen Lenox, a real person. His step was lighter than it had been all morning.

He was not as surprised as he would have expected a month ago to realize a growing part of him wished he were a permanent part of the joyful, chaotic, and accomplished Wynchester clan. After all these years, Stephen was amused to discover himself not to be a reclusive misanthrope after all. That was a misdiagnosis. It turned out, he simply had not yet found his people.

Until now.

"Tell us about your house," Tommy said. "Is it tiny bachelor lodgings, or some sprawling estate filled to the brim with gigantic contraptions like those in the Great Hall?"

"It's a formidable size," he admitted, "with lots of room for machines, though I tend to take them down after a few months and reuse the materials into something new and better. Which means there's plenty of room for..."

Elizabeth. An arsenal of swords. Visits from family.

Tommy's eyebrows shot up. "Plenty of room for more machines?"

Stephen's throat grew tight. The nonchalant response he'd intended to make garbled on his tongue.

Saving him from replying, Marjorie chose that moment to skid into the room with a dash of moss-green paint on the tip of her nose and her husband, Adrian, trailing close behind.

"There you are!" She hunched over, hands on her knees, to catch her breath. "We've been looking everywhere for you."

"Why? Is there a problem with one of the machines?"

"Oh, we finished setting up over an hour ago."

"An hour ago?" Stephen dug out his pocket watch and gaped at the time. It was almost nine o'clock already.

Marjorie stepped forward, an object enclosed in her fist. "To thank you for your lovely gift, Adrian and I made you a good-luck token for the battle ahead."

Stephen held out his hand.

She dropped a locket on a chain into his palm.

"Thank you." Stephen stared at the gold locket in his hand. The craftsmanship was excellent. It reminded him of a locket he had once seen in a royal portrait, gracing the neck of—

Marjorie kicked his toe. "Open it."

Stephen released the clasp. His heart skipped. Inside the locket was a miniature of Elizabeth. It was a portrait from only the bodice up, yet managed to convey all of her fierceness and fire.

"Thank you," he said again, this time his voice thick with emotion. Stephen hadn't believed himself the syrupy sort of romantic to wear a lover's likeness, but he knew already he would wear this one for the rest of his life.

"Adrian made the locket, and I did the portrait. I was inspired by the way you look at my sister. I want you to always be able to gaze at her, whenever you'd like."

Stephen tried to swallow. Or to smile. Or do anything besides stare unblinkingly in all his syrupy romantic gooeyness at the beautiful miniature of the woman he loved.

This was the perfect gift and the worst gift all in one. The most bittersweet of souvenirs. After all, he would not need to gaze upon a portrait in a locket if there was any hope of keeping the actual woman in his life.

He pressed the locket to his chest. He and Elizabeth were still in the castle. Perhaps it wasn't too late to trap his bloodthirsty princess in a turret and lock himself in with her.

Marjorie stepped forward. "I'll clasp it around your neck."

"You can't reach his neck," Adrian said dryly. "I'll do it."

Stephen relinquished his gift only long enough for the chain to be secured, then tucked the locket beneath his shirt next to his skin. The gold was warm, as though it was the kiss of Elizabeth's fingertips touching his heart, and not a heart-shaped piece of metal.

"I'll cherish it," he promised Marjorie and Adrian. "Thank you."

And yet the true gift was not the locket, but rather a hard truth put so clearly into focus: Stephen didn't *want* Elizabeth to be reduced to a memory. He wanted the real woman.

Now and forevermore.

37

Elizabeth did a second round of stretches after breaking her fast. Getting out of bed had required additional time this morning. Sometimes when she rushed, her body seized up to punish her. After verifying she had no current pain, she took extra care to ensure she began the day as limber and strong as possible.

The others were packed into a side parlor, crowding to look out of a trio of arrow-slit windows.

Stephen made room for her at once and took her hand in his. Or tried to. She had to pass her sword stick to the opposite hand first, in order to twine her fingers with his.

And then she looked out the window.

Reddington's army was still there. They'd camped out front all night. A proliferation of tents lined the edge of the forest. Soldiers milled about in army regimentals, cleaning weapons or eating hunks of bread.

Adrian shook his head. "I can't believe he's convinced this many people to live as though they were a real squadron."

"Or to believe Reddington a real general," added Kuni.

"His Grace, the emperor of entitlement," Jacob muttered.

"They know who and what he is," said Philippa. "It doesn't matter. Proximity to a viscount's son can be life-changing for those in the outer edges of the beau monde. Being an officer in Reddington's army gives cachet to those who couldn't afford to purchase rank in the real military."

"Besides, camping out is what those who reenact battles do," Elizabeth reminded them. She did not mention she'd once wished to be one of them. She'd believed joining their number would be visible proof that she was just as good as any man. That you didn't have to be one hundred percent able-bodied to have just as much value as anyone else.

"That's true," said Tommy. "It's clear weather, so to them it's all in good fun. A nice, wholesome activity for the whole family."

Adrian watched the men below. "They may have signed up for a lark, but are they truly prepared to wage actual battle?"

"They're loading a real cannon," Marjorie pointed out.

"And they've pulled it much closer than where it stood in yesterday's trial," Tommy said. "If they fire from this distance, the castle will take a direct hit."

Stephen pointed. "Here comes our nemesis now."

Reddington was once again in full uniform atop his white stallion. He turned his horse to face the castle. With a sword in hand and a euphoric expression, he looked the very picture of a general leading his troops into a battle in which victory was assured.

There were now two page boys armed with flower petals. To Reddington's left was a drummer boy, to his right, a trumpeter. Flanking them was a full marching band, interspersed with several flag bearers solemnly waving the distinctive red, white, and blue of the Union Jack.

"As if Reddington stands for the entire United Kingdom."

"As if he'll be standing at all after today," Elizabeth replied.

Stephen lowered his voice. "What percentage are you?"

"Eighty-five," she murmured back. It was the best she'd felt in years.

He squeezed her hand. "Then you're unstoppable."

"All that matters is stopping Redding—"

"Hear ye, hear ye," boomed from the front lines. Reddington once again held a speaking trumpet to his lips. "The battle royal shall begin in—"

The castle echoed with earsplitting pops as though a thousand bottles of champagne had opened one right after the other. A screeching sound followed, then a series of bright flashes, as though lightning were streaking out from the castle's towers. Feathers fell outside the windows like snow, and the faint scent of gunpowder and burnt honey mingled in the air.

All went silent.

"What," Jacob asked, "was that?"

"Oh, just my alarm," Stephen explained. "I set it to deploy when one hour remained before the scheduled confrontation."

Elizabeth pointed over her shoulder. "There's also an hourglass lowering in the Great Hall, if you prefer to watch the time run out."

"I don't think we will need to," Graham said dryly. "Reddington has numerous faults, but lack of punctuality does not appear to be one of them."

Now that the surprise of Stephen's alarm was over, the speaking trumpet once again rose to Reddington's lips. "The battle royal begins in one hour! If you wish to save your souls, hand over the castle posthaste. Otherwise, I shall take my due by force. Prepare to be besieged!"

"Save our souls?" Adrian repeated. "That's a little dramatic, isn't it?"

Marjorie snorted. "Everything Reddington does is dramatic."

"And now he's going to dramatically punch a hole through the castle wall with a cannon." Jacob peered out the window.

"What kind of frosted teapot destroys his own castle?" Kuni asked.

"A desperate one," Graham said. "He already sold tickets for the Waterloo reenactment he scheduled to take place on this property. His image will crumble if he cannot follow through as advertised. He has to save face with his soldiers, or they'll stop following him."

"His men adore reenactments," Marjorie added. "The more spectators, the more motivated his soldiers will be to fight to win."

"Reddington has nothing to lose by fighting," Jacob agreed. "The publicity gained from a siege, whether successful or not, will only bring more volunteers and more spectators to the main event—even if he must hold the reenactment on his adjacent land instead of at Castle Harbrook."

"Do you think he *will* retreat to his property?" Marjorie asked. "Regardless of who prevails in today's battle royal?"

"*We* prevail," Elizabeth answered. "We must defeat him so resoundingly, his remaining men would prefer to defect rather than expose themselves to further public humiliation."

Throwing knives appeared in Kuni's hands. "I'm ready. Are you?"

"We're all as ready as we can be," said Stephen. Then he told them, "Whispering walls are on all four sides, but you must be near the locations I showed you for your voice to carry to the turret."

He and the others had set up the murder room and arranged the other machines as traps around the perimeter of the castle.

Elizabeth and her siblings all nodded their understanding. "And your spy tubes?"

"In perfect working order. I checked the telescopes and mirrors less than an hour ago. I'll be able to monitor what's happening, and set off levers to deploy appropriate defensive and offensive measures as necessary."

"Defeating Reddington and his men is only the first step," Elizabeth reminded them all. "We need to ensure the well-being of the castle itself for the use and safety of all the children in Miss Oak's orphanage. Harbrook is going to be their home. It's up to us to protect it."

An eerie, plaintive howl ripped through the castle. The air filled with the scent of singed grass. What sounded like a thousand feet stomped at once on the ceiling overhead, followed by the din of hundreds of glass jars full of pebbles being shaken at once. Metal squeaked against metal seconds before an explosion of bright yellow dandelion petals and sunflower seeds poured down from the battlements like sheets of rain.

"Another alarm?" Jacob asked politely.

Stephen nodded. "The fifteen-minute signal. We're running out of time before the first shots are fired."

"Just one shot," said Elizabeth. "The muskets aren't loaded, and they only have the one cannon. It might eventually make a hole in the wall, but it should take several minutes to load up another ball. Of course, if the stone crumbles enough, soldiers with bayonets could crawl through and—"

"Elizabeth," Jacob said in warning.

"Nothing to worry about." Kuni brandished her daggers.

Elizabeth lifted her sword. "Welcome to the battle royal."

38

Stomach sinking, Stephen stared out the window at Reddington's army. Those were real soldiers outside. With a real cannon and real arrows. Dutifully following Reddington's every wish and command. And what Reddington wanted was to oust the Wynchesters and install himself as king of the castle. "There's got to be another way."

Philippa and Jacob flanked the window.

"Kuni and Elizabeth are impressively lethal," Jacob said, "but two warriors cannot defend against an entire army, no matter how skilled they may be."

"Let me try to reason with him." Philippa took the speaking trumpet and swung the flared end toward the arrow slit. "Cease fire, Reddington. It's over. The countess's will and testament proves without a doubt—"

"Bring it here," Reddington's voice boomed, "and His Grace will have the document appraised by his own independent authorities."

"They're not independent if they're in his pocket," Graham muttered. "Of course he'll claim it's false."

"Or destroy the document," Elizabeth agreed. "We have to take the will to Miss Oak. She'll want to speak to us in person. Her lawyer will corroborate the contents."

"We can't go anywhere," Marjorie said. "We're surrounded."

"Then we'll deliver the will to Miss Oak once we win the battle royal," said Philippa.

Kuni arched her brows. "*You* are advocating for war?"

Philippa sighed. "What choice have we got?"

Kuni handed her a dagger.

Philippa dangled it gingerly by the hilt.

"Never mind, give it back." Kuni held out her hand. "A neophyte is more likely to hurt herself than her enemy."

"I can throw a dagger," said Philippa.

All the Wynchesters spun to look at her in shock. "You *can*?"

"Remember when my book club spent a month studying archery a couple of years ago? It wasn't all theoretical. Once we'd learned everything we could about the equipment and memorized the stratagems, we spent several afternoons engaged in hands-on practice. After we met Kuni, it seemed logical to do the same with daggers."

"It seemed logical." Tommy kissed her on the cheek. "That's the most Philippa-est thing you've ever said."

"What about swords?" asked Elizabeth.

"Swords were one of the first weapons we studied. We're not as gifted in combat as you or Kuni, but I can thrust and parry without hurting my wrist or losing my grip."

"Swords it is," said Elizabeth. "Give Kuni her dagger back. She has a limited supply, and I have a plethora of rapiers. Unless you'd prefer a battle-axe?"

Philippa returned the dagger. "That's a contingency plan to the contingency plan. I'd rather leave the bloodying of enemies to you."

Elizabeth flashed her teeth in a cobra-like grin. "With pleasure. Today, we defend Castle Harbrook to the death."

Adrian blanched. "Uh..."

"She means Reddington's death," Kuni assured him.

"Nobody's death," Jacob reminded them all. "Both sides agreed to no murdering."

"That leaves plenty of room for damage," Philippa pointed out. "Even if Reddington keeps his word."

"Wait." Graham placed a palm against the stone wall and leaned out the window. "I hear—"

"Horses! Reddington *did* summon the cavalry." Elizabeth strode over to the loophole to look.

But it was not a second squadron of soldiers that came into view. The dirt road before the castle suddenly filled with hackney carriages, out of which spilled dozens of spectators with picnic blankets, opera glasses... and conspicuous slips of paper in their hands.

Stephen sputtered in disbelief. "Reddington sold *tickets*? To a legally dubious violent attack against his neighbor?"

Of course he had. Elizabeth had requested an impartial witness, had she not? Now there were dozens of them.

"Contingency number fourteen," Graham said. "A public battle royal."

"We cannot allow innocent bystanders to be harmed," Stephen warned them.

"They'll be safe," Elizabeth said. "No one would be foolish enough to venture into the line of fire."

They watched with trepidation as more carriages arrived, along with several pockets of chattering onlookers on foot.

"Crowds can be dangerous," Stephen said.

"Especially crowds rooting for the enemy," Graham agreed. "Easily stirred to mob violence."

"Will Reddington take care not to harm them?" Jacob asked.

Stephen considered this. "I think so. He wants to be admired and celebrated. Which won't happen if he's perceived as the bully tyrannizing innocent unarmed citizens."

Outside, so many arrows struck the door that it sounded as though it were raining.

"Do something," Philippa whispered.

Elizabeth pointed the speaking trumpet through the window loophole. "Your Grace! Such unsportsmanlike conduct does not befit a gentleman such as yourself. You agreed that both sides would have an equal number of representatives, not nine ordinary people versus an army of ... Fifty? Sixty?"

There was a pause. Then, "One hundred and four soldiers."

"That's it," Philippa whispered. "We're doomed."

Stephen shared the same sentiment.

Elizabeth raised the speaking trumpet. "There are witnesses all around you. Your opponent has no army. No arrows. No cannons. Do you think anyone will respect you for perpetrating a massacre on a handful of unarmed civilians? The public will vilify you. No one will attend your reenactments, save to jeer and throw rotten fruit."

An even longer pause. Then, "You cannot expect me to forfeit all of my advantages. This is a siege, not tea with the Queen."

"You gave your word. No more than nine of you versus the nine of us. Should a blade draw blood, that soldier is out. The first general to yield, loses. And to ensure fairness, there shall be no arrows, no bullets, and no cannonballs."

"Just because you couldn't outfit and prepare a proper army—"

"I'm sorry, I couldn't hear you. Did you just say you're afraid you'll lose a fair fight?"

"His Grace's men are unmatched at any configuration. The odds will never be in your favor," Reddington boomed back. "Terms confirmed."

Elizabeth lowered her trumpet. "He said yes?"

The others nodded. "He said yes."

She frowned. "I don't like it. He agreed before, too. He thinks he's tricked us. Again."

"Then what do we do?" asked Stephen.

Elizabeth unsheathed her sword. "We fight back. Everyone ready?"

The Wynchesters lifted their various fists and weapons. With and without daggers in hand, each member of the family touched their fingers to their hearts, then lifted them to the sky.

"Uh...Do I do that, too?" Stephen quickly copied the motion, hoping he got it right.

Elizabeth kissed him on the cheek. "I'll explain the Wynchester salute later. Right now, we need you to get to your turret posthaste. We can't win this battle without you."

"Not terrifying at all," Stephen muttered. But at least they had a plan. Several plans.

"Places, everyone!" Graham ordered. "Once we draw first blood from all eight of Reddington's men, he'll have no choice but to yield. Don't let your guard down for a moment. He'll be desperate to draw first blood from *us*. On your marks!"

The Wynchesters scattered. Stephen ran down the corridor and up the narrow spiral staircase to the topmost tower, which not only had the best view of the property...but also now contained several new toys and multiple levers to pull.

Stephen hoped this gambit was going to work.

39

⟨⟨⟨

Stephen burst into the topmost turret with a gasp for air.

By his count, he and the Wynchesters were at least on the fourth or fifth contingency plan already. The aim was to limit bloodshed— *No murdering*—but when one was defending oneself at sword-point, anything could happen.

This cylindrical tower boasted four windows, one for every direction of the compass. Stephen dashed to each in turn, squinting an eye into the mirrored telescoping tubes that gave him a full view of each side of the castle.

Up here, the windows were not arrow embrasures, but rather full open rectangles one could tumble out of, if one was not careful. Stephen was not worried about himself; he had the good sense not to lean out of a tower window while the castle was actively being attacked.

The stone edges of each window were covered with ropes and chains that connected to the levers and pulleys he could use to detonate various attacks.

Half of the Wynchester family was far below in the dungeon, awaiting any breach through the trapdoor. Elizabeth and Kuni remained stationed at the only other entrance, guarding the scarred front door with their swords and daggers.

Stephen hoped that door remained closed and barred for as long as possible. With luck, Reddington's men would tire themselves and become easy prey once their morale had lowered and their energy was depleted.

Which might be what Reddington hoped for the Wynchesters, too.

From the front window, Stephen had a perfect view of the invading army, without any need for his spy tubes—yet.

Down below, Reddington handed his speaking trumpet to one of his men and leapt down from his white stallion with worrisome agility. He might not have fought in His Majesty's army, but he unquestionably looked the part.

He kept his sword in hand as a lanky young boy in regimentals led the horse back to the forest to be tied to a tree. When the lad finished, the boy retook his place amongst the other men. Three rows of soldiers in red regimentals genuflected to Reddington in perfect unison, as if they had practiced this maneuver as much as or more than archery.

Reddington pointed his blade at eight burly men in turn, each of whom rose and stepped forward, muskets in hand. The bullet chamber might not be loaded, but the sharp bayonets protruding from each long muzzle could cause plenty of damage.

As if that weren't enough, swords and daggers hung from the soldiers' hips. Reddington had clearly taken Elizabeth's keep-your-blades challenge to heart. Stephen hoped the eight brawny men stepping forward had been chosen for their intimidating size, and not for their swordsmanship. If Reddington had scrounged up master fencers…

Stephen placed his leather helmet atop his head and adjusted its attached field glass over his left eye. Seeing long distances with one eye and up close with the other played havoc with one's vertigo and depth perception, but closing one at a time left both of his hands free to engage in more important matters.

A bell tinkled in the cupola above him. He smiled. One chime meant all was in place in the dungeon. Nonetheless, he hurried across the turret and tilted his ear toward the whispering wall.

Marjorie's voice floated up loud and clear. "Tommy and Philippa are hidden inside their paintings, and Adrian is ready with lengths of rope."

"Understood and standing by," Stephen answered. "Ring thrice if you need assistance."

He placed his unobstructed eye on the spy tube leading to the dungeon. They couldn't see up here, but he could see down there—sort of. This was the longest series of mirrored telescoping tubes he'd ever connected. The dim torchlight in the dungeon was not ideal, and the spy tubes could not change angle or pivot, but Stephen could still make out two of his machines next to three open cells.

The untrained eye would not *know* that these were machines, however. The shadowy contraptions looked like nothing more than unnecessarily elaborate wooden frames for two eerily life-size portraits, one of an elderly man and the other of an elderly woman.

Marjorie and Adrian were out of sight, but Stephen had no doubt that they—

A bugle sounded from the front lines.

Stephen jerked back from the spy tube and leapt across the turret to the front-facing window.

Reddington and his well-armed eight still stood below, but they were not watching the front door. Their gazes were fixed high up on the castle walls. As Stephen watched, a projectile appeared from far above the soldiers' heads and splattered on the grass before them.

A tomato, courtesy of Graham Wynchester.

Reddington's face ruddied, and he pointed his sword up at the side of the castle. "You have daggers, men. Get him!"

Stephen lowered his eye to the castle-facing spy tube as eight knives soared toward the castle.

None struck their target.

Graham nimbly spidered along the gray stone exterior, pausing only to hurl rocks from the bulging leather satchel draped across his chest.

Stephen returned his gaze to the front-facing tube.

"Yowch!" One of the untapped soldiers in the audience rubbed his shoulder with a vexed expression.

"I said, *get him*," Reddington bellowed.

Six of the eight foot soldiers took off in hot pursuit, throwing daggers at impossible-to-catch Graham as they chased him around the side of the castle to the rear.

It was all Stephen could do not to cackle in anticipation of the surprise to come.

The soldiers drew to a stop several yards short of the trapdoor. Stephen tugged a cord that led to a bell in the murder room. This was Elizabeth's sign that her skill as a mimic was required posthaste.

He could not see into the murder room or hear the words she spoke, but according to contingency plan eight, she was calling out, "Over here, men!" in Reddington's voice.

Her trick worked, as the soldiers took off running to obey.

The moment the soldiers crossed the trapdoor, Stephen flipped the lever.

Howls of surprise rang out as the men's feet found empty air and they fell twelve feet to the hard stone floor below.

After resealing the trapdoor, Stephen ducked his eye from the exterior telescope to the interior dungeon spy tube.

The soldiers had landed on the stone floor in a graceless, inglorious heap. That made six fallen soldiers versus four waiting Wynchesters— an uneven pairing, if not in the way the soldiers imagined as they scrambled to their feet.

To them, only Marjorie was visible in the darkness, looking tiny and scrawny and pathetically easy to capture.

"A hostage!" shouted one of the soldiers, his voice distant but audible through the whispering wall.

As they advanced obliviously between the dim portraits, the lifelike paintings twitched. Tommy and Philippa stepped out of the canvases with weapons in hand. Silently, they swung large wooden clubs at the backs of the heads of the two closest soldiers.

The men dropped like lead balloons, unconscious.

The other soldiers spun about, goggling at their fallen comrades—and the spectacle of two octogenarians bearing wooden clubs before them.

Tommy and Philippa wasted no time swinging their weapons at their attackers, but this time, the soldiers drew their swords. Unfortunately for them, the soldiers did not anticipate Adrian sneaking up behind them with wooden clubs of his own. Down went two more soldiers.

Only two remained to defend themselves against four Wynchesters. The startled men reached for their swords, but it was too late. They were no match against the speed and surprise of the attack.

In no time, Marjorie and Philippa had all six soldiers' hands tied behind their backs and their ankles bound tight. Tommy and Adrian dragged the men into the waiting cells. The iron doors locked tight.

Stephen's blood sang, thrilled that his machines had given the Wynchesters a tactical advantage. They were winning.

Marjorie and Adrian disappeared from his line of sight. Tommy and Philippa retook their positions.

Stephen hurried back to the other side of the turret in time to see two of Redington's extra soldiers break away from the rest of the idle regiment and disappear into the forest. Since six of the eight active combatants had been captured, only Reddington and two final men remained. Fortunately, the castle door was still shut tight. There was no way Elizabeth would allow—

The clang of metal on stone sounded behind him, and Stephen spun around.

"My apologies for startling you," said Graham. "I wanted to bring you the weapons we confiscated from the soldiers who fell through the trapdoor."

Stephen collected the stray sword and handful of daggers and placed them on a wooden chair beside the open archway leading to the spiral stairs.

"The battle is almost over," he said with a grin. "Reddington is down to two men."

Graham smiled back at him. "We couldn't have planned it to go any better."

"You literally planned every possible contingency," Stephen said dryly. "Of course it would go your way."

"Elizabeth is the war general. But with Reddington, one never knows—"

The bugle sounded again.

Stephen arched his brows at Graham. "White flag of surrender, already?"

They hurried to the front window and peered below.

Reddington was pointing his blade at six new men, who each stepped forward in obvious delight at being chosen as replacements for the six captured soldiers.

"That unscrupulous *cheater*," Graham exclaimed in outrage.

Stephen groaned. "I knew he agreed to the negotiation terms too quickly. We failed to specify nine men in *total*. Reddington is attacking with nine at a *time*."

Graham ran a hand over his black curls in frustration. "He won't surrender easily."

Stephen calculated quickly. "It will take forever to vanquish one hundred men, even if we had enough supplies and could stave off exhaustion long enough to try. Perhaps Elizabeth can still convince him to—"

Graham snorted. "She wants this fight as much as he does. I'd wager it's killing her to be trapped behind a locked door with so many armed soldiers to defeat on the other side."

A dull *thwack* echoed in the forest.

"What was that?" Graham scanned the horizon.

Stephen closed his unobstructed eye and searched the forest with his field glass. "An animal?"

"Maybe." Graham looked unsettled. "And maybe we need another contingency."

"The original distraction worked brilliantly," said Stephen. "Do it again."

"With pleasure." Graham retrieved a fresh satchel of rocks and slipped out through the window. In seconds, new projectiles soared down at the men below, several of whom shouted in surprise at being struck on the head and shoulders with rocks the size of fists.

Blood trickled down from two men's foreheads.

"First blood!" Graham called. "They're out!"

Reddington wasted no time replacing the injured soldiers, then pointed up at Graham. "It's a man, not a giant spider! Squash him!"

The soldiers let fly with their own daggers.

Graham scrambled nimbly out of harm's way, disappearing behind the turret to lure the new crop of soldiers to the trapdoor.

They followed at full speed initially, then slowed when they rounded the second corner to the rear of the castle and realized there was no sign of their missing comrades.

They didn't dither for long. In the bare seconds since they had paused, seemingly wild cats encircled them from out of nowhere.

Before the soldiers could do more than tighten their grips on their swords, the cats sprang, claws and incisors out, tangling with the soldiers' legs and biting through their stockings.

The soldiers shrieked and windmilled in panic—right over the trapdoor.

Whoosh. Another special delivery to the dungeon.

Some of the cats tumbled inside along with the men. The felines not only landed on their feet, but also happily partook of the treats the Wynchesters had prepared to thank them for their part in the battle. The soldiers, on the other hand, were herded straight into the waiting cells and locked in tight with their brethren.

Rather than watch through the spy tube as the trapdoor was disguised anew, Stephen hurried back to the front of the turret.

Without wasting a moment, Reddington quickly replaced all eight men.

"You pair, guard me," he barked at the largest two. "You six, go and find out what's happening. And for God's sake, be careful."

The new, significantly less burly soldiers exchanged doubtful glances, as if being sent off into a magical forest after finding out pixies and goblins were indeed real after all.

"Close," Stephen murmured. "You'll see."

40

Three of Reddington's men headed to the left of the castle, while the other three circled around the right.

A loud screech sounded from the far turret. Hawks filled the sky. One by one, the birds dived. The soldiers fled from the attack in panic, running right onto the waiting trapdoor. The first few fell in by accident, succumbing to gravity in the blink of an eye. The others witnessed the trick and skidded to a sudden stop.

Briefly.

The hawks wasted no time clawing at the men's hair and uniforms. The rest of the panicked soldiers had no choice but to run, hurling themselves into the gaping hole right behind their comrades in order to escape the vicious talons streaking down from overhead.

Stephen cackled in glee.

Out below the front window, Reddington was furiously appointing new replacement soldiers. He could not fathom what had happened, but he had seen the hawks and heard the shouts and swiftly realized that he had been bamboozled.

Another loud *thwack* sounded in the forest.

The dungeon bell chimed three times. The code for trouble.

Stephen rushed to the spy tube. Four Wynchesters were visible, with no cats or enemy soldiers in sight. All must have gone according to contingency plan number nine.

"What's happening?" he called.

"We're running out of room in the cells for prisoners of war," came Tommy's voice up the whispering wall.

"Blast." Stephen swiveled his field glass. "Let me see what Reddington is doing."

"I think they're going to rush the door," came Graham's voice from the front of the turret.

Stephen spun around in surprise. Graham had entered silently this time. There was even a fresh sword and two more daggers lying atop the wooden chair.

Out the window below, Reddington and his men were advancing toward the main entrance.

The women inside the castle were having none of it. Daggers flew out from the arrow slits on either side of the wooden door. One of the blades narrowly missed striking Reddington in the chest, and tore a strip from the uniform of the soldier beside him instead.

"First blood," called a voice with a Balcovian accent.

The wounded soldier was immediately replaced by a fresh combatant.

"These narrow embrasure windows are for shooting arrows, not throwing daggers," Graham said apologetically. "In open air, Kuni doesn't miss. She's aiming to scare, not to kill."

"She's doing an excellent job. Look, they're retreating!"

Reddington and his soldiers backed up several yards until they were out of range of the flying blades.

"Maybe not retreating," Stephen allowed. "More like reevaluating."

Another loud *thwack* sounded in the forest. This time, followed by a thundering boom. A tall elm crashed forward from the line of trees.

Axes in hand, a half-dozen soldiers swarmed the fallen tree, hacking its branches free until they were left with nothing more than a long, thick trunk.

"A battering ram," Stephen breathed. "The men weren't retreating. They were changing tactics."

"Contingency number sixteen," Graham said with a grimace.

Precisely eight men hefted the heavy trunk and aimed it toward the castle.

The spectators wisely arranged their blankets near the safety of the forest, watching the skirmish with rapt expressions and eager shouts.

Stephen gripped the stone windowsill. "Here they come..."

Daggers sailed through the castle loopholes as the men approached. Fat, wet, red splotches appeared on their uniforms.

Graham blinked. "Did Kuni just—"

"It's Marjorie," Stephen said in delight. "I made a slight modification to her and Adrian's machine before placing it before the upstairs windows. We may not have bullets, but we have plenty of red paint."

In the confusion, Reddington replaced his paint-splattered men with fresh soldiers.

The men visibly gritted their teeth against the onslaught of daggers and paint, charging forward with their battering ram until—

Boom.

"It didn't work!" Graham crowed.

"Not yet," Stephen agreed. "It can take a few hits to break down a door. What happened to the ladies' daggers? This is the perfect time to attack, whilst they're readjusting for the next strike."

"Shite." Graham glanced around the turret, then started stuffing the daggers confiscated from Reddington's men into an empty leather satchel. "Our side is running out of supplies."

Boom.

The walls of the castle vibrated with the impact. Stephen dropped the satchel to race around the turret, righting his displaced equipment.

Gaining confidence, the soldiers backed up to give the battering ram one last running start.

Boom.

This time, a sickening crack accompanied the boom, followed by the dull thud of a gigantic, heavy wooden door falling flat against a stone floor.

Stephen grappled for his telescopes and pulleys. "They're in?"

"Not yet."

He rushed over in time to see the two warrioresses spring out from the new hole.

Kuni, whom Stephen had previously only witnessed wearing various confections of eye-searing pink, had donned black-and-gold Wynchester regimentals for battle, two knives gripped in her fists.

Elizabeth was also wearing Wynchester regimentals. Stephen's throat went dry at the sight of her looking like a vindictive goddess in tight-fitting pantaloons and a tunic of chain mail. Rather than knives, she clutched a deadly sword in each hand.

Expertly, she twirled both swords, then struck a battle pose.

"Kuni has only two daggers left." Graham scooped up Stephen's bag of knives and tied a sword to his leather belt. "I'm going down there."

"You know how to fence?"

"Aim for the enemy," Graham answered dryly. "You control the ship." With a grin, he nudged Stephen. "It's nice to have a puppet master in the family."

Before Stephen could formulate a reply, Graham was out the window and gone.

"Attack!" shouted Reddington.

All eight of his appointed soldiers rushed Elizabeth and Kuni, swords and bayonets held high. Metal clanged against metal.

Graham dropped down into the middle of the melee. He tossed his wife the bag of daggers and beat back Reddington's men as best he could.

The crimson paint-water had ceased flying from the upper windows. Either Marjorie and Adrian were out of ammunition, or Reddington's army had caught on to the ruse.

"Get the leader," Reddington screamed, pointing his blade at Elizabeth. "We win the moment she yields. Bring me her head on a pike!"

Half of the crowd roared its approval. The other half looked confused... and concerned.

Reddington's face twisted into a mask of fury and vengeance.

This wasn't a game anymore, if it ever had been. Reddington would never allow himself to be humiliated in front of witnesses. He wasn't pretending to wage war. He was out for blood, and wanted Elizabeth's literal head on a literal spike.

The man had to be stopped.

Stephen watched with his heart in his throat. Elizabeth was trying her hardest. Graham fended off one of the soldiers, while Kuni held back three, leaving Elizabeth to fight four at once.

She disarmed two in short order, then wounded a third, leaving only one to—No. Reddington had nominated replacements already. It was one against four again. Elizabeth wounded a second, then disarmed a third, and then... stumbled. Sickeningly.

To say Stephen suffered an immediate apoplexy would be understating the matter. He nearly flew out the window just like Graham, except that for Stephen to do so would be to invite instant death. He could not aid Elizabeth whatsoever.

Already, two new soldiers advanced to replace the latest pair.

Stephen's stomach roiled.

Elizabeth gathered both swords with one hand. She glanced up over her shoulder at the turret where she knew Stephen was watching. She pistoned her free arm into the air, and made three quick number gestures with her empty hand.

One. Zero. Zero.

She tossed one of the swords back into her other hand just in time to defend herself against Reddington's newest batch of soldiers.

One-zero-zero. One hundred. She was telling Stephen not to worry. That she was one hundred percent Elizabeth. That Reddington was going down, because he held no chance against a berserker fighting at one hundred percent.

Of course, that number was a wild overstatement. By Elizabeth's own admission, she rarely even felt eighty percent, and even that had only occurred on a handful of occasions. Which she knew Stephen realized. She also knew he was zero percent calm when it came to her well-being, which was why she was trying to reassure him.

Stephen wouldn't trust Reddington if the man claimed water was wet, but he did trust Elizabeth. More importantly, she was her own woman, which was why Stephen loved her. And no matter how he felt about the unfair situation, she was right about one thing:

She was a warrior. And there was nothing anyone could do to stop her.

41

Elizabeth knew the moment she heard the tree fall that Reddington was up to his usual tricks. She had no intention of being pre-
dictable, either. This was war. Wynchesters played by their own rules
and had wiles of their own in store.

"She cut me!" The soldier Elizabeth was fighting jumped backward, forgetting to parry in his shock.

"Of *course* I cut you." After she'd wounded or disarmed no less
than two dozen soldiers in a row, were these men somehow still
befuddled at the thought that a woman could fight back?

Reddington replaced the injured man at once.

She took advantage of the closest soldier's distraction and flipped
his sword out of his hand, garnering even more surprise.

Tommy claimed the soldiers' dazed expressions were in part due
to the Wynchester women's costumes. Elizabeth did look nice in
pantaloons. She could feel Stephen's hungry gaze on her, four stories
overhead.

Or maybe that was his anxiety she felt. He had a lot of that, too.

"Ah-ah," she cautioned when the soldier before her attempted to
pick up his fallen sword. She whipped her own blade between him
and the fallen sword.

He ignored her and attempted to snatch up the handle anyway.

She sliced open the back of his calf for his trouble.

"Yowch!" He hopped backward on one leg, unleashing a string of venomous, curse-filled insults as he limped back to camp.

Another soldier immediately took his place. Which made things tricky, since she was concurrently dealing with three others.

Unluckily for Reddington, no faux soldier could ever come close to meeting Elizabeth's skill with a blade. Unluckily for her, there were seventy more of the relentless vermin left to conquer. They needn't be legendary swordsmen to tire her out from sheer numbers alone.

Aside from a single unfortunate misstep—which Elizabeth knew Stephen had not missed from his lookout perch—she was holding her own with ease.

But her limber parries and fluidity of motion would not last forever. At the moment, there was the barest whisper of discontent in her hips and joints, but it could flare into full-on rebellion at any time.

"How are you doing, Kuni?" she called out in Balcovian.

Her sister-in-law had been muttering a steady tirade of colorful curses herself, the majority of which were either completely made up or amusingly inaccurate translations. Elizabeth made a mental note to have Kuni define "snoodish shalloon" later.

After they won. Which of course they were going to do.

"*Alles goed*," Kuni shouted back.

All is good. Really, Balcovian wasn't so very complicated. At least, not the list of close cognates Elizabeth had managed to memorize. She might not have Philippa's gift with linguistics, but Elizabeth and her siblings all spoke English, French, and sign language. Balcovian was trickier, but half the battle of learning a new tongue was believing that you *could*.

She hoped the same sheer determination would carry her through today.

"Graham?" she called out. "How about you?"

Her brother was really the one Elizabeth wished to check up on.

Kuni could not only hold her own, but in fact was holding herself back. Like Elizabeth, for Kuni the hardest part of this battle was defeating enemy soldiers without killing them, which would have been the most efficient path to take. The rest of Reddington's men would have surrendered by now, if they realized their lives depended on it.

Yes, yes, the agreement was no murdering, and now there were children in the audience. But—

"Should've...taken you up on...fencing lessons," panted her brother.

Damn it. Exactly what Elizabeth was afraid of. She and Kuni could fight battles in their sleep, but Graham—despite being impressive physically—was not used to hand-to-hand combat. He was more of the "let me climb this sheer wall and leap from parapet to parapet in order to spy through windows" persuasion. The only time Graham ever touched a sword was when he was annoyed Elizabeth had left one on the dining room table. Again.

He and Kuni were fighting back-to-back. Graham's longer sword kept soldiers at bay. Those who ventured too close received a bite from one of Kuni's daggers.

The situation would have been even worse for Reddington's men if Kuni still *had* a reserve of daggers. Unhindered by narrow arrow slits, she could throw a knife between the eyes of her enemy from twenty yards away. If she still had knives to throw. And if she were allowed to aim between the eyes.

"*En jij?*" called Kuni. And you?

"Seventy percent," Elizabeth called back in Balcovian. "They don't stand a chance."

More like sixty-five percent. Or sixty. Certainly a far cry from the one hundred percent she'd signed up to Stephen to stop him from worrying. Sixty percent was no problem. Sixty was a normal day. A good day. Any day she could swing a sword at an enemy was a *great* day. Elizabeth would not complain about sixty percent. The trick was to win this fight before her thermometer dipped any lower.

"How many soldiers are left?" she called out in Balcovian.

Back-to-back, Kuni and Graham turned around so that he faced Reddington's camp. Graham had uncanny spatial ability that allowed him to register details and count vast numbers in the blink of an eye.

"Forty-nine," he answered.

Good God, they'd barely dispatched half of them? The whispering in her joints grew to a murmur.

"How's Stephen?" she asked as her sword crashed against an enemy soldier's blade, spinning the handle up and out of his hands.

"Impressively competent," replied her brother.

Despite being no doubt anxious and worried, Stephen was also capable of single-handedly manning a 360-degree command center with bells from each floor and telescopes and whispering walls on every side and dozens of levers and pulleys that detonated disasters he'd designed out of nothing more than an empty apothecary bottle and a piece of thread.

She loved that his machines had been such a boon to the mission. The trapdoor was brilliant, as were all the other tricks, from false portraits to hot paint catapults. When they finally beat Reddington, the first thing Elizabeth was going to do was tell Stephen he—

"By the bobbled horse-flowers," gasped Kuni.

"What is it?"

"We're out of daggers!"

Elizabeth tossed over the sword in her left hand without breaking stride from her current parries.

Long black braids swinging, Kuni caught the blade by its hilt and immediately employed it in the destruction of her enemy's dapper red coat. She and Graham were still fighting back-to-back...or at least, Kuni was still fighting. Without a blade, Graham was reduced to his fists. He was quick and strong, but speed and power were no match against the slice of sharp steel.

"Augh!" Kuni cried out.

Shite. "What happened?"

"Lost the sword," she gasped. "Hadn't practiced with that one and I—oh!"

She and Graham rolled out of the way as two soldiers swung at them in unison.

With a burst of tenaciousness, Elizabeth bloodied the arms and chests of all four of her attackers, giving her siblings a few seconds' respite before new replacements arrived. She tossed her final sword to Graham, who handed it immediately to Kuni.

In seconds, the tip of Kuni's blade met her opponent's cheek.

"Huzzah!" cheered Graham.

Elizabeth felt less like exultation. Four new soldiers were bearing down, and *they* had swords in their hands.

She bit her lip and risked a glance overhead at Stephen's turret. She couldn't see him, but she knew he was up there worrying her head was about to be chopped off and stuffed onto a pike, which normally would be a laughable concern, but under these circumstances—

A blade arced through the air and stuck into the ground an arm's width from her body.

"Last sword!" came Stephen's distant shout.

"One is all I need," she murmured, and yanked the blade up from the grass.

The sword wasn't one of hers, which meant wielding it wasn't quite as natural as breathing. But all she needed was a blade.

"Aargh!" Kuni yelled again. "There went my last weapon, too!"

"Go to the murder room!" Elizabeth called out in Balcovian. "If they make it inside, the traps will take care of them. I'll hold them off as long as possible to give you a head start."

How long was "as long as possible"? Sixty percent had now come and gone. She was at fifty-five. Maybe fifty.

And there were forty more soldiers left to go.

42

Elizabeth swung her sword against one soldier's blade, then another. She felt her muscles resist as each new strike reverberated up her arm.

If four against one had been difficult, eight against one was impossible. Even for her.

Time to draft a new contingency plan.

Jacob was readying the next round of attack animals, and Stephen was preparing to launch a formidable sequence of machines—but Elizabeth was done playing games. She was ready to fight the battle she'd been waiting for, and settle the matter once and for all.

Reddington thought Elizabeth Wynchester wasn't good enough to join an army? That a woman could never be his match? He was about to find out just how wrong he was.

"Reddington!" she shouted. "Are you truly such a coward?"

Through the blur of swords before her, she saw him puff up with bluster and outrage. "What did you call His Grace?"

"A coward! Whilst you watch in safety, you send your entire army to attack one girl," Elizabeth shouted loud enough for all the soldiers to hear. Loud enough to reach the spectators in the back. "And you call yourself a hero?"

The soldiers she was fighting hesitated at this new characterization. It was momentary, but all she needed was an opening.

One after another, their swords littered the ground. Fresh red scratches opened across their chests and shoulders.

Reddington turned toward his remaining army in search of more men.

"Must we drag this out until you're the last man standing?" she yelled. "Or can we settle the battle now, like gentlemen?"

He scoffed. "You're no gentleman."

And neither was Reddington. "Like generals, then."

He would soon find out Elizabeth wasn't one of those, either. She was a berserker. Second to no man.

The crowd cheered for him to take her on.

"Very well." Reddington strutted forward, a prima donna swanning in the footlights. When he finished swaggering up to her as dramatically as possible, Reddington gave a mocking bow.

"To first blood," Elizabeth reminded him, and wielded her sword.

To the last drop would have suited her better, but she would take what she could get. At least it was finally one-on-one, instead of one versus eight.

Reddington did not acknowledge her words, other than to raise his sword and swagger.

Elizabeth was exhausted and her opponent well rested...and the best swordsman of any other in his troops. This would not be easy. She would have preferred to face Reddington when she was still at eighty percent, not fifty.

"*En garde!*" Reddington yelled.

All he cared about was showmanship. These soldiers would follow their arrogant leader to the ends of the earth, and he wanted to keep it that way.

Plus there was the audience to consider. The townsfolk had purchased tickets expecting a good show. Reddington intended to give it to them.

So did Elizabeth. They wanted a head on a pike? With pleasure. But it would not be hers.

She gave Reddington her best cobra smile.

With brisk strokes, she met him thrust for thrust, parry for parry. To her chagrin, she realized his pompous *en garde* hadn't been all for show after all. In the split second she'd spent curling her lip at his histrionics instead of attacking, she had let *him* take the lead. Elizabeth was now on defense, rather than offense, reacting to his moves instead of launching counter-strikes of her own.

She felt the sting on the back of her hand before she saw the blood.

"*Damn* it," she spat in frustration.

He'd done it. Ice water sluiced through her veins. Her siblings would have to try their best without her.

And none of them could duel like Elizabeth could.

Reddington saw the line of wet blood drip from her hand and smirked. Rather than raise his fist in victory, he swung his sword toward her neck.

She dived out of the way just in time.

"Yield!" he commanded.

In relief, she realized his refusal to agree to cease at first blood had worked in her favor. The battle would end only when one of them surrendered. And it would not be Elizabeth.

She panted, gathering strength from her very marrows. "Not today, and not ever."

This wasn't a show. This was a real fight to the finish.

"What's that?" Reddington mocked her. "A weepy boo-hoo-hoo from a little girl who didn't realize she was up against a—"

She slashed down, then immediately back up, catching him off guard—and nicking the underside of his chin. Red blood dripped down onto the bright white of his cravat.

"You'll pay for that," he snarled.

Probably. She was already sinking below forty-five percent.

"You won't be alive to find out," she shot back, and rained down blows as fast and as hard as she was able.

Reddington was halfway across the lawn before he realized she had backed him up for twenty yards in front of hundreds of witnesses.

He let out a roar of rage and charged her.

She ducked and rolled at the last moment, kicking out a leg to trip him as he passed—a move that cost her five more percentage points. She was down to forty. Nonetheless, she followed it up with a swipe of her sword across Reddington's buttocks, slicing the bottom half of his coattails clean off.

Her enemy looked as though he wanted to beat her with his bare hands. Elizabeth wouldn't give him the chance.

She was on him before he could scramble back to his feet, swinging at him from above, forcing him to defend himself from a prone—then fetal—position.

"You *lose*," she shouted.

With a final thrust and spiral, she spun his sword out of his grip and sliced her own blade down toward his neck.

Reddington cried out in fear, turning his head and closing his eyes to block out his final moment of life before she extinguished it forever.

The tip of Elizabeth's blade buried itself into the grass-covered soil instead, the sharp side of her sword coming to rest a quarter inch from Reddington's throat. The thin skin of his neck brushed against the blade with every shuddering breath.

Dizziness rushed through her. This rich white bully of a man with a perfectly working body and all the privileges bestowed upon him by the blue blood of his viscount father lay helpless at her feet. The toes of a once-scared little girl deemed so worthless that her own family had traded her for a used dog cart.

She held the power. And she would wield it to make a better life for all the children soon to find a home in Miss Oak's orphanage.

"It's over, Reddington," Elizabeth said softly. "Surrender, or I shall liberate your head from your body and toss your dripping skull into the crowd."

He glared at her with eyes as murderous as she had ever seen, but he could not deny the truth. The battle was over. She had won. He had been bested in front of his entire army and a hundred ticket-holding witnesses.

She felt all those eyes upon her. Not in pity or relieved superiority, as was so often the case when passers-by glimpsed a young woman gripping a cane as she struggled to navigate a world that had not been built for people like her. If passers-by even registered her presence at all.

They watched her in awe. These spectators weren't counting their lucky stars that they were not her. They *wished* they had lives half as interesting. That their enemies would cower at their feet, vanquished once and for all.

Bitterly, Reddington banged his palm against the grass in a clear gesture of surrender.

Elizabeth jerked her gaze toward the crowd to make sure everyone present had witnessed the moment of unequivocal defeat.

They had.

She grinned at them. Not just to prolong Reddington's humiliation, but to impress upon the witnesses that Wynchesters *win*. If any of the ticket holders were ever in trouble, they now knew whom they could call upon. She and her siblings eagerly took any opportunity possible to champion those who could not advocate for themselves and put unfair circumstances back to rights.

Elizabeth allowed her blade to touch Reddington's throat one last time. Then she leapt away, swinging her sword toward the sky and holding it high in the air. Despite the exhaustion in her bones, she let out her best berserker cry of triumph.

Reddington's soldiers stared at her in blank stupefaction.

The rest of the crowd went wild.

43

At the sight of Elizabeth holding her sword to Reddington's throat, Stephen dashed down the narrow spiral stairs. His boots slipped on the worn gray stones in his race to reach her. Kuni and Graham had already burst outside. Stephen in red and the other Wynchesters in black-and-gold family regimentals reached the murder room at the same time. They streamed out the door into the front garden together.

"Victory to Castle Harbrook!" Jacob's amplified voice shouted through the speaking trumpet.

The crowd cheered.

Kuni and Graham were hugging Elizabeth, but they parted in order to allow Stephen access. He pulled her into his arms and swung her in victorious circles.

"You did it!" He covered her face in relieved kisses. "You squashed Reddington like the dung beetle he is."

Elizabeth laughed and kissed Stephen back, her eyes sparkling. "And I managed it at a measly forty percent!"

"Humph," he said. "Speak for your body. As for your sword-wielding, you never slipped below one hundred percent Elizabeth."

Elizabeth tipped the back of her head toward the vanquished dung beetle. "He never dipped below one hundred percent Reddington—which was his downfall."

Stephen glanced over Elizabeth's shoulder at the scene. "He's still surrounded by an adoring public, I see."

"He wishes he were." Jacob grinned. "They want a refund for their tickets to the upcoming Waterloo anniversary reenactment. They've decided Reddington is nothing at all like the Duke of Wellington, and they're demanding their shillings back."

Marjorie threw her arms around Elizabeth and Stephen both. "You two were phenomenal! Elizabeth won the war, but you helped us win the battles. Your machines are marvelous, and the trapdoor absolutely divine."

Stephen's entire body felt electric with excitement and energy and pride. It wasn't just that he couldn't recall the last time he'd won against a bully. He couldn't remember ever being part of a team like this at all.

"You are just as talented at throwing paint as you are at creating portraits with it," he demurred. "*All* of you played your roles perfectly."

Tommy stuck her thumbs in her waistband and grinned. "All we did was follow the plan."

"There were at least twenty potential plans," Stephen reminded her.

"And I think we implemented all of them," Graham agreed with a laugh.

They clapped shoulders and exchanged hugs for a few more minutes until Philippa gasped. "Oh no, the prisoners of war! They're still locked in the cells. Come on, Tommy, we must let the men return home."

The two rushed inside over the fallen door without a backward glance.

Graham pulled a small journal from his waistcoat. "That battering ram did real damage. I'm making a note to replace Miss Oak's castle door posthaste."

"*I* need to replace it," said Elizabeth. "The wood was missing quite a few chunks before Reddington and his men showed up."

Stephen gave her an indulgent smile. "That's my berserker."

At least, he wished she was his.

She nestled into him and sighed happily. "Nothing gives me more joy than to see Reddington and his army fall to a woman, a tinker, and a family of orphans. And my souvenir, of course." She held up her wounded hand. "A future battle scar!"

Jacob peered at her hand. "That's not going to scar."

"*Damn* it." Elizabeth scowled at her superficial war wound as though it had ruined her day.

Another carriage pulled up along the side of the road.

"Too late, you missed it!" yelled one of the departing picnickers. "The girl won!"

Elizabeth grinned.

"That's not more townsfolk arriving for the show," Graham told Stephen. "It's our hackney."

"We own a few carriages that double as hackneys for missions where we need to be discreet," Jacob explained.

A familiar, sheepish face emerged from the not-a-hackney's door.

"The Earl of Densmore!" Adrian exclaimed.

The awestruck earl took in the chaos of limping soldiers and chattering picnickers cluttering the length of the castle's lawn. After a long moment, he jogged up to Stephen. "I leave you alone for one month..."

"It's been over four months," Stephen corrected his cousin. "You said you'd be gone for two days."

The earl winced. "I lost track of time?"

"You lost your castle, too," said Elizabeth.

"Technically, it never was your castle," Kuni added. "We defended it all the same."

Densmore pointed at his feet in horror. "Is that *blood* splattering my boots?"

"It's red paint," answered Marjorie. "Mostly."

"Excuse me for a moment," said Graham. "I must send our driver on one more mission."

"Paint?" Densmore repeated. "Why on earth is—"

A swarm of soldiers streamed out from the gaping castle entrance, several of them sporting impressive knots on their foreheads.

"You!" Reddington marched up to the cluster of Wynchesters, the frayed stumps of his severed coattails flapping with each stride. He jabbed his finger into the earl's lapel. "This is all *your* fault, Densmore."

"I have no idea what's happening," the earl protested.

"You apparently didn't know what was happening the last time I saw you, either. You promised me a castle these infidels claim you do not own."

Densmore had the grace to flinch with embarrassment at this accusation. "At the time of that particular gameplay, ownership was somewhat unclear—"

"Do you want to know what's clear?" Face flushed, Reddington smashed his worthless IOU into the earl's chest. "Your word is worth as much as this paper. None at all."

Without waiting for a response, Reddington spun around in a huff, giving the earl his back. He stomped off to lead his men through the forest and away from Castle Harbrook.

Stephen turned to his long-lost cousin. "You *are* a rogue, you know."

"I know." Densmore hung his head. "Thank you for coming to my rescue yet again. I suppose you've left things better than how you found them? If a bit more cluttered?"

"If you're referring to my machines, yes, I might have installed one or two. And if you're referring to your finances...also yes. Your coffers are heavier than ever, and you've given all your employees a raise in salary."

Densmore made a sheepish expression. "How would you like to be earl?"

"Not on your life." Stephen leapt away from his cousin. "Take that back."

"What I mean is...I could really use your help. Would you be my man of business? You can name your price. You'd be the one in charge of your salary anyway."

"You can't afford me," said Stephen. "I have tinkerings to tinkle."

"And you'd earn fifty percent of all capital gains due to your investment advice, starting from the moment you stepped onto this property four months ago."

"I'll accept a fair commission, though I shan't take a position on your staff."

Densmore nodded dejectedly. "Who in their right mind would?"

Stephen let out a sigh. "But I will help you find and train appropriate staff so that your other holdings are never in jeopardy. At least, unless you gamble them away."

"I'm through wagering," Densmore promised. "And drinking. New leaf, I promise."

Stephen slanted him a skeptical look.

"I mean it," his cousin insisted. "I'll prove it." He pulled a folded piece of parchment from his inner breast pocket and slapped it into Stephen's palm. "Here. Give this to its rightful owner."

Stephen unfolded the paper and grinned. "The deed to the castle?"

"Mother always said this pile was to become her and Aunt Oak's orphanage. I know my sudden flight was corkbrained, but I ran away to keep Reddington from getting his hands on the deed before we could find Mother's will."

"You're not all bad," Stephen said grudgingly, and slung his arm around his cousin. "Come, allow me to introduce you to the Wynchesters."

One by one, he explained who each was, and how he or she had contributed to the vanquishing of a villain.

Densmore bowed to each in turn. "It sounds like this is very much *my* honor."

Stephen squeezed Elizabeth's uninjured hand. Not to comfort her this time, but to comfort himself. While the rest of the Wynchesters were relating excited stories about how this person or that person had been brave and brilliant and had triumphed, Stephen was facing what all this exuberance really meant:

The mission was over. His cousin no longer needed him. The Wynchesters no longer needed him. Elizabeth no longer needed him. He could pick up and go home now, just like the picnickers and the soldiers.

It had been fun while it lasted, but he and his machines were now superfluous. His part was through. Thank you and goodbye.

He wasn't ready. He might never be ready. But the time had come.

"There's our carriage," said Graham as the not-a-hackney returned into view.

"That was a fast errand," said Densmore. "Did you send it just to drive down the street and back?"

"Close. Come on." Graham waved them over to greet the carriage.

The driver leapt out, but Graham was already at the door. With a grin, he handed down a wonderstruck Miss Oak.

"What on earth happened here?" she asked as she glanced around the stained and trampled lawn.

"Exactly what I said," muttered Densmore.

She rapped him on the shoulder with her fan. "Nephew! No doubt you were at the root of all this trouble."

"One of the roots," said Jacob. "Reddington was the main thorn."

"But I ripped him from the ground and threw him away," said Elizabeth. "And now he's honor bound, before dozens of impartial witnesses and one hundred of his own men, to leave Castle Harbrook in peace forevermore."

Miss Oak brightened in relief and joy. "Truly?"

Elizabeth grinned at her. "The castle is yours."

Stephen handed her the deed.

Miss Oak hugged them all.

"We'll clean up the lawn after the last stragglers have left," Graham added. "Come with us to the parlor, in the meantime. We've got something else you've been looking for."

"I'll buy you a new front door," added Elizabeth. "For now, pretend it's a whimsical wooden carpet decorating the open entrance."

Miss Oak's eyes widened.

"I'll ring for tea," said Stephen. "I think we could all use a cup."

When they reached the parlor, Marjorie and Philippa handed out the cups and saucers from atop the tea cabinet.

"This is the deed," said Miss Oak, "but without my sister's will—"

Elizabeth hurried over to the emptied cabinet and placed her finger above the thorn-shaped secret button. "Ready?"

Miss Oak leaned forward. "Is that a fresh wound on your hand?"

"Pah," said Elizabeth. "That's nothing important. It won't even scar. Watch this!"

She pressed the button, which caused the spring-loaded panel to fly open.

Miss Oak gasped. "A secret compartment!"

Elizabeth pulled out the countess's will, and handed it to Miss Oak. "Yours, at last. I don't even think I got blood on the parchment."

Miss Oak unfolded the document. "My sister's handwriting! You found the will, just as you said you would." She pressed the papers to her bosom. "How can I ever thank you all?"

"It's not settled yet," said Elizabeth. "You inherited the castle, but no funds with which to support it. I've not yet discussed details with my siblings, but I think we—"

"But I do have funds," said Miss Oak. "Mr. Lenox set up a trust for me. The interest alone will more than cover the expenses of staff and meals and ongoing castle maintenance."

"Of course he did." Elizabeth grinned at Stephen. "You wily fox."

He blinked innocently.

Miss Oak tucked the will and the deed into her reticule. "Need I still worry about Richard Reddington?"

"Not for a single second," Graham assured her. "Your papers are in order, and the castle is legally yours. If you're amenable, Marjorie will create a spare copy for you and your original solicitor, while the original documents will be held for safekeeping by a trusted lawyer who frequently handles Wynchester affairs."

"Thank you," said Miss Oak. "That sounds wonderful."

"Reddington is so used to money and status making his every wish come true," said Elizabeth. "I'm glad this time, it's Miss Oak and her sister's wishes coming true."

Miss Oak smiled. "Not just me and my sister. This will mean the world to several new employees and one hundred worthy children, who now will have a stable new home. Thank you. You'll never know how much this means to me. To all of us."

"We have some idea," Tommy murmured. "Call on us whenever you please."

Maids arrived with the kettle and cakes, and soon the chatter turned to plans for the future rather than the trials of the past.

Stephen was glad Miss Oak knew exactly how she intended to utilize the trust he'd set up for her and her school. Even if that meant Densmore's aunt no longer needed Stephen, either. Like the

Wynchesters, she now had all the tools she needed to live the life she wanted. A life that had nothing to do with an eccentric tinker.

When the tea was over, Stephen glanced out the window to discover even the castle itself no longer needed him. He'd planned to help clean up the detritus on the lawn, but the servants had already completed the task.

Reddington was long gone, as were his men and the ticket holders, so there was no one to chase away. Stephen could order a new door, but Elizabeth was handling that. All that remained for him to do was to gather his things and vacate the premises so that Miss Oak could get started building her new school.

"Well," said Graham. "Time to pack our valises."

"I never unpacked," said Kuni.

"I can help you dismantle your souvenir machines," Stephen offered.

"Adrian and I remember how to do it," Marjorie said. "Besides, we need the practice more than you do."

She and the other siblings looked at Elizabeth, who cleared her throat and glanced out the window.

"Ugh," she said loudly. "It will be a long drive back to London."

Stephen pressed his lips together at the unspoken rejection. *Ugh, a long drive.* Not: *Ugh, how it pains me to leave you, Stephen.*

"The torture will soon end," Jacob said dryly. "All the swords you missed so much are at home in your armory waiting for you."

Elizabeth brightened. "And I may have expropriated a new one to add to my collection."

"The sword you defeated Reddington with?" Marjorie asked.

Elizabeth smiled. "The sword we all defeated Reddington with."

Her siblings laughed and cheered.

Stephen wished he felt like laughing and cheering.

All this talk was an extended goodbye. A permanent goodbye. Not only wasn't Elizabeth tearfully begging for their time not to come to an end, but she also hadn't even bothered to inquire about Stephen's direction so that they could exchange the occasional letter.

When the war ends, the soldiers go home.

And the tinker returns to solitude.

"Well," said Tommy. "Shall we load up our carriages and hand the castle over to our client?"

Now? Already? They wouldn't even pause for luncheon?

Stephen shot an anguished look over at Elizabeth. Her eyes were already on him. When their gazes met, she dropped hers at once... but not before he glimpsed a matching flash of torment. Or maybe her pain had nothing to do with him at all. Maybe it was the battle, catching up to her. Maybe what she really wanted was to be done with Dorset—and Stephen.

In any case, he couldn't allow her to walk out of his life without at least trying to be part of hers.

He strode over to her. "Might we speak privately for a moment?"

She nodded and followed him into the castle's corridor.

This was not the romantic setting of Stephen's dreams. He wished he'd had time to construct an elaborate set, using every trick at his disposal to tip the odds in his favor. Instead, he was going to have to plead his case with nothing more than himself... and a flood of anxiety more suffocating than any he'd ever experienced before.

She raised her eyebrows at him.

He tried to remember how to speak. His usually deep voice came out in a croak. "Stay with me," he blurted.

She took a step back. "None of us can stay. The castle belongs to Miss Oak now, remember? Footmen are readying my siblings' carriages for the long drive home."

"I know. My residence is in London, too. You could—" Stephen's words bubbled in his stomach. He was botching this completely. Shite. He had to start anew. "Marry me. Please."

She blinked. "What?"

He reached for her hands. "I have never known happiness like these weeks spent with you. Please allow me to devote the rest of our lives to making you just as happy. This hasn't been a traditional courtship—"

"Duels, dungeons, and catacombs are the *best* kind of courtship," she assured him.

Some of his anxiety eased, and he lifted her hands to his mouth to kiss them. "You haven't seen my home yet, but I hope you'll love it. If there are any modifications you'd like me to make before you move in, just say the word and I'll—"

Her smile vanished, replaced by a look of horror. "You want me to abandon my family?"

Stephen's anxiety ratcheted up higher than before, making his muscles twitch with panic.

"You won't be abandoning them," he stammered. "I live five miles away, not on the other side of the world."

"I *won't* be abandoning them," she repeated unshakably. "Not now, and not ever. It felt awful when Chloe left, and she's in London, too."

What could be more definitive than *not now, and not ever*?

His chest hollowed. "If you don't see any hope of a future between us—"

"Of course I do." She pulled his hands to her bosom and gave a little bounce. "You must come live with us."

"Live in that house with . . . your entire family?"

She nodded happily.

His skin turned clammy. Stephen tried his best to keep his voice calm and steady. "That's very kind of you to offer, but there's not enough room for me and my machines. Which are as much a part of me as . . . as your swords are a part of you."

"It's a very large residence," she assured him. "Each sibling has their own spare room to do with as they will."

"One room. To do with what they will." His stomach roiled. "My love, I have an entire house to do with as we wish. You can have a whole floor for your armory if it pleases you. We can visit your siblings as often as you'd like. Doesn't it make more sense to live where we both can be comfortable?"

She dropped his hands. "I'm comfortable in the room I've lived in for over twenty years."

"Are you?" he asked softly. "Or is it what you've grown used to?"

"What about you?" she snapped. "If you stay with us, we're only five miles away from your precious machines. You can visit them whenever you want."

He took a deep breath and let it out slowly. "I see we're at a stalemate. If you're not ready to leave your family, I won't pressure you to do so."

Her forehead lined. "That's it, then? Battle over? We go our separate ways?"

"I hope not. I want to spend every minute of the rest of my life with you. If you ask it of me, I'd build you the tallest palace in the land, with a cabled conveyance that sails you from our tallest turret straight into your family's sitting room. I'm open to any compromise at all that will give us a life together in which we both have the space we need to be our true selves."

She crossed her arms and squinted at him.

He pressed on. "But if that's not what you want, I won't force you. If you don't feel that being with me is a *good* choice, then it's not the choice you should make." Even if the loss of her killed him. He tucked a stray hair behind her ear. "How about you come and visit *me* when and if you see a mutual path forward, and we'll resume our discussion then?"

She lifted her chin. "Fine."

There. She'd agreed to something, at least. A pact Stephen already regretted, because he would miss her desperately from the moment she climbed into her carriage. And now he'd locked himself in a position where he couldn't chase after her without undermining her free will.

No calls. No letters. No courtship.

Just Stephen, five miles away, hoping for a knock on his front door. Or a battle-axe.

"I should return to the parlor," she said. "My siblings need me."

He held up his palms in acquiescence.

When they reentered, Marjorie and Adrian were just pushing to their feet.

"There you are," said Marjorie. "There's still plenty of light for the journey. Adrian and I can break down the machines and arrange for hired carriages to transport them later."

"I'll collect my animals now," said Jacob.

The rest chimed in with how they would help. They had clearly done this before. At this rate, they would be out the door in less than an hour.

"I've a reading circle tomorrow," said Philippa. "Do you think we'll be back in time?"

"If we drive straight through." Graham looked at Elizabeth. "Are you up for a long ride?"

She hesitated.

Stephen's heart stuttered. Was she worried about the seats and the bumpiness of the road, or was she realizing that she, too, could not bear to be separated from Ste—

"Of course we can drive straight through," Elizabeth said loudly. "I can do anything."

His chest seized. Of course she could do anything. He had no choice but to let her go.

In no time at all, the Wynchesters were packed and ready. The hired carriages to cart all of Stephen's other creations and supplies wouldn't arrive until morning. Which left him nothing to do but stand there on the side of the road to wave goodbye.

And hope his broken heart didn't show on his face.

Elizabeth was the last to climb into a carriage, pausing just outside the open door.

Stephen gave up on being stoic. He sprinted to the carriage before it could swallow her whole. Instead, he wrapped his arms around her and pressed his frantic lips to hers, telling her without words that she was the most exquisite berserker he'd ever known. His favorite person, whom he would miss more than he'd missed anything else in his life.

She squeezed him back. And kissed him.

And then she let him go.

44

❦

*E*lizabeth could not stand being cooped up in a carriage for this many hours.

Not because of her exhausted joints, which pained her. Or her aching hip, which hated her. Or even the endless monotony of bumping over rocks and ruts again and again, mile after godforsaken mile.

It was because the carriage was taking her away from Stephen.

Philippa's furtive, commiserative glances made Elizabeth feel like her heretofore unknown emotions and barely constrained hysteria weren't ridiculous at all. That it might, in fact, be understandable, were Elizabeth to leap from the moving carriage and crawl back to Castle Harbrook on her knees if that was what it took.

But Philippa was a romantic. She spent her free time with her nose in some star-crossed lovers saga or another. When Philippa wasn't actively practicing romance with Tommy. Or performing both tasks at the same time, as she was now, with her head on Tommy's shoulder and an open gothic novel on her lap, and her eyes...on Elizabeth, damn it, and not on the pages of romantic melodrama at all.

"Um," said Philippa.

"I'm fine," Elizabeth snapped preemptively.

The only thing worse than being seated across from a pair of snuggling romantics...was sharing the other seat with an even worse romantic. Jacob's sad-puppy brown eyes had been *oh-you-poor-thing-ing* her for the entire journey back to Islington.

Only Tommy wasn't acting like Elizabeth's inner turmoil was visible all over her face like an outbreak of measles. It was worse. Tommy was acting like she believed Elizabeth's bravado and bought her nonchalance at leaving behind the sole non–family member who had ever made Elizabeth feel truly at home.

"Bet you're glad to be rid of that tinker," Tommy said cheerfully.

"Mm," Elizabeth managed noncommittally.

"A full month with a stodgy professor type must have been torture," Tommy continued.

Elizabeth kept her gaze firmly out the window. "Torture."

"Once you're back to your real life, you can resume your search for the warrior of your dreams, just like you've always wanted. Someone who swashbuckles at your side, rather than peers down from a turret like a princess locked in a tower."

"Shut up, Tommy," Elizabeth whispered desperately, then risked a glance her sister's way.

Tommy was gazing at her with an expression of such innocent, absolute blankness that Elizabeth knew then and there her sister had been needling her on purpose.

"I liked Stephen," said Philippa.

"I liked him, too," said Jacob.

Elizabeth *loved* him. And she'd walked away rather than say so. Chose *safety* rather than risk and romance.

Because admitting she cared meant giving the universe the power to hurt her. Elizabeth never gave anyone that power, if she could help it. She hurt enough on her own. The rest of her body might fall apart, but her heart was the one thing she could protect.

Even if right now, it felt more like it was breaking.

"Bah," said Tommy, keeping her obnoxiously blank face pointed straight at Elizabeth. "Our sister has sworn for years never to settle for less than a warrior or warrioress. 'Must love swords' is requirement number one. Requirement number two is a personality characterized as 'a remorseless killing machine with a love of unnecessary bloodshed.' Then something about hulking muscles—"

"Stephen has surprisingly defined muscles," Elizabeth mumbled.

"Does he? Well, that's hardly enough to tempt Beth the Berserker. What else can a scholar so insipid have to offer?"

"He's methodical," Elizabeth said.

Tommy shuddered. "You hate anything methodical."

"He's a thinker."

"Your least favorite activity," Tommy said with authority. "You always say there's no sense wasting time thinking, when you could be impaling someone with your sword."

Stabbing someone like Tommy.

"He's careful and deliberate," Elizabeth said.

"Two more words that don't describe you."

Elizabeth thought about the joy Stephen took in his machines. "He loves anarchy."

"That one's a good match," Tommy allowed. "The rest of his so-called accomplishments—"

"—seem like they balance you," Philippa said softly.

Elizabeth didn't respond.

"Sounds like a fairy tale to me." Jacob stretched out his feet and crossed them at the ankle. "Stephen settles you down when appropriate, and unleashes you as necessary."

"He's Pandora, and Elizabeth is what's in the box," agreed Philippa.

"Stephen would never keep me in a box," Elizabeth said. "He likes me unrestrained."

It was true, she realized. Stephen had never once tried to change her. If anything, he had gone out of his way to enable her to be the most Elizabeth-est Elizabeth possible. He'd offered her the space to be her true self, whatever that looked like.

Others saw weakness, and pitied her. Or made teeth-grinding comments about how she inspired them to feel better about their own perfect lives.

Elizabeth's life *was* perfect. She was happy to be a cane-wielding berserker. Stephen never doubted her. She was the one who had doubted *him*. But she'd been wrong. He did not see her as something that needed to be fixed. He saw her as someone who should be allowed to run wild.

"His fine qualities don't matter," she forced herself to say. "The case is finished."

"Mm-hm," murmured Jacob beside her. "The case certainly is."

Meaning, if she admitted that the most romantic interlude of her life was over, then . . . She had no one to blame but herself.

"Well," said Tommy. "I'm sure you told Stephen very clearly how you feel about muscular, methodical, anarchic tinkers like him."

Elizabeth swung her gaze back outside the window and blinked rapidly to clear her eyes.

She didn't share her feelings with anyone. She claimed not to *have* any, save for uncontrollable bloodlust and a soft spot for her favorite hedgehog. Of course, that was before she'd walked away from the handsomest, kindest, cleverest, sweetest, and quirkiest person she had ever known.

What was she supposed to have done, rip off his cravat and say, *I love you*? Re-creating Buckingham House out of feathers and grains of sand would be easier. She'd rather fight Napoleon's actual army with a wooden sword at ten percent capacity than make herself vulnerable on purpose. The best shield of all was the Wynchester castle back home.

Wasn't it?

Philippa placed her hand on Elizabeth's knee. "How *are* you doing?"

"Still fifty percent," Elizabeth responded automatically.

Her voice cracked on the final syllable. No matter how her body waned and waxed, now that she'd left Stephen, Elizabeth would be stuck at fifty percent forever.

One solitary, lonely half of what might have been.

45

Stephen hauled himself up from his comfortable padded chair that lately felt like a bed of nails. He trudged down the hall and into his workroom. He'd been here for days, and still hadn't opened a single box after returning home from Castle Harbrook.

Three days of staring sullenly at an unlit fireplace while the forgotten tea cradled in his hands grew cold.

Three days of press-up after press-up after press-up. Anything to relieve his anxiety. None of it worked.

Three days of wishing he were still standing in for his cousin. That Reddington was still a puffed-up peacock determined to lay public siege on someone else's castle. That Elizabeth were there at Stephen's side, on the battlefield and in his bed.

Three days was an eternity.

It normally took Stephen less than three hours to unpack after a trip, no matter how many crates of new supplies he'd bought. He adored unpacking. Each item that passed through his hands sparked inspiration for a new contraption, a new trigger, a new outcome.

The problem was, he didn't want a new idea. He wanted the fantasy in his head to become real. Elizabeth was the one thing Stephen didn't want to build up or tear down or alter. He wanted to install her in this very room and keep her exactly as she was, forever and always.

But he didn't have her. He'd never truly had her. She wasn't a thing a man could *have*. She was someone who had to give herself willingly, who had to choose *him*, again and again, not just as a temporary diversion but as a permanent installation in her life.

But there had been no sign. No visit. No letter. Not even a messenger crow.

She'd made her choice. And the answer was no.

In defeat, he turned to the pile of boxes shipped home from the castle. He lifted a chisel from his worktable and forced himself to pry the lid from a wooden crate in a civilized manner, rather than take a hatchet to it as he'd prefer. There were no berserkers here. Only a reclusive tinker. He'd lost himself in his machines before, for decades at a time. He could do so again.

The contents of the box conspired against him. The wooden crate was not full of planks and pulleys and interlocking gears as he'd anticipated, but rather, the broken pieces of Elizabeth's sweetly hilarious attempt at making a machine for him as a gift. Her contraption had never worked. It had fallen apart at the first touch.

Much like Stephen felt now.

He dropped to his knees before the open crate and lifted out the topmost nonsensical piece. What had this crooked bar been for? Who knew? Did Elizabeth even know? A choking laugh garbled in his throat. He couldn't bear to repurpose the parts in some other machine. Nor could he bring himself to attempt to fix her creation himself, and make a working contraption of it.

The thing had barely been standing when Elizabeth presented her design to him, yet it was perfect just as it was. It wasn't her invention's function—or lack thereof—that meant so much to him. It was the intent to give him something that he did not have. Something he might like. He had filled the empty spaces in his heart with machines before. Her logic was sound. But it was not a lifeless wooden structure that he needed most.

He craved Elizabeth.

Slowly, Stephen removed each piece from the box and placed it in a row along the floor. If he was careful, perhaps he could rebuild it exactly as she'd had it. It wouldn't be quite like having her back—and if he so much as hiccupped, it would fall apart all over again—but it would make him feel like he still had some connection to her, no matter how gossamer.

Then again, it was a kiss-delivery machine. No matter how perfectly Stephen managed to reassemble it, without Elizabeth here... There would be no more kisses.

The empty room seemed to whisper, *What did you think would happen?*

Yes. A fair question. What *had* he thought would happen? A woman like that...A man like him...It had been foolish to fall in love. Of course she wouldn't stay. She was a transitory tempest, and he the empty land laid waste in her passing.

One could not reason with a tempest. One could love it from afar, and one could not blame it for its trail of destruction. He was the architect of his own loneliness. Always had been. Hanging back, holding his tongue, hiding himself away.

And then came Elizabeth. She had smashed her way past his barriers just like she'd done to the castle. And once his defenses were breached, to Stephen's surprise he discovered that he liked her there. That life with her was infinitely better than life without her.

So what was he going to do about it?

Stephen pushed to his feet. He wasn't just about to try something new. He was going to try his *hardest*. Prepare his best argument, in the event she ever actually did attempt to communicate with him in the future. He'd have the perfect gift on hand for the woman he hoped would be his bride.

Roses? Bah.

Stephen had a berserker to woo.

46

Elizabeth crouched in total darkness. She was awaiting the sound of approaching footsteps before she sprang from the shadows. Elizabeth hated waiting. Springing up and slicing down were second nature, but biding her time was an absolute nightmare.

To distract herself, she took inventory of her body. Despite holding an uncomfortable position for what felt like weeks, she was still a solid seventy-five percent. Possibly it was the return to the warmth and safety of home that had invigorated her after a month in a drafty castle. Or perhaps it was the new mission, which had consumed her thoughts from the moment she stepped foot back in Islington.

She enjoyed infiltrating unknown territory, at least. That part was fun.

The waiting, on the other hand...Lurking in the shadows alone with no sounds but her own breaths, no smells but dust, nothing to see but blackness—well, it gave a skulking interloper plenty of time to think.

And all Elizabeth could think about was Stephen.

One more hour with him wouldn't leave her satisfied. She wanted more than that. She wanted to spend *every* hour with him. Clothing optional. Even swordplay optional. What mattered was not the activity, but whom she shared it with. And the person she longed for most was Stephen.

She was glad his cousin was a complete disaster. If the Earl of Densmore had been competent in his duties, Stephen would not have been at Castle Harbrook.

She was grateful her siblings had all been busy, and had therefore been forced out of pure necessity to send Elizabeth 120 miles southwest to Dorset all by herself. If they had come with her from the beginning, or if Jacob or Graham had been sent instead, Elizabeth would never have spent that blissful time with Stephen. Or discovered she indeed had the capacity to fall in love.

Elizabeth apparently also had a limitless capacity to bollocks it up. Not only had she walked away from the person she most wished to keep close, but had also wasted the past few hours of her life hunched in an extremely uncomfortable shed despite it becoming increasingly obvious no one was going to come and open the door.

With a sigh, she rolled back her shoulders and eased around the sharp edges of dozens of jutting wooden boxes and pushed open the door.

Well, *pushed* anyway. The door did not budge.

Elizabeth pushed harder. The hinges squeaked and the door moved only slightly, but it was enough to rattle heavy chains against the outer side.

No one was coming. She was locked in!

The dust in the musty air now tasted a bit like panic. She didn't mind dark spaces, and even now had gained an affection for wooden boxes, but this was not the moment to stand around waiting to be rescued. *She* was the one who intended to do the conquering.

She certainly wasn't going to let a locked door stop her from trying. Not with Stephen on the other side.

Elizabeth unsheathed her sword with a flourish. Or tried to. It was a semi-flourish, interrupted by the sharp edge of a wooden crate, and twenty full seconds of swearing as she picked splinters out of the skin of her hand. Swashbuckling in an enclosed space sounded dramatic, but in practice it was bloody near impossible.

She was going to do it anyway.

Once her sword was free, she positioned herself halfway between the locked door and the hulking crates and swung her sword with all her might.

A satisfying crack exploded into the wood before her, and a stream of dust-filled sunlight dazzled her eyes. Without waiting for her vision to adjust, she swung her sword again and again, concentrating instead on dislodging one of the individual panels that made up the door.

At last it popped free, and sunlight poured into the storage shelter. One skinny panel might have been wide enough for Tommy to slip through, but wouldn't do for Elizabeth. So she pried at the next one, fully expecting footsteps to come running at any moment to investigate the destruction unfolding in the rear garden.

Nothing. No one. Not even a maid, a footman, a gardener.

The security in this place was absolute rubbish.

She squeezed out through the hole she'd carved into the door and brushed dust and splinters of wood from her dress. She'd looked nice when she'd left the house this morning, but now she looked like she'd spent the day wrestling with a wooden crocodile. Bites were missing from her skirt, and her hands were pricked with blood.

Elizabeth shook the extraneous shards from her hair and turned her gaze toward the house. A short wooden ramp connected the storage shed to a rear door that might have been a servants' entrance. Tall hedgerows blocked the house from the neighbors' view. Out front, an imposing stone wall with a thick iron gate indicated no visitors were welcome.

Luckily for Elizabeth, she wasn't a visitor. Not in the traditional sense. She'd been delivered inside a wooden crate, hidden amongst a dozen other such crates. A Trojan horse, if you will.

Which she'd *specifically* warned Stephen to check for.

She was tempted to chop down the next door out of pure disgruntlement that her advice had gone unheeded, but Marjorie had provided her with a special lock-opening key. Besides, Elizabeth was tired of picking splinters from her skin. It was on to the next contingency plan.

She removed the special key from the hidden pocket Tommy had sewn in Elizabeth's skirt, and inserted it into the lock. After twisting it a few times and banging the end with the hilt of her sword the way Chloe had shown her, the mechanism sprang open, and Elizabeth gained access to the interior of the residence.

It looked like... Well, it looked a lot like the storage structure she'd just been locked inside, honestly. This room was twice the size of the largest parlor at home, and filled floor-to-ceiling with shelves and boxes and contraptions.

Her quarry, unfortunately, was nowhere in sight.

She sheathed her sword and carefully picked her way forward, testing each slat of the parquet before placing her full weight on it. A good thing, too, since one of the panels had a slight give to it, indicating it was either a trapdoor to a hidden dungeon, or a lever that would have filled the air with nettles and stinging wasps. Her darling anarchist was nothing if not consistent.

A few more steps, and—Ha! A trip wire! The thin strip of string a mere inch from the floor would have been invisible to anyone not specifically searching for just such devious methods. She stepped over it gingerly, taking even more care with her balance, lest the vibrations of her footfalls cause gears to turn and pulleys to raise, unleashing a trough of boiling oil on her head.

By her count, she dodged no fewer than fifteen more near disasters before reaching the door on the other side of the workroom. The handle was unlocked. Unlocked! Then again, perhaps she was being lured into another murder room.

She cast a suspicious eye at every surface as she crept through the silent house. It was surprisingly pretty. For a man repulsed by the notion of entertaining guests, Stephen had surrounded himself with plenty of beauty. There was a guest room that appeared untouched, and a study that seemed likewise unused. She imagined Stephen spent most of his time in his workroom, when he wasn't...wherever he was at this moment. Was he even on the premises? Had she broken in too early?

But, no—the next door was ajar, and low voices spilled out from the interior. Elizabeth caught her breath and flattened against one wall of the corridor.

Only when she was convinced that whoever was on the other side had not heard her approach, did she peek through the crack between the hinges. A man and a woman were seated at a small table, engaged in a game of cards. Casino, if Elizabeth had to guess. She'd also guess that these were Stephen's servants. He'd mentioned only having a single maid and a single manservant. Elizabeth would have to give them lessons in defending against Trojan horses, too.

She eased past the door and continued on down the hallway.

Contingency plan five, she mouthed to herself. That was the one where she shook a trail of rose petals to his bedchamber, and arranged herself naked atop the—

There he was! Beside the bed. Fully clothed, alas. On his side, facing away from her, engaged in a dizzying series of press-ups on the floor.

She didn't move a muscle.

He sensed her anyway, his head jerking up from the floor. His eyes widened at the sight of her. "*Elizabeth*? But how—?"

"What did I *tell* you about Trojan horses?" she scolded him before she remembered that wasn't how she'd intended to start off at all. "Wait. Forget about the Trojan horse for the moment."

He sprang to his feet. "I definitely want to know about the Trojan horse. You're covered in sawdust. Did you come in an actual wooden horse? How did my servants not see that?"

"An important discussion we can have with them at another time. But I didn't pay this call to upbraid anyone. I came to beg forgiveness."

He sat on the edge of the bed and stared at her. "Forgiveness for what?"

Elizabeth took a deep breath and leaned her hip against the wall for physical and emotional support. She was going to have to talk about her *feelings*.

She should have brought Jacob as an interpreter. He was the poet of the family, not Elizabeth.

She gripped the handle of her sword one last time, then tossed it aside. It clattered noisily to the floor.

Stephen raised his brows.

Elizabeth tried to smile bravely. It probably came out like a grimace. She removed the daggers from her bodice and threw those to the ground as well.

Her dress, she'd chosen for a reason: She could remove it without assistance. Elizabeth untied the ribbon beneath her bodice. The back of her gown loosened enough to slip the cording free, which tugged the sleeves down over her shoulders.

Stephen sat up straight. "What are you doing?"

"Removing my armor."

The dress fell to the floor. Elizabeth lifted her chain mail up and over her head, then added it to the growing pile at her feet. She was now wearing nothing more than silk stockings and a cotton shift. Her fingers itched for the comfort of her sword. She left it where it lay.

Then remembered a hidden knife tucked into her garter, and added that to the pile as well.

"I stand before you, defenseless." Elizabeth straightened and clutched her hands together. "I've never felt more vulnerable. I've never *been* more vulnerable. But it's not the lack of armor and weaponry that makes me this way. It's how I feel about you."

He started to rise from the bed. She held up a palm to stop him. If she didn't get through this now, she never would. And he deserved all the words in her heart.

"I'm sorry I walked away. I wanted to stay with you forever from the very beginning. I never frighten, but my feelings for you terrify me. So I chose safety. The familiarity of the known instead of the adventure of a lifetime."

"I didn't mean to frighten you away."

"*I* did that. I couldn't even admit to myself that this short time with you had filled me to the brim with happiness. I don't like people, much less need them. And yet you slipped in through the tiniest crack, sand filling my empty hourglass, until I was so full of contentment and peace, that I felt I did not deserve this much joy."

"Elizabeth, you deserve *all* the joy."

"I should have told you I was falling in love as soon as *I* knew it. Instead, I bottled the truth inside, as if that way I could keep myself safe. I thought I was guarding my heart, but my silence broke our bond instead. Instead of protecting what I cherished most, I abandoned you out of fear."

His eyes watched her with hope.

Softly, she said, "Without you, I will always be fifty percent of what we could have had."

"And what could we have had?"

"Everything. I don't want to walk away or say goodbye. I want to be with *you*, Stephen. Here, or wherever you happen to be. I love you.

I lost my heart to you weeks ago, on a string connected to a pulley connected to gears that launched an arrow straight into my chest. Nothing could stop me from loving you. You're stronger than any force I've ever known."

"Impossible." He rose to his feet and stepped forward. "You're the strongest force *I've* ever known. My first glimpse of you was as Beth the Berserker, and you've given me no reason to doubt your strength any moment since. I did not strip you of your armor. You chose to remove it. And as for me..."

She held her breath.

"I've been defenseless from the moment you swashbuckled your way into my life," he said softly. "I love you, Elizabeth Wynchester. I love you two thousand percent and rising. You're phenomenal and fearless and...How did you get into my house?"

"Through the murder room."

"Through the murder room," he repeated. "How did you know where all the traps were?"

"I didn't. But I know you." She gave him a crooked smile. "Don't worry, I didn't destroy anything. Even I could see that it wasn't an environment where I could hack my way through with a sword."

He took her hands. "I'm glad you didn't."

"The storage shelter, on the other hand..." She winced. "You might need to replace a few panels."

A startled laugh escaped him. "You were inside the barn?"

"I was delivered with your latest supplies earlier today. You always immediately unpack every crate. I was so certain you'd pry open mine at any moment." She swallowed. "Is it unromantic to hide in a wooden crate? I fear my methods may always be a bit abnormal."

He placed her arms around his neck and wrapped his own about her. "In case it was unclear whilst you were picking your way through a murder room...I am not a man who craves normal."

"What do you crave?"

"You. Always and only you." He covered her mouth with his.

Elizabeth kissed him back for all she was worth. He loved her, thorns and all. They tumbled together onto the bed.

"Say you'll marry me," he murmured between kisses.

"Hmm," she teased. "I'll think it over. Does this proposal come with jewelry and my own army?"

"No," he said. "But I did commission you a bejeweled claymore. I can turn it into a ring if you'd rather have—"

She silenced him with a kiss. "I was yours at 'bejeweled claymore.'"

"That's more like it." He trailed his kisses down to her bosom. "Now I'll never let you go."

"Where would I go?" She tugged his shirt from his waistband. "I'm finally home." She glanced down. "I'm also shedding wood shards onto your elegant bedsheets."

He tossed his waistcoat aside and grinned. "I'll try to think of a way for you to make it up to me."

47

Stephen had not expected to ever return to Castle Harbrook, but he and Elizabeth could not think of a better place to embark upon a new start than where it had all begun.

The special license had been simple enough to obtain. Stephen's cousin had spoken to the archbishop on his behalf, as part of his apology for all the trouble he'd caused. Densmore was here now, standing next to Miss Oak and the school instructors on the castle's front garden.

Elizabeth grinned up at Stephen from beneath her veil.

He couldn't wait until the end of the ceremony. He wanted to kiss her, to hell with pomp and circumstance. But there were a hundred schoolchildren watching, so he would have to save a thorough ravishment until he and his wife could share a moment in private.

The curate turned to Stephen. "Wilt thou have this woman to thy wedded wife, to love her, comfort her, honor and keep her, in sickness and in health, and forsaking all others, keep thee only unto her so long as you both shall live?"

"I will."

The curate turned to Elizabeth and asked the same question. Technically, the curate was supposed to instruct her to *obey*, but the man was a friend of the Wynchesters and had therefore agreed to accidentally forget that phrase, lest Elizabeth break her vows before the end of the ceremony.

"... and, forsaking all others, keep thee only unto him, so long as you both shall live?"

Elizabeth grinned at Stephen. "I will."

There were no sniffles in the crowd. Only cheers of joy and the clapping of hands when at last the curate pronounced them legally wed.

"And now," said Elizabeth, her green eyes twinkling. "We get to do the good part!"

The curate stepped back, his expression shocked and alarmed.

"Not *that* 'good part,'" Stephen assured him. "We'll attend to consummation later."

Elizabeth held out her hand. "My bejeweled claymore, if you please."

Jacob placed the hilt into Elizabeth's open hand.

"Kneel before me, husband," Elizabeth commanded.

Stephen dutifully sank to his knees.

"Who gives this man to the Wynchester family?"

Silence reigned amongst the hundred-plus spectators.

"Uh..." Densmore stammered. "I suppose... I suppose that would be me?"

The children cheered.

"I have no idea what I'm doing," the earl murmured. "I've no idea what any of you are doing. But if it makes you happy..."

"I've never been happier," Stephen said, and meant it.

Elizabeth hefted the claymore. "Step aside, if you would please, Lord Densmore. You don't want to get splashed by blood if I chop off an ear."

Startled, the earl leapt backward. "Did you just say—"

"Mr. Stephen Lenox," Elizabeth bellowed, as though her husband were not kneeling two feet in front of her. "Do you, before these witnesses, pledge to uphold the spirit and service of the Wynchester family, at play and on missions, legal or not—"

The curate blinked. "Did you just say—"

"—for causes great and small, upholding justice and striking bloody vengeance—"

"No vengeance," said Jacob. "Bloody or otherwise. We went over this."

"—and restore justice wherever it is needed, for as long as we all shall live?"

"Indeed I shall." Stephen touched his fingers to his chest and lifted them to the sky.

"Then by the power vested in me by me," Elizabeth continued, touching the sword first to Stephen's right shoulder, and then to his left, "and also fully and irrevocably bestowed upon me by my supportive family, who has agreed that I alone am equal to the task of knighting this and all future Wynchesters—"

"*Did* we agree to that?" murmured Tommy.

"I don't think we were asked," replied Philippa.

"—therefore I hereby declare you a full-blooded Wynchester!" She pressed her fingers to her chest and lifted them toward the sky.

All of the Wynchester siblings did the same.

Elizabeth hauled Stephen to his feet and kissed him, then stabbed her bejeweled sword up to the heavens in victory.

Whistles and cheers erupted from the audience. She sheathed the sword. The students danced around them in glee as Stephen and Elizabeth's family burst forward to give them happy hugs.

"Welcome to the family," said Jacob.

Stephen's heart swelled. He laced his fingers with his bride's and swung their clasped hands high in the air before leaning in to give her another kiss.

"About that good part," she murmured against his lips. "Think they'll notice if we don't attend our own wedding breakfast?"

He grinned back at her. "Let's find out."

EPILOGUE

*E*lizabeth stretched out on the sofa in the Wynchester sibling sitting room. She and Stephen almost hadn't left their house today, because Elizabeth had awoken to her hips and joints threatening mutiny. But rather than continue with the planned fencing practice—or hole up and pretend nothing was amiss—Stephen had fed her pistachio ices in bed until she informed him she could at least make the short trip from their house to her siblings'.

The rest of the family had seen her in such a position countless times. Stephen was now part of the family, too. He not only loved every part of her, from the working bits to the not-always-working bits, but also believed she was a formidable knight at all times. Even when lying in repose atop a pillow-strewn sofa with her ankles in her husband's lap so that Stephen could rub her feet.

The massages weren't because he thought her weak. He rubbed her feet every night, no matter what percentage she was at that day. And all she had to do to be showered with ices was whisper the word "pistachio" and Stephen would be out the door like a shot.

"Wait," said Jacob. "I cannot possibly have heard you correctly."

"Stephen allows me in his workroom, even when he's not there," Elizabeth repeated, her voice dreamy. "He blows things up all the time, and told me to feel free to blow up whatever I please as well."

Her siblings' gazes swung toward Stephen, who shrugged indulgently. "What's good for the goose..."

"Married life together is marvelous," Elizabeth said with a happy sigh. "You should see my new dagger-sharpening device."

"I'm never leaving one of our children alone with you in that workroom," Chloe said sternly.

Elizabeth and Stephen squeezed each other's hands in mutual relief. Chloe's baby was now *crawling*. She and Stephen would rather be set upon by hornets.

They grinned at each other. Elizabeth was pretty sure her grin was wider. Even when her hips were at fifty percent, with Stephen she was always one hundred percent Elizabeth.

Graham glanced at him askance. "Now that you're a Wynchester, I intended to offer you your own room in the western wing to do with as you please. We might have to add a 'no explosion' rule."

"We have plenty of space at our house," Elizabeth assured him. "Space to be ourselves."

"And speaking of explosions," Stephen added, earning a sideways glance from all the rest of the Wynchesters, too. "It's not exactly a souvenir, but I finally had a chance to make a machine for the Faircliffe family."

"Speaking of explosions?" the duke repeated dubiously. "Did we mention the baby?"

Chloe plucked her crawling devil-child up from the floor and clutched him protectively to her chest. "What kind of machine is it?"

"A combination clock and cradle. The weights powering the clock also drive pulleys that rock the cradle on curved feet."

"That *sounds*...nice," Faircliffe admitted.

Chloe narrowed her eyes. "What *else* does it do?"

Elizabeth and Stephen exchanged innocent smiles.

Faircliffe covered his face with his hand and sighed.

Mr. Randall appeared in the doorway. "There's a strange caller. A cobbler distraught about the escapade Jarvis Wynchester pulled yesterday night. Something to do with disgruntled ferrets."

"Er...Do you mean *Jacob* Wynchester?" Philippa asked.

"Not me," Jacob protested, cradling Tickletums the hedgehog. "I was at my poetry club last evening."

Elizabeth's mouth fell open. "Someone pretended to be one of us?"

"Pretended to be Jacob, at least," said Marjorie.

"Well, I won't stand for it." Jacob bristled. "Or the mistreatment of ferrets."

Elizabeth arched her brows. "You don't know that they were mistreated."

"They were disgruntled, weren't they? Why would a ferret be disgruntled unless something was horribly amiss?"

"A question we ask ourselves daily," Stephen murmured.

"Quick." Tommy turned to Jacob, her eyes twinkling. "The ferrets need their hero."

He leapt to his feet. "If this takes a while, will one of you feed my animals whilst I'm gone?"

"*No*," all his siblings said at once.

"I'll do it," Stephen offered. "I logged all of the schedules and safety procedures."

"Of course you did." Elizabeth grinned at him. "I'll watch Tickletums."

"I can put together an automated feeding machine to handle any future absences," Stephen said.

"That may become our new routine. Now that Jacob is the only unmarried Wynchester," Elizabeth added slyly, "he may have to handle more of the cases."

Jacob sent her a flat look. "There are more cases than ever."

"Then maybe you should think about adding another Wynchester to the team," Elizabeth teased.

"I don't have time or interest in courtship," he said firmly.

"Says the lonely soul who writes endless sonnets about love," she murmured. "And has enough free time to train or rehabilitate an entire barn full of animals."

"I don't write sonnets," Jacob protested. "You've never even read my work."

"He doesn't deny his poems are about love," Elizabeth stage-whispered to Stephen.

Mr. Randall cleared his throat. "What shall I tell the caller in the entryway?"

Jacob handed the hedgehog to Elizabeth and rushed off to interview the visitor.

Elizabeth and Stephen exchanged mischievous grins and snuggled closer together, with Tickletums in their lap. Whatever was happening certainly sounded like an adventure. And wherever Wynchesters found adventure, love was rarely far behind.

"Want to stay here and see what's happening?" Stephen murmured into Elizabeth's ear. "Or would you rather go home and watch me launch my biggest trebuchet ever?"

"That better be a metaphor," she whispered back. "When I take off this chain mail, I'll be ripe for the plundering."

He grinned and kissed her. "May all Beth the Berserker's wishes come true."

DON'T MISS JACOB'S STORY,
COMING IN SUMMER 2025!

ACKNOWLEDGMENTS

As always, this book would not exist without the support of many wonderful people. I was lucky enough to have two fabulous editors this time: Leah Hultenschmidt and Sabrina Flemming. Thank you to the whole team at Forever, including Dana Cuadrado and Estelle Hallick. And to my brilliant agent, Lauren Abramo, for your wisdom, encouragement, and friendship.

My utmost gratitude goes to Rose Lerner, who makes every book better. Erica Monroe and my early reader crew—thank you so much for your feedback and enthusiasm.

Full disclosure: Please forgive my creative license with the catacombs. These were inspired by the ones in Paris, and though I've no reason to believe there was anything similar at this time in Dorset, if anyone could stumble across hidden tunnels filled with skeletons, it's Elizabeth Wynchester.

Enormous thanks to intrepid assistant Laura Stout, for being my right hand (even when you broke yours!), and for taking care of everything I cannot from Costa Rica.

All the cowriting dates with Alyssa, Mary, Ava, Joy Club, and Coven—you guys keep me grounded, and I love you for it. Thanks also go to Darc, Lace, Shauna, Susan, and Team #1k1hr for the texts from the trenches and all the mutual support.

Muchísimas gracias to Roy Prendas, who makes every single day happy ever after. *Te adoro, mi poporiquísimo.*

And my biggest, most heartfelt thanks go to my amazing, wonderful readers. You're all so fun and funny and smart. I love your reviews and TikToks and Bookstagrams, and adore chatting with you in the Ridley.VIP newsletter list, on social media, in person, and in our Historical Romance Book Club group on Facebook. Your enthusiasm makes the romance happen.

Thank you for everything!

ABOUT THE AUTHOR

Erica Ridley is a *New York Times* and *USA Today* bestselling author of historical romance novels. When not reading or writing romances, Erica can be found eating couscous in Morocco, zip-lining through rainforests in Costa Rica, or getting hopelessly lost in the middle of Budapest.

You can learn more at:

EricaRidley.com
X @EricaRidley
Facebook.com/EricaRidley
Instagram @EricaRidley
TikTok @EricaRidley